'Beautifully written, intelligent,
uncompromising – highly recommended.'
Sunday Times bestselling author Sophie Hannah

'Propulsive.'
New York Times

'*Gone Girl* meets *We Need to Talk About Kevin* . . . a twisty,
delirious read that will constantly question your sympathies
for the two characters as their bond continues to crumble.'
Entertainment Weekly

'A deliciously creepy read.'
NY Post

'Gripping.'
InStyle

'A wholly original and terrifically creepy story.'
Refinery29

'A totally engaging and unnerving read. Debut
novelist Stage has convincingly created one of the
youngest villains ever, and readers will be unable
to resist the urge to meet Hanna.'
Booklist

'Unnerving and unputdownable, *Bad Apple* will get
under your skin and keep you trapped in its chilling
grip until the shocking conclusion.'
New York Times bestselling author Lisa Scottoline

Bad Apple

ZOJE STAGE

CORGI BOOKS

TRANSWORLD PUBLISHERS
61–63 Uxbridge Road, London W5 5SA
www.penguin.co.uk

Transworld is part of the Penguin Random House group of companies
whose addresses can be found at global.penguinrandomhouse.com

First published in Great Britain in 2018 by Bantam Press
an imprint of Transworld Publishers
Corgi edition published 2019

A CIP catalogue record for this book
is available from the British Library.

ISBN
9780552175012

Typeset in 12.25/15.5 pt Fournier MT Std by Jouve (UK), Milton Keynes
Printed and bound in Great Britain by Clays Ltd, Elcograf S.p.A.

Penguin Random House is committed to a sustainable future
for our business, our readers and our planet. This book is made
from Forest Stewardship Council® certified paper.

1 3 5 7 9 10 8 6 4 2

For my dad,
John Stage

Bad
Apple

HANNA

MAYBE THE MACHINE could see the words she never spoke. Maybe they blazed in her bones. Maybe if the people in the white coats blew up the pictures they'd see her thoughts, mapped like mountains and railroad tracks, across her ghostly skull. Hanna knew nothing was wrong with her. But Mommy wanted them to look. Again.

The room in the hospital's dungeon carried the threat of needles and smelled like lemon candies tinged with poison. When she was little, the machine scared her. But now, seven, she pretended she was an astronaut. The rocket ship spun and beeped and she scanned the coordinates, double-checking her course. Through the round window, tiny Earth dropped from view, then she was in the darkness with the glimmering stars, zooming away. No one would ever catch her. She smiled.

"Stay still, please. Almost finished—you're doing great."

The flight director watched her from his monitor. She hated all the ground control people, with their white coats and lilting voices, their play-dough smiles that flopped into frowns. They were all the same. Liars.

Hanna kept her words to herself because they gave

her power. Inside her, they retained their purity. She scrutinized Mommy and other adults, studied them. Their words fell like dead bugs from their mouths. A rare person, like Daddy, spoke in butterflies, whispering colors that made her gasp. Inside, she was a kaleidoscope of racing, popping, bursting exclamations, full of wonder and question marks. Patterns swirled, and within every secret pocket she'd stashed a treasure, some stolen, some found. She had tried, as a little girl, to express what was within her. But it came out like marbles. Nonsense. Babbling. Disappointing even to her own ears. She'd practiced, alone in her room, but the bugs fell from her mouth, frighteningly alive, scampering over her skin and bedclothes. She flicked them away. Watched them escape under her closed door.

Words, ever unreliable, were no one's friend.

But, if she was being honest, there was another reason—a benefit. Her silence was making Mommy crazy. Poor Mommy made it all too clear, over many desperate years, how badly she wanted her to talk. She used to beg.

"Please, baby? Ma-ma? Ma-ma?"

Daddy, on the other hand, never begged or acted put out. His eyes lit up when he held her, like he was witnessing a supernova. He alone really saw her, and so she smiled for him and was rewarded with kisses and tickles.

"Okay, all finished," said the flight director.

The ground control people pushed a button and her head slid out of the giant mechanical tube. The rocket ship crashed back to Earth, where she found herself in a crater of ugliness. The blobby people emerged—one with her hand outstretched offering to take her back to Mommy, like that was some sort of reward.

"You did such a good job!"

What a lie. She hadn't done anything but come back to Earth too soon. It wasn't hard to be still, and not speaking was her natural state. She let the woman take her hand, even though she didn't want to go back to moody Mommy and another suffocating room. She'd rather explore the hospital's endless corridors. She pretended she was walking around in the intestines of a giant dragon. When it exhaled its angry flames, they'd catapult her forward into another world. The one where she belonged, where she could race through a gloomy forest with her trusted sword, screaming the call that would summon the others. Her minions would charge behind her as she led the attack. Slash, crash, grunt, and stab. Her sword would get its taste of blood.

SUZETTE

SHE SMOOTHED DOWN the back of Hanna's hair where it had gotten rumpled during her test.

"See, not so bad. Now we'll see what the doctor says." Her tight smile forced her eye to twitch. She dabbed at the corner of it with her index finger. A terror clawed beneath her skin, making small rips in her equilibrium. Doctors' offices, medical buildings: institutions of torture. They pressed on her like a heavy slab. Hanna sat with her elbow on the chair's armrest, head on her hand, absorbed and expressionless like she became in front of the TV. Suzette glanced at the framed print that held her daughter's interest. Squares of watery color. She tried to guess, by the movement of Hanna's eyes, if she was counting the total number of squares, or collecting them in groups of similar shades. Hanna pretended to be unaware of Suzette beside her, and she read the usual rebuke in Hanna's refusal to look at her. After so many years, she'd lost track of the moments for which she was being punished.

Perhaps Hanna was still angry at her for running out of bananas. She'd slammed her fists on the table, glaring at her naked bowl of cereal. Or maybe Hanna couldn't forgive some perceived slight from the previous night, or week, or month. Hanna didn't know that Suzette had resisted bringing her in for another CT scan—500 times the radiation of a single X-ray—but relented to Alex's wishes. Her husband's concerns remained rooted in the pragmatic insistence that something might yet be physically impeding her verbal progress. He didn't see what she did, and she could never tell him what was really wrong— that it had all been a mistake: She didn't know how to be a mother; why had that ever seemed like a good idea? So she played along. Of course she'd have Hanna tested again. Of course they needed to know if anything was physiologically awry.

She considered her daughter. They looked so much alike. Her dark, dark hair. The big brown eyes. If only she'd inherited some of Alex's fairness. She had Hanna put on a nice dress, brand-new knee socks, and Mary Janes. Suzette wore a silk shirtdress, loosely belted to show off her figure, and shoes that cost a fortune. It was silly, she knew, for both of them to dress up for a medical appointment, but she feared situations in which her mothering might be judged, and at least no one could say her child looked neglected or ill. And Suzette had so little opportunity otherwise to wear her finer clothes when all she did was stay home with Hanna. She used to dress up for Alex's office parties and loved the way his lustful eyes followed her around as she sipped wine and chatted, enjoying the rare company of other adults. But no babysitter would ever come back, and they finally gave up. Alex, considerately, made the gatherings rarer and shorter, but still. She missed the casual normalcy she once had with Fiona and Sasha and Ngozi. She never asked if Alex talked about her at work, or if they all acted as if she no longer existed.

Nervous about what the doctor would say—how he might criticize her—she patted a jumpy rhythm on Hanna's arm. Hanna pulled it away, lowering her chin as the colorful, blocky print continued to mesmerize her. Suzette held each part of her body too tightly—her crossed legs, her tense shoulders, her hands curled into fists. It made the tender part in her abdomen twist and squeal in protest and she fanned her fingers, trying to make herself relax. It was her first big outing since The Surgery, eight weeks before. They did it laparoscopically this time so the superficial part of the recovery was faster, though she'd asked the doctor to fix her horrible scar while they were there.

The misshapen canyon of a scar had always bothered her, falling in a deep, wonky six-inch diagonal on the right side of her navel. Alex insisted it was part of her beauty, her strength. A marking of survival, of the suffering she'd endured as a teenager. She didn't need any reminders of those lonely and disgusting years, of the enemy within or her own mother's deadly indifference. As it was, that first surgery at seventeen put such a fear in her that she'd put off Dr. Stefanski's recommendation for another resection until her intestines were in danger of perforating. In the beginning, the stricture only caused a bit of pain and she reduced the fiber in her diet. She'd expected her heavy-duty medication—an injectable biological drug— to eliminate the worst of her Crohn's symptoms. And it did. But as the inflammation receded, scar tissue built up around a narrowing in her intestine.

"Don't take too much!" she'd pleaded with the surgeon, as if he was about to rob her, not restore her to health.

Alex had kissed her white-knuckled hand. "It'll be fine, *älskling*, you'll feel so much better, and be able to eat so much more food."

Yes, reasonable assessments. If it wasn't for her inconsolable fear of losing so much small intestine that she'd lose the inalienable right to shit on a toilet like a normal person. People did it every day—lived with ileostomies and bags attached to their abdomens. But she couldn't. Couldn't. The very thought of it made her start shaking her head until Hanna twitched, glancing at her with a sour frown as if she was already stinking up the room.

Suzette got herself back under control, at least so far as her daughter would notice. But her dark mind played on, resistant to more-comforting distractions in the weeks since her surgery.

What if she got another fistula?

That was the thing that haunted her every day since she agreed to schedule the procedure. The last time, it developed about six weeks after her emergency resection. She'd woken up one morning feeling as if she was sleeping on a brick, but the mass had been in her own belly, a pool of waste that needed to be drained. It had been eight weeks since The Surgery, so maybe the danger had lessened. Alex said his usual "one day at a time" platitudes. Dr. Stefanski said no no, just keep doing your injections, your inflammation markers are low. But in her head the oozing puss and shit waited in the wings, and what if

Alex had to play the role her mother played, nursemaid, replacing the soiled packing in a wound that wouldn't heal—

A quick knuckle rap on the exam room door dispelled her thoughts. Sometimes the presence of a doctor only made her trauma worse, but this one was here for Hanna, not her. And she was here as a good mother, a concerned mother, unlike her own. She pressed her palm against her tingling abdomen and made herself smile as the new doctor gusted in, grayer than the last one. His eyebrows needed a trim and Suzette struggled to maintain eye contact with him with his nose hairs on such display.

"Mrs. Jensen." He shook her hand.

He pronounced her name as everyone did, incorrectly. It didn't bother her as much as it did Swedish-born Alex, who, after nineteen years in the United States, still couldn't accept that Americans would never make a *J* sound like a *Y*. The doctor sat on the rolling stool and brought Hanna's records up on the computer.

"No changes from the scan she had . . . When was it? Two and a half years ago? No abnormalities of the skull, jaw, throat, mouth . . . upon examination or on the scan. So that's good, right? Hanna's a healthy girl." He smiled at Hanna's turned-away head.

"So . . . There's no . . . ?" She tried not to sound as disappointed as she felt. "She should be finishing first grade and we can't even send her to school, not if she doesn't speak. We don't feel like she needs a special class—she's smart, I homeschool her and she's very smart. She can read, do math—"

"Mrs. Jensen—"

"But it won't be good for her—it's not good for her, to be so isolated. She doesn't have friends, won't interact with her peers. We've tried to be supportive, encouraging. There has to be something we can do, something to help her . . ."

"I know an excellent speech language pathologist, if Hanna is having trouble—"

"We've tried speech pathologists."

"—she can be tested for any number of things. Verbal apraxia, semantic pragmatic language disorder . . ." He scrolled through her online chart, looking for something. "Maybe auditory processing disorder, though she presents atypically for that. Has she had any of these tests?"

"We've tested her for everything. Her hearing's fine, no muscle weakness, no cognitive problems. I've lost track of all the tests, but she takes them, seems to think they're fun—but she won't say a word."

"Won't?" The doctor turned to face Suzette.

"Won't. Can't. I don't know. That's . . . We're trying to find out."

Suzette squirmed as the doctor flicked his overeducated attention between the two of them. She knew what he was seeing: the daughter, lost in her own head; the mother, a carefully groomed, but wound-up mess.

"You say she can read and write? Can you communicate with her that way?"

"She'll write out answers in her workbooks, she doesn't seem to mind that. We know she understands. But when we've asked her to write what she's thinking or wants—any type of actual communication . . . No, she won't speak to us that way." Her interlocked fingers started hurting and she glanced down at them, a little surprised by how forcefully she'd been twisting them. She took hold of her purse strap and started strangling it instead. "She can make noises—so we know, maybe, she could make other sounds. She can grunt. And squeal. Hum little songs."

"If it's a matter of her refusing . . . *Won't* requires a different type of doctor than *can't*."

Suzette felt her face reddening, as if her hands had moved to her throat, squeezing the life from her. "I—we—don't know what to do. We can't go on like this." She gasped for air.

The doctor wove his fingers together and gave her a sympathetic, if lopsided, smile. "Behavioral difficulties can be just as difficult to manage as physical ones, maybe more so."

She nodded. "I always wonder . . . Am I doing something wrong?"

"It causes strain in a family, I understand. Perhaps the next thing to try . . . I could recommend a pediatric psychologist. I wouldn't recommend a psychiatrist, not until she has a diagnosis. In this age, they're so quick to write prescriptions, and maybe this is something you can work through."

"Yes, I'd prefer that, thank you."

"I'll send a referral through your insurance company . . ." He turned back to the computer.

Suzette worked the kinks out of her purse strap, feeling slightly dizzy with relief. She tucked a piece of Hanna's hair behind her ear.

"I try to avoid toxic things," she said to the doctor's

slouched back. "Not that all medication is toxic, but like you said, society's so quick to find a pill for something, never mind the side effects. But if it's not a disability . . . An organic solution, that sounds good." She turned to Hanna. "We're going to work this out. Find someone you might talk to."

Hanna took a swat at Suzette's fussing hand and curled her lip in a snarl. Suzette shot her a warning glare, then peeked at the doctor to make sure he hadn't seen.

Hanna bolted to her feet, crossed her arms, and stood by the door.

"In a minute, we're almost finished." Suzette made her voice sound endlessly patient.

Spinning back around on his stool, the doctor chuckled. "I don't blame you one bit, young lady, cooped up at the doctor's on a sunny day." Suzette stood as he did. "The referral will probably take a few days, then you can schedule something directly with Dr. Yamamoto. She's a developmental child psychologist and has a great way with kids, very established. And hopefully Hanna will connect with her. They'll print out all the information when you check out."

"Thank you so much."

"She might even be able to recommend some schools for you."

"Perfect." She looked over at her daughter, not surprised to see the angry scowl on her face. Through bad behavior, Hanna had made herself unwelcome at three preschools and two kindergartens. Suzette had come to believe that their mother-daughter relationship would improve only when they had some distance—when

Hanna went off to school. And Suzette wanted their relationship to improve. She was tired of yelling "Hanna, stop!" and maybe she shouldn't yell, but there were endless reasons—small and large—why she'd needed to. Plucking all the leaves off the houseplants. Pulling on every loose thread, no matter what it unraveled. Mixing a cocktail of orange juice and nail polish remover. Throwing balls against the glass wall of their house. Staring at her and refusing to blink or budge. Hurling sharpened pencils like darts across the room. Hanna had creative ways to amuse herself, and most of them were intolerable.

Since the doctor confirmed there was nothing physically wrong, then, for the sake of her own health and sanity, it was time to convince Alex that they needed to find a school for Hanna. Maybe someone else would succeed where she hadn't in disciplining the girl. She couldn't phrase it to him as a desperate need for her own time and space; she couldn't make it all about herself. Hanna behaved quite lovingly in his presence, and often he saw silliness where she saw mischief, and her more-provocative antics he ascribed to intelligence. He remained blind to his own hypocrisy, all the things he explained away as normal while exalting her precocity. So that would be her argument: Gifted Hanna was bored; she needed more stimulation than what she was getting at home.

One way or another, she wouldn't let Hanna continue to derail her life.

Hand in hand, they engaged in a silent contest of who could squeeze the tightest, as Suzette smiled at the nurses on their way out.

HANNA

SOMETIMES MOMMY WAS an octopus with a sharp blade in each hand. It seemed fair to Hanna that when Mommy bruised her heart, or made her feel all icky crumbly inside, that she should be able to hurt her back. She didn't like Dr. Caterpillar Eyebrows scanning her with his X-ray vision, trying to find out what was wrong with her. She didn't like how Mommy talked about her, like she was broken. Bad. Worthless. And to make it worse, it was all an act. Mommy just wanted to find a good reason to return her. She'd seen her do it before, in line at a store.

"This is defective—can I get a refund?"

She knew Mommy wanted to get rid of her; she was always trying to leave her behind. That's what school was all about, though Hanna had other reasons to resist. The noises. The grabby children. The piercing red panic of not having her own space. By the age of four she was on to Mommy's other tricks, like the babysitters. It was unacceptable; Mommy was failing her tests to prove her motherly love. And the more she failed, the more opportunities Hanna tried to provide for her to redeem herself. Though she wasn't always sure of the rules to their war games. And when she scrunched up her brain, she couldn't quite remember who had started it.

Abha. She was the last babysitter. Hanna always remembered her name because it reminded her of ABBA, a musical group from where Daddy was born. He liked to sing the "Dancing Queen" song to her, holding her as they twirled and bopped around. It wasn't Abha's fault. Hanna was ready to burst before the girl even rang the doorbell. She wanted to dress up and go to the party and have Daddy's friends smile at her and say nice things that made her feel like she was full of bubbles. Not stay home, forgotten, with another bug-eyed stranger.

She remembered tiptoeing into Mommy's room. When she saw Mommy in the bathroom, standing in front of the mirror in an oil slick of a dress, she dropped to her hands and knees and crawled over to Mommy's side of the bed. It wasn't Hanna's first spy-and-capture mission. She knew all of Mommy's habits, like the way she always picked out her jewelry before getting dressed, and then left it sitting like lost treasure on her bedside table. Mommy planned to wear a pair of sparkling little hoop earrings and a swimming-pool colored gemstone that dangled from a delicate chain.

Hanna plucked the earrings from the table and whisked them away to her room.

There wasn't much time—Mommy looked almost ready to leave—so she tucked the earrings into a little hole in Mungo's back. Mungo was a very, very old stuffed monkey who loved to help Hanna hide things. She quickly changed into her shimmery lavender dress. It was a teensy bit small, she hadn't worn it for a while, but it was the fanciest thing in her closet.

When she bounded back into her parents' bedroom, Mommy was still in the bathroom, leaning against the snowbank sink that glittered with suspended ice crystals, putting on mascara. Hanna waltzed in, holding out the ruffled hem of her dress as she did a couple of spins. It was still such a pretty dress, even if it was tight across her shoulders.

"I thought you were putting on your pajamas." Mommy's reflection glared at her with one misshapen eye.

Hanna did a little jump, then pointed at Mommy. *Go go go,* she said in her head.

Mommy stuffed the brush back into the tube and turned to her. Hanna thought for sure she would notice how special she looked, so dazzling and grown up and ready for the party. She giggled, thinking about how Daddy would carry her around and say, doesn't my squirrely girl look beautiful.

"I told you before. And Daddy told you this morning. It's for big people, no kids will be there, and it's all stuff you don't eat or drink. And you need to go to bed soon. The babysitter will be here any second . . ."

Hanna tilted her head back, squawking in protest. As Mommy strode out, she scrambled after her, gripping the edges of the shimmery dress in her fists. It wasn't fair. Mommy had floated around all day—have to get this done before the party, Mommy needs to change for the party— it was all so obvious. She'd sounded so chipper confirming with the babysitting company, and checking in with Daddy: Do you need anything? Should I pick up anything else? Hanna had to eat her supper alone while Mommy stood in the little downstairs bathroom, putting up her hair. It was all Mommy wanted all day. To stop thinking about her. To leave her behind.

Hanna reached out and let her fingertips whisper her desire, gently, on Mommy's naked arm. It was the way she said "please." Tears knotted up in her throat.

But it was too late. Mommy stared at her bedside table.

"Where are my earrings?" She fastened the little necklace, even as her eyes searched. Tugging up her dress, she got down and peered along the floor, running her hands over it like maybe the earrings had turned invisible. When Mommy looked at her, they were at eye level. "Did you take my earrings?"

Hanna didn't move. Didn't even blink.

"They were diamonds. An expensive gift from . . . Did you take them?"

The doorbell rang.

Mommy stood. Her belly went in and out as she breathed, glaring down on her.

"Please, Hanna. The last time, those were just . . . They had no value, but . . . Please."

No moving. No blinking.

The doorbell rang again.

Mommy chuffed and marched out. Hanna chased after her. Maybe Mommy would lose her temper and send the babysitter away and then tear apart the house in search of the earrings. What a sight that would be, Mommy making a mess! Hanna would "find" them and return them to her. And Mommy would be so happy, she'd take Hanna with her to the party.

In her dark and shiny dress, Mommy moved like a crashing wave, spilling down the stairs toward the front door.

"Hi, thanks so much for coming—I'm Suzette, this is Hanna."

"Hi Hanna, I'm Abha." She had straight black hair that fell in a swoop over her shoulder when she bent to smile in Hanna's face.

"Come in. She's not verbal yet—"

"Is she potty-trained?" Abha asked, stepping inside.

"Oh yes."

Hanna roared like a lion who'd stepped on a thorn. Stupid Abha would regret thinking she was a baby; she was *four*.

Mommy showed her the kitchen—help yourself—and how the TV remote worked—in case you want to watch something.

"I have some studying to do, after Hanna's in bed."

"You're at Pitt?" Mommy asked.

"Yes, third year."

Hanna followed the tour upstairs, growing more disappointed and growly. Mommy clearly still intended to leave her with the babysitter, even without finding the precious diamond earrings.

"Hanna might throw a little fit about wanting to sleep in our room—she's tried that with other sitters before—but she knows she's supposed to sleep in her own bed." Mommy flicked on the light in Hanna's room. "She can watch TV for about fifteen minutes after I leave, then she should come up to bed. You can read her a book."

"It looks like Hanna's dressed as a princess—are you a princess?"

It's a party dress, you dodo.

"She has clean pajamas under her pillow."

Abha held her hand out to Hanna. "Want to watch a little TV? What shows do you like?"

Mommy led them downstairs and Hanna did *not* take Abha's hand. "She knows which channels she's allowed to watch. Our cell numbers are on the fridge . . ."

Hanna ran ahead and leapt onto the couch. She heard the dress rip a little, but so what—she'd show Daddy and he'd say, time for a new one. She pushed the little buttons that controlled the big TV . . . But Mommy wasn't done talking to Abha.

"Um, I'd asked the agency for someone really experienced, because Hanna"—she met Hanna's eyes across the room—"can be a handful. I just want to make sure, you're really—"

"Don't worry. I'm certified in CPR, I know how to treat a choking child. I was a nanny for a year for two-year-old twins, I'm a big sister, a little sister, an aunt—I've been around kids my whole life."

"Okay, I just don't want you to . . . It can be hard because she doesn't talk. So please, call if things . . . It's fine to call us."

"I will, don't worry."

"Goodnight, baby. Be good." Mommy blew her a kiss that evaporated before it reached her on the couch. "Why don't you go put on your pajamas before you watch TV. Are you sure you don't know where my earrings are?"

Hanna turned up the volume on the television, but she still heard when Mommy left, shutting the door behind her. Abha sat down near her, and Hanna fought the urge to swing on her long hair. The babysitter smiled, but Hanna only glowered in return. Until a pang in her tummy gave her the most wonderful idea.

She sprang up and jumped over the back of the couch, racing to get upstairs.

"Changing into your pj's?" Abha asked.

Hanna nodded, grinning, so excited to execute her plan.

She was already half out of her dress before she got to her room. She threw it on the floor.

A minute later, she stood in the threshold of her bathroom, panties at her feet, and started wailing. For good measure she let out a shriek or two, in case Abha couldn't hear well over the television.

The startled babysitter bumbled up the stairs, and Hanna made sure to keep crying, even though she wanted to laugh, as Abha took in the problem: the puddle of pee and pile of poop she'd left on the floor.

"Oh no, did you have an accident?"

Hanna nodded, still crying.

"We'll just get everything cleaned up, it's okay." But Abha crinkled her nose and Hanna knew the mess was disgusting. That's what Abha deserved, for thinking she might not be potty-trained.

She let Abha clean her off and dress her for bed, even

though Hanna could have managed it all herself. One foot over the other, she leaned against the hallway railing, eager to see Abha's technique for cleaning up pee and poo. She knew how Mommy would do it—had even seen her do it once, when Hanna, at two, had legitimately not made it to the potty in time. Mommy had gloves and cleaning stuff stashed under every sink, but Abha didn't know that.

Abha stood with her hands at her waist, weighing her options. "Does your Mommy have spray bottles and sponges in the kitchen?"

Hanna nodded, sucking in her lips so she wouldn't grin. It was turning out to be not such a bad night after all. She skipped after the babysitter, thrilled by her every move.

Abha took off all her silvery rings and set them on the kitchen counter. Hanna took such interest in them, she barely noticed Abha anymore. She nodded when asked a question, and let the babysitter return upstairs alone with her paper towels and gloves and cleaning stuff.

There were four rings, each one enticing in its own way. But in the end she chose the smallest one, with a braided band and a reddish stone in the middle. She knew Abha would ask her later "What happened to my ring?" and she didn't want another round of blinking-and-not-moving, so she opted to go to bed. But first, she hid the remote control so Abha would be stuck watching loud cartoons all night.

The mess was gone when she reached the top of the stairs, and Abha was on her hands and knees, scrubbing the floor. Hanna yawned and headed for her room.

"Ready for bed?"

Yup.

"I'll just finish up and come tuck you in."

Before slipping into bed, she offered Mungo another treasure to keep safe. She heard Abha next door, scrubbing up her hands under a gush of water. When she came in a few minutes later and put the back of her hand on Hanna's forehead, it was still a little damp.

"Feeling okay?" she asked. Hanna nodded. "Good. Want me to read a story?"

Hanna shook her head. She only liked Daddy to read to her. But she pointed to her cheeks, one, and then the other, so Abha would kiss her goodnight.

Smooch. "Sweet dreams." Smooch.

When Abha went to sit back up, Hanna grabbed hold of a thick chunk of her hair. It seemed possible that it might be strong enough to swing on. She gave it a little yank, testing it.

"Hey."

Abha tried to pull her hair free, but Hanna wouldn't let go; she gripped it in both hands.

"What are you doing?"

Hanna just gazed at her, a satisfied smile on her face.

"I have to get up now."

But Hanna wouldn't give up the grip on her hair.

"Hanna . . ." Abha tried to pry her fingers off, but that just made Hanna squeeze as tightly as she could. She yanked it again, bringing the babysitter's face closer to hers. Abha looked a little freaked out.

"Stop it, this isn't funny."

Yank.

"Ow! Hanna!"

Hanna kept pulling. Slowly. Closer. Knowing Abha couldn't pull her head away without making it hurt worse.

When they were nose to nose, they engaged in a stare-off.

"I'm telling your mother."

Hanna shrugged. But Abha had bad breath. She didn't want the babysitter in her face forever. Time to make a move.

Ruff! Hanna barked. To her own ears it sounded very authentic.

It startled Abha enough that she jumped backward and yelped. Tears stood in her eyes as she pressed one hand against her scalp, and grabbed her shank of hair in the other.

Hanna laughed and let go.

Abha gave her a crazed look. She hurried from the room, switching off the light and shutting the door.

Hanna knew she wouldn't come back in, even to inquire after her missing ring. Abha would probably tell Mommy and Daddy everything, but that was good. Mommy would wonder if she stole Abha's ring, or pooped on the floor on purpose. But Daddy would say, Poor *lilla gumman* isn't comfortable around strangers.

When Hanna awoke many hours later, the house was dark and quiet. For the night's final act of revenge, she fished the jewelry out of Mungo's plush back. But on second thought, she put the ring back; she liked it, maybe she'd want to wear it someday, when she got bigger.

Plop! Plop! Two diamond earrings, into the toilet. For good measure, she had a quick pee before flushing everything away. She remembered watching the shiny baubles circle and spin before the tidal wave carried them away forever.

Mommy never set her treasures beside her bed again. Or called in another babysitter. The memory of it made Hanna grin, but it was hot in the car and she was hungry. A part of her wanted to get back in the tube, where she could spin around like a ship in orbit. Sometimes she couldn't tell where she wanted to be. Far away in outer space? Or closer than close. Sometimes she wished she could remember being in Mommy's tummy. Were they both really happy then? When their blood was all jumbled up and they shared a mystery?

SUZETTE

SHE TUCKED THE little travel pillow against her abdomen before fastening the seat belt. It wasn't such a necessary precaution anymore, but sometimes when she hit a pothole it made her wince. She described for Alex how it felt, feeling the places inside her knit back together. Once, on a slow day at Phipps Conservatory in their early months of dating, they meandered from room to room, lingering in front of whatever odd plant caught their attention. The sweat dripped from their temples as they stood shoulder to shoulder in the sun-filled glass enclosure, entranced as they watched a grassy plant burst upward in spurts of growth. The sound attracted them first—they could hear the plant growing!

"That's how it feels inside sometimes. Like little bursts of mending. It's like I can feel filaments reaching out, webbing together. Like that plant we watched grow at Phipps."

"Must be weird," Alex had said as he gently caressed her tender flesh.

"It doesn't hurt exactly, but it startles me." And it was reassuring that her body knew how to put itself back together. Though she still willed it to mend correctly, without the aberration of another fistula.

Suzette concentrated on the traffic; midday Oakland was always a mess. She regretted not going in the other direction. She could have stopped by Alex's office if they'd gone that way—his firm owned a building on McKee Place that had once been a church. He and his partner, Matt, had fully remodeled it, keeping the main room—open and airy—as a conference room with an immense table made of recycled paper. She knew Hanna loved the atrium, which had once been the altar. They'd installed skylights so the trees would reach for the light. Visiting Daddy would have been a treat; he'd give Hanna his effortless kisses and affection. Sometimes it bothered Suzette, how Hanna lit up in his presence, becoming as loving toward her daddy as he was toward her. It wasn't that Suzette had never tried to be more loving, but her efforts waned as Hanna continually pushed her away. Still, she'd behaved very well through her appointments; she deserved a little reward.

"So Hanna, I want to thank you for being so good today." She looked in the rearview mirror, but Hanna wouldn't meet her eye. "Why don't we stop at Trader Joe's and you can pick out a little—"

Hanna burst into happy clapping. Suzette smiled, pleased with herself.

"You're becoming such a big girl. And the doctor had good news: you're totally fine. Perfect health. It might be a good time to start looking for a school. It's been a while and you'll probably like it better—"

Hanna slammed her hands against the window, shrieking as if she'd awakened in a coffin.

"Stop it!" Suzette didn't think Hanna was strong

enough to break the glass, but the girl seemed determined to try. Suzette regretted spoiling their good moment.

"Okay! You wouldn't be going to school now, not right now. We'd be looking for the fall—"

Hanna kept pounding on the window, squawking in anger.

Suzette wanted to whip around and slap her knee, but the cars inched together nose-to-tail; she couldn't risk turning away. Why had she said anything? Another of her stupid parental fails. The light mercifully turned red and she put on the brakes. She snapped off her seat belt so she could turn all the way around.

"Stop it right now! We're not going to Trader Joe's if you keep acting like a brat!"

Hanna switched off her tantrum. They competed in a stare-off, which Suzette lost when she glanced at the stoplight. But she quickly reengaged with her daughter.

"You think this is funny? These games you play? Someday it's gonna get you in real trouble. You're not going to get your way forever."

Hanna smiled. And nodded her head.

A car beeped at them. "All right!" Suzette put her foot on the gas and the car lurched forward. With one hand, she refastened her seat belt. "And I expect you to behave well in the store—you behave well, and you can pick out what you want."

Suzette saw the smug grin on her daughter's face; Hanna might have thought she'd won, but the issue of school wouldn't be dropped that easily. She'd get Alex on her side before they brought it up again. Meanwhile, if she was lucky, she could appease Hanna with a bag of dark chocolate–covered blueberries, and hope they could maintain the peace for the rest of the day.

In the store, Hanna dropped her favorite items into the cart while Suzette pushed it along, lost in thought. Alex. Naked. Alex's mouth. Alex's comforting arms. Alex's torso and the way they fit together. She didn't love his trendy beard, but he looked good in it. More reddish than his corn-silk hair, and he kept it fairly short. He liked his beauty products. He liked beauty—Suzette's, their daughter's. He dressed well and kept himself fit, but he wasn't tradi-tionally handsome. His features were too crowded in the center of his face; when they first met, she had an impulse to pinch his cheeks and stretch them out, giving his eyes, nose, mouth a little more room. But the minute he started talking to her by the coffee machine at her first and only post-school job, he exuded such warmth and interest. His kindness transformed him, making him so easy to talk to. And so gorgeous.

They were all the way to the refrigerated section when Suzette realized she'd forgotten the bananas. She scanned the cart, pleasantly surprised that Hanna hadn't picked up any strange items, just her Puffins, a jar of peaches, a bag of organic tortilla chips, and a frozen spinach pizza. Suzette experienced a rare bloom of pride, hopeful that she'd managed to teach Hanna about healthy food choices.

"Did you want to get your blueberries?" she asked as they backtracked past the fruit, nuts, and chocolate.

Hanna grabbed up multiple bags of various chocolate-covered fruit.

"Hey, how about just one of each." That was still more than she usually allowed, but she wanted Alex to have proof of the reward she'd given to her. She knew how he envisioned their family: his good daughter and his perfect wife. The loving, caring mother who successfully eased her daughter's fears of the scary machine and found a new path to try on the quest for their sweet child's health and happiness. (The perfect, devoted wife who worried her family was slipping away. She'd spent years in the pre-Alex abyss and couldn't survive another descent.)

When Hanna didn't listen, Suzette plucked the extra pouches out of the cart. Hanna only whined a little, half-heartedly stamping her foot.

"It's still four times what you usually get."

Flashing a triumphant grin, Hanna bounded off to the produce section.

From elsewhere in the store, a young child was crying. Recognizing the long, determined wails of a tantrum, Suzette felt immediate sympathy for the parent. The cries increased in volume when she reached the produce area, where a mother struggled to hang on to an erupting toddler in one hand as she pushed a full cart with the other. The toddler's screaming grew louder and more determined, and Suzette made out individual words—Want! No!—as he raged.

Just as she was about to tell Hanna to stop licking the lemons, Hanna abandoned them to go watch the tantrum. Suzette kept a watchful eye on her and quickly placed bananas and apples, Brussels sprouts and salad fixings into the cart.

"Hanna, come on."

The toddler, red-faced, tried to wrestle out of his mother's grasp. When he realized he couldn't, his body went rigid and he howled at the ceiling. The other shoppers made a wide arc around the commotion, their faces pinched and judgmental. Hanna stepped right in front of the bellowing little boy, bending at the waist as she put a finger to her mouth. Sssshhh.

It startled him for a moment and he quieted.

"Hanna, come on—we're ready to go."

"She's a sweet little girl," said the other mother.

"Thanks." Suzette, not trusting in Hanna's sweetness, extended her hand, knowing Hanna wouldn't take it, but hoping she would move along.

The toddler exploded again, this time with Hanna as the object of his rage. He lashed out at her with a sloppy punch and resumed screeching.

"Brandon, you know better . . ." said the other mother.

Before Suzette could stop her, Hanna drew back a closed, determined fist and struck the boy on the side of the head.

The boy tottered, stunned, then dropped to his bottom.

"Oh no!" Suzette rushed over, tugging Hanna away. "I'm sorry—we're so sorry!"

The mother scooped Brandon into her arms, her face alight with shock. He burst into tears, breathy cries of pain.

"Is he okay? I'm so sorry!" Suzette glared down at Hanna. "We do not hit people!"

Hanna pointed at the boy, her silent way of condemning him as the instigator.

The mother held him away from them, checking his eye, his ear, the soft spot along his temple. She bounced him, trying to soothe his tears.

Reading the hateful, how-dare-you-make-my-day-worse glower on the mother's face, Suzette clutched Hanna's hand and escaped to the checkout lanes. She would have just left, abandoned the cart, and fled in shame. But things would get worse if Hanna had to leave the store without her treat.

Suzette's hands shook and she babbled as the cashier scanned her items.

"Hanna, you absolutely know hitting is wrong. And he's just a little—it doesn't matter, you can't hit people, ever. That is not okay, and you know that is not okay . . ."

Hanna sighed, bored. Suzette kept her head down as they left the store, certain everyone would recognize her as the mother who couldn't control her violent child. Slugging a toddler.

"I can't believe you did that."

After buckling herself into her car seat, Hanna gazed at Suzette, expectant and unblinking. She tilted her head and quirked her mouth, and Suzette knew exactly what she was threatening. A tantrum of her own, unless Suzette handed over the goods.

Suzette put the shopping bags in the front seat, far from Hanna's reach, and dug out a pouch of dark chocolate–covered blueberries.

"This is *not* a reward for what you did in the store,"

she said before handing them over. "You earned this by being good at the doctor's, but Daddy and I will have to talk about what you did, because hitting is unacceptable. Okay?"

Hanna grinned, tearing open the bag, and God help her but Suzette saw nothing but devilish pride in her daughter's face. She wanted to rip the pouch from her hands. But she was too tired. Too tired and she just wanted to get home.

It was always too much to hope for that an entire day would go well.

As they drove, Hanna nibbled her blueberries and hummed a nasally tune that almost made her sound cheerful, normal. Suzette prayed the chocolate would be enough to mollify her until Alex got home, when Hanna could be counted on to put on her angelic mask and become Daddy's good little girl.

HANNA

THEIR HOUSE WAS different from the other houses on their tight Shadyside street, like it was from the future. She loved it because it was safe, and familiar, and Daddy designed the whole thing. He always said Mommy helped him with the inside, but Hanna knew she just picked out the furniture—stuff not so different from things she'd seen in the IKEA catalog. Everything was white or natural-looking wood. But the magical part was all Daddy's doing: the glass wall that overlooked the big garden, even from the second floor. The space-age stairs. The cool cleanness of the whole interior, better than a flying saucer.

The L-shaped living room couch was custom-made. Hanna liked to leap off the built-in slats that stuck out at the ends. Mommy always yelled "Stop standing on the tables!" but to Hanna they looked like diving platforms. She liked to stick her fingers in the potted plants to see if they needed to be watered, but Mommy always yelled at her for sprinkling dirt on the floor. Mommy liked things to be clean. And she liked to yell, when Daddy wasn't around. Hanna liked to play in the walled-in garden, the high fence and hedges a barrier that obscured the other houses, and hid them all from the neighbors' curious eyes. No one bothered her as she ran around saving all the passengers from the sinking ship. She filched the money from their pockets and the gems from their necks before pushing them into the lifeboat. Sometimes she galloped around and around, astride her magnificent gray horse.

She stood in front of the giant television, flipping through the channels.

"Hanna—it's not time for TV, you haven't done any schoolwork today."

Behind her, Mommy put away the Trader Joe's stuff in the cabinets that reminded her of fog. When she was little, she climbed onto the counter and carefully took out all the plates and bowls. She was about to hoist herself in, wanting to see the foggy cabinet from the inside where she imagined it would be like being in a cloud. Then Daddy scooped her into his arms. "Whatcha doing, little monkey?" He wasn't mad and she giggled.

She kept pressing the buttons on the remote control, aware of her sticky fingers. She saw it in her mind, and then it happened: Mommy marched over and grabbed the remote. She made her disgusted face. "You've got chocolate . . ."

Mommy clicked her tongue and switched off the TV. She carried the remote back with her to the kitchen and got a paper towel and the fancy spray bottle and rubbed away Hanna's cooties. Hanna grinned behind her hand, licking it clean.

"Come on, we'll start with a little spelling bee, it'll be fun. You can impress me with all the hard words you know." Mommy got some supplies out of the cupboard where they kept the school things.

Hanna trudged over. She sat on her knees in a chair at the big tree-slab table that hovered between the kitchen and the living room.

Mommy stuck a pencil into the electric sharpener, whirring it until it was sharp enough to poke out an eye. Hanna liked that part, and watched as Mommy did a second pencil. Mommy handed them both to her, and slid over a piece of paper.

"We'll just do a few. It'll be a short school day. First word: *love*. I love sleeping. You love the color yellow. *Love*."

As Hanna wrote down an answer, Mommy tucked the reading book under her arm so Hanna couldn't see the answers and went back to the kitchen to get herself a glass of water and two white pills. She swallowed the pills as she came back.

"Got it? Ready?" Mommy sat across from her, looking weird and wobbly as she rubbed at two spots on either side of her head.

Hanna held up her paper so Mommy could see what she'd written.

Hate

"Nice try. But this isn't word association. Do you want to spell out *love*?"

Hanna shook her head. She knew Mommy tried to be her most extra patient when they did schoolwork, because it was Important. Daddy said that all the time, so Hanna usually tried her best so Daddy would gush about how smart she was. But she needed Mommy to understand how it would be if she forced her to go to school. Mommy should never have brought it up.

"Okay, we'll do a different word. How about . . . *summer*. In a couple of months it will be summer. Hanna's *Farmor* and *Farfar* come to visit every summer."

So easy peasy. Hanna wrote something on her paper, then turned it around to show Mommy.

Bitch

Mommy's sigh half-melted her and she could barely keep her floppy-self sitting upright. "That's not a nice word. I'm not even surprised you know how to spell it. Could you please spell the words I'm asking you to spell? The sooner we finish this, the sooner we can move on to other things."

Hanna sat poised, ready for the next word.

"*Strawberry*. *Straw-berry*. She couldn't eat just one strawberry."

Hanna covered the paper with her hand so Mommy couldn't see what she was writing.

"That seems a bit long for one word—what are you spelling over there?"

Hanna giggled and kept writing. When she was ready, she held up her masterpiece.

Fuck Mommy. She is week and stupid.

A vein squiggled next to Mommy's eye and she clenched her jaw.

"Okay, that's it, you can work on your own for a while." As she got up, Mommy reached for the spelling test.

But Hanna was ready: she tore up the page into little pieces and sprinkled them on the table.

"Of course, no evidence for Daddy. Hanna, I don't want to do this with you right now. I know you couldn't have loved the CT and new doctor—don't you just want the rest of the day to be easy?" She scooped the paper scraps into her hand.

It wasn't just easy, it was fun. And here was Mommy, losing her patience. Bad, bad Mommy. Maybe she'd make a report card on Mommy and show it to Daddy, with a big fat failing *F*. But Mommy wasn't quite ready to give up. She opened another workbook and spun it around so Hanna could see it.

"You can read this short section . . . It's about ancient Egypt: the Pyramids, and the Pharaohs—they're like kings and queens, you'll like that. And then on the next page. Look, you'll get to write something out using hieroglyphs— that's like a secret language. You can write Daddy a secret message. Okay? Write him whatever you want. Tell him you hit a baby at the store. Tell him you've mastered spelling profane words." She headed for the kitchen. After sprinkling the spelling test into the recycling bin, she gathered up her cleaning supplies and trusty rubber gloves. "And by the way, you used the wrong spelling—it's w-e-*a*-k. Because Mommy is not a day of the week."

Hanna wasn't sure whether to laugh or scowl. She didn't like to be corrected. But she always enjoyed seeing

Mommy like this, in her natural state of hating and giving up. If only Daddy could see it, then he'd understand that Mommy was phony. When he was around, Mommy was kissy and helpful. But it was an act she couldn't keep up. If Hanna kept trying, Mommy's face would dribble off and Daddy would shriek and toss her out of the house.

Hanna experimented with sounds as she read through the paragraphs. "Nya. Bya. Fya. Pwa. Bwa. Dwa." She liked how French they sounded. She turned it into a repetitive singsong. "Dee dee dee dee dee dee dee dee dwa bwa pwa. Mee mee mee mee mee mee mee mee nya fya bya."

Mommy glanced at her over her bucket of vinegar and water. "Little more reading, little less singing."

"Bee bee bee bee bee bee bee, laa laa laa laa laa laa laaaaaaaaah! Di dee do do di dee do di ba ba baaaaaaah!"

"If you want to be vocal, *say* something. You're only giving away the fact that you *can* say something."

Hanna squished her lips together and batted her eyelashes. Mommy glared at her for a moment and went back to scrubbing the already clean kitchen. What a dumbo.

She liked how the Pyramids looked, but she wouldn't want to live in one. No windows. Then she read that they were tombs for the Pharaohs. Homes for dead people. Weird. They were buried with gold and food. Weirder. Like dead people would wear jewelry and get hungry. It reminded her of some research she'd done online. On Daddy's computer (because he let her use it sometimes). Fairy tales were full of ghosts and witches—people who weren't like regular people, capable of fascinating and creepy things. Once she even wore a black dress and a pointy hat for Halloween. She was desperate to know *But are they* real*?* and heaped her library books about witches onto Daddy's lap. He misunderstood. He patiently read them with her, but didn't understand what she was trying to find out. She googled it on her own.

Yes. Witches were real.

There were lots of them, especially in the golden days. Her search on "real witches" led her to Mother Shipton and Agnes Sampson. She'd read about young girls who were burned alive or tossed into a river to drown, weighted with stones, while the stupid villagers cheered. Nobody liked witches, that much was clear, but Hanna couldn't understand why. It made her giggle, thinking about the fun games she could play if she had a witch for a friend. Maybe such a friend could finally help her do what she'd struggled to do on her own: make Mommy go away and never come back. After digging around some more, curious about the witch hunts, she found a big list of people who were killed. One of them had a name she very much liked and still remembered—a pretty French name with soft letters, not like the ugly *n*'s that trampled through "Hanna Jensen."

She silently tested the words *Marie-Anne Dufosset* with her lips and tongue. Maybe if she repeated it enough, the French girl would come to her in spirit and be her bestest friend. She and Marie-Anne could make up songs and sing them together. Marie-Anne could teach her how to cast spells with the words no one else understood. Spells that would make Mommy's heart explode.

Marie-Anne Dufosset. Marie-Anne Dufosset.

Ha, it worked! Marie-Anne helpfully instructed her on how to get her vocalization just right.

"Nya nya, nya nya. Boo dee boo dee baaa! Bwa bwa bwa bwa loo lee loo lee laaa!"

Mommy tilted her head. Hanna loved the look she gave her—the one that said *I give up*.

"Fine." She gathered up her bucket and sponge and, head held high, marched away. Up the space-age stairs and into the master bedroom.

Hanna cackled. It was a start. They had made Mommy disappear.

SUZETTE

SHE TENDED TO the house as if it were a newborn, needing constant attention to thrive. She knew what squalor looked like—a grimy bucket or chipped bowl beneath every exposed pipe, every ceiling a topographic map of peeling paint—and as long as she was with Alex she need never see it again. To enjoy the tactile sensation, she went around the house barefoot, and the bathroom floor was her favorite: cool, smooth stone. The tingling against the soles of her feet traveled all the way up to her throbbing head, offering more relief than the Tylenol. In circular scrubs, she worked her way across the quartz countertop. Alex spared no expense to make the master bathroom the spa she longed for. A long trough sink. A soaking tub with sleek, oceanic curves, large enough for the two of them to share like a womb. The shower with its pair of rainfall nozzles, so they could stand together and close their eyes, transporting themselves to distant places—misty Ireland, balmy Thailand. Toilet. Bidet. A tall window, the bottom half frosted. Everything white. Everything clean. The only thing he hadn't been able to give her was a skylight, because of his third-floor home office.

It had been an extravagance: Gutting the whole house;

reframing for larger, more efficient windows throughout; moving the interior stairwells. He'd only just started Jensen & Goldstein, but Pittsburgh was a hot market for home-owners and businesses wanting Scandinavian-inspired green renovations: the most modern finishes, state-of-the-art recycled materials, creatively readapted objects and architectural bits. They employed—and were hired by—bright young visionaries. The firm, and its reputation, grew quickly; they designed or rehabbed interesting homes and buildings all around the city. After their office was featured in a local newspaper, repurposing old churches became one of their specialties. So Alex turned the house that once looked so unimpressive, purchased right after their wedding when they were both twenty-six, into their dream home. They'd already decided they would have a child and Suzette would be a stay-at-home mom, at least for a few years.

It was a mistake, she realized, to examine the mirror for smudges, because all she saw was herself. A charred but unexploded stick of dynamite. She peeled off her gloves. Smoothed down her hair. Fixed the smears of mascara. She took off her belt and lifted her dress to examine the healing scars. Three laparoscopic ones, each about an inch long, lay strategically around the newly remade one: The canyon of uneven flesh removed; the skin pulled together tight and stitched back up in a tidy line. It was better. Not better enough for a bikini, but maybe in its new form the old trauma would start to dissipate.

She'd told Alex about her health problems on their second date, a picnic in the park, because they'd kissed after the first movie-pizza date, and she was afraid that if things grew more intimate he'd be repulsed by her scar. It was hard for him to understand everything at first, because he hadn't been raised in such a dysfunctional household, but he listened, really listened. His attention was comforting, and she told her life story for the first time. How, at thirteen, the stomach pains started, followed by almost constant diarrhea. Her world spiraled downward.

"My mother shrugged it off. Said it happened to her at the same age. Hormones."

"But . . . When you never got better?" Alex asked.

"I didn't think of it as being sick anymore. It became normal."

But what she and her mother called normal, other people called Crohn's disease.

She retreated from the world and became afraid of food; maybe if she stopped eating, her stomach would get better. But it didn't. On the night before her seventeenth birthday, she lay awake as her intestines twisted and screamed with wrongness. Sometimes she wished she'd had the bravery to lie there and accept her slow and agonizing death. Instead, she awakened her mother.

They arrived at the hospital, and her mother played her best parlor trick and transmogrified into a commonplace person. She wore nice clothes and a facial expression of parental concern. When the triage nurse asked how long Suzette had been having abdominal pain, she said it started overnight. Her mother, in her mother costume, nodded and asserted that it was out of the ordinary. "I brought her in straightaway."

Suzette declined to have her mother present for the exam.

The doctors ravaged all her virginal orifices in search of a diagnosis. Suspecting appendicitis, they performed emergency surgery and found her lower intestines in a knot.

Her mother wasn't there when she awakened in a dark room, a tube in her nose, her midsection alight with a throbbing exigence for which she had no words.

Weeks later, when it seemed as if she'd recovered well, she developed a fistula—a slender channel that grew from the site of her bowel resection to the surface incision. She found herself on the operating table with a cloth across her eyes. They cut into her jugular and inserted a central line without anesthetic. "Young people can handle the pain," the surgeon explained to someone she couldn't see. She didn't scream (though she wanted to). But she never forgot (though she wanted to). They put her to sleep a few minutes later to reopen her abdomen.

The idea was to keep the incision open and let the fistula heal on its own. Shit and puss oozed through the hole for the better part of four years. Four years during which it seemed impossible that she would ever live a regular life, or do ordinary things like kiss a boy or have a job. She thought often about killing herself, but she developed a career plan and eventually got herself into art school. And then there was Alex.

"If I hadn't met you . . . The freakish existence of my life might have gone on forever."

He kissed her then, with tears in his eyes. And months later, he admitted that he fell in love with her on that second date, seeing her so vulnerable, and inspired by her astonishing resolve and inner strength.

A light hand rapped on the other side of the door.

Suzette clenched her jaw and shut her eyes. Go away. Go away. Please go away.

Tap-tap-tap.

"Just a minute." She let the dress slip back down to her knees. Gave her right abdomen a comforting little rub to encourage the healing.

Tap-tap-tap.

"Mommy needs a minute."

Tap-tap-tap. Tap-tap-tap.

She ripped open the door, her teeth bared. "What is so fucking important?"

Her daughter looked so small. The picture of a good girl in a pretty dress. Her mouth hung open a bit, in fear or shock. The workbook dangled from Hanna's left hand, and in her right fist she gripped the pencil.

She'd only come to ask a question, to get help. A better mom would have known that. Or at least not have lost her temper so quickly.

The brittle bones in Suzette's chest collapsed. Even the easy things were hard. "I'll be down in a minute. Sorry. Be right down to help you."

She shut the door and quickly locked it so Hanna wouldn't see her cry.

For several moments she paced, huffing in and out like a runner at the end of a race. Get it together. Get it together. Get it together. A twinge, electrical, poked beneath her incision like a warning. This is what anger, frustration, stress of any kind did to her: sent her body into overdrive, signaled the soldiers to come out and kill, and everything they shot was collateral damage. Life with an autoimmune disease. She couldn't afford prolonged periods of distress, and she worried how her murky internalization of being Hanna's frustrated mother was taking its toll.

The ileostomy bag taunted her—*I'll make you more disgusting than you've ever been. You'll have to handle a nub of your own intestine and make sure your bag of shit doesn't overflow.* How was she going to turn this around and not let it become her inevitable future? Being a stay-at-home mom was meant to be part of a low-stress solution; it wasn't a choice made because she lacked drive or talent.

When they met, before Alex had his own firm, she was an interior designer—as ambitious and adept with her work as Alex was with his. They were paired on a project, the green-loving newbies who clicked into a companionship that became inseparable. But the overtime and juggling of deadlines took its toll. It was her first career position. Her ambition started to crumble as her wretched bowels became more unpredictable. Shit shit shit.

She didn't need to work after they got engaged and she moved into his apartment. She thought she'd do some freelance work, but mostly she cooked and cleaned and waited for Alex to get home. Her Crohn's quieted down. She started sketching again—not just elegantly functional interiors, but more-abstract things from her imagination. After starting Jensen & Goldstein, Alex brought her in as a consultant on a part-time basis and let her choose the projects that appealed to her. She credited him with loving her back to health.

Then she got pregnant.

She'd expected a spiritual revelation; instead, her pregnancy demarcated the beginning of an extended sense of loss. Loss of self. Loss of Alex as the sole and cherished member of her tribe. Loss of her regained health.

Her body became more and more foreign, more and more distressed. In the middle months when she was meant to be gaining and expanding, all systems rebelled. She had so much cramping and diarrhea that she struggled to gain enough weight during the pregnancy. Dr. Stefanski advised her to double her daily intake of Imodium, but the drug he promised would help the most would have to wait: the biological injections were too dangerous to risk on a growing fetus. The exhaustion was so debilitating they considered hiring a full-time nanny if her health didn't improve after the birth. She started to hope the baby would come early, not caring if it was slightly premature. She needed relief and wanted the medication, no matter how toxic.

She tried, during her worst moments, to hold on to the earliest days, the glorious days. When she and Alex beamed with radiant light. Their love had created a living, breathing creature who would someday hold the universe in its eyes and look at everything with wonder. But when it reached a size that she could feel within her, it seemed not like a baby but like a mass. And then they made the mistake of rewatching *Alien* and she burst into tears, knowing that's how her baby would emerge, a monster that would tear her apart.

"It's just the Crohn's, she's fine," Alex cooed, drying her tears, caressing her extended mound. "Right after she's born, we'll get you on the new meds."

As much as Alex tried to comfort her, she couldn't stop the flashbacks, not when a pregnancy was, after all, a medical ordeal. Not a spiritual awakening.

She dreaded all the necessary doctor appointments where she was supposed to surrender her own privacy and fears of being tortured for the benefit of the baby. Like it was already someone else's body and their needs superseded her own. The minute she felt herself getting selfish and resentful, she thought: this is how it started, how my mother came to hate the responsibilities of motherhood. And then she'd have a change of heart and embrace her precious, fragile creature, and of course she'd do whatever it took. Endure the indignities of invasive exams because her beloved baby monster needed her, and she would prove that her instincts were strong, in spite of learning nothing from her own mother. Nothing but what not to do. Suzette vowed—with a savagery that put a spark of fear in Alex's eyes—she'd never be a mother who dismissed her child's pain. She'd never not care, she'd never be indifferent toward her child's quality of life.

"Of course you're not like that," he said. "You're a loving, talented, wonderful woman—you'll be a wonderful mother. Full of love and life."

But it was his love that created her life. Did she have enough of her own love to spare? The baby wasn't supposed to remind her of an internal mass of pooling waste. The forty weeks weren't supposed to be remembered for the new pains of a Crohn's flare-up, or the demanding medical regimen that modernity required. She told Alex many times she wished they could go rent a farm, and while harvesting the cabbages she'd squat in the earth and give birth. In the end, she had her epidural and pushed like a champ, and it was worth it for the look on Alex's face as he held their newborn daughter in his arms. The moment sealed it for him: Hanna was perfect, and Suzette his hero. In the years since, she did everything possible not to disrupt his mirage of familial tranquility; at least one of them was consistently happy.

Her health and digestion improved dramatically after starting the injections, but it remained a source of guilt that she'd never nursed Hanna. What unintentional harm might her baby have suffered? Might Hanna have developed differently with the early benefits of her milk's precious antibodies? Suzette tried to compensate by laser-focusing her love as she fed Hanna a bottle. She cherished Hanna's infancy. By the time Hanna was three months old, she prided herself on her knack for mothering. Baby Hanna was like an ever-changing work of art, with those expressive eyes, her little eyebrows that wiggled with concern.

It should have kept getting better as Hanna grew into a toddler and started establishing her own identity. She and Alex prepared themselves for tantrums and rebelliousness, and looked forward to hearing her say "No!" and "Mine!" But while the tantrums started on schedule, other milestones were left behind. At first, when they started to worry about her verbal skills, helping Hanna gave Suzette a purpose unlike anything she'd ever experienced. She worked with Hanna every day, enunciating words, trying to make fun games out of teaching her. But more often than not, Hanna stared at her with an unnervingly skeptical look, then burst into smiles when Alex entered the room. Suzette tried for a long time, but as the years went on the constant failure was a punch to the gut. A gut that couldn't take much more trauma.

She pulled the rubber gloves back on. Sometimes she wished she had a full rubber bodysuit. It was armor against the germs—the drug compromised her immune system—but more important, the gloves made her feel purposeful. They symbolized hard work and productivity, cleanliness, and ultimately beauty. It was something she strove for, physical perfection. Her own might always be flawed (though she compensated as best she could), but the house was something she could master. Through the effort, she manifested her worth.

She set the bucket on the floor and got down on her hands and knees. And scrubbed along the path where she had paced, erasing her own invisible footprints.

Usually, such methodic movements lulled her into a spacey, unfocused state. A place where she could decompress. But she worried about what to tell Alex. Good news: nothing's physically wrong with Hanna. Bad news: the problem might be in her head. Would he be upset? He never saw Hanna do things like lash out at a much younger child, and disbelieved much of the bad behavior that her kindergarten teachers had reported. He was convinced they were exaggerating because Hanna wasn't milestone typical. They'd started referring, between themselves, to "Hanna's disability," and while Alex insisted the world was becoming more tolerant and inclusive of such differences, the elite schools they'd enrolled her in were not.

"She's so smart, way above average, even without being verbal," Alex had boasted many times.

Suzette knew he still hoped for full, if delayed, integration. Had enough time passed? Would Hanna be ready by fall? Perhaps the new developmental psychologist could help them prepare her. It worried Suzette that Alex didn't know everything—she'd stopped the daily updates years before when she saw the growing annoyance in his face. He made her feel like a complainer; incompetent. Their time together went more smoothly without the behavioral reports. But if she repeated the doctor's assessment—that refusing to speak required very different treatment than being unable to speak—then Alex would have to accept that some-most-all of Hanna's willfulness was intentional. Their daughter was playing with them, in different ways. Fucking with them. Manipulating them for her own sadistic purposes.

She threw the sponge into the bucket and cautioned herself to stop. Accusing a seven-year-old of sadism might be taking it a bit too far. But though Suzette had tried, she couldn't figure out her daughter's game. She loved the girl so effortlessly when she was a baby, a toddler. People told her those were the hardest times, before a child could speak her needs, but for her they were the easiest. Baby Hanna had simple, intuitive needs. Girl Hanna was a box within a box, each layer wrapped in a bow that was really a trickster's knot. Once, she and Alex had orbited each other, their hands clasped together as gravity spun them in perfect circles. The addition of Hanna made it all wonky.

An image flashed behind her eyes. A runaway

asteroid, knocking Hanna out of their orbit. If it were just the two of them, they could find their equilibrium again.

Tap-tap-tap.

She blinked away the treasonous thought.

Hanna was still there? She hadn't gone back downstairs? Suzette sat back on her heels and didn't respond.

Tap-tap-tap. Tap-tap-tap.

"I said I'll be right down."

Whap-whap. Hanna slammed her palm on the closed door. Kicked it. Uttered a high-pitched squeal of protest.

"Hanna! Go downstairs! Move on to another question that you can do on your own and I'll be down in a minute!"

She waited, listening, hoping to hear an exasperated *humphh* of defeat and the retreating sound of small feet. But no. The doorknob jiggled. Tentatively, then more insistently. Hanna kicked the door again.

They didn't spank. And Alex never even yelled. The only profanity he used in front of her was in Swedish. But the kid was pushing it. Suzette unlocked the door and whipped it open.

"For fuck's sake, Hanna. Why don't you ever listen to me?"

The girl stood there, arms loosely at her sides, considering her mother. Then her eyes rolled back until they were solid white. Dead nothingness in the sockets.

"Because I'm not Hanna," the girl whispered.

HANNA

"WHAT?"

That's all Mommy said. Then she shook her head, harder and harder so her eyeballs rattled around. She clutched her tummy and slammed the door. Hanna pressed her ear to it. The lock clicked. Mommy moaned, but she didn't cry or scream. It got too quiet, so Hanna raked her fingernails down the door's wooden grain. Water ran and splashed. She got down on her belly to peer into the crack of space beneath the door, but all she could make out were Mommy's feet, standing in front of the sink.

Not quite the reaction she'd been hoping for—she thought Mommy would be more impressed. Or scared. And in case she had been more inquisitive, Hanna had a list of short answers at the ready, stuff she remembered from her Google search. It was a little disappointing that Mommy didn't want to know about her special friend. Poo-poo to her; Hanna would try again later.

She skipped out into the hallway and dropped her schoolbook at the top of the stairs. There was nothing fun to do in her room, so she padded down the hall and up to Daddy's attic study. By far, it was the best room in the house. The angled ceiling made it so cozy, like the walls were giving her a hug. Daddy's study revealed that he and Mommy were nothing alike. He had a mess of stuff, though he kept his big worktable tidy. A squooshy chair, a fluffy rug, and shelves and shelves of books and weird things. Light poured in through the windows in the roof. She picked up one of his models—her favorite, the Viking ship—and carried it over to the window that looked out over their street. The glass came all the way to the floor, so she sat and watched a bubble car try to squeeze in between two silver tanks. The bubble car just fit, and the lady who got out grabbed her yoga mat from the trunk and hurried off down the street.

Daddy always said he liked Shadyside because they could walk everywhere, which reminded him of the city where he grew up. He always talked about Sweden with a big smile on his face. She often wanted to ask him about where he was from. Sometimes he told her things, like how he'd left with his parents when he was a teenager because *Farmor* got a position at Carnegie Mellon University. *Farmor* was proud that her son followed in his footsteps, which baffled Hanna because *Farmor* and *Farfar* later moved all the way across the country, to Tucson, Arizona, and Daddy had not once tried to walk there.

She bobbed the Viking ship in an invisible sea. When it landed, she stormed ashore with her battle-ax, ready to chop up the villagers and steal their gold. Daddy said most Vikings were farmers who did little, if any, raiding, but she had no interest in being a boring farmer. When she had all the gold she could carry, she put the boat back and turned off the light. She passed her parents' big bedroom, but inside, the bathroom door was still closed. She scooped up her book and pencil and headed downstairs.

She was still in front of the TV, practicing writing in hieroglyphs, when Daddy got home from work. She ran to greet him. He was so tall, so he always got down on one knee to give her a hug.

"How's my squirrelly girl?"

She jumped up and down as her fingers played in his cantaloupe-tinged beard and his coffee breath tickled her nose. Daddy was the most handsome man in the world. He dressed nicely, in crisp shirts and colorful ties, and his favorites were the ones she picked out for him. When she grew up she'd marry him, and then Mommy wouldn't be competition anymore.

"That good?"

She nodded like her head was huge, and flashed a big smile of uneven teeth. It bothered her that they were falling out, but Mommy said it was normal. They celebrated every time she lost one, but to her it remained a horror. She liked her little baby teeth. She didn't want a snarling mouth of adult-size teeth. Not until the rest of her face had grown up, too.

Daddy put his lunch kit on the counter and took out the used containers that once held his food.

"Where's Mommy? Did you have your big round and around scan today?"

Affirmative, said her head.

"How'd that go?"

She mushed her lips together and shrugged.

Mommy slunk down the stairs, perpetually alert for Daddy's voice.

"My two girls, in fine dresses," he said.

Mommy stood on tiptoe to give him a kiss. "It was better before, with the belt and the shoes." She glanced at Hanna with red-rimmed eyes.

"Have you been crying?" Daddy asked.

"Tired. A little stressed."

Immediately concerned, he took Mommy's hands. Hanna hung by the kitchen counter, watching everything.

"Everything okay with . . ." He flicked his head toward her.

"Yes." Mommy flashed a fake smile. "Let's talk later. I need to start supper."

"Need help with anything?" He pressed in close, his eyes glued to her.

"Help Hanna with her homework?"

"Sure, *älskling*. Sure you're okay?"

She nodded like a clackety-clack skeleton that was about to fall apart. Daddy was reluctant to let her go, to leave her alone, but finally he reached out to Hanna.

"Okay squirrely girl, it's you and me. What are you working on today?"

Hanna scooped up her book and the pair of deadly pencils. She pointed up—way, way up.

"Want to work in my study?"

Excited, she grabbed his hand and did a little gallop.

"Sounds good to me."

Daddy started pulling off his tie as they headed up

the stairs. At the landing, Hanna turned back to look at Mommy. She stood with a hand on her hip, studying the contents of the refrigerator. She caught Hanna's eye, so Hanna smiled and waved. Mommy's mouth shrunk into a tight line.

SUZETTE

USUALLY SHE MADE Alex something a bit nicer, a bit more involved, but she didn't feel like chopping vegetables and messing with ingredients. She just wanted to get him alone. To tell him what Hanna said.

What did it mean? Could Suzette have misheard her? Were they just nonsense sounds, one of her little singsongs? She could've sworn she heard an accent. It didn't make any sense. Hanna's first words should have been something to celebrate, but Suzette writhed with uncertainty. And dread. If she heard Hanna correctly . . . If she wasn't Hanna . . . Around and around, the doubt and terror spun. Was one of them going crazy? Both of them? And those empty eyes still made her crackle with fear.

By the time they all sat down to her basic garlic-and-olive-oil pasta with last night's leftover veggies and a fresh salad that Suzette declined to try, she questioned if she should even tell him. It was too easy to imagine him over-looking the specificity of Hanna's ominous words in favor of celebrating the achievement of speaking. Or, knowing Hanna, she'd screw up her face, puzzled, and act completely baffled by Suzette's announcement and pretend it never happened. Whose side would Alex take then? Even

Suzette thought it more likely that, mired in worries, she'd misinterpreted what she saw and heard. A nightmare mingling with life, not reality.

She let him dominate the conversation, grateful for the upbeat normality of his presence. He filled her in on Jensen & Goldstein's latest success, a commission for an all-new, all-green structure on a tiny empty lot of prime downtown real estate.

"They're going to give us a lot of freedom in choices of materials. We'll really be able to make a unique statement. I've always wanted to take a crack at a really skinny, unusual space."

"This house was practice," she said, trying to share his enthusiasm.

"Definitely—I showed them some of the pictures. You should help us with the interiors; they like your style. Nothing complements my clean lines the way your aesthetic does."

Her fine, considerate, supportive man, always trying to include her.

"*Skål!*" She clinked her wineglass against his. "And congratulations."

She hoped her happiness for him seemed genuine, because it was, to the degree that she could muster it. He went on and on as she moved bland pasta around her plate with a fork. She couldn't *not* tell him—this was something they'd been waiting for. If only Hanna had said something—anything—else.

"It's going to be four stories, and we're thinking of ways of making it look like a ship, round windows . . ."

What a heartwarming moment it could have been, if the girl had come to the door and said "Mommy." She hadn't heard any semblance of her name on her child's lips since she'd babbled "mamamama" as a baby. Alex would have been so proud—of both of them—if she could have made such an announcement. He would have kissed and cooed over them both, allowing her the victory of good mothering.

What sort of mother had a child who showed up like a demon to announce she wasn't even your daughter? And if Hanna didn't think she was Hanna, was she more disturbed than either of them had ever considered possible?

". . . while still making it fully handicapped accessible. Matt suggested long sloping walkways to connect—"

"Hanna spoke today."

Alex and Hanna stopped chewing in unison, turning their high-wattage shock on her in unison.

"Hanna what?"

"She spoke. Said words. Out loud."

A grin started to eclipse his face. "*Älskling* . . ." Then he turned from her to Hanna. "*Lilla gumman*, that's so—"

"She said she wasn't Hanna."

The grin faltered. "What?"

Suzette shrugged. "That's what she said. 'I'm not Hanna.' With her eyes rolled so she looked like . . . I don't know what she looked like. Something . . . monstrous."

Alex got that unseemly look that befell him when he was perplexed, or thinking too hard, where his features morphed together like the continents retracting, becoming the formless blob of Pangaea. Clouds of doubt whisked across his face. He put on a smile to try to mask the confusion.

"Is that what you said, *lilla gumman*? Did you talk to Mommy?"

Suzette expected Hanna to shake her head. And she did. She didn't expect her to go wide-eyed with fear and huddle beside her father. Hanna slapped her palm repeatedly against her little chest, pleading with Alex to understand.

"You're Hanna?"

She nodded and started whimpering, her eyes filling with tears. She slapped her chest harder.

"Of course you're Hanna; no one's saying you're not Hanna. You didn't talk to Mommy?"

She shook her head again and reached out for a hug.

Suzette sighed, exasperated, and propped her elbow up on the table so she could rest her weary head. Why had she fucking bothered?

He squeezed Hanna and kissed her hair. "Why don't you go up to your room for a little bit so Mommy and I can talk."

Suzette saw the moment Hanna registered her victory. And changed tactics. She pointed to the living room, the television, but Suzette had no intention of coddling her false anguish.

"I think you've watched enough TV for today."

Hanna slammed her foot on the ground and angrily shook her head.

"You did. I heard it from upstairs, the entire time I was in the bathroom." Alex quickly turned to her, a question on his face. "I wasn't feeling well," she said to him.

She didn't look at either of them as she got up to clear the table. "You can play in your room with some of your toys. Or read a book?"

She knew what was happening behind her: Hanna would put on a sad face and try to get Alex to cave to her desires. Half the time he did; a true diplomat, he evenly divided the amount of time that either one of them would be mad at him. But tonight he was on Suzette's side.

"Listen to Mommy. I'll be up later to read you a story."

Hanna drooped and trudged out of the room. Suzette watched her daughter's dainty feet move slowly up the stairs. She expected her to glower at her from the landing, but Hanna quietly retreated to her room.

Alex caressed her back as he joined her at the sink. "So what's going on?"

"That's what she said. She knocked on the door when I was in the bathroom and said, 'I'm not Hanna.' I knew you wouldn't believe me."

"It isn't that I don't want to believe you—I'd love for Hanna to speak. But that seems like a weird . . . I can't see her saying that, what does it even mean—"

"I have no idea—"

"And she seemed pretty scared . . ."

Suzette leaned her back against the counter and massaged the sore spots under her eyebrows, her thumb on one, index finger on the other. Hanna's announcement had worsened her headache.

"You weren't feeling well today?"

"Being there, at the medical center . . ."

He kissed her forehead and started massaging the

rest of her scalp. "Have you thought more? About finding someone to talk to?"

"I'm not crazy, she really—"

"For the PTSD. I hate that you get like this, maybe someone can help. Did you take any Percocet today?"

She lurched away from him.

"I was not on drugs! I was not high. I knew I shouldn't have told you."

"There's nothing wrong with taking it, if you're still having pain—"

"Alex. Are you even listening?"

For a moment they stood there, still and watchful as hunters. Or the beasts about to be shot.

"Yes. I was listening. And I was trying to find a logical explana—"

"There's no logical explanation, just forget it. Forget it."

She dumped their leftovers into Pyrex containers and shoved them into the refrigerator. Alex studied her, his expression cautious.

"Was she whispering? Was she maybe just singsonging—"

"Yes. I'm sure that's what it was. Because she couldn't possibly be a different child with me than she is with you. She hit a toddler while we were at the store."

"When?"

"Today. I took her for a treat."

"I can't help it if I don't see—if I'm not always there—"

"There's the rub of it." She reached back into the refrigerator and grabbed the half-empty bottle of white wine. "She's smart enough to make sure you never believe me."

She scooped up her wineglass from the table and carried it over to the couch, refilling the glass on her way. She set the bottle on the coffee table and stretched her legs out, flipping on *PBS NewsHour*. After a moment, Alex joined her, refilling his own glass as he settled in beside her. Neither of them said anything through an entire segment analyzing extreme weather events and the impact of climate change.

Finally, he slipped the remote out of her hand and lowered the volume. He eased closer to her, his head on her shoulder.

"I'm sorry."

Maybe this was her moment, when Alex was being contrite. "She's bored. She's too smart to just . . . be with me all day. And I'm tired . . ."

"I'm sorry, I shouldn't have had you schedule her stuff so soon after your—"

"No, I'm glad. I'm glad we went. The new doctor was helpful."

The peace brokered, they angled toward each other, the news program forgotten.

"He found something?"

"Nothing's physically wrong with her—we can definitively put that concern to rest."

"That's good, right?"

"I think so. He suggested a psychologist—a developmental psychologist, and was quick to say not a psychiatrist, because he didn't think she needed medication—"

"Okay . . ."

"But, maybe there's something else going on. Something . . . There could be something bothering her, holding her back."

Alex took a moment to consider her words. "That makes sense. We understand her so well. But I hate to think that she won't have opportunities, and people won't get to know her. I don't know why she . . . But from all the sounds she makes . . . She's so expressive, and I think she *can* talk—"

"You do?" She sucked in her lips to keep from pointing out his hypocrisy.

"Maybe it was something she struggled with at first. Maybe she's self-conscious about it. Sometimes I wonder if she talks to herself, and has a lisp or something and doesn't know how to fix it, doesn't want to sound different. Maybe she's become obsessed . . . That's what worries me most, I guess. That she's telling herself negative things. And because we don't know what they are we can't undo them."

Suzette squeaked her finger along the rim of her glass. Typically, Alex had a different explanation for Hanna's continued silence: the hopeful possibility that she might be self-conscious, not defiant.

"Well . . . I'm hoping the therapist can reassure her, in some way that we can't. I just wish . . ."

Alex cupped her cheek with his hand, his face earnest and full of compassion. "I know you just want the best for her. Don't feel like you've failed."

She wasn't sure anymore which failure should bother her most. That Hanna wouldn't talk, that Alex wasn't fully on her side, or that she'd lost faith in her own instincts. For far too long they'd tried to justify, each in different ways, Hanna's aberrant behavior. Should one of them have suggested a psychologist sooner? Were they behaving more like Suzette's mother than they realized?

"This is a good thing to try. Dr. Yamamoto sounds very experienced," she said, her tone more urgent than she'd intended, as if they could yet ameliorate whatever damage might have been caused to Hanna by their delay.

"And I'm fully supportive." As he reached out to her, his face softened. "I don't mean to make you feel like you're on your own, and especially . . . You need to heal and be well. I don't always know how to help, but I want to . . ."

A tiny, hard rubber ball came bouncing down the stairs. A second later, another one followed. At the bottom, they sprang about wildly and Hanna scampered down after them. She spun in circles, trying to catch them.

"Hanna. Go back to your room, please."

Hanna ignored her. She caught one of the balls and bounced it again, loping after its drunken movement as she swayed and held her arms out for balance.

"Hanna?" Suzette got up and walked around the couch, her arms crossed, her back to Alex. She didn't want him to see how she strained to control her temper. She wanted to lash out, scream, "Or whoever the fuck you are!" but couldn't. "Can you play upstairs until we're finished?"

A ball bounded past Suzette. Without even giving her a glance, Hanna flew after it.

"*Lilla gumman?* Mommy and I are talking. Go on up, I'll be up soon."

Plodding as she gathered up her bouncy balls, Hanna finally drifted upstairs.

Hanna's rebukes had become minor, but constant, acts of torture. A pinching of delicate skin. A solitary, but well-aimed, punch. Suzette felt purple and damaged, and didn't have the energy to hide it.

"She always listens to you," she said, sinking back down so she was perpendicular to Alex.

"She doesn't see me as much."

"She likes you better."

"That isn't true."

"It is."

"She doesn't speak to me either, *älskling*."

There was that. Maybe it was a victory, however fiendish, that Hanna had spoken to her first.

"Maybe it's time to give Sunnybridge a call," he said.

Suzette held her breath. She couldn't let it all gush out and reveal her relief. Slowly, she reached for her wineglass and took a sip.

Alex had always been reluctant about Sunnybridge. The stupid name aside, it was an alternative (hippie) school that focused on the arts, and he thought it wasn't academically inclined enough. When Hanna was still a baby, they'd debated between sending her to Green Hill Academy or the Frick School, which both proved to be impressive and pioneering in their academics.

Hanna was asked to leave Green Hill after five weeks. Suzette and Alex sat before a small panel of teachers and administrators and were informed that Hanna just wasn't emotionally ready for kindergarten. Her "inability to

interact" proved to be "more troubling than anticipated."
Alex, especially, grew offended as the meeting deteriorated
and the teachers' polite façades fell away. He'd never seen
Hanna "snarl aggressively" and couldn't believe their accusations that she "hid toys just so the other children couldn't
use them" and "broke things to be spiteful." They feared
that eventually Hanna would hurt another student—"We
suspect her of setting the cafeteria trash bin on fire"—at
which point Alex demanded a refund for the remaining
tuition and stormed out.

Suzette meekly apologized to the staff and hurried
after her husband.

Before the Green Hill Academy expulsion debacle,
she'd known Alex to have the least arousable—and quick
to dissipate—temper of any human she'd ever met. But for
days afterward, he simmered.

So Suzette got Hanna enrolled at the Frick School, and
Alex's mood returned to normal. Hoping it would help,
she gave the new teacher a heads-up on the ways that
Hanna had struggled at her previous school.

Suzette knew the young woman, with a delicate snail
tattoo on her wrist and the tiniest stud in her nose, had no
idea what she was in for. But she hoped—prayed—that
Hanna would respond to her youthful, boundless energy,
be enamored of her snail (or the rebellious mini piercing),
and try to please her. Suzette had already decided she'd
shield Alex, as best she could, from the truth if it didn't
work out. He'd never shown a remote or depressive side
until the expulsion, and she couldn't handle him in such a
state for a prolonged period.

When Suzette picked her up after her first day, the teacher remarked, "She might be quiet but she's not shy, quite the little spitfire." The end was already in sight. On her fifth day, the young woman twisted her long fingers in worry and reported that Hanna wasn't adjusting well. She wouldn't stop breaking all the crayons into little pieces. But worse, she liked to grab the goldfish out of its bowl. They'd caught her at it a few times, until they finally found the goldfish dead, scattered among a collection of similarly sized plastic animals. On her eighth day, Suzette was called in after Hanna had pretended to pass out from hunger. It was one thing for them to question if Hanna had ADHD; it was another for them to doubt Suzette's parenting.

Suzette didn't wait for another day. She withdrew Hanna from school. And told Alex the obvious part of the truth: without an ability to speak, Hanna grew frustrated among new people. Suzette offered to homeschool her. She'd already taught her to read and do simple arithmetic. Alex embraced the idea—embraced her.

For Alex to finally come around to the idea of Sunnybridge meant perhaps he was realizing there was a bigger problem. He hadn't, as she'd feared, been insulted by the idea of a psychologist. Maybe he had a more selfish desire, with the new downtown commission, that she'd have more time to help him. Maybe he'd become infected by her fear of rotting intestines and shitting in a bag. She couldn't always tell what motivated him: someone else's best interests—hers, their daughter's—or his own. But it was possible that a school with a more playful approach would be a pleasant distraction for Hanna.

"It's April already, too late for this year," she now said, filling her glass with what was left of the wine. "But I can see if they'll admit her for second grade."

"I'm sure they will." He was nothing if not loyal to his daughter. "She's so academically advanced for her age, they'll see she's a silent genius." The delicate skin around his eyes crinkled as he smiled.

"I'll set up an appointment."

Alex leaned forward and kissed her. "See? Therapist. New school. It's all going to work out. Maybe she'll even be talking by the fall—maybe we'll have lots of schools to choose from."

Did he really believe that?

Alex got up, stretched his long limbs. "Better head up. Should I say anything to her?"

"Yes—that would be great. I made the mistake in the car, I thought she might be more open to school since it's been awhile. She doesn't realize what she's missing. Maybe if it comes from you . . ."

She carried their wine goblets to the sink.

"What do I tell her about the therapist?"

"Maybe focus on . . . Something just for her, without us. Maybe just plant the idea, a different kind of relationship, someone who isn't a parent or grandparent."

Alex nodded. "I'll keep it really low-key. I don't think she handles pressure well, being on the spot."

"Yes." She couldn't help sounding relieved. "I'm glad you understand. *Jag älskar dig.*" She knew how it pleased him when she expressed her love for him in Swedish.

"*Jag älskar dig.*" He blew her a kiss and took the steps two at a time.

Alone in the empty downstairs, it was easy for Suzette to imagine what it would be like. With her schoolbooks back in the cupboard, there was no trace of Hanna. And if the girl were in school, she'd have six hours a day to herself. Maybe she'd start sketching again. She could become a valuable member of the Jensen & Goldstein team, not a ghost on the periphery. She could take a cooking class. Or a dance class. She could start a blog. She could grow a real garden, full of fresh organic vegetables to feed her family. She wouldn't always eat the vegetables—sometimes her finicky digestion rebelled against brightly colored, hard-to-absorb foods. But in her mind, the act of growing would earn her a prize. Better than store-bought, and truly local.

It seemed possible that's what all the other mothers were doing, the ones whose children spent their days at small, expensive schools. They probably already knew how to knit socks and sew their own clothes. They probably stood side by side with their husbands to thatch the roof and jury-rig a composting toilet. Suzette wanted to do better. She longed for more-practical life skills, and knew Alex would support her endeavor to negate their carbon footprint.

She wasn't opposed to hard or dirty work, even if she had a lot of catching up to do. More ways to strive for perfection, and prove her worth.

HANNA

DADDY PULLED THE blinds across her big window that looked out over the backyard; she had the smallest but coziest room in the house. But she liked it best when Daddy was there with her, adding his splashes of color and movement to her plain cubicle. She'd given up years earlier trying to color the white walls with her fat toddler crayons, as Mommy always painted over it. "Why won't you use all the paper we bought? Or the coloring books?" Mommy said her toys could be colorful, her bedding and books. But the toys were kept in perfectly arranged stacks of white bins, and the yellow comforter couldn't fill the entire room. She wished she could blow into it and make it puff up into a giant sun, or a hot air balloon that would carry her away.

Mommy wanted her to keep her drawing and painting contained to the easel that stood soldierly in the corner. So Hanna left the big sheets of white paper perfect and unused. It wasn't just to disobey Mommy, who used to plead "Just a little picture? A tiny one? Too small for anyone to see?" That was when Mommy was still in her sad phase, before it turned to anger.

She didn't give up. On every Christmas Eve and the

third night of Hanukkah, Mommy gave her art supplies. Hanna loved how the pencils and crayons looked, with their pointy unused tips. She liked the quarter-size circles of watercolor paint, like frozen puddles from a dripping rainbow. She didn't want to mess them up. If she took the Magic Markers out of their perfect nest, she'd never be able to put them back in the right order. She liked Mommy's presents, but she'd never do with them what Mommy wanted. Hanna made sure Mommy saw her holding them sometimes, running her fingers over the tops of the crayons, making gentle swirls in the dry rainbows of paint. Sometimes she kissed the colors she especially liked. Mommy never got mad then. She watched, very still, her eyes wet with tears. Hanna couldn't tell if she was happy or unhappy, though sometimes Mommy frowned. But she kept buying the beautiful packages of color, and that's all that mattered. Every win for Hanna was a you-lose for Mommy.

He slid a book from the shelf above her head and sat beside her, ready to read.

" 'There was a forest under my bed, one I had been cultivating for quite some time.' "

Daddy had the faintest of accents and *there* sounded more like *dere*.

" 'It was quite a tropical place, suitable for molds and monkeys and very small things that—' "

Daddy said *tings dat*.

" '—might enjoy swinging on vines of hair and bouncing on trampolines of spider webs.' "

Hanna smiled, anticipating the next line.

" 'I had been suspicious for a while of the existence of

an UnderSlumberBumbleBeast. I heard noises coming from beneath my bed as I lay in the dark trying to sleep.' "

Hanna so wished for a messy under-the-bed, but Mommy and her mops and buckets would never let such a forest grow beneath anything in the house. Hanna wanted funny-looking friends like the ones in the story, which is why she always picked it for Daddy to read.

" 'Sometimes I heard scratching sounds like it was scavenging for food.' "

Hannah wished she could sprinkle her floor with crumbled granola bars. She wanted to feed the little beasts.

" 'Other times it sounded very much like a tiny bug singing at the bottom of a tall glass. Once I could have sworn I heard something driving a bus up a very steep hill, the engines grinding and the brakes squealing. The conditions under my bed were ripe for an UnderSlumber-BumbleBeast, that I knew.' "

Stuff. That's what Hanna needed to attract her own under-the-bed friends. Bits of stuff for them to form themselves out of, broken old toys and sticky pieces of half-eaten candy—things Mommy would pinch up in her rubber gloves and throw away.

Mommy came to the door. She leaned against the jamb, watching beautiful Daddy as he read.

" 'Since I had never seen one, I wasn't sure how to anticipate its arrival. I rather thought it would introduce itself one night—I had whispered 'Hello?' so many times, so certain of the existence of a creature under my bed. But I never heard a reply. Maybe it was shy. Or perhaps we didn't speak the same language—' "

Hanna waved her hand, a shooing gesture, at her mother. Daddy glanced at Mommy, then fanned his fingers lightly over the open pages of the book, like giant moths landing in a field.

"Mommy can stay and listen. Maybe she likes this story too."

Hanna made a sharp, guttural grunt and gave one hard shake of her head.

Daddy frowned at Mommy. "We don't get as much Hanna-Daddy time as you get Hanna-Mommy time."

"It's fine."

She saw the hate-you-don't-forget-it in Mommy's glare before she left. Someday Mommy would open her mouth and have teeth made of shards of glass. She'd give Hanna that hateful look, and then start eating her own hands. It would be gross, but she almost wanted to see it.

She just needed to push Mommy a bit further. Fortunately, Marie-Anne was helping her come up with some very excellent ideas for making Mommy go-away-die forever.

Daddy resumed reading, and she stuffed the sunshine comforter under her chin and smiled.

" 'As I hung there over the edge of my bed, flashlight searching, I suddenly saw him! (I assume he was male because of the mustache.) He squinted in the beam of bright light, holding up an arm that looked like a lollipop to protect his sensitive eyes. 'Wow!' I said. We were looking right at each other! I wondered if I looked as strange to him as he appeared to me. His body was about the size of a yam, and he wore a pair of sky-blue knitted shorts.' "

Hanna and Alex giggled together, sharing an image of a yam with a mustache in a pair of knitted shorts.

She didn't remember falling asleep, but when she woke, it was dark and Daddy was gone. She hung her head over the side of the bed, like the little girl in the book, to see if any UnderSlumberBumbleBeasts were tottering around. She kept a compact purple flashlight on one of the shelves above her bed, but even on maximum brightness there was nothing but smooth, clean, Mommy-perfect floor. She got out of bed, tugged down her soft hedgehog nightgown, and tiptoed to her dresser where she pulled out a few random things. A white sock. A brown barrette. A red hair band. She peered into one of the bins that held her art supplies, but couldn't, in the end, mess up any of her crayon or pencil or marker sets.

It was an inadequate collection, but better than nothing. She tossed them under her bed. Maybe she'd get a day or two to gather up more things before Mommy gasped in horror at the accumulated mess. She'd seen Mommy on her knees so many times, her vacuum wand a sword, her mission the annihilation of every colony of dusty invaders, no matter how small. It might not be enough time for an UnderSlumberBumbleBeast to assemble itself, but it was worth a try—and then she'd hide it somewhere safe from Mommy.

She heard a noise she recognized but couldn't decipher. She crept from her room and down the hallway, toward the glow that emerged beneath her parents' door. Breathy grunts and gasps. She'd heard such noises her whole life and knew it was the secret language Mommy and Daddy used when they were alone together. It bothered her that they never spoke it with her, though she'd tried on several occasions to duplicate their sounds. Daddy laughed, telling her she sounded like a cave girl. Mommy wrinkled her eyebrows and looked scared. "Please use your words." Hanna supposed she hadn't gotten the articulation just right and that's why they didn't understand her.

She listened a minute longer. The grunts and gasps, devoid of meaning, were a bit scary. Mommy sounded like she was drifting around a spaceship, on the verge of running out of air. Daddy's voice kept punching something, again and again. She'd tried, when she was younger, to enter the conversation. But they stopped as soon as she came into the room. After that, they instructed her to knock first, especially when people within a room sounded busy—though she should interrupt only if it was an emergency. But they were never going to communicate with her in the language she found more interesting than words. Maybe it was only for adults, or maybe it was for only two people at a time (they never spoke to anyone else in the guttural tongue). Sometimes she wanted to ask them, in the language she refused to speak, "Why won't you include me?"

She went back to her room, impressed with her magical ability to not make a sound. Not only could she withhold her words, but her feet stepped across the floor like she was made of air. A phantom, floating. A witch, reincarnated.

*   *   *

A few hours later, printouts in hand, she came down from Daddy's study to a hallway filled with morning light. Her feet grew warm in its triangle of sunshine as she stood by the window that looked out over their private yard. She scanned the well-trimmed bushes and ankle-high grass, the wooden wall and the roof of the neighboring house. The blooming daffodils waited in a tidy row in front of the hedge, like an army about to charge. The tulips weren't finished yet and their pink heads looked like arrows, ready to burst. Someone's cherry tree blew a soft snow of white petals into the yard. She sniffed the glass, wanting the aroma of flowers, but got only the household smell of Mommy's vinegar concoction.

She'd expected Daddy to get up awhile ago; she'd already dressed, brushed her hair, and worked on her special project. After looking up some stuff on Daddy's computer, she printed off a bunch of pictures onto recycled office paper. It didn't matter if the pictures were a little crinkly or splotchy. The online images were from very old photographs, and she printed some of them in color so they were brown and white instead of black and white. With one thing still left to do, she crept off to her room to hide the photos.

Pressing her ear to her parents' door, all was quiet within. There was no particular rule about going into their room while they slept, so she carefully turned the door handle and slipped in. Daddy lay long and naked on his side of the bed. She could almost see all his man parts—properly called a penis—but his leg, bent upward, blocked the complete view. He had one arm under his pillow and the other across his chest. His mouth was parted and he breathed in and out, unaware of her and everything else.

She gazed at Daddy for several moments, then resumed her mission. She picked up Daddy's phone from the shelf beside his bed where he kept a few scattered things within easy reach: two books, some tissues, a mostly empty glass of water, a pickle jar full of loose change. She walked around to Mommy's side of the bed.

Mommy lay in a similar position on her right side, her knees tucked up. She gripped the pillow between praying hands, and dark hair made stripes across her face. Mommy's boobs flopped to one side, and Hanna decided that if she had to grow extra body parts, she'd rather have a tail. She couldn't see Mommy's new scar, but she liked the old one better. A purplish worm held between fleshy lips of white skin. She touched it once when she was very young, in a dressing room at the mall, but Mommy pulled away like it hurt.

She took a couple of steps backward and held the phone horizontally so she could get a picture of Mommy's whole sleeping form. She slept on the window-side of the room, and even with the blinds drawn she was still softly illumin-ated. Hanna pressed the button, and the camera made its little clicking noise. She pressed it a second time for good measure, and that's when Mommy lifted her head and sucked in air, like she'd been lying there dead the whole time. It was a wonderful thought. Mommy pushed the hair out of her face and blinked several times, and Hanna could have run from the room, but she didn't.

Instead, she slid her feet along the floor until she was

right against the bed. Mommy eased away from her, a look of confusion on her face.

"Hanna? Do you need something?"

She bent at the waist. Lower and lower until her face hovered above her frightened mother.

"My name. Is Marie-Anne. Dufosset," she whispered in Mommy's ear in her bestest French accent. Mommy didn't think she'd played that *French by French* computer game more than once. But she had.

As Mommy pushed herself up on her elbow, the abrupt motion made her boobs jiggle. Hanna smirked, and Mommy pulled the sheet up to cover herself.

"What?" Mommy glanced over at sleeping Daddy. Then she spoke more softly. "I'm glad you're speaking, baby. What did you say?"

"My name. Is Marie-Anne. Dufosset. Don't forget." Her voice still sounded weak and soft, from lack of use.

The word "who" formed on Mommy's lips, but Hanna giggled and skipped out of the room, with Daddy's phone still in her hand.

SUZETTE

SHE MADE ALEX'S coffee, Italian roast, dark and strong just as he liked it. Even though he was running late, Hanna managed to lure him up to his study. Something to do with his phone and the picture she'd taken. He'd protested only for a second; as eager as he was to start brainstorming ideas for the new downtown skinny building, it wasn't like he couldn't—or didn't—set his own hours or work at home over the weekend. She wanted to think it was harmless, that Hanna had come into their room to take a picture of her. But her queasy vulnerability lingered, and not just because she'd been naked. Hanna—or whomever she was claiming to be—wasn't some innocent, normal kid.

Normal children loved cameras and taking photos; she remembered as much from her own childhood. Every few years, her mother had given her a new camera—Polaroid, then film, then digital. Her mother, in spite of other deficits, was big on gift giving. And her presents were usually well chosen and beautifully wrapped. As an adult, Suzette understood this had been her sole means of expressing love. She'd saved most of the nicer ribbons, still had them in a special box: shimmery fabric in metallic and holiday plaids. In her mind, the wrappings became the hugs she never received.

She sent a text telling him his coffee was ready. Right after it went through, her phone pinged with an email notification. A smile came to her face as she read the message.

Alex bounded down the stairs, with Hanna at his heels.

"I promise I promise I promise, my lips are sealed," he said.

"What are you promising?"

Alex slid an invisible zipper across his closed mouth. Hanna hung on to her hero's arm, jumping up and down with malicious glee.

"If they're really sealed, I guess you won't be needing this." She set his gleaming, steaming travel mug on the other end of the counter, out of his reach. Whatever Hanna had gotten him to do for her was unlikely to be a pleasant surprise. It bothered her that Alex could be working against her, even if he wasn't fully aware of what he'd been drawn into. Hanna didn't have fun secrets. The last time Suzette had hoped her daughter was doing something sweet, Suzette opened a small gift box filled with spiders. The long-dead ones were crumbling, but some still twitched, and a few were very much alive. Not a fun surprise—even if Alex joked that Hanna was like a cat, bringing her favorite person a precious mouse.

"No no no, the coffee is innocent in all of this." He winked at her and reached for his mug, seemingly oblivious to Suzette's genuine annoyance.

"Fine. So guess what, I have great news." She wanted to tell him while they were all together, in case Hanna reacted badly. Maybe she would throw a fit that he would not only witness, but also have to deal with. Suzette handed over his mug.

"Thank you, *älskling*." Alex kissed her on the cheek. He sipped his coffee and leaned against the counter, waiting for her to divulge the news.

She brought the email back up on her phone. "I sent Sunnybridge an email last night, and I just got a reply. They'd be happy to sit down and talk with me. They even have time today, if I'm available."

"Sounds good." He turned to Hanna, who stood stoic and suspicious. "Remember, *lilla gumman*? I told you last night about a new school, for the fall? A more fun school than the others we looked at."

"I think we should go this afternoon—what do you think?" She made herself sound sweet and innocent, though a part of her hoped the goading would work.

Hanna only glared at her. She turned and ran up the stairs, and a second later her door slammed shut. Suzette sighed, disappointed by the lack of drama. It would make convincing Alex of her revised idea more difficult.

"Don't worry, any school is a big change. She'll need time to wrap her head around it. We'll have all summer—"

"I might ask if they can take her now," she said, all pleasantness gone from her voice.

Alex froze, startled. "Now? There's only two and a half months—"

"You haven't noticed her behavior?"

"Not particularly."

"She's getting very manipulative. The way she plays us.

She makes sure only I see what she does, so when I tell you . . . You can't corroborate anything. The hitting. Spelling bad words. *Talking* . . . she's taunting me. What did she drag you upstairs to do for her this morning?"

"Nothing. A project." He squirmed in his skin a bit. "She's trying something, I guess. I think you'll like it, actually."

Though she wasn't cold, she zipped up the gray yoga jacket she liked to wear around the house and stuffed her hands into the pockets. She wanted to get properly dressed and call the school back, but Alex remained fixated on her and she wished he'd look away.

"Fine. I'll handle it myself."

"Hey." He reached for her arm as she started to walk away. "I don't disagree with you that she should be in school, you're probably right—she's bored, she needs a change—"

"I need a change. You don't know how she is. She puts on her best face for you. Always sweet for you."

"No, I believe that. But it's so late in the school year, we already talked—"

"I cannot stay here, cooped up with her! You're not listening to me."

"I am. *Älskling.*" He took her in the great wingspan of his embrace.

Usually his arms were such a comfort, but she already felt too confined—burned out by the day-to-day trials of mothering Hanna, and the chronic disappointment of her own body. She wanted to run full speed into their glass wall and didn't care if, like a bird, she broke her own neck.

She'd run at it again and again until it was smeared with her blood.

She pushed him away and fought back a scream. She saw her wild-eyed panic mirrored on Alex's face. It didn't belong there, that frightened, uncertain look. It quelled a bit of her own anxiety and she wished she could swipe her hand in front of his eyes, past his nose and mouth, and restore the easy face he usually wore.

"I'm sorry, you just don't . . ." She took a step away from him. Fidgety, she pressed a hand to her mouth, trying to keep the words from falling out. "She's doing things. I don't know what she's doing, but she's playing games—"

"What things?"

"Who is Marie-Anne Dufosset?"

"What?"

Oh, that look he gave her. Like she'd revealed her insides to be just cogs and springs and explosions of fluff.

"Marie-Anne Dufosset! Is this some story you've been reading to her? Some French thing you watched together? Someone you told her about?" She stepped toward him, pleading with her hands. "Who is she?"

"Suzette, stop."

At the sound of her name, she stopped—moving, ranting, breathing. Not that she minded Alex's Swedish endearments, but in the absence of ever hearing her own name, sometimes she forgot she had one.

"I don't know who Marie-Anne Dufosset is. Why would I know that? What does that have to do with . . . ?" Such perfect, innocent confusion. Devoid of anger, and oozing with concern.

Had she lost her mind?

"I'll google it. Never mind. You're late. I need to call the school."

"Do you want me to . . . I could stay? Go with you? I shouldn't leave you like—"

"I'll figure it out, it's fine."

He did that thing she loved and took hold of her upper arms while resting his forehead against hers. Beneath the coffee, he smelled like toothpaste, and his body radiated warmth. She breathed him in. He stood there, letting her absorb him.

"I'm sorry, I didn't mean to freak out."

"Suzette—we'll do whatever we need to do. Your health is as much a priority—I don't want you to get sick again—"

"I know, I have the shots, they help . . ."

"Still, I've never seen you so rattled. I could work at home more—"

"You were just home for two weeks, you can't be my nursemaid forever—"

"Was it better?"

Just thinking of how much easier it had been made her drumming heart settle into an easier rhythm. Those two full weeks after The Surgery had been like a vacation. Alex around to help with everything; Hanna on her best behavior. "Yes," she admitted.

"I could do half days at the office."

"You can't."

"I can. So don't get upset if the school says she can't start now. We'll get her enrolled somewhere for the fall.

And I'll be here more, okay? Maybe we'll switch it up, and you can head into the office sometimes, it's been awhile—would that help?"

"Maybe. I don't know. I feel tired. All the time."

She'd tried explaining it to him before, how her energy existed in precious spools that came unwound faster than she liked. He tried, but couldn't really understand any more than she could about how it felt to be someone else. She gauged herself against what she saw other people do and how they moved through the world, their days filled with work and errands and chores and social lives and home lives, and no one else seemed too tired to live. But for her, by four o'clock in the afternoon she was often too weary to even stare at the television. What no one understood about her cleaning was how mindlessly purposeful it was for her. She needed to disconnect a few times a day, like a battery in reverse that recharged when it wasn't plugged in. It was part of having Crohn's disease, though the gastro-enterologists weren't interested in that part. Dr. Stefanski told her to take the matter up with her primary-care physician. It helped when Suzette kept a regular schedule for eating and sleeping. Sometimes a bit of light exercise in the morning spurred a burst of energy. But as she got older—as her days stretched out with Hanna—it seemed as if nothing helped. She was becoming a wind-up toy with a faulty crank.

"You need to tell me. More. Let me help you," Alex pleaded.

Suzette nodded and finally wrapped her arms around her husband.

"You don't have to do it all today," he said.

"I want to. I need to, it'll be fine. You should go, I know you want to get started."

"Let's talk more later, okay?"

They kissed, and he grabbed his coffee and car keys, shuffled into his shoes, and left.

She'd once imagined herself as a woman who wouldn't need a man. She'd survived without a father, after all. The world didn't revolve around men. But after she fell in love with Alex, she learned the truth of it: she never wanted to live in a world without him again. He smoothed the searing edges of happenstance and gave her a life that wasn't capricious or cruel. She knew she could never live so well on her own, with the compromised income of compromised energy. And she'd worked so little that if she managed to qualify for disability, the payments would be meager. Together, they were the nurturing cycle of a life that mattered. Sun, soil, rain, roots, fruit, sustenance. Joy.

She called Sunnybridge and took the appointment they offered for eleven o'clock.

When she went upstairs, Hanna's door was closed. She pressed her ear to it and listened. And heard what sounded like scissors cutting paper. Alex said she was making a project, but Suzette assumed it was something on his computer, not something that Hanna might assemble by hand. The thought of her working industriously in her room actually gave her hope. Maybe she'd finally use some of her markers or pencils. She didn't know why Hanna never used them, especially because she knew she liked them. It wouldn't even bother her if, later, she found scraps of paper littering the floor. In fact, the possibility made her smile.

"I'm taking a quick shower—everything okay in there?"

Hanna rapped her knuckles on the floor, like a knock—the code they'd developed for those times when they couldn't see her, but needed a reply.

"Okay." She hesitated for a second, debating whether to caution her to be careful with the scissors. She decided against it; Hanna wouldn't like her hovering, or babying her.

Suzette enjoyed sixty seconds of hope, imagining what her daughter's creation might be. She had faith in Hanna's creativity, though it had rarely been applied in conventional ways. Maybe it would be the next stage in a welcome, albeit strange, process toward communication.

Her hope ended when she closed the door to her room and googled *Marie-Anne Dufosset* on her phone.

She felt defenseless in her nudity, even with the bathroom door locked. She couldn't stop imagining Hanna wielding a pair of large scissors, stabbing her to death in the shower. It was a gruesomely melodramatic concern—especially since Marie-Anne Dufosset was barely a footnote in history. But according to Wikipedia, in 1679, at the age of eighteen, she was the last woman burned as a witch in France. That the article gave scant evidence the teen had ever done anything remotely witch-like was beyond the point. That Hanna even knew of her and had some reason to admire her—to invoke her spirit—was concerning enough.

Now that she knew the name of the game—Scare Mommy—she should be able to defend herself. But goose bumps rose on her skin, even under the heat of the water, when she thought about her creepy daughter. The whites of her eyes. Her ability to sneak up on her as she slept.

HANNA

FUN. THAT'S WHAT they'd promised her in preschool, and then kindergarten. She'd lasted longest at Green Hill Academy. Five whole weeks during which every day was a challenge. A challenge to not throw herself against the walls in protest (they peeled her off the one time she tried it and sent her to a roly-poly nurse, who held an ice cube to her forehead before calling in Mommy). A challenge to turn the dumply and squiggly children into things to play with: living, breathing toys. Pushing them into place only got her in trouble. Nobody approved of the ways she had fun.

It had been no fun sitting on an orange square of carpet, watching one day as three children built a tower of interlocking plastic bricks—like Legos for a giant. They squabbled about who got to add the next one, and which color it should be. Hanna couldn't understand why they were even trying to work together. Curly Hair only liked the blue blocks. Hot Pink Glasses kept trying to boss the other two around. Nose Picker was contaminating everything he touched with his green boogers. He kept a finger in his nose even when he wasn't picking it, like that's where it lived.

Hanna finally had enough and got up from her spot.

She stood in front of the plastic tower, eyeing its construction. What a bunch of doodoo heads. They could have used the blocks to make a nice pattern, red yellow blue, red yellow blue. Or two blue, two red, two yellow.

"You can play with us," said Hot Pink Glasses.

Like Hanna needed her permission. The three little pigs waited for her. Did they think she was going to add a brick to their tower? Or pay them some sort of sappy compliment?

The thing they made hurt her eyes. She kicked it in the center block, sending the tower crumpling to the ground. Not the most fun she'd ever had, but it was better than sitting around.

"Hey!" said Hot Pink Glasses.

Curly Hair burst into tears.

Hanna walked away and maybe someone, an adult, called after her, but she didn't care.

Playing outside wasn't much better. Everyone ran around the playground shrieking in a way that pained her ears. A pair of do-goody best friends in matching floppy braids played with striped jump ropes. Hopping. Skipping. Getting their feet tangled up. Laughing. Hanna thought it would be a much better game if she could tie the rope around one of their necks. And then maybe she—would any other children help?—could drag her along like a pull toy and watch her wriggle and scream. That would be fun.

One day she approached a circle of kids, who squealed and giggled as they compared the special things they could do. A girl stuck out her tongue, stretching it so it kissed the tip of her nose. A boy made his eyes splay in, so he looked like a defective doll.

"I can wiggle my ear!" a girl shrieked, holding back her hair as the other children leaned in to see.

As they took turns seeing who could curl up the sides of their tongue, Hanna jumped up and down until they all looked at her. Grinning, she rolled her eyes back into her head, a trick she'd practiced in the mirror for years while washing her hands after a pee. She'd expected the others to offer up impressed ooohs and aaahs like they did for everyone else. But while still blinded, her eyes snuggled in her skull, she heard the receding screams as everyone ran away.

After that, on most days Hanna just stood there in her uniform, dark blue jumper and white shirt, watching. She looked like one of the kids, even if she didn't feel like them. Daddy loved her little uniform, and it was the initial reason she thought kindergarten might be better than preschool. But it wasn't. Just like in preschool, she could never run fast enough to get to the swings first. The other kids buzzed and swarmed over everything, and she wasn't sure if, once out of doors, they grew stingers like bumblebees, so she kept her distance.

Since the beginning of the school year, she'd kept her eye on a particular girl whose hair fell like golden beams of light. Hanna didn't think it was fair that Sunshine had such perfect hair—the color of Daddy's. Sometimes she gazed at it, longing to take a knife to Sunshine's scalp and remove her fine locks. Hanna imagined herself proudly wearing the wig she'd make, unbothered by the stray trickle of blood that might dribble down her forehead.

During art class, Hanna would stand at her easel and wear her plasticky smock, but she wouldn't paint. At first Mrs. Smiley tried guiding her hand as Hanna clutched the brush. She dipped it in the tempera paint and made swooping strokes on the paper. But whenever Mrs. Smiley let go, Hanna let go, too, and the brush splattered to the floor. Mrs. Smiley gave up trying soon after that and let her just stand there. But one day, Hanna thought of a way to have fun while the other kids were busy with their messy, drippy masterpieces.

Everybody knew Sunshine was particularly fond of fruit punch. She refused to drink water and shrank away from milk like she'd been offered a glass of poop. At first she was the only one who got fruit punch at snack time, but then the other kids grumbled and pleaded, and Mrs. Smiley blew out her cheeks and filled everyone's cups with Sunshine's red elixir. But then the parents caught on and didn't want their children drinking Red Dye Number Forty Sugar Water—that's what Mommy called it—so Sunshine had to have her snack alone.

While Mrs. Smiley was busy with the other children, Hanna found a cup of red paint. She carried it against her body so no one would see. And while no one was looking, she stole an extra Dixie Cup and slipped into the bathroom with the miniature sink and toilet. The bathroom with its tiny fixtures was her favorite thing about kindergarten, and she almost wished Daddy would redo the bathroom she used at home. She poured a wee bit of the red paint into the cup, then filled up the rest with water.

Diluted, it looked convincingly like Kool-Aid.

Mrs. Smiley was helping Nose Picker, whose painting was the same murky green as his boogers. Sunshine painted flowers. At least Hanna assumed they were flowers. They also could have been tall people with very punk hairdos. She stood beside Sunshine and smiled. People could be easily won over with a smile; she learned that as a baby.

"Don't push me," Sunshine said, pouting, taking a step back. Maybe Hanna had given her a little shove or accidental bump once or twice in the past, but that wasn't what she had in mind.

She shook her head, so Sunshine would know she was safe. The girl still looked wary. Hanna held out the cup full of red. *You'll like this.* Sunshine's eyes went hungry.

"Fruit punch?"

Hanna nodded.

"Oh. Thank you." Sunshine was such a polite girl. Mommy would like her. Mommy made sure Hanna knew about *please* and *thank you*, even if she wouldn't say the words out loud.

Sunshine took big gulps from the cup and swallowed it down. Hanna couldn't stop herself: she reached out and stroked the girl's fine golden hair.

But before Sunshine got all of it down, she gagged, choking on the liquid still in her mouth. It dribbled down her chin like blood.

Hanna smiled, thinking of a better trick with crushed pieces of glass.

"Uckkkhh! That's gross—Mrs. McNally . . ." Mrs. Smiley came over. "She made me drink this."

"What is it?" The teacher took the cup and sniffed it. Once. Twice. "Paint? Did you give Aria paint?"

Hanna shrugged. If they had any imagination they could *pretend* it was fruit punch.

The teacher *tsked* as she thumbed the red dribbles from Sunshine's chin. "I'll take you to the nurse, just in case, it's not toxic, but . . . And you . . ."

Hanna went to Green Hill Academy's principal's office.

She couldn't remember how many times in total she was sent to the office. But she remembered the last time. Hanna had had no way to explain that she was *helping*. She found ants on the floor around the cafeteria garbage can. Performing a public service, she stepped on all of them. The next day they were back, so she stepped on them again. She finally decided they must have a nest inside the garbage can, where new ants were born every day. Daddy kept some matchbooks in his study, pretty ones from different places. They were easy to steal, so she took the pack with the bright blue heads because she liked them best. She only meant to help the school with their stubborn ant problem, and no one actually saw her drop the match into the bin. But they saw her standing near it, delighted by the whoosh of flames. They didn't even let her go back to class after that. She sat in the office until Mommy and Daddy flapped in, indignant on her behalf.

"She doesn't even know how to light a match!" said Daddy.

It turned out well because she never had to go back to Green Hill Academy. But after her parents talked with the principal and a couple of teachers, everything got touchy-shifty at home because Daddy was in a bad mood.

After Green Hill, she lasted two weeks at Frick before Mommy withdrew her. Hanna had pretended to pass out during story time because she hated how her teacher read aloud, adopting squeaky voices that made Hanna want to stop up her mouth with flaming rags. They rushed her to the nurse's office—more a cubicle, compared with Green Hill's—and asked her lots of yes and no questions so she could nod and shake. When Mommy came to pick her up, the nurse sounded very stern and said Mommy shouldn't withhold food as a punishment because young children need calories and nutrients for growing bones and brains and blah-blah-blah.

It was hard not to laugh when Mommy froze like a startled bird, her head at an angle as her beak opened and closed.

"What? I've never . . . Did she tell you that? Hanna?"

Hanna really was hungry; it wasn't a complete lie. And she'd seen tons of kids get sent home for sniffles and puking and all varieties of "I feel sick." Not the most fun she ever had, but an effective strategy.

"It was just . . . At suppertime we have a rule, to eat what's on the table—it was my mother's rule too—eat what's there, or don't eat supper. It's not . . . So she ate a little, and I always try to have things that I know she likes, but she didn't want any more . . . There's no snacking later, if you skip supper—we can't reward her for that. So . . . She had breakfast, her regular breakfast . . ."

Mommy got red in the face and the nurse said, "I

understand, we just need all the parents to take responsibility for their children's nutrition—"

"We do—I do."

"We don't want the children to fall over dead."

That's not exactly what the nurse said, but Hanna—and Mommy, too—knew that's what she meant.

After that, the squeaky-voiced teacher spoke to Mommy for a few minutes.

"The writing's on the wall," Mommy said as they left. And that was the end of the Frick School, though Hanna was innocent of scribbling on anyone's wall.

Hanna thought that would be the end of school forever. Mommy started teaching her at home and Hanna "soaked up everything like a sponge." Mommy sounded impressed when she said that, and Hanna accepted it as a compliment because she knew how much Mommy loved to clean. Being at home was mostly better, less running around and more time to do what she wanted. It tried Mommy's patience sometimes, but Hanna considered that a good thing because you can't get better at something without practice, and she wanted Mommy to become more patient.

But here they were. In the car. Heading for some new place that they'd promised would be fun—more fun than the other places, but what was that supposed to mean?

At least she had some time to think on the way. And she was bigger and smarter than the last time they'd tried to send her to school. With a little effort, she wouldn't have to wait long for the fun to begin.

SUZETTE

IT WAS A fairly long drive to Sunnybridge, through downtown traffic and out to the South Hills. She listened to
WYEP on the radio, the independent alternative station.
Sometimes she glanced at Hanna, buckled in the back in
her car seat, and was surprised to see her head bobbing
along with the music. She'd never shown much interest in
music, in spite of Alex's valiant efforts. Whereas Suzette
bought her art supplies, Alex bought her CDs, and then an
MP3 player, a child-size pair of conga drums, a ukulele.
She never so much as tapped a drumhead or plunked one
of the ukulele's strings, though she watched with apparent
interest as Alex demonstrated. After she took Hanna to an
audiologist and ruled out any hearing problems, they
started worrying that some of her delays were a result of
confusion. As a baby and toddler, Alex spoke to her in
Swedish and she in English. They knew many people had
successfully raised bilingual children that way, but still
blamed themselves initially when Hanna didn't speak.
When her interaction skills receded a bit, they feared she'd
descended into autism, but she remained attuned to her
daddy's voice even though he couldn't coax her into
responding, either vocally or through music.

An ad came on, a request for listeners to support independent radio. Suzette turned it down until it was barely audible. Alex, under his company's name, made donations every year to support 91.3 and the local PBS television station. She considered Hanna in the rearview mirror, safely strapped in, and out of reach, her eyelids heavy with sleep. It was her best moment to try to draw her out.

"So Hanna. I looked up Marie-Anne Dufosset."

The child's head twitched at the name and she lifted her eyes, but only to gaze out the window.

"She must have been a very interesting girl. And what a tragic end. Burned at the stake with her mother. And they weren't even witches."

Hanna turned to meet her eyes in the mirror. Hoping to dispel some of her unease about her daughter's newly acquired persona, Suzette attempted to dismantle the threat.

"That was the thing about the whole witch craze, which you probably didn't know. People were very superstitious back then. Sometimes, to save yourself from an accusation, your only choice was to name other people—the real witches. Only they weren't really witches either. So that's what happened in the case of Marie-Anne Dufosset. Someone else was accused first, and she ended up naming lots of other people—including Marie-Anne—in an attempt to save herself. But it's true I guess, that Marie-Anne was the last person burned at the stake. Just as innocent as all the girls and women who came before her."

Hanna shook her head. "You're so stupid."

She pronounced it *stu-peed*, and Suzette was struck by

the girl's consistent French accent. But Suzette made her face a mask, not wanting to reveal the victory of having made Hanna speak. "How so?"

But Hanna turned back to the window.

"If I'm wrong, you could explain it to me. Hanna? Marie-Anne?"

That got her attention. She had to give it to the girl: she played her game well. Suzette had to focus on where she was going; they were almost to the school and she didn't want to miss the turn. But she was aware of Hanna studying her profile, calculating her next move.

Suzette parked the car and Hanna unbuckled herself. The building's exterior and the surrounding grounds weren't as well maintained as the other—more expensive— schools they'd visited. The playground equipment was just a few years from turning to rust. A muddy field lay scattered with fluorescent orange traffic cones and underinflated balls of various sizes and colors. It looked as if it had been a public school once, possibly abandoned for lack of modernity. There was a big sign by the front doors with an overly large, dangerously spiked yellow sun.

To her shock, she felt a little hand slip into hers. Maybe Hanna really did harbor fears about the prospect of school.

As they made their way up the walk, Hanna spoke again, in her soft new voice. "Do you trust me?"

Suzette considered how to respond. It seemed wrong to lie when asked so directly—and it being their first real conversation.

"No," she said.

"Good. They were right to burn me."

Zey. Like a French movie star.

The little hand squeezed hers more tightly. A flicker of fear coursed through her; so much for dissuading her daughter from her chosen idol. For a second, Suzette considered turning around—jumping in the car and racing to Jensen & Goldstein. Alex might not even care about the specifics of her words, just that she was saying more things. And what if Hanna, silent for so long, chose her school interview to affirm her new identity? It was surprisingly easy to imagine her describing her life as Marie-Anne Dufosset—who's initials, not lost on her, were MAD—a misunderstood but, in this case, not quite innocent young witch.

They walked down the hallway with its slightly dingy lighting and pockmarked cinder block walls. The half-size lockers, with their chipped yellow and orange paint, were dented and dinged. The ammonia-laced disinfectant tickled her nostrils, but at least the school was clean, even if it reminded Suzette more of a war zone than a place for nurturing young minds.

A classroom of children trailed past them, single file, with the middle-aged teacher bringing up the rear. She wore a shapeless peasant top with a faint coffee stain down the front. Suzette experienced a rare but vibrant flashback of her father: he always had a coffee cup in his hand and stains down his shirt. She remembered him laughing, unaware of the brown liquid spilling over the cup in his hand. Suzette smiled at the memory and the teacher smiled at her. A moment later she released her class through the front doors, and upon passing the threshold the kids transformed from quiet to squealing.

"See? You'll get to play outside," Suzette said to Hanna, intent on selling her child on the school and the school on her child. Though doubt weighed her down as she saw more of the school.

Everything stank of not enough money, and even the art displayed on the walls looked like the work of ordinary children tasked with cliché assignments. Trees drawn as green circles set atop brown rectangles. The ubiquitous house with a pointy roof and a front door flanked by two misshapen windows. Not what she was expecting from a school that boasted of its creative commitments. Alex would hate it. She hated it.

They found their way to the office, where an administrative assistant, a woman in mom jeans and a slightly shrunken T-shirt that she kept tugging down, smiled and pointed them to a row of chairs just outside the principal's door.

"Mrs. Wade will be right with you, she's just finishing a phone call."

"Thank you."

Suzette and Hanna waited side by side on the hard chairs. They'd sat in so many waiting rooms, for doctors and specialists and schools. Waiting made Suzette nervous—it usually led to disappointing conclusions. Absently, she accordioned her purse strap into smaller and smaller pieces, releasing it when there was nothing else to fold, and then started again. Based on the poor physical conditions of the school, Suzette wondered how many of the students were on scholarship and not paying the full, albeit modest, tuition. If the school was desperate for money, perhaps that could work in their favor. They could promise other financial gifts, dependent upon Hanna's acceptance. She tightened her grip on the purse strap, realizing there was no "they" and Alex would be appalled by every aspect of the bribe; he wouldn't believe Hanna needed it or that Sunnybridge deserved it.

She studied the administrative assistant, hunched over her computer. Her reddish hair revealed blackish roots. Whenever her shirt rode up, Suzette could see the elastic of a sensible pair of underpants. Everyone she'd seen so far was super casual, and Suzette was torn between thinking the staff didn't make very much money, or they simply weren't interested in appearances. It made Suzette self-conscious. She'd deliberately made a point of not overdressing, intent on portraying the image of a laid-back mom. Perfectly faded jeans. Perfectly white T-shirt. Effortlessly slouchy, loose-weave cardigan for the chill that still crept into the April air. She'd never had a "problem" with overdressing until she met Alex. He loved her body even when she didn't and encouraged her to show it off with well-tailored clothing. Sunnybridge reminded her of her ragged high school years—a time marked by deterioration and disappointment. It didn't put the school, or her mood, in a winning place.

When it really mattered, during the time when teens declared their individuality by conforming to a peer group, her mother refused to support her fashion interests. Suzette wanted everything from dELiA's catalog: maxiskirts and platform flip-flops and especially the stripe-down-the-side Postman pants. She would have killed for anything with

Julius the Monkey on it. Her mother thought the trends were silly or unflattering and asserted her considerable authority to say "no." No to the clothes she liked. No to driver's ed. No to hanging out with boys after school. She said no to everything that might possibly have allowed Suzette to fit in, or even be normal. She gave reasons like money and homework and bad influences, but Suzette didn't believe her mother had considered any of her desires long enough to actually formulate a reason. Her mother followed a script that she learned from her own parents: Teens have no judgment; don't cave to their selfish desires; put your foot down.

Her mother did agree to let Suzette shop at thrift stores, "because they're cheap." Suzette thought her second-choice style was cool. Patterned polyester shirts and men's jeans rolled to midcalf. Her classmates weren't impressed, but that wasn't what killed her social life. As her health got worse—her mortifying diarrhea—she dropped her extracurricular activities, like theater club, where she once enjoyed designing and helping to build the sets. Then she started saying no to social gatherings, even casual ones with a couple of once-good friends at their favorite coffee shop. Eventually people stopped asking her anywhere. She spent poisoned hours alone in her room. They were bad years, and her mother never noticed. In spite of her own problems, Suzette spent more time taking care of the necessities than her mother did. Cooking, cleaning, walking to the supermarket, tending to their small yard. Instead of thanking her, her mother often quipped, "That's the only reason I wanted a kid, so I could have live-in help."

She was lucky to have been able to graduate from high school on time, having missed weeks of class following her bowel resection, and weeks more after her fistula developed. Her school counselor made sure she got all her assignments to work on at home, and encouraged her to come back to class. Suzette had resisted at first, certain everyone would smell the shit seeping through the bandage beneath her shirt.

For three years after graduating she rarely left the house, except to do the marketing and go to the library. But she made productive use of her hours alone—studying, drawing, researching. The highlight of her life became the monthly delivery of magazines with glossy pictures of beautiful houses and contemporary furniture. Hours and months and years of magazines and clipping out pictures and organizing folders and laying everything out like puzzle pieces of What Could Be. Her mother changed the packing—thin sterile strips of cotton—twice a day in her wound that wouldn't heal. By the time she felt physically able to handle college, she was so socially awkward that she focused solely on classes. The other students were only a few years younger, but she felt so far behind them—in life, in love; she pushed herself to graduate from the Art Institute a year early. Her portfolio was impressive enough to earn her a position at the firm where Alex was a rising young star. And he became the person who helped her, at twenty-four, finish growing up.

He recognized her talent the first time they worked together. "Naturally gifted," he called her. "With a profound aesthetic." Their friendship blossomed quickly, and then she boldly asked him out one day, determined to seize back some of the chances she'd missed. Sometimes she still thought of how he smiled in reply—relieved and momentarily shy—before nodding and suggesting a thousand things they could do, like going out with her had been on his mind for longer than was possible. After their first couple of dates their lives fell into an easy rhythm. She told him everything about her inexperience in the world, and her concerns that she'd never catch up. He taught her how to drive, and not only didn't ridicule the deficiencies she considered backward about herself, but praised her determination and self-awareness.

"You had no one," he said, with a hint of pride and sadness.

Suzette didn't fully agree. "I had my mother. Way too much of my mother." It shamed her that she hadn't been able to escape sooner, that they'd stuck together in such a sickly, co-dependent, useless sort of life.

But Alex hadn't allowed her to dismiss it all so easily. "You did the best you could. Learning so much on your own, making the best of an impossible situation. And you did it. You're here. Your life brought you to me."

Sometimes she dared to think what would have become of her if she hadn't met him. She wouldn't have made it. Life—and her mother—would have taken her down. She couldn't erase certain indelible images from her childhood. Her mother's rattling snores as she slept her life away, oblivious to her responsibilities as a parent (or hiding from them). Her mother's daft-eyed spaciness as she sat on her throne in the living room, consumed by the television, blowing her nose and tossing her dirty tissues into a pile on the floor. Her laziness was made possible by her husband's early death—a generous life insurance policy and help from his family. Her mother called it depression. It began as mourning, but never went away. If Daddy hadn't died when she was four . . . Another thing Suzette tried not to think about.

Parenting was hard for her. But she tried to be responsible in the ways her mother was not, with a reliable schedule and healthy food, a desirable wardrobe and constant investment in Hanna's well-being. Suzette started out fully determined to be everything she would have wanted for herself. But Hanna didn't want what she had to offer. Maybe if she could just get her enrolled in school, and work on this weird new witch identity with a therapist—at least she was talking!—they could start again. It worried her that her mothering was too much of one thing and too little of another, but somewhere along the line she lost track of which and what.

Mrs. Wavalene Wade—as identified by the lettering on her door—popped out of her office. Older and plumper, but just as casual as the rest of the Sunnybridge staff, she flashed a warm smile and gestured for them both to come in.

"Sorry to keep you ladies waiting. I'm so happy you were able to come in today."

"Thank you for seeing us on such short notice." She held up her index finger, gesturing to Hanna to wait a minute. Hanna sprang from her chair and followed the adults into the room. Suzette's facial muscles tightened in annoyance, and she feared that Hanna would remain oppositional throughout the meeting.

Mrs. Wade closed the door behind them and went around to sit behind her (messy) desk. Her office was filled with bookcases of (messy) books and a menagerie of children's sculptures made of clay and play-dough. A mobile made of plastic straws and felt-covered cardboard stars dangled from the ceiling. Struck again by the sub-standard artwork, Suzette pondered the possibility that the problem might be budgetary: perhaps Sunnybridge couldn't afford the extensive art materials of the more elite schools Hanna had previously attended, with their foiled papers and lap looms and fancy wooden beads. She declined to comment or inquire, and remained standing.

"I was hoping we could speak alone, just the two of us, for a few minutes?" she said.

Hanna plopped herself into one of two chairs across from the principal's desk. Suzette fought the urge to breathe flames through her nose.

"Yes, of course. But since you're both new to our school I always like to start by getting acquainted, hearing a bit about each of you, and telling you a little about us." The principal gestured toward the empty chair.

As she sat, Suzette registered Hanna's victorious smirk.

Mrs. Wade, in appearance and mannerisms, reminded Suzette so much of a character she'd liked on *Nurse Jackie* played by Anna Deavere Smith—the boss of a drug addicted nurse. Suzette couldn't shake the feeling that she was about to be busted for something. Hanna turned her attention upward, toward the wobbling mobile.

"I'm Wavalene Wade—the principal here and one of the original founders of the school."

"I'm Suzette, and this is my daughter, Hanna."

"Hello, Hanna."

Hanna held her gaze on the ceiling, seemingly unaware of being spoken to.

"She doesn't talk that much—that was one of the things I wanted to talk to you about."

"Sure, we'll have time for that. So, I gathered from our brief conversation that both you and your husband are creative people?"

"Yes, Alex is an architect, specializing in green materials and technology—"

"Wonderful!"

"I'm an interior designer by trade, but for the past few years I've mostly been a stay-at-home mom."

"And Hanna's creative too?" Mrs. Wade turned her genial grin to Hanna, who continued acting as if she were unaware of the adults in the room.

Suzette faltered. She didn't want to bullshit her, but the truth was almost shameful. They hadn't had even a scribble to clip to the refrigerator since Hanna was three. They had no way to justify—based on their child's performance—enrolling her in an artistic school. Only Alex saw any potential there. She saw Sunnybridge slipping away from them as she and Hanna failed a test that had only just begun. Desperate to not lose the school as an option, Suzette decided to stretch the truth, in whatever ways she needed to. She'd be grateful for even a few weeks' reprieve, if Hanna's behavior ultimately got her expelled. Something—anything—was better than nothing.

"As my husband would say . . . Hanna . . . She expresses herself creatively all the time, even in how she moves through the world."

"Wonderful! So, if I understood correctly, you've been homeschooling her?"

"That's right—she's exceptionally bright, we're already working on second-, even some third-grade material."

"But you'd be looking at enrolling her in second grade for the fall?"

"Well . . ." She gripped the hem of her sweater, twirling the extra fabric around her finger. "If there was any way . . . I know there's only two months or so left in the school year, but Hanna is really . . . She's at a point where she really wants to have other kids to socialize and play with." In her peripheral vision, Hanna's jaw clenched and her nostrils flared at the lie. "So we were hoping . . . Could she jump into the first grade and finish the year with you?"

Mrs. Wade bobbed her head a bit, weighing the possibility. "It's not completely out of the question, but I'm not sure, since she hasn't been in school before, if that would make for the smoothest transition." She looked at Hanna. "How do you feel about it, Hanna? Are there things you're looking forward to doing in school?"

Suzette held her breath, unsure how Hanna would

respond. Once upon a time, she could have counted on her to remain mute and disinterested. She was almost as startled as Mrs. Wade when the girl began snarling like a vicious dog.

Hanna looked the principal right in the eye, her teeth bared, and emitted a guttural growl followed by a volley of savage barks. Fearing what her daughter might do, Suzette gripped Hanna's forearm.

"Hanna! Stop it!"

The girl didn't stop. Mrs. Wade inched away in her rolling chair as Hanna rose from her seat, the barking growing more rabid.

Suzette saw nothing of her once beatific baby in that ferocious face, no trace that Hanna had ever been the toddler who smiled when she and Alex sang to her. In her place was a feral animal. Even her eyes shone with cruelty, and Suzette feared there was something—someone—else in there. She wanted to grab Hanna and shake her, shake the demon loose and scream "Give her back to me!" But she couldn't, not as a stranger watched.

"Stop it, Hanna!" She didn't want to do it, invoke that other name, but desperation drove her. "Marie-Anne, stop it this instant!"

And Hanna stopped. She smiled, smoothing out her flowered skirt like a girl at a tea party as she sat back down. She even folded her hands on her lap and beamed at Mrs. Wade like she was eager to be asked another question.

For a moment, neither woman spoke. They both gazed at Hanna, horrified and unsure how to react. Suzette sank back into her chair, trembling with defeat. She felt herself growing pink with shame. How could she explain her daughter? To Mrs. Wade. To Alex.

But Mrs. Wade quickly recovered.

"I see what you mean about having a few private words." She came from around her desk and opened her door. "Hanna, would you like to wait in the outer office for a minute? There are some books on the table, if you'd like to read. And some crayons and paper."

Hanna sashayed out of the room. Mrs. Wade watched her get settled in a chair, then closed the door and returned to her desk.

Suzette sat with one elbow propped on an armrest, holding her hand over her eyes as if shielding them from the sun. She wanted to hide. She wanted to rewind the day back to when Hanna and Alex were still in his study. She could throw a few things in a bag and slip out before any-one noticed she was gone . . . No. Not unless Alex would sneak away with her.

"I'm so sorry," she said.

"It's all right. Why don't you tell me, now that it's the two of us, what sort of issues you're having."

Suzette grabbed her purse. "I'm sorry, I shouldn't have come here——" She stood, ready to bolt.

"Wait, please. I've been teaching kids for thirty-five years, I've seen everything. Let me help you." She extended her hand toward the chair, until Suzette finally crumpled back into it.

Unable to find the words at first, she just shook her head. "It wasn't always this bad—not like this. She . . ."

She closed her eyes and saw a curtain of red. She blinked hard, trying to clear the blood from her vision. Mrs. Wade's expression was like a beacon of hope, so full of calm understanding. "I've tried so hard and I don't know where I went wrong and I don't know how to fix—"

"But you're trying to figure it out, that's the important thing." She folded her hands atop her desk, committed to the conversation.

"She never liked me. No, that's not true. When she was a baby . . ." Suzette knew she was oversharing, but the words spilled out. "But at some point this war began. And I'm losing. I'm losing it. And I can't tell my husband because, I try but . . . He doesn't see it. And where would I be? I'm supposed to be a good mom, the mom I never had, that's what I wanted. That's what I promised him, what I promised myself."

Mrs. Wade leaned back in her chair, crossing one leg over the other, like they were two women who'd known each other forever and always sought the other's counsel. "Being a mother is the hardest job in the world. And every other mom understands that. I can't tell you how many parents—it's bittersweet, of course they want to spend as much time with their kids, but it's such a relief when they're finally in school."

Suzette nodded in firm agreement. "I thought everything would get better. Kindergarten. But she didn't talk. That's how it all started. We tried doctors, there's nothing physically wrong. But every place I've tried to enroll her. And every babysitter. It's like she wants to torture me—just me."

"I know it seems that way—feels that way. But sometimes kids don't know why they do what they do. They want something but don't know how to express it. And for someone with the communication difficulties that it sounds like Hanna has had . . . Have you tried therapy?"

"We're going to. A developmental psychologist. The pediatrician recommended someone."

"That's good. That's a good start."

"I never have anyone to talk to about this." She refused to let herself cry, even as she wished for a mom like Wavalene and the routine comfort of an older woman's wisdom.

"Being a mom can be a lonely job too, sometimes other people don't see that. The child's the center of your universe. And I think your idea to enroll her in school is a good one. But even though she's on target intellectually . . . I know it's disappointing, but sometimes the idea we have of who we want a child to be doesn't fit with who they are. It might not be reasonable to expect Hanna to thrive in an environment of typically abled kids. Have you heard of the Tisdale School?"

She shook her head. "Alex would never accept enrolling her in a school for special kids."

Mrs. Wade shrugged, impossible to ruffle. "Define 'special.' I've personally seen some very bright children with autism and other behavioral issues do very well at—"

"Do you think she's autistic?"

As Mrs. Wade spoke, she leaned forward over her desk and wrote something on a piece of copy paper. "I think many things are on a spectrum, and our society is fairly unforgiving unless people fall into a very narrow range that they've determined to be 'normal.' I pass no judgments—and you and your husband shouldn't either. You know your daughter isn't less of a person for being different." She handed her the paper. "Dr. Gutierrez is the principal there. Call him, tell him I recommended Tisdale for Hanna—we've known each other a long time. They'll probably take her right away."

"Oh my God, thank you so much." The looping cursive spelled out a place of salvation, a phone number that glowed with promise, and the name of someone who might finally help. Take Hanna off her hands. "Thank you so much."

"Sometimes the hardest part is seeing what's right in front of you. But when you find a place that's a good match for her needs I think the whole family will be happier, even Hanna." Mrs. Wade escorted her to the door.

"I think we've been in some denial because she's so smart." The two women shook hands. "I can't thank you enough for all your help."

"Happy to do it. I hope it all works out for you." She peered over toward the waiting area. "It was nice to meet you, Hanna."

Hanna threw down the book she was reading and marched into the hallway. Catching up to her, Suzette strode along beside her as they plowed toward the exit.

"Good job. For once you performed in front of the right person. Worked out splendidly."

She cast a sideways glance at her daughter, long enough to catch the uncertainty and worry on her face.

Suzette grinned, amazed by the triumphant turnaround of their day. She'd call Dr. Gutierrez as soon as they got home. And she'd have to figure out the best way to discuss it with Alex. But if the Tisdale School would take Hanna— and it sounded most probable that they would—she'd let nothing get in the way.

Suzette thought of the prize looming ahead of her. Time. Rest. Peace. The return of her sanity.

HANNA

MOMMY MADE HER favorite lunch: a grilled cheese sandwich and apple slices sprinkled with cinnamon and the bestest vanilla almond milk. She ate at the table alone and watched Mommy in the garden, on the other side of the glass wall, pacing up and down as she talked to someone on the phone. When she came back in, she was even happier.

"We are so close, Hanna-Suzanna-Fofanna-Banana!"

Her happiness and high energy were abnormal. Mommy had turned into a balloon, and she wanted to pop her with a pin and watch her fizzle-fuzzle into nothingness.

She couldn't figure out what she'd done wrong. The principal had looked genuinely scared when she'd barked at her, but Mommy left the school bouncing up and down. Was it a school for bad children? Had she played right into their hands? Never mind. She had a million more tricks to show them. She knew what adults liked and didn't like: rabbit-like girls who kept still and never raised their voice were good; dragon-like girls who roared and stomped and flew and generated their own fire were bad. No one could make her stay at SunnyBunnyPooPooBridge if she didn't want to.

After lunch, Mommy wanted her to do a page in her

math book. She opened it and left a pencil in the crevice between the pages. Hanna liked doing math problems. They were like puzzles but not silly; numbers lived in a pure world of yes or no. But she also wanted to finish her special project, which she was counting on to erase Mommy's upbeat mood. Not wanting to appear too eager, she took the book by a corner edge and slid it off the table. She put the pencil between her teeth and made a show of trudging up the stairs.

"Why, of course, Hanna, you may do your work in your room if you like. I'll come up in thirty minutes and check on your progress."

Mommy sounded like a robot who was about to overheat. It almost made Hanna laugh, imagining her frozen in place as wisps of smoke trailed from her ears. She'd start to melt from the inside and collapse onto her knees, eyes wide and dazed, as brain matter dripped from her nose. Daddy would come home and find her like that and realize Mommy had been a phony all along.

Once upstairs she hurried to her room and shut the door. She had thirty minutes before Mommy would come and check on her. She wanted to be ready.

Daddy had questioned the photo at first—"Why is Mommy naked?"—but Hanna simply shrugged and shut her eyes as she steepled her hands beside her ear in a gesture of sleep. Daddy shrugged, too, and printed the photo in black and white as she requested. Before leaving for Sunnybridge, she had trimmed away the white edges—from Mommy's picture and the ones she'd printed in secret (they all knew Daddy's password was BlueAndGoldForSweden). Now everything was ready for assembly, so she tore a sheet off the tablet of heavy paper on her easel and got down on the floor with her glue stick.

There were lots of pictures on the Creepy Photos website, but she'd rejected the ones where the people might be mistaken for alive. She liked the ones of the women in their coffins. Or lying stiff as a board on white fabric with lacy edges. In truth, she liked the dead children best, held in their mother's arms, or in tiny coffins, or surrounded by living siblings who looked merely bored, not scared—as if death were so every-day-not-again-here's-another-one. But she wanted Mommy to see only the other ladies, the other Mommies.

Some of them lay amid arrangements of flowers. Or among a gathering of relatives who wore funny old-fashioned clothing. Nobody smiled except in one, where the dead woman had a rectangular grin and empty, open eyes. She wished there was a photo of Marie-Anne Dufosset, all crispy after her burning, but cameras hadn't been invented then. The text that accompanied the photos on the website said sometimes they were the only pictures a family might have of a loved one. People didn't document their whole lives on the internet back then—that was news to Hanna—so instead they invested in postmortem photography. She wished she could see a dead person in real life. Even in black and white to match the other pictures, Mommy just looked like she was sleeping, not dead. But it was the best she could do.

She glued Mommy's picture next to one of a particularly ugly woman whose eyes were so sunken in, the lids didn't fit over the eyeballs anymore. Her mouth was a gash of thin lips locked in a permanent grimace with two wonky teeth sticking out. The woman was in such an advanced state of rotting that Hanna wondered why they'd waited so long to take the picture.

When she was finished, she wiped her gluey hands onto uneven remnants of paper, then folded them into wads and tossed them under the bed. She blew on all the tiny paper slivers until she got dizzy, but successfully corralled them with the other scraps and bits that she was hoping would transform, under the magic of night and nobody looking, into an UnderSlumberBumbleBeast. The glue stick and scissors went back into their designated cubby, and she made sure everything looked tidy and perfect. Finally, she set her masterpiece on the easel, where it stood in graphic black and white, its appearance in the room a new scream that could not be missed.

She sat on her bed and zipped through the easy peasy math problems. Something tickled in her belly; she was so excited for Mommy to see her picture. She almost wanted to summon her. She could stand at the top of the stairs and shriek; that always worked. Mommy would come running, afraid she'd poked herself with the pencil (which she did once, just to test its sharpness), or gotten a paper cut, or found a bug with a thousand legs in the bathroom. Mommy hated those bugs more than anything. If they weren't so stupidly fast on their thousand thin-as-a-hair legs she'd catch them just to see Mommy scream and flap her hands like she felt them crawling all over her body.

Wasn't thirty minutes up yet?

She opened her door so Mommy would come right in. That's when she heard her on the steps. She leapt back onto the bed and made herself look busy with schoolwork. It was hard not to grin or giggle.

"Need any help? Look at you, working so hard." Mommy stood with one hand on each side of the doorjamb, like it was a frame and she was posing for a picture.

Hanna grinned so wide all her teeth showed. She shook her head.

"Got it all figured out?"

She nodded.

Then Mommy saw it. She crept over to the easel, her eyes like question marks.

"What's this?"

Hanna made a high-pitched tittering noise in the back of her throat as her mother's bugged-out eyes traveled over the pictures.

"Hanna, what is this?"

Mommy scanned faster and faster, taking in the fancy dressed corpses and the one that was different: her, naked, sleeping the sleep of death.

"Did you make this, is this why you were taking a picture of me?" Mommy didn't sound happy anymore. Her voice sounded like someone was strangling her. "Why did you make this? Am I supposed to be dead?"

Hanna dragged a finger across her throat, then let her head loll as she flopped back onto the bed, dead.

"It's not funny! Where did you get all these . . . Horrible . . . Why did you do this? Hanna? Hanna! Marie-Anne, goddammit!"

Hanna sat bolt upright, so happy to let her friend share in the credit.

"What's wrong with you?"

Hanna crossed one leg over the other and folded her hands on her lap. An angel. Mommy's teeth gnashed and she looked like a scream was snaking its way up her throat but got clogged in her mouth.

Mommy snatched the collage off the easel. For a second she looked about to rip it in half. But she stopped.

"You think Daddy's going to like this? You think he's going to be proud of you? I'm going to tell him about everything. Every fucking word you said today, the barking, this. Nails in your own coffin, little girl."

Mommy was still shaking, but she held her head high and left the room. Hanna heard her go into the master bedroom and shut the door.

She pushed her lower lip against her teeth and chewed it. Had she miscalculated? Would Mommy really tell him everything? Would Daddy be mad at her? Such a thing was hard to imagine.

She got an idea. A so-good, brilliant idea. She threw off her yellow cotton cardigan and examined her arms. She gripped her right hand around her left forearm and squeezed. Her fingernails turned pink, and when she released her hand it left a faint white impression of her fingers. Then it faded away. But it was still a good idea.

She shut her door. Never mind Mommy's threats; she knew Mommy would hide away until it was time to come out and make supper, make everything look normal for when Daddy came home. Hanna had lots of time to figure out the next part. And Mommy telling Daddy lots of crazy things would make it all even better.

A pair of tights might work. There were lots of tights, rolled up in a color-coordinated row in her dresser. She picked a thin stretchy white pair and wrapped it around her forearm like a tourniquet, pulling it as tight as she could. She pulled and pulled, straining with the effort, even after her poor left hand started to feel numb.

SUZETTE

CURLED FULLY CLOTHED in the dry womb of the tub, she could still see the collage—and its double—if she turned her head even slightly. It leaned against the bathroom counter in such a way that the mirror reflected it. Why had she left it there to taunt her? She reached up and grabbed a fluffy white towel and folded it into a pillow, intent on waiting. As she slid down deeper, the mirror and Hanna's demented artwork disappeared from view. But she still felt herself slipping, regressing, becoming the pathetic person she never wanted to be who needed someone else to take the next step. It was Alex's turn; he needed to do something. Hopefully it would work out better than when she needed her mother.

By the age of nineteen, she was used to taking the bus into Oakland alone for all her medical appointments, even to the surgeons' office. Sometimes the open incision on her abdomen would start to heal over. Only it wouldn't always heal from the inside. The fistula still wanted to drain and it needed the exterior pathway through her skin. Her doctor injected her skin with something that would numb it, and it hurt like a bee sting, sharp and sizzling. She didn't really know what he was doing and was too intimidated to ask.

Two years into her official medical nightmare (the years she suffered without being taken to a doctor conveniently didn't count) and she never knew what anyone was doing. Things happened. And she suffered the consequences. With her skin numbed, he ran a scalpel through her closing incision, returning it to its gaping-maw condition.

It didn't hurt, not really. After the initial surgery to let the fistula drain, something must have happened to the nerve endings all around the incision. When she was in the hospital they gave her morphine each time they changed the packing. That it remained numb was a mercy, as otherwise the process of stuffing it full of cotton would have meant years of excruciating pain.

So she let him cut her open, and then he folded over some four-by-four bandages and taped them on her belly. She went everywhere in a daze, having become accustomed to being a recluse, so it was neither surprising nor alarming when she bled through the bandages while sitting on the bus. She bled through her T-shirt, the blood dripping onto the waistband of her jeans as she walked home from the bus stop.

They kept a supply of four-by-four bandages in the living room, where her mother changed her packing twice a day as she lay on the couch. Suzette didn't have enough hands to do it herself—she helped by holding the wound open—but it was just as well that she never had to look directly at her own separated flesh, or see how deep it went; the very thought was nauseating. They had a hospital vomit bin full of medical things—sterile jars of cotton packing, paper tape, scissors, tweezers. But as Suzette stood there bleeding, she couldn't find any four-by-fours. It was late afternoon. Maybe if she was lucky, her mother was getting hungry and wouldn't mind getting out of bed.

"Mom? Mom?"

"Hmm?"

"I'm bleeding. We're out of bandages."

"I'll get up soon," she said in a groan, not even rolling over or opening her eyes.

Suzette changed out of her stained clothes and affixed a sanitary pad to her bleeding wound. She was quite proud of her resourcefulness. With a sketchbook and a head full of dark thoughts, she settled back in her room to wait. Her mother slept for another hour.

When she came home from the store with the supplies, Suzette lay on the couch, the helpless patient once again. When her mother took off the sanitary pad, the wound gushed a dark stream of blood that was almost black. Her mother, uncharacteristically, winced. The gaping wound took almost an entire bottle of the cotton packing—five yards—which her mother delicately tucked between her raw flesh with a pair of surgical tweezers. By then, it was more of an ordeal for her mother than it was for Suzette, and she was glad.

The next day her mother drove her back into Oakland, a scant half-dozen blocks from the previous day's destination. Not for a medical appointment, but a treat. Sometimes her mother did that: offered wordless apologies in the form of a shopping expedition. It made Suzette aware that her mother knew, on some level, how much her drawing and dreaming meant to her. She let Suzette pick out anything she wanted at the art store. Professional quality pencils. Sketchbooks with paper in various sizes and textures. Then they went across the street for lunch at Alibaba's, their favorite Syrian restaurant. Suzette got her usual, the cheese pie, and tasted bits of her mother's hearty order of side dishes. She always wondered if they looked like a normal mother and daughter, sharing a day out. Or did people notice her mother never made eye contact with her, never initiated a single word of conversation. In her mother's silences, in the fog she drew down like a blind, Suzette was left to ponder what thoughts consumed her days and nights. Did she have a vivid fantasy world? Or just endless moments of regret? Even amid her own suffering, Suzette never stopped feeling sorry for her mother.

Pushing herself up with her feet, she surfaced, like a periscope, over the edge of the tub. With a more focused viewing, she appreciated the merit of her daughter's work: the pictures were neatly cut out, laid out in a balanced way, and glued with care. Maybe she should have just complimented her on a job well done instead of falling to pieces.

She launched herself out of the bathtub, huffing with annoyance. "I'm the adult!"

Snatching up the towel, she neatly folded it and put it back on the rack. Her daughter was just a little kid—she couldn't really hurt her. And even if Hanna ever became violent, she could overpower her. Pouting in the bathroom was ridiculous.

"I'm the adult," she told herself again. "I'm the mother—not the daughter."

Her phone was downstairs but she knew exactly what

she would do: message Alex a picture of Hanna's collage. She tucked it under her arm and marched out of the bathroom.

She started for the stairs, but turned back and went to her daughter's closed door. She fought a series of impulses. With her hand in a fist, she considered knocking. But then her features turned hard and mean and she drew back the fist like she wanted to punch something. As she exhaled, the anger left her and her hand fell defeated to her side. Maybe she should just peek in on her, make sure she was okay. Suzette spent years alone in her room, in pain. She couldn't stand to think of Hanna in pain, alone, helpless to communicate her true needs.

She glanced down at the grotesque face that Hanna had pasted beside her own, a woman whose frail body lay succumbing to decomposition. The shape of the woman's skull was clearly visible with the skin stretched tight across her bony nose and cheekbones. Suzette's concern evaporated. She reminded herself she *was* helping her daughter—Tisdale specialized in working with children with individual needs. Let them figure it out.

Her phone sat on the kitchen counter where she'd left it. She dropped Hanna's masterpiece onto the floor so she could stand above it, manipulating the camera to get the entire collage in the frame. But in the end, she focused on her sleeping self and the grotesque woman beside her so the point wouldn't be lost on a small screen. She typed in a message: This is what your daughter did w the pic she took of me. Made a collage of dead people. We need to talk.

She clicked send. Setting the phone aside, she checked

on the salmon that was thawing in the refrigerator. She didn't really like salmon, but it was Alex's favorite. She'd make her husband and daughter a salad of organic microgreens, from which she would eat only a few bites. She was just thinking of ways to jazz up the brown rice that would be the bulk of her own meal when Alex called.

"Hey."

"*Hej*."

"You got the picture?" she asked.

"Yes . . . She made that?"

"Yeah, beautiful, isn't it? Look, I need to catch you up on some things, and I think it's best in person. Can you come home?"

In the silence that followed she heard an unspoken "no."

"We're in the middle of *fika*," he said.

Suzette rolled her eyes. Sometimes Alex seemed a trifle too attached to his Swedish traditions. Having an organized daily break for coffee and pastries was great, charming, so civilized—but hardly something he needed to stay at work for.

"Great, so they won't mind if you leave."

"It's the one time of day we all get to chat about what we're working on."

She rolled her eyes again. He didn't have that many employees, and they were the most expressive, congenial, collaborative bunch of coworkers ever—he ran a friendly ship. She knew the truth: he didn't want to leave the pastries behind.

"Alex, please—remember what you said this morning?

We need to talk about Hanna and school." She could almost see him through the phone, looking with longing at the steaming freshly brewed coffee, the plate of yummies that he had delivered every day from a local bakery. "Finish your pastry, then come home?"

"*Tack, älskling.*"

She heard the smile in his voice. The whole thing struck her as childish, but at least he was coming home. It was likely he'd hoped to avoid another confrontation, especially so soon after their rocky morning. But maybe she could also ease up on her dessert rules. They rarely had sweets at home, except on holidays—which, come to think of it, was not infrequent in the Jensen household. She and her Jewish mother hadn't celebrated much of anything. Her mother came from a family that sent only boys to Hebrew school, so she never learned the prayers that accompanied holidays and rituals. Her maternal grandparents—whom Suzette had barely known—had expected her mother to marry a Jewish man who would lead them in their Jewish traditions, but she opted for a *goy* instead. An unhealthy *goy* with a bad heart. Her mother's side of the family kept their distance, and after Daddy died, they disappeared.

Suzette still remembered seeing, as a four-year-old, her father wrapped in white muslin—like a mummy, a monster. She hadn't felt sad then, as everyone cried around her, only afraid. But for her maternal grandparents it was the final insult: the muslin was a Jewish tradition, one her mother clung to because she thought embalming was grisly; for her parents, it was a sacrilege. He was buried at

Homewood, not the Jewish cemetery, and as he was
lowered into the ground Suzette's mother wept hysterically.
She fell to her knees and almost tumbled into the grave. It
seemed possible, looking back on it as an adult, that some
part of her mother had slipped under the earth with her
father, never to resurface.

Maybe Alex was overcompensating, but he liked to
celebrate everything. He bought books about the Jewish
holidays, which they honored alongside their own slightly
less consumer-oriented versions of Christian holidays, as
well as his beloved Swedish ones, like Midsummer. They
even did their own version of Walpurgis Night, which
they'd celebrate in less than two weeks. They couldn't have
a bonfire in the backyard, but they'd set up the portable
copper fire pit and sing songs to welcome in the spring. She
wasn't much of a baker, but every October 4 they celebrated
Kanelbullens Dag—Cinnamon Bun Day—and she baked
accordingly from her mother-in-law Tova's time-honored
recipe. Maybe she should indulge her family in more than
treats of chocolate covered fruit or nuts or nondairy ice
cream. They ate healthily otherwise and might like it if she
learned to bake. It wasn't as if Suzette didn't love chocolate
chip cookies.

It was suddenly easy to imagine them both getting fat
someday, if Alex spent less time at the gym, or she relented
to the call of the doughnuts and cupcakes and fried onion
rings that, ironically, were easier to digest than raw vegetables and whole grains and every other consciously
healthful food. She knew better than to ever try becoming
a vegan; one navel orange, devoured over the winter with

slurping glee, landed her in excruciating pain and another round of tests. That's when they found out how bad the narrowing in her intestine had become. Sometimes she struggled with resentment watching her family eat a meal that she'd prepared. People took eating and shitting for granted, like the continuous beating of their hearts, the inevitable protection of their skin. They didn't think about their intestines doing everything wrong, fucking up the basic process of digestion. Sometimes food was a marauding enemy, threatening and bludgeoning. She couldn't tell Alex how cheated she felt sometimes, or jealous. She looked normal and he accepted her near-normality.

She slipped back upstairs and put a big hot-water load of towels in the washing machine. The sound of the wash cycle, the rhythmic churning and frothing, always comforted her. She lingered there, her hand on the machine, taking in its faintly oceanic vibrations.

Hanna came out of her room and spotted her in the laundry alcove. She thought the girl would have changed into something more comfortable, the leggings and T-shirt dresses she liked. But she still wore the skirt and cardigan from their morning outing. She gazed up at her with the expression Suzette had come to learn meant "I'm bored."

"You could play outside for a bit? It's a nice day."

She wriggled her face around, apparently weighing the merits of the suggestion, but then looked up with her slightly hopeful "anything else?" look.

"I'm still irritated with you, you know. About that picture. But I have to say, you constructed it very well."

Hanna gave one sharp bob of her head in agreement.

"You are a smart and capable girl . . ."

Hanna reached out and placed her hand on the washing machine, a mirror of her mother. Suzette read the question on her face.

"I like the way the vibration feels. Someday . . . You don't believe it now, and I'm sorry if you're afraid, but once you're in school—"

The girl let out a vicious bark.

"—things will be so much better. For you, us."

Hanna snarled and yipped, growing more and more savage. Suzette stood there, passive and unimpressed.

"I should have brought my phone up, so I could record this—a little more evidence so Daddy knows who you really are."

Hanna stopped barking but held her mother in a hateful stare. She whipped her head toward Suzette's extended arm, opening her mouth as wide as she could.

Suzette pulled her vulnerable arm in and instinctively pressed her other hand against her daughter's forehead to keep her at bay.

"We do not bite! You know better!"

Hanna clacked her teeth together, biting the air, twisting her head against her mother's resisting arm.

"Stop it!"

She made growling noises in her throat: rabid, dangerous sounds. Grabbing Suzette's arm, Hanna tried a new tactic in her fight to get close enough to bite her.

Suzette jumped out of the way, flailing her arms, trying to swat her away. "Hanna! You fucking little . . . !" She thought she'd be strong enough, should the need arise, to overpower her. But she was afraid—afraid she was wrong and afraid of feeling her daughter's teeth breaking through her skin, clamping onto her bone. She recalled a story, splashed across the internet, of a woman and her dog. One night, after drinking too much, the woman passed out, and while trying to lick her awake, her pet dog became anxious and manic. The woman lay unconscious and the dog kept licking. Her skin became raw, her nose started to bleed. Excited by the blood, the dog ate her entire face.

She could almost feel Hanna biting through her skin, tearing off a long and bloody strip of her flesh. The girl-dog kept advancing and she retreated, slapping at her.

"Stop!" Suzette howled again and again. "You're going to end up in a fucking mental hospital, is that what you want?"

The girl-dog vanished as suddenly as she'd appeared. Suzette struggled to control her ragged tear-choked breathing. Her heart screamed in her chest. The word "hate" formed in her mouth, but she didn't give it a voice.

"Why? Why are you doing this to me?"

Her daughter's slight shoulders drooped, her head tilted a little to the right. She almost looked sad.

"Je suis Marie-Anne. Je m'appelle Marie-Anne!"

She sounded so desperate, begging to be understood. She also sounded, to Suzette's ears, so perfectly, natively French. But what could she know beyond a few words from the French computer game she'd refused to play? *Impossible.*

They faced off for a moment, before Suzette snatched her daughter's arm. She gripped her tightly and dragged her down the stairs. Hanna tried to wrest free, digging at her mother's clenched fingers, but Suzette asserted her superior size, her superior strength.

Down the steps. Across the great room. She opened the door that led to their enclosed garden and practically tossed the girl outside.

"Go play!"

She slammed the door and locked it. Hanna glared at her from the other side of the glass. She tested the door, confirming that it couldn't be opened. Unflustered, she set her hands at her waist and jauntily walked off into the yard, like the queen of Nothing Matters.

Suzette breathed in and out, a bull deciding whether to charge. She flicked the lock open and stuck her head outside.

"I'll be right here watching you! And Daddy'll be home any minute!"

Hanna looked back at her long enough to shrug, then went to her stash of toys that they kept in a storage box alongside the house. Suzette reclosed the door and locked it.

She could kill Hanna.

No, she couldn't.

She could.

She'd never.

She might.

Once, only once in her life had she ever wanted to tear someone apart. It lasted only a moment. Scrawny Ira Blumenfeld thought it was funny one day, before their sixth-grade art teacher came in, to snip off an inch of her hair. Was she supposed to laugh? Were the other boys?

She'd always been friendly with Ira—she was still healthy then, still had friends. But the rage it set off in her. Because her mother butchered her hair once, too lazy to take her to a salon? Whatever the reason, she grabbed scrawny Ira Blumenfeld by his neck with both hands and nearly threw him across the room.

The shocked look on his face extinguished her rage, and for years afterward she remained puzzled and guilt-ridden by her outburst of violence. But now, she felt it again.

Hanna was safer on the other side of the glass.

In her reliable rubber gloves, she used a clean cloth and window cleaner and worked her way across the glass wall. For a while, Hanna played with her Hula-Hoop in the middle of the yard as the two of them kept careful watch of each other. Now, the Hula-Hoop lay forgotten and Hanna stood just on the other side of the glass, inching along as Suzette sprayed and rubbed, stepped to her right, sprayed and rubbed. With a certain glee she was able to spray it on Hanna's face without actually damaging her. But a sense of disappointment remained that with all her effort and rubbing, she couldn't make her daughter dissolve with the dust and oily smudges.

It registered on Hanna's face before Suzette even heard the door open behind her: Alex was home. She lit up, grinning, and ran for the door. She tugged it, but it wouldn't open. Suzette peeled off her gloves and met Alex in the center of the room. As they kissed, Hanna banged on the glass.

"Don't bang on the glass, *lilla gumman*," he called out.

She tugged ferociously on the door and he understood. "Is it locked?"

"Yes. She's fine. Let's just talk while she's out playing—"

"She wants in." He brushed past Suzette and unlocked the door.

"—please, Alex, we can't talk if she's in—"

Hanna ran into her father's arms and Suzette swallowed the rest of her plea. It was such a defeat to see him on his knees, and her, so sweet, kissing his cheek, hugging him around the neck. What had he done that was so much better, that earned him all of their daughter's love? Alex fussed over her and she giggled.

"How's my squirrely girl?"

At his question, Hanna turned sheepish, frightened eyes toward Suzette, then turned back to her Daddy. Wincing as if she was in pain, she tugged up the sweater sleeve on her left arm.

Suzette couldn't see exactly what she revealed, but horror dropped onto Alex's face. And he turned that horrified face to her.

"What is it?" She felt fear brewing once again in that fragile place inside her, the place that could soften and fail and destroy her equilibrium.

"Did you do this?" he asked.

"What?"

She stepped closer, and Hanna, wearing a pout, extended her arm.

Four screaming red bands, already bruising, marred her delicate skin.

Suzette gasped, concerned for her daughter's injury. She became aware of both of them looking at her, condemning her, escorting her onto the gallows and nodding for the hangman to drop the floor. She swung before them, jittery and unable to beg for her life.

"I didn't . . . !"

She saw in their faces: they didn't believe her.

Had she made those marks? When she yanked Hanna down the stairs and across the room? She didn't think she'd gripped her so forcefully. And it hadn't been for more than a minute. Could she have caused such damage to her child?

"Alex, I swear . . ."

Hanna pointed at her, but looked at her father. The fire in his face. He'd do worse than let her hang. He'd gather the kindling and strike the match himself.

Suzette shook her head. "You don't know what she was doing! She was trying to attack me. She tried to bite me, she was growling and biting—"

"*Lilla gumman,* I need you to go to your room while I talk to your mother."

"—I only took her by the arm, it wasn't . . . I didn't . . ." She tried to take hold of her daughter's arm, gingerly, to examine it further, but Hanna hugged it against her body. "I'll get you an ice pack." She hurried to the freezer, aware of Alex lobbing fireballs at her back.

"I swear, Alex . . . I don't know what happened." She wrapped a reusable Freez Pak into a dish towel. She tried to hand it to Hanna, but he took it from her and placed it gently on their daughter's swollen arm. He picked her up and carried her upstairs.

"Only leave it on for a few minutes at a time, otherwise it'll get too cold," she called to him.

He didn't acknowledge her.

"Make sure there's enough fabric against her skin . . ."

"We've got this." He disappeared without looking at her. His condemnation reverberated around the room.

She pressed her fingers to her lips and for a moment forgot to breathe.

Did she do it?

She was sure she didn't.

Almost sure.

Pretty sure.

The cracks formed and doubt broke her open.

She couldn't remember.

What had she done to her daughter? In that moment when her hatred blacked out her reason?

Nothing.

She'd done nothing to Hanna.

It was Marie-Anne Dufosset. She was the problem.

That fucking little French witch.

HANNA

SUPPER WAS WEIRD. Fishy fish and Mommy and Daddy with a wall between them, thicker than the garden glass that had separated her from Mommy. Daddy gobbled up his fish like a hungry bear while Mommy picked at hers like the pink flesh was human meat.

"I think we should talk about what happened," she said in a sad cartoony voice. "What preceded—"

"Not in front of Hanna."

She perked up, interested. It had turned out even better than she had planned, and she really truly didn't mind if they wanted to talk about her. It would be like watching a very good game, like what no one but Daddy called football where the men ran around in such a hurry, kicking and chasing after a ball that would explode if it stayed still for too long.

"It affects Hanna, and she was involved—"

Daddy glared at Mommy as she put her cheek against her palm. Her head looked heavy enough to break her wrist.

Hanna fought the urge to smile. She ate her rice one tiny grain at a time, wedged between the tines of her fork.

So it went for fifty-two grains. Mommy kept glancing at Daddy, but he'd never seen anything more interesting than his plate of food. He took a second serving of salad.

"She wasn't accepted at Sunnybridge," she said into the silence.

He kept his chin down but tilted his eyes up, making him look a bit evil. "Not now."

"Don't you want to know why? Hanna knows—there's no reason not to talk about it in front of her. I wish she would tell you herself. Or show you—"

"Suzette—"

"—how remarkably talented she is at imitating vicious dogs. Can you do your little barking routine for Daddy?"

Hanna didn't mind if they talked *about* her, but she didn't want Mommy talking *to* her. She studied how Daddy ate his greens, stabbing them onto his fork, folding over any pieces that were sticking out, opening his mouth to receive them. She imitated him.

"I don't like the tone you're using to talk about our daughter," he said.

"She's not a baby. She needs to be held responsible for what she does. And you have no idea what she does. She's a girl of many talents. Hanna knows how to sabotage getting into a school, or staying at a school. She knows how to print pictures off the Internet. She knows how to research stuff online—all on *your* computer."

"She should know how to do those things."

Mommy's mouth dropped open at his response. Then Daddy squirmed a little.

"The computer stuff. That's the age we live in."

"She barked like a dog to terrorize the principal of Sunnybridge."

Daddy put his fork down. He looked at Hanna for a long time, but she didn't want to meet his gaze. She concentrated on her rice, one grain at a time. Onto the fork. Into her mouth. Eventually Daddy turned back to Mommy.

"That's why we were talking about the . . . other thing . . ." He tried to communicate something silently to Mommy, and Hanna grew annoyed. Mommy didn't look too happy, either.

"You know I'm waiting for the approval from our insurance—"

"You don't have to. We can afford it."

"Well Mrs. Wade, the principal, helped me get in touch with the Tisdale School and we have an appointment there tomorrow. And this school specializes in kids like Hanna."

Hanna looked at her, startled. Kids who were learning to be witches?

"What does that mean?" Daddy asked, his voice a threatening rumble.

Mommy didn't answer him for a long time. They made laser-beam eyes at each other, trying to suck out each other's brains with just their thoughts.

"The pediatrician said . . ." She finally blinked and turned away. "There's a difference between *can't* speak and *won't* speak. Hanna had some more things to say today."

Hanna pressed the fork tines against her tongue. She imagined how it looked, skinny parallel rows of nubbly tongue poking through. She paid keen attention now, to

Daddy especially. He looked like he'd been struck by a wayward lick of lightning.

"She really spoke? Not just . . . What did she say?"

He turned to her, and Hanna could see his hope that she'd say something to him, too. But Marie-Anne wasn't interested in him. Daddy didn't understand this was for the best.

Mommy sighed. "She said she was Marie-Anne Dufosset—remember, I asked you? A seventeenth-century witch—well, the last person in France burned as a witch."

Now Daddy looked like he was trapped in a pinball machine. The little silver balls bounced off his face, his brain, making his eyes go wobbly. He looked from daughter to wife, back and forth.

"She said . . . ? You said . . . ?"

"I don't know what it means, Alex. I'm not bullshitting you and I have no idea what . . . *Hon skrämmer mig, ibland.*"

It didn't matter that Mommy tried to hide her words in Swedish. Once upon a time, Daddy always spoke Swedish around the house. "She scares me, sometimes." That's what her mother said. Hanna felt a tickle of relief. Her little canoes of rice traveled down their river into her victorious belly. She was still winning.

"*Lilla gumman,* is that what you told Mommy? I'd like to hear it too."

She hummed a high-pitched version of the theme to *Star Trek*, her favorite show. Daddy didn't really sound like he believed Mommy, but it didn't matter. She'd never prove her mother right, and then Daddy would have to choose whose side he was on.

"We'll talk later," Daddy said to Mommy as Hanna moved her hand like the *Enterprise*, traveling around the stars.

Mommy nodded, her face still tight and unsettled.

Daddy wore what he called pajamas—old gym pants and a T-shirt—though she knew he slept all naked. He opened the book to the Post-it where they'd left off and sat beside her on the bed. She gripped her comforter, paddling her legs beneath it like she was swimming, so excited.

"Right, so . . . 'I let my eyes acclimate to the darkness. My constellation stickers glowed on the ceiling. I concentrated on what I could hear: the television from downstairs; my older sister brushing her teeth in the bathroom. Then I heard it! *De-ding, de-ding*. It sounded like my Under-SlumberBumbleBeast was riding a squeaky bicycle and, with his lollipop hand, ringing a tiny bell. I grinned. But then there was a honking noise. And a crash. Wait a minute, this was all wrong!

" 'I hung over the side of the bed with my flashlight, hoping my UnderSlumberBumbleBeast was okay. But it wasn't just him—there were others! They must have been sleeping when I first met Lollipop Hand. Now I could see several . . . One, two, three, four, five. And each one was different! I was immediately relieved, as it would be lonely to be a singular beast living in the forest of my under-the-bed forgotten things.' "

At that point Mommy slipped into the room. She bent over and kissed her on the forehead.

"Goodnight. Sweet dreams." Hanna wiped off Mommy's kiss with the back of her hand. "I'm really sorry, about before. I didn't mean to lose my temper. I shouldn't have grabbed you like that." She spoke the words to Hanna, but then she turned toward Daddy and her fingertips grazed his shoulder.

"We're just going to read a little more," he said.

Yay, Daddy was staying! Mommy threw her a kiss. "Love you." Then she blew away like a ghost.

Hanna slapped her hand against the book so Daddy would keep reading.

"Okay, I know you love this part . . . 'Lollipop Hand picked himself up and wiped the dust from his sky-blue knitted shorts. It looked like a second UnderSlumberBumbleBeast had lost control while trying to steer a lopsided airplane with only one wing. I worried for my lollipop-handed friend (who hadn't been wearing a helmet), but he chased after the beast in the airplane (who had a Monopoly die for a mouth) and the two of them bickered and flapped and spun their parts. I was relieved they were okay, and I was about to suggest they drive around in different quadrants, so they'd each have enough space, when I saw something lurking in the far corner that almost made me scream. I lay flat against my pillow and stuffed sheets into my mouth.' "

Hanna stuffed her own sheet into her mouth, though she giggled with anticipation.

"Don't chew on that," Daddy said, and she opened her mouth so he could pull out the saliva-tinged edge of her bedding.

"'I took a deep breath and told myself to be brave. I wanted to see that many-legged thing—was it friend or foe? Was it going to attack the other little beasts? Or crawl up the side of the bed and pounce on my foot? I dared to lie on my stomach and peer under the bed again. Lollipop Hand and Bad Airplane Driver must have kissed and made up. The UnderSlumberBumbleBeasts were all in a circle, dancing the Hokey Pokey! I even saw the one that had frightened me—the one with so many legs. They were just pencils—new pencils and stubs of pencils—framing its head like the petals of a flower.'"

Hanna squealed and kicked back the covers. She grabbed her flashlight and flopped over the edge of the bed to peer beneath it, just like the girl in the story. She gestured to Daddy: come look.

In the beam of her light she revealed her treasures: scraps of paper, the sock, the hair band, the barrette, a faded coin purse shaped like an owl, a twist tie she'd stolen from a drawer in the kitchen, a tiny plastic fluorescent-green stegosaurus, two colored pencils in undesirable booger-y shades. It was a miracle they'd survived so long without Mommy reaching under to decontaminate the world she was building.

"Are you trying to make your own UnderSlumber-BumbleBeast?" Daddy asked, sitting back up with a pink grin on his face.

Hanna's heart puffed so it was about to burst. She nodded.

"Very clever. Hmm. We'll have to protect it from Mommy."

She nodded so hard she bounced up and down on her knees.

"Last time I told her you were working on a little project, it didn't go so well. I wouldn't have printed that picture of Mommy if I'd known about the other ones. Putting Mommy next to all those dead people wasn't nice. And having my password doesn't mean you can abuse your computer privileges."

Hanna sat cross-legged with her pillow on her lap, punching it halfheartedly.

"Maybe . . . I could ask her not to clean so much in here? We can tell her you can do it yourself. You think that'll work?"

She chewed on her lip. A padlock would be better. But she agreed. Daddy tucked her back into bed. He planted kisses all over her face.

"*Lilla gumman?* I know you want friends. And you can have real friends too—little girls and little boys. I have friends—every day I like to go to work and see my friends. Then I like to come home and see you and Mommy. That's what it's like to go to school too. You go there and see your friends, and then later you come home."

She shook her head and chewed on the edge of the sheet. He gently removed it from her mouth and folded it back down.

"I know you're worried about it, and it can be scary at first, going somewhere new. But that's where you're going to find your friends. Okay? Be brave for Daddy?"

She really didn't want to disappoint him, but she couldn't explain why she didn't want to go to school. She tried to nod but her eyes just turned up to the ceiling. She wanted a friend who looked like a yam in a pair of sky-blue knitted shorts. A nocturnal friend. A kind of ugly, broken friend.

A friend who could be taken apart if she grew bored with him.

Daddy planted three more kisses on her cheek. *"Jag älskar dig."*

She loved him, too. So so very much.

The little girl in the book had glow-in-the-dark constellation stickers on her ceiling, and Hanna wished she could have some, too. Maybe she'd put them on her Hanukkah list. It would be nice to look at them on those nights when she couldn't fall right to sleep. All sorts of weird images came into her head when she thought about school. Mommy was really determined this time, and it sounded like the Pissdale School was almost a done deal. She thought of worms swarming over the rotting body of a bunny that had once been adorable. Now it was mud and dried blood and oozing eyeballs and matted fur and the worms ate it up, yummy yum yum. She thought of armies of ants carrying away their bounties of food. Leaves and slices of bread and sticky red Tootsie Pops and severed fingers. The images frightened her, and she didn't know where they came from or why, or how to tell them to go away and leave her alone.

She wanted Daddy.

She knew they were downstairs, probably on the couch, with the lamps set to glow and the corners of the room in shadow. Sometimes an isolated word or two, spoken in anger, floated upstairs through the floor. Mommy saying "it's not" or Daddy saying "you can't." She heard a loud "Tisdale" and a louder "retarded" and a high-pitched booming "they're not and that's terrible."

Hanna tiptoed into the hall. She sat on the top step where she could hear everything perfectly.

"That's what we've wanted all along—a place that understands her." Mommy sounded very convincing. Daddy didn't say anything in response. She heard the clink of a glass being set on a hard surface.

"They have to have academic standards too—" he said.

"Of course."

"—it can't just be life skills, or . . . Whatever they teach in remedial classes, she knows how to tie her shoes."

"I keep telling you it's not remedial. They have small classes but also work one-on-one with the kids so they can address specific needs. But it's still a school, they want to teach them, and the website says a lot of the kids end up mainstreamed by middle school. Not everyone starts in the same place. Hanna has her own particular issues."

"No, I know."

It got quiet again.

"Maybe it's stupid, but I was wondering," Daddy said. "When she spoke . . . What was her voice like? Her pronunciation?"

"She sounded . . ." Mommy hesitated. "French. And like she hasn't used her voice very much. But everything she said was clear, if accented. Her pronunciation . . . You'd be proud. Excellent. She picks up so much."

"Very smart."

"Maybe too smart. I wish you could've seen her. So you'd understand. And I truly, truly . . . I'd never hit her, I'd never—"

"I know."

There were kissy-smoochy sounds.

"Sometimes I think . . ." She waited a long time to hear what Daddy thought. "Maybe, I've been the bigger problem all along. I didn't want . . . I just thought she needed time."

"Maybe she did, at first."

"Did they tell you how much the school costs?"

"It's not on the website; they said we could discuss it tomorrow."

"So, expensive."

"Probably."

"Put it on the credit card, doesn't matter how much. There isn't a ton in the cash account, but I'll move some things around."

"Thank you."

Grown-ups talked about boring things in boring ways and it was almost enough to put her to sleep. But then Mommy made a gasping noise and she hoped for a moment that Daddy was strangling her. Mommy giggled, very much alive, and then there was a flurry of papery noises but no talking.

Hanna eased down the stairs on her butt. A little farther, a little farther, until finally she could see everything that was going on. Their clothes lay in random piles on the floor. Mommy and Daddy stood entwined in front of the couch, their hands running around like lost animals and their mouths like yucky suction cups, all over each other's faces. Marie-Anne wanted to find something to light on fire, a paper airplane that she could sail into the room where it would ignite the couch. Mommy might swallow Daddy but he didn't seem aware of the danger. Poor Daddy could die of his own cluelessness.

They made weird noises that Hanna began to recognize. The throaty whines and breathy gasps.

In a rush, they tore off their last bits of clothing and then they were naked, and Hanna saw Daddy's sculpted bum and Mommy's breasts looked sharp and ready to shoot. He picked her up and she wrapped her legs around him and then in a swift gesture they were on the couch, Daddy on top. He put his thing inside her and Mommy groaned, and he hovered above her and his bum went up and down, flexing with the effort. They were speaking it then, the language of adults, and now she understood what went with it. The savagery, out of control.

Hanna hoped for a minute that Daddy might kill her this way, as it looked so gruesome, but Mommy came more and more to life as he pumped himself against her. Like he was blowing up a bicycle tire, restoring it to usable condition. She hated Daddy for a minute then. He could have left her flat and lifeless and eventually Mommy would turn to rust like her old tricycle, dead from lack of use.

Mommy gripped his strong arms and threw her head back, and Daddy rode her back to life. He pumped her full of everything he had and they made all their mutant noises that were part of something she'd only faintly grasped before: sex. The strange physicality of it somehow left them wordless.

Hanna slid over into the protective shadows against the wall, got to her feet, and retreated back to bed.

She would get her chance. It remained disappointing that Daddy hadn't let Mommy wither and die when he'd had the chance. But maybe she could undo Daddy's life-giving efforts. Marie-Anne could help, and the devil would come along soon—he always visited his witch children, she'd read—and then they'd be even more powerful. As she grew stronger she could take advantage of Mommy's weaknesses. Could Mommy die of cleaning too much—could she be scrubbed to death? And Mommy needed a lot of medication. If something bad happened to her medicine, would something bad happen to Mommy?

Or maybe . . . Mommy was always fussing about how she looked, and she glowed whenever Daddy said she was beautiful.

Maybe if Mommy was uglier.

Maybe Daddy wouldn't love her as much.

And she wouldn't want to leave the house and Hanna would never have to go to Pissdale.

SUZETTE

FRESHLY FUCKED AND the sun was shining; oh, what a beautiful day—and soon they'd be heading off to Tisdale. Things were back to normalish with Alex, though it remained an easy source of disappointment that every conversation they had was about Hanna. In their early years, they could spend an entire day side by side with sketchbooks, silently taking in the beauty of the plants and the array of people at Phipps Conservatory. They could lose hours and hours hand in hand, walking around a museum or strolling through Frick Park or the cemetery. At night, they would lie together and the words would come. The things they'd observed about the people at Phipps, the draw of certain places for selfie and group photo opportunities: in front of the green and gold sea monster of a desert plant; beside or beneath one of the tangled and sexual Chihuly sculptures. Or they'd compare what they'd seen at the museum, enthralled by how differently their brains interpreted a piece of art. The cemetery would inspire them to talk about their beliefs in the universe, and how they hoped their decomposing bodies would become part of a forest one day.

They could stay up all night, saying "Remember . . ."

or "Did you see . . ." Sometimes they'd doze and maybe they'd awaken to nibble at each other. They lived and breathed in extended silences followed by bursts of amazed nose-to-nose chatter that they were together, alive, in sync, in love.

After one final stretch, Suzette sat up. Out of her peripheral vision, she saw something dark on her pillow. Her mind scrambled for answers, not understanding, even as she touched what appeared to be human hair.

Her hair?

It didn't make sense. She'd experienced a bit of hair loss years earlier when she'd been on 6-mercaptopurine—a medication she'd refused to stay on precisely because of the horror of seeing strands of her hair floating into the bathroom sink as she shook her head. But what was on the pillow was too much, too evenly . . . cut.

She touched the left side of her head. Oh God.

Hanna.

Hanna who knew how to sneak into her room as she slept.

Hanna and her fucking scissors.

Suzette stumbled into the bathroom, pawing the severed strands as she turned on the light.

No no no . . . ! Chunks were missing from the left side of her head. Too much to hide, and she'd look like a freak if she didn't try to fix it. But fixing it would mean . . . How many inches would have to be cut?

Tears blurred her vision. Why why why was Hanna such a little shit? Suzette could already hear Alex tut-tutting about kids and their inevitable urge to try haircutting at least once. But Hanna had never hacked off her own hair. Suzette held the butchered parts flat against her head. Could she go punk? Shave off one side and leave the other long? Would Alex like it? Or would he grimace, disgusted?

"Fuck!"

She pulled it back in a ponytail, relieved that only a few pieces, now too short, dangled alongside her face. She'd deal with it later. Hanna was almost in school, almost out of the house.

"Just get her out of this fucking house," she muttered under her breath. She clenched her fists. Don't strangle her. Don't strangle her. Alex would never forgive her if she tightened her hands around their daughter's throat.

Suzette sat at the table, holding the syringe pen in her fist to warm it to her body temperature, staring at nothing and wishing for things that wouldn't happen. It crossed her mind that she must look like her mother—was she becoming too much like her? Without Alex, it would be so easy to . . . And suddenly her mother's lifelong mourning seemed plausible. Maybe her father was her mother's sustenance, as Alex was hers. Maybe his absence was space that only expanded over time, such as she imagined would happen if she didn't have Alex. The expanding dissolution of her stability, her health, her sanity. She shuddered away the image, the fear of what she could yet become. Alex was coming around a little. Of course he couldn't process Hanna's insane words, but at least he hadn't refused the possibility that they emerged from her mouth.

The medication in the syringe was viscous, and refrigeration made it thicker; it would sting even more if it went in gluey and cold. As she waited for it to warm up, she pondered the previous day's drama. She still couldn't understand what had happened with Hanna or how her arm became so red, so promising of bruises. *Don't touch her. You can't control yourself.* She'd dragged her to the car more than once over the years, kicking and screaming after a shopping trip tantrum. There had never been any evidence to give away her momentary inability to parent as placidly as Alex desired. Fortunately, by nightfall, he resumed speaking to her, seemed to forgive her even. At least his penis had.

Hanna was better at holding grudges. Had the mutilation of her hair been an act of retribution?

Suzette heard stockinged feet on the stairs and the slight squeal of hands pushing erratically against the handrail. She considered yelling at Hanna to wait a minute—she preferred to do her injection without an audience—but couldn't risk the words that might erupt if she opened her mouth. Not yet. Not while her own vengeance bubbled in her thoughts. Hanna padded closer, wearing patterned monkey knee socks, denim shorts, and a T-shirt given to her by Matt and Sasha—Alex's partner and his wife— upon their return from Ireland, their last excursion before the twins were born. A green Guinness T-shirt with its harp logo on the front—they'd brought one for each of them, and for everyone in the office. Suzette wouldn't even ask her to change. So what if she wore a beer T-shirt to her new school? She was exhausted and beyond trying to impress anyone. She'd have her put on a sweater or hoodie, though, to cover the fading marks on her arm.

With the bottom of her shirt tucked into her bra, she tore open the alcohol prep pad. She wiped it in hard stripes against her lower left abdomen—she never used the right side, even before the recent surgery; it didn't seem right to inflict more pain there. The tops of her thighs were fair game, but they were too sensitive. The nurse had given her a set of rules to follow, but Suzette learned some better tricks. Broken rule number one: she used the same approximate area for every shot, administered every two weeks. Hanna leaned against the table and watched. Suzette had explained the process to her many times over the years. How the syringe pen worked—"I never have to see the needle"—and how the medication changed her cells at a biological level to prevent inflammation—"Sometimes the body attacks itself." It was hard to explain to a kid; Suzette struggled to understand it herself.

She pulled off the gray cap at the bottom of the pen, the part that would go against her skin. Then she pulled off the red cap that revealed the press-button. Broken rule number two: she didn't pinch her flesh as the nurse had instructed; it hurt more that way, forcing the thick medicine through a compressed space. She didn't talk it through with Hanna this time, just got herself ready, took a deep breath, and exhaled slowly. She depressed the button that plunged the medicine into her flesh and counted silently to ten.

Ten seconds. That's how long the injection hurt, building to a gasping, stinging climax.

And then the pain receded. She pressed a clean cotton ball to the spot and held it lightly, rubbing it in small circles to help distribute the medicine and reduce the lingering sting. Hanna, as she occasionally liked to do, peeled the wrapper off the Band-Aid and handed it to her mother.

"Do you think this makes up for what you did to my hair?" A tiny speck of blood bubbled from the injection site. She plastered the Band-Aid over it and dropped her shirt.

Hanna, smiling, reached for one of the too-short pieces that hung by her face. Suzette jerked away from her touch.

"Get away from me!"

Hanna grinned with her upper teeth overlapping her bottom lip. Suzette worried for her ability to maintain control. She'd never before been so repulsed by the sight of her child.

"Daddy will see this, he'll know what you did."

Hanna shrugged. And Suzette couldn't shake the feeling that they shared the same thought: Alex will throw her away now. Hanna saw it as a victory, while Suzette feared it more than she could ever admit. Not that Alex was so shallow; not that his interest in her was only superficial. But of course her appearance was important to him. And she wasn't always confident about what she had to offer as a woman, as a wife. She owed him at least her best attempt at presenting an attractive exterior, even if it was a guise to distract them both from the memory of shit oozing through her belly. Or maybe she was only ever trying to convince herself. *Not hideous. Not disgusting.* Protectively, she held her hand against the damaged side of her head.

"Get your shoes. And a sweater. We're going to school." She scooped up the detritus that went into the garbage, then dropped the used syringe into the red sharps box that she kept high up in one of the kitchen cabinets.

Hanna uttered a pouty wail, crossing her arms.

"Go. You and me, looking . . . worse for the wear. Put on your damn shoes."

As Hanna's protest collapsed, her body slumped. She mewled and halfheartedly stamped her foot. Her head fell toward her chest, sending her fine hair spilling forward. Suzette couldn't stop herself; she reached out and touched it. Her daughter's hair was still as soft as when she was a baby. Suzette grew wistful, remembering how everyone in the delivery room exclaimed over her daughter's headful of dark hair. On another day she might have combed it, or put it in two braids, or at least gotten it out of her face with a pair of colorful barrettes.

Not today.

Hanna slapped at the car window as Suzette drove past the playground.

"If you're good, we'll stop by after our appointment."

In truth, Suzette longed to spend the day in the park, too, though not with Hanna. It had been a gloomy winter and the return of the sun made her want to bask in its light and warmth. She turned down the side street toward the school, which bordered Frick Park. It made her think of Alex, years ago, in the autumn, golden leaves crunching beneath their shoes. He talked about mushrooms. She

concentrated on the feel of his bones, his fingers inter-
twined with hers.

Regent Square was a quaint neighborhood with a bust-
ling few blocks of shops, surrounded by residential streets.
From the outside, Tisdale looked like any other repurposed public school (she'd be sure to phrase it that way to
Alex) with its classic and solid architecture. A respectable
building to house the young sons and daughters of all the
elite parents who had hoped for a more prestigious institution for their children, but instead had to accept the best in
a private, but not yet college track, education. Troubled
children, special children, children exceptional in the
wrong ways, perhaps even kids with actual disabilities.
Some of them overcame their earlier adjustment problems
well enough to matriculate elsewhere, into fine schools even,
and Suzette hung on to that hope for Hanna's brighter future.

Inside it had been fully remodeled and everything was
bright and modern. They took a left past the front doors
and followed the sign toward the office. A young teacher
emerged from another room holding the hand of a boy,
maybe a couple of years older than Hanna, who wore a
bright red helmet. The young teacher said hello and led
the boy up the stairs. Hanna watched them go, a storm
brewing on her face. She turned to look at her mother, an
accusation forming in her expression.

"No, you're not like him. You won't have to wear a
helmet. There is a spectrum to behavioral disorders, and
they can help all different kinds of children here." She
made it sound as if Hanna was so lucky; Hanna clearly
wasn't buying it.

Footsteps came running up behind them. "Mrs. Jensen? Am I saying that correctly?"

They stopped and let the running man catch up with them. "It's *Yensen*—"

"That's right, I know you told me on the phone, and I couldn't quite remember, knew it wasn't Hensen. I was just hurrying to our appointment—I'm Dr. Gutierrez." They shook hands.

"So nice to meet you."

"David to coworkers and parents, and Mr. G to most of the kids. Hello, Hanna. Look at you, all ready for spring."

Hanna barked—*ru ru ru*—followed by a throaty growl. Mr. G didn't miss a beat.

"I love dogs; we're going to get along so well."

As they followed him into his plant-filled office, Suzette couldn't shake the impression that he was a Latino, and possibly gay, Mr. Rogers. He wasn't overly effeminate, but there was something in the lilt of his voice, the grace of his movements, the ease with which he moved about the School of Imperfect Children. He even wore a V-neck sweater and sneakers that squeaked on the polished floors.

So close to her meeting with Mrs. Wade—another calm and confident principal—it seemed obvious to Suzette that managing children, especially difficult ones, was a job best suited to someone with a middle-aged or older level of experience. Twenty-eight wasn't a young age to give birth to a child, but it alleviated a bit of her self-loathing, her sense of failure, to see how much better a mother she might become by her fiftieth or sixtieth birthday. It suddenly made sense why people were so eager to be grandparents: by that point they'd achieved some level of competence with their off-spring, or at least were more accepting of their own deficiencies. Even her mother had been excited to become a grandmother. She, more than any of them, spoiled Hanna with excess gifts of toys and clothing, though she'd died before the girl's problems started to set in.

Her mother's death remained a source of guilt for Suzette: she shouldn't have been living alone. Her situation had deteriorated after Suzette moved in with Alex. No one was there to pick up her piles of dirty Kleenex or keep the sinks from growing a thin layer of mold. When Suzette hired a housekeeper to do the cleaning and laundry, her mother complained that the woman was a thief and fired her. She fired the two replacements as well—one for lazi-ness, one for giving her the creeps. After that, her mother insisted that she didn't want strangers in her house. Some-times Suzette and Alex took her out to Alibaba's, and they always had her over for their not-very-Jewish seders—Suzette could still taste the nasty gefilte fish of her youth—but it wasn't enough. Her mother even once said, "I miss your cooking," which was a complicated, overwhelming compliment.

She was still a couple of years too young to qualify for senior housing, but Suzette had started researching it any-way. Not even generous Alex ever suggested their home as a possibility for her. Shortly before she died, her mother complained of a sore throat, but Suzette didn't take it more seriously than any other of her frequent sinus com-plaints. Suzette hadn't even thought to suggest she see a doctor; eventually the infection spread to her bloodstream. Officially, her mother died of sepsis. Suzette sometimes wondered if she actually died of irony, but there was little comfort in such black humor. It scared Alex; he kept saying "That could've been you," because what if her childhood illness had been fatal, not chronic? Her mother didn't have a single, practical life skill—not even the instinct to preserve her own life. It broke Suzette's heart.

As Mr. G led them into the Botany Lab, Hanna made a beeline to the long table covered with starter pots of tiny plants.

"Careful," Suzette said. She considered it a good sign that Hanna seemed so engaged in the tour, but it was easy to imagine her ripping out all the plants.

"We grow all sorts of things here—beans and tomatoes and flowers—and when they're a bit bigger you can take them home and plant them in your own garden. Would you like that?" Mr. G asked Hanna.

To Suzette's shock, Hanna nodded.

They visited the Bouncy Room next—an open space with padded floors and big, rideable rubber balls. Hanna jumped right on and started bounding around the room.

"She seems to like it here," Suzette said, tingling with optimism.

"All the kids love this room. It lets them work out any aggressive behavior in a safe way—or just have fun."

Fifty minutes after walking through Tisdale's front doors, Suzette left feeling a bit silly that it had never been on their list of prospective schools. She carried the student handbook under her arm, which included all the school policies, dress code (in fact, beer T-shirts—even fancy ones from Ireland—were not okay, though Mr. G admitted to loving a good stout), and contact info for the other students and parents. Even Hanna seemed resigned to the reality that she would join the first-grade class come Monday. They accepted everything Suzette told them about Hanna's academic progress without insisting on any preliminary tests, and Suzette was more than glad to hand over the credit card when Mr. G's assistant said they'd prorate the fees for the rest of the semester. Mr. G promised the school would send her and Alex daily emails for at least two weeks on how Hanna was adjusting, with suggestions of things they could say or do at home to ease her transition.

She drove to the playground a couple of blocks away and parked the car. Hanna shot out and headed for one of the complex climbing rigs. Suzette didn't even care that she tossed off her hoodie and left it on the ground. She picked it up and dusted it off. She sat on a swing, kicking her feet along the rut as she swung languidly back and forth, and called Alex.

"I have good news about Hanna." What a triumph to finally be able to say that. She didn't even need to exaggerate about how well Hanna responded to the school's carefully considered environment.

"I'm glad, Suze. This will be good for her. And you."

The words were right, but Suzette didn't think he sounded enthusiastic. She knew it wasn't the school he'd dreamt of for his child.

"It's a starting place," she said. "She has to start somewhere."

"No, you're right. It's a beginning, a good beginning. *Tack, älskling.* You're a good mother, don't forget it."

"*Tack.*" And she felt it, too, in that moment. Maybe she was a good parent. Persistent. And blessed with a clarity that he didn't have. Maybe she'd made some mistakes, but who didn't?

He started to say goodbye and she almost blurted out about waking up and finding hair on her pillow. The image that came to her—tiptoeing Hanna, with outthrust scissors—made her shiver. At the last minute she changed her mind. Alex didn't like it when she focused only on Hanna's mischief. She'd call Meri and see if she could see her right away—as soon as they left the park. Maybe Meri could give her a new hairstyle, restore her confidence. Maybe Suzette could still get Alex to call her beautiful.

She watched her daughter clamber on the underside of the rig, swinging from arm to arm. A strong girl. A girl who moved with purpose and wouldn't let herself be pushed around.

Maybe she'd still grow up just fine.

HANNA

SOMETIMES SHE WASN'T sure if she remembered it exactly right. When people asked her how old she was, she was still only holding up two fingers, but the leaves were starting to change so she was probably almost three. So the memory was more or less right, and she knew what Mommy meant even then, when she was two, not-yet-three, because she saw Mommy crumbling. And heard in the silences all of Mommy's regret.

Lunch. Must have been a weekend, because Daddy was around somewhere. But only she and Mommy were at the table. Mommy used her favorite plate, the one with three little sections with a fox, a squirrel, and a rabbit. Little bits of colorful food were in each section. Strawberry slices and grapes cut in half; yellow and orange cubes of cheese; teeny tiny carrots and crunchy sugar snap peas. Stuff she still liked to nibble on.

The only thing she couldn't remember is why she didn't feel like eating.

Mommy sat with her, nibbling a sandwich. She remembered Mommy kept gazing at her, but her eyes looked off, blank like the ones in the dead fish she'd seen at the deli.

Hanna wasn't sure if Mommy was really in there, so she threw a carrot at her.

She blinked. "Hey. No throwing. Eat your lunch."

Mommy hunched back down, blowing out her cheeks. She went still. As Hanna watched, sometimes Mommy forgot to keep chewing and the sandwich looked like it was about to fall out of her hand. Hanna didn't like it. Was Mommy dying, like a toy that needed to be wound up? Was there a little slot in her somewhere, like on a phone, where she could be plugged in? She was too big to drag around if all her parts stopped working. Hanna wanted her to come back to life; she threw a grape at her.

"Hey. Why are you throwing everything?" She tapped at Hanna's plate, like that would make her hungry.

Hanna wanted to say *Why?* She wanted to say *Stay here don't go away don't look so weird*. She squeaked out a noise instead.

"Eat a little, something from each—you like these."

Hanna put a piece of cheese in her mouth, sucked it a little, then took it out and dropped it on the floor. She and Mommy did one of their games, where they watched each other and neither of them spoke. And the whole time Hanna dropped pieces of her lunch on the ground, one tidbit at a time.

"Don't you ever get tired? Just completely tired?"

Hanna blinked hard in surprise, and maybe that meant she'd lost the game, but she didn't care. Mommy didn't usually talk to her like she did to Daddy, but it was interesting, so she stuck a carrot in her mouth and waited to see what she would say next.

"Do you ever wish . . . Maybe you don't even know who you are yet, so you probably don't ever wish you were someone else. Not that I know who I'd want to be. Not someone I know, just someone . . . else. Maybe someone without . . ."

Hanna didn't like what Mommy was saying, so she threw the carrot right at her eye.

"Hey!" She bent over and picked up the other bits that were littering the floor. "Don't waste food. Do you want me to take it away?"

When Mommy started to pull it away, Hanna pulled it right back. Would Mommy really take her food away? Just because she wanted Mommy to stop being weird? She put a grape in her mouth and started chewing.

"I was just trying to make conversation. I always do all the talking and it's like I just talk to myself all day. I didn't think it would be so lonely. I didn't think you'd be so hard to spend so much time with. You make me miss Alex, Daddy, who he was before."

Hanna missed Daddy, too. She spit the chewed grape into Mommy's face.

"Hey, Hanna! That's not how we eat our food, you know better. Chew and swallow, don't put everything on the floor. If you don't want to eat then just . . ." She flicked the grape onto her own plate.

Mommy deflated again, with a look on her face that Hanna thought meant there wasn't a point. Hanna wasn't worth the little energy she had left.

Hanna glared at her. She stuffed a grape in her mouth,

a strawberry, a cheese cube, another cheese cube, another grape. And made a show of chewing, chewing.

"Thank you. See, that wasn't so hard."

When it was a nice mushy consistency, Hanna got up on her knees and spit the whole glob in Mommy's face. It struck her cheek, then started to dribble down. Hanna giggled.

Mommy scooped the mash from her face. For a second Hanna thought she might cry. But Mommy got up and came around and forced the glop back into Hanna's mouth. She held her hand there, making it so Hanna couldn't open her lips. She couldn't spit anything back out, but she could also barely breathe.

"Chew."

Mommy's eyes looked scarier than the dead fish and she pressed hard against Hanna's mouth. Hanna whimpered and tried to chew, but it was too tight and her teeth only gnawed on her cheeks as the gloop started slipping down her throat.

She started to gag but thankfully her tears made her throat too tight so nothing else went down that way, and that's when Mommy burst back to normal—"Oh my God, I'm so sorry!"—and lifted the plate to her mouth so she could spit it all out.

Mommy patted her back and wiped her chin and Hanna coughed and coughed.

"I'm so sorry, I don't know why I did that. Oh, baby." Mommy scooped her onto her hip, bouncing her, kissing her. "I'm so sorry. You're okay, I didn't mean to do that. I

don't know why I did that. I love you, baby, I love you."
She kissed her cheek so many times.

But Mommy wasn't full of love. She was full of fear.

Daddy came in then. Had he been upstairs? Outside?
Both she and Mommy were crying. Daddy ran over like a
superhero.

"What's wrong?"

"She was choking."

"Is she okay? You okay?"

Hanna reached her arms out to Daddy and he took her,
bouncing her just like Mommy did. "Just scared?"

"It really scared us. I don't know what happened."

"Everything's okay now," Daddy said. And it was.
With him, Hanna felt safe.

Mommy gave her a sip of water to drink and smoothed
out her hair. "You're okay now. We're okay."

Hanna gazed at her, in a new way. A kind of game that
wasn't fun, but deadly serious. Like a war. She thought
Mommy even understood. She stayed all big-eyed and
hovering. Finally, Daddy gripped Mommy's arm.

"It's okay, she's fine."

"I can't do this, Alex."

"You can. It happens. Look, totally fine."

"I don't understand her anymore—"

"She'll start talking soon."

"I don't know what she wants, I don't know what she
needs. I think maybe . . . Do you think there's anything
wrong?"

"With her hearing?"

"Maybe."

"You can hear Daddy, can't you?" And Hanna replied with a big grin. "That's my girl."

To show Mommy there was nothing wrong with her, she reached out her arms. Mommy hesitated, but Daddy held her out for Mommy to take.

"See, she's all good," Daddy said.

But Hanna felt it, how Mommy couldn't relax with her in her arms. How Mommy wanted to drop her.

She knew then, she needed to test Mommy. To find out what she was made of. Was she a sandcastle that would melt away as the water lapped ashore? Or was she made of rockier stuff? Daddy never crumbled. Hanna was determined to give Mommy every possible chance.

Mommy owed her—and more than the empty apology that tumbled so easily from her lips. She understood then how words could hide a deeper truth. But actions. That's what *Farmor*, Daddy's mom, said, and Daddy agreed: actions speak louder than words. So Hanna would act, and give Mommy a chance to act in reply. And then she'd know. If Mommy passed or failed.

SUZETTE

HANNA HADN'T TAKEN regular naps for years, but it was obvious by the time they slunk back into the house, their limbs all loose and poorly directed, that they were both wiped out. Suzette felt on the verge of collapse, and she'd sped home after her emergency hair appointment when she saw Hanna drifting to sleep in the backseat, hoping to get her into the house before she'd sufficiently rested.

They stopped in the kitchen and Suzette filled two glasses with cold water. They gulped in unison, which made her aware—for the billionth time—how similar she and Hanna were. Sometimes Alex remarked on it, how they'd both stand with one leg crossed in front of the other, or with their arms folded exactly the same way. They could sit like mirrored bookends on the couch, watching television in exactly the same position.

"I'm going to lie down for a little bit. You seem kind of pooped too. Have fun at the park?"

Hanna nodded without looking at her. Finished with her water, she opened the dishwasher and put her glass on the top rack.

"Thank you. You've been most very, very excellent today. Except for . . ." She pointed to her new layered bob, angled a little from the back. The left side still had a couple of slightly shorter layers, but most people wouldn't notice. Meri suggested long bangs, swept off to the side. It was a very different look for her, but it was fresh, and modern. Hanna, indifferent, took off and galloped up the stairs. Suzette filled her glass with more water and followed her up.

Hanna was already lying on top of her comforter, looking through the weird book that Alex often read to her. Suzette paused in her doorway.

"I'll leave my door open, if you need anything. I won't be asleep for very long, I just need to . . ." Fall into a coma. Wake up in a new body. Hanna ignored her, so she retreated to her own space.

She set her water on the bedside shelf, but before putting her phone down she opened the camera. Using the selfie mode, she examined her new look. Definitely shorter than she was used to. But it was still feminine, pretty-ish. Stop being so tragic. It was hair, it wasn't like Hanna . . .

Poked out her eye.

It could have been worse.

She flopped onto the bed, ready to sleep. Beams of sunlight poured their hopeful, generous energy into the room. They knocked on her eyelids but she held them tight. Her thoughts became jumbled-up images and sound bites of the school, like Mr. G was narrating a promotional video. Then came blessed nothingness.

At some point the nothingness ignited into a dream, a sexual dream. Suzette, a gauzy-clad nymphet, lay among immense patterned pillows in a room whose many windows contained no glass. The ever-aware part of her mind suggested that such a room would exist in a tropical place. But when the focus shifted past the fluttering sheer draperies, she saw not the wild greenery of the tropics, or sand or ocean, but towering mountains. At their base lay a body of reflective blue water. She knew, as one knows things in a dream, that she was a concubine, one of many, and through a distant room came the moans of passion as another whore enjoyed the pleasure of their master. She longed for him to come to her, give himself to her, fuck her like she was the only one he really cared about . . .

Deep sleep left her. Her director-self called "Cut!" and a clapboard signaled the end of the scene. She had no interest in a stupid dream about someone else's pleasure. But as she awakened, the audio portion of the dream remained—a feminine voice, groaning. She pushed herself up to her elbows, confused. Was the window open? Maybe a neighbor was enjoying the sunny afternoon, fucking *en plein air*? Though it didn't really seem like something the neighbors would do.

She glanced at the clock glowing on her shelf. She hadn't slept that long, maybe twenty minutes.

With a dawning horror, she realized the gasps and moans were coming from within her house, from down the hallway.

She shook off the remnants of her nap and barreled out of the room, unable to process what was happening or what she expected to find. The sounds led her to Hanna's room—

Who's raping my child?

Hanna lay on the bed beneath her yellow comforter in her small but sunny room. For a moment, Suzette thought she'd found her engaged in an exuberant experiment in masturbation. Hanna's denim shorts lay on the floor with the smiling curl of her pink striped underpants, and she could see the girl bucking and writhing beneath the comforter. But her hands were gripping it and her head was moving in such a way on her pillow like someone was thrusting against her.

Suzette stood there for a moment, unsure what to do. What was even happening? Her daughter's knees made a tent of the fabric and she moved and sounded like she was enjoying a fine afternoon of hearty intercourse.

"Stop it! What are you doing?"

Hanna looked at her, neither startled nor embarrassed. She smiled as her invisible lover resumed making love to her. Suzette grimaced, inhaling with disgust even as it scared her to see her child gasp and writhe like a fully sexualized adult. She ripped back the comforter, but of course no one and nothing was there. Hanna pulled her knees together and turned over onto her side, giggling.

"What are you doing?" She snatched up the panties and shorts and restrained herself from throwing them at Hanna's face. She dropped them next to the pillow, her hand shaking. "Get dressed."

"That's how I get my power. From the devil, when he comes to me."

Her voice sounded different—mature and confident. It spooked Suzette. She stumbled backward a few steps. "Marie-Anne?"

Hanna sat up, covering herself with the comforter. She maintained unblinking eye contact with Suzette.

"I like it when he comes to me. It feels so good. He loves me and he puts his thing in me and fills me with the world."

"Leave my daughter alone!" She didn't know whom she was saying it to. The invisible demon with his fire-hot phallus. The long-dead witch who made her daughter claim she was Marie-Anne. Her mouth went tingly and she backed out of the room. She wanted to vomit. Her daughter needed help, but not this smiling thing who writhed so happily beneath the covers. This girl needed to go away, leave them all alone. "Go, just go—go!"

But it was Suzette who left, heaving, running for the bathroom.

Her mouth still tasted like the sour gut-spoiled remains of her lunch, but she didn't care. She had to find the papers from the pediatrician's office. They should have been in the folder, the one they kept in a file box in their walk-in closet that contained all of Hanna's medical and immunization records. Had she misfiled it? Misplaced it?

She turned, feeling a presence behind her. Hanna, fully dressed, wore a familiar and non-threatening question—"What are you doing?" But she didn't have time or patience. She sprang up, scooped the girl around her ribs, and carried her back to her room. Hanna's face asked "What's going on?" as she hung over her mother's arm, but she didn't otherwise protest.

"I don't have time for this. Play with your devil friends. Read your books. I'm sorry, but something's wrong with you . . . I have to find out what." She deposited the girl in her room and shut the door.

This time, she locked her own bedroom door behind her and fell back to her knees as soon as she reached the closet; she dug through the file box again. She considered calling Alex. But she could already hear him, confusion in his voice, stuttering about how everything had been fine—better than fine—not two hours ago. How could she explain what she heard, and then saw, and what their daughter—was she still their daughter?—said while her little-girl underpants lay abandoned on the floor? Their practically indestructible recycled rubber, better than other people's floor. Alex still used photos of their house in the company's portfolio. Oh, yes, they looked the part. As long as no one knew what went on within that house. She couldn't expect Alex to really help—not until he got to experience firsthand Hanna and her other self, the self who knew more than any seven-year-old should.

She found it, stuck between two hanging file folders. She flipped to the last of the stapled pages, where the doctor had included the information about the referral to . . . Dr. Yamamoto. They might hear from the insurance company any day, but it couldn't wait. She dialed, shaking like she'd narrowly regained her balance at the edge of an abyss. It went to voicemail. Her words came out in a panicked flurry.

"Hello Dr. Yamamoto, my name is Suzette Jensen and I was referred to you by my pediatrician. I'm . . . We're having an emergency and I urgently need to speak with you and make an appointment for my daughter. Please, as soon as you get this. Please, as soon as possible. Thank you." She recited her phone number twice, just in case.

After disconnecting the call, she tossed the phone onto the bed. She paced the room in long strides. Maybe she should see someone, too. The possibility of it came up from time to time. Part of her hesitation was not being able to figure out how to get a whole hour to herself. She didn't want to drag Hanna with her, leave her alone in someone's waiting room to do God knows what. But it was getting increasingly worse. The medical PTSD, the fear that motherhood had been a terrible mistake, the guilt that she wanted to undo it but couldn't. She felt unhinged, like any large noise would force her body parts to separate and trail off into space in a slow-motion explosion. She wanted sleep. Real sleep. Maybe this was a dream, too, a dream within a dream and she could laugh to herself about it later, how she'd lost track of the levels of unconsciousness.

It struck her, replaying it in her head, that Alex cared only about what Hanna's words had *sounded* like, not what they meant. But they needed to know where the delusions were coming from. Dr. Yamamoto could help her sort that out, of course she could. And the good therapist would help keep her fears from tumbling into the unreasonable—the supernatural. Left to her own degenerating uncertainty, it was too easy to imagine googling "experienced exorcists Pittsburgh PA" as if there'd be a local or regional list. It almost made her laugh, the progression that started with speech pathologists and auditory specialists. She didn't even believe in possession or exorcism. But until she understood what was wrong with Hanna, despair might lead her there.

Her phone rang. She recognized the number immediately, having just called it. It brought her back to earth a little: she needed help. What was Hanna going to do next?

"Hello?"

"Mrs. Jensen?"

"Yes—"

"Hi, I'm Beatrix Yamamoto—"

"Thank you so much for calling me back so quickly."

"Happy to. Glad I had a break in my schedule. You sounded kind of panicked on your message—"

"Yes—"

"Is there any sort of emergency? Does one of you need immediate help? Is this a 9-1-1 situation?" In spite of the implied urgency of her questions, the therapist sounded calm and levelheaded.

Suzette was already grateful for her help; in an instant Dr. Yamamoto put the crisis in perspective, something she had been unable to do. She perched on the edge of her bed and the mania and dread started seeping out of her. Her spine softened; her shoulders relaxed.

"No. No, nothing like that."

"Good. I'm glad to hear it. I'm booked the rest of the day, but I could see you on Monday. I work from my home, in Squirrel Hill."

"Yes, perfect. Do you have something in the afternoon, after school?"

"Let's see . . . Four o'clock?"

"Perfect, thank you."

"And I have a few minutes now, if you want to tell me what's going on?"

"Yes . . ." Suzette walked as she talked, back and forth, but in an absent sort of way, without her earlier frenzy. She filled the doctor in on Hanna's medical history, and the recent efforts she'd made to get her into school.

"Things just accelerated so quickly, with her behavior. And it should be good that she's finally talking, but the things she's saying . . . And only to me."

"What was she saying?"

She took a couple of breaths and looked out the window. A squirrel scampered out along a tree branch. No houses imploded. No zombies lurched down the street. The normality of it all was a comfort. The woman across the way knelt on a pink gardening pad, planting something in her flower bed. A group of teenagers went past in their huddle and she saw flashes of school uniforms and crazy hair and cell phones and earbuds and arms filled with bracelets.

"Well, the first thing she told me . . . She said she wasn't Hanna. Later she told me she was a witch named Marie-Anne Dufosset. My husband didn't seem that concerned, said she must have read about it online. Or maybe he didn't believe me at all. That's part of it, the problem. It's such a cliché, you know, from horror movies. And the woman starts to experience things and the man dismisses her and she becomes the crazy one."

"Is that what you think is happening?"

"Maybe. Sometimes I feel like it's true, maybe I am going crazy. I don't understand what she's doing. I don't know what it means, I don't know what I'm supposed to do—"

"Did something happen before you called me?"

"Yes . . ."

"I know you're upset. And I know whatever happened was upsetting."

"Yes . . . My daughter . . . I heard her, in her room. And when I went in there . . . It was like she was having sex. Making these noises—very, very realistic noises. And at first I thought she was masturbating, which is fine, we'd have no problems with that. But then she looked at me, smiling, and told me the devil was fucking her, basically— that the devil was fucking her and she liked it."

"Mrs. Jensen, I have to ask you a serious question—"

"Okay."

"To your knowledge, is there any chance your daughter has been sexually abused?"

"No!" The bile ignited within her again; she tasted it rising in her throat. She'd kept her daughter safe, she'd always kept her safe. Except for the radiation from the CT scans, and whatever pollutants they were all subject to in their toxic world. It was too horrible to think about, but she needed to not get defensive; now more than ever she didn't want the doctor jumping to the wrong conclusions.

"I don't see how she could have been." She swallowed down the horrible taste at the back of her tongue. "She's been with me, at home, almost all the time. And Alex *never*—I mean never. He is a mature, kind, sophisticated man . . . He's Swedish," she said, stupidly, like that would convince her, like no Swedish men ever molested their children.

Oh, God. She covered her mouth, afraid Dr. Yamamoto might have heard her gasp. She'd almost forgotten about last year, when Alex had started growing facial hair, on his way toward a beard. He'd trimmed it to a goatee with a kind of elongated mustache.

"Do I look super cool?"

Suzette remembered how she'd replied. In front of Hanna. "I think Daddy looks like a Scandinavian devil."

It made Hanna giggle. Alex smirked—and returned to the bathroom to reconfigure his mustache.

Could Alex possibly have . . . ? When Hanna said "he comes to me," could she have meant her father, the Scandinavian devil?

No. No, not Alex. She banished the absurd thought. "No, it isn't possible."

"I understand it's an upsetting prospect. But it's something we'll need to clarify. It's not uncommon for children who have experienced inappropriate sexual contact to act out in some way."

"But with Hanna." She felt the perspiration in her armpits, the sweat of renewed panic congealing on the back of her neck. It was all so crazy, she'd never be able to make anyone understand. "I just . . . I think it's something else." *Not Alex.* "This witch she's claiming to be—this weird sexual thing is some sort of offshoot of this persona, this other person she's . . . I can't explain it, I know it doesn't make any sense."

"It's hard, and it's complicated—I understand. Maybe over the weekend you could do something for me, which might help for our appointment on Monday."

"Of course."

"Write down, as precisely as you can, everything your daughter has said. Everything she said, and everything you can remember about what was going on at the time, and how you reacted. Young children can find strange and creative ways to react to things they don't understand. Her not speaking for so long is one issue that we'll need to address. But what she has *chosen* to say now is another issue. It might take some time, but we'll sort this out."

"I'll write down everything I remember. Thank you so much, Dr. Yamamoto. For listening to me, and taking this seriously." She was back to where she'd started at the beginning of her conversation, feeling like this woman would calmly and methodically get to the bottom of the problem.

"Please, call me Beatrix. And I know it's scary, I understand. There's nothing scarier than loving a child and not understanding what they're trying to tell you—"

"Yes," she said, her breath making the word an exclamation mark.

"But you're taking all the right steps. And we'll sort this out. So try to have a good weekend—"

"You too—"

"And I'll see you and Hanna on Monday."

She hung up feeling—for the first time in a very long time—vindicated. The doctor said she was taking all the right steps—a statement that implied action was necessary. She said they'd sort it out. In her mind, Beatrix—with her lovely, soothing voice, her confident manner—bore the majesty of a powerful and beautiful woman. She'd understood Suzette was afraid and hadn't dismissed her in any way. She needed to do better around Hanna and Alex—not show them how she could become flustered and disturbed. That Beatrix had thought of sexual abuse ahead of demonic possession proved she was grounded in reality, something Suzette needed to keep in mind when Hanna next attempted to torment her. She couldn't imagine when or how she might have come into contact with someone who would abuse her, but maybe she could help rule one person out.

Over the weekend, in addition to compiling her notes about Hanna's communication efforts, she'd check Alex's search history—see if there was more beyond Hanna's morbid interests. It would invite new questions about his secrets—for creepy kinks and other taboo fetishes—if he was visiting pornographic sites about witches or dead people. But that seemed unlikely. Throughout their relationship, Alex never hesitated to enumerate his reasons for hating pornography whenever the subject arose. By ruling out porn, she expected to free Alex of any suspicion. He couldn't—in any way—be the source of Hanna's perversions. Beatrix needed to know she and Alex weren't the problem; it would help Beatrix's ability to treat Hanna.

She sent Alex a text asking him to bring home their favorite Thai food for supper—a bit of a celebration.

Maintain normalcy. Look like everything's fine.

When she came out of her room, Hanna's door was

still closed; she pushed away the unwelcome images of what might be happening within. Between their rooms was the laundry alcove and Hanna's bathroom. Suzette kept a stash of cleaning supplies beneath every sink in the house. In need of comfort, she slipped on her rubber battle gloves.

Hanna's door creaked open as Suzette emerged from the bathroom with a bucket. She went to the stairs and sat on the second step. From there she scrubbed the top step. Then she scooted down to the third step and scrubbed the second step. Hanna peered at her over the hallway railing. The little spy monitored everything.

"Better come down now, before all the steps are wet."

The girl zipped around to the top of the stairs. In her monkey knee socks, she descended like a dancer *en pointe,* with only her tippy-toes touching the damp wood. When she was safely on the dry landing, Suzette turned to address her.

"Since school starts on Monday"—Hanna stopped in mid-escape and met her mother's eyes—"you don't have to do any schoolwork today, if you don't want to." Excitement and disbelief wavered on Hanna's face. "Really. You can have the whole weekend too, to just have fun. Sound good?"

Hanna's face lit up and she burst like a firecracker down the rest of the stairs. She disappeared into the living room and a second later the television came to life with giggly cartoon voices.

"Good Mommy. Nice Mommy." Suzette smiled without mirth. "Can't ruin Mommy. Or scare her to death."

It was in all their best interests to keep the coming days as drama-free as possible. Monday—with a new school and therapist—would be challenging enough.

Her wet rag demolished a universe, one step at a time. Worlds that would never grow. Forests that would never mature. Vinegar-infused annihilation. At least in one area of her life she was powerful and divine. She worked in the only direction she could go. Down.

HANNA

NOODLES FOR SUPPER! Mommy and Daddy were both in smiley moods, but Hanna suspected Mommy was merely trying a new tactic. She was a good opponent. She had big reactions to things and then sulked off to her room to regroup. When Daddy first saw Mommy's new hair, his smile wobbled and Mommy looked scared for a second, tugging on the layers like she could make them longer. Hanna hoped Daddy would chuck her ugly butt out of the house.

"You don't like it?" Mommy asked.

Then Daddy beamed at her, reaching for her like she was a snow angel who'd fallen to earth and his warm hands would make her melt. "It's a surprise—but look at you. Radiant."

Mommy, who knew how ugly she was, breathed with relief. Sometimes Daddy was too nice.

"What inspired this?" he asked.

"Your daughter. Who cut off half my hair while I lay in bed sleeping."

Hanna heard the steel blade in her voice, the thing Mommy wanted to stab her with.

Daddy's face grumpled. *"Lilla gumman . . ."*

He turned to her, frowning. Hanna thought she might have blown it, and felt squiggles of fear swimming inside her.

"Doing something like that—it can be dangerous, for one. You shouldn't be using scissors like that. And it's a violation—do you understand what that means?"

She shook her head, aware of Mommy watching Daddy with big eager eyes.

"Well, at least there's no harm done." He winked at Hanna. "Mommy looks more beautiful than ever."

"Alex!"

Mommy clutched her chopsticks, ready to spear him with them, but Daddy reached out and squeezed her hand.

"It was wrong," he said, "she shouldn't have done it— but I love the way it frames your face. You can't be mad at me for liking that."

Mommy sagged a little. One side of her mouth lifted in a smile. He twinkled his eyes at her and dived back into his food. While he wasn't looking, Mommy turned to her and gave her a see-you-haven't-beaten-me smirk.

Hanna gave her a not-for-long grin in reply.

As Mommy and Daddy ate with their chopsticks, their hands looked like giant stick bugs, monsters *click clacking* as they devoured noodle cities. Hanna had to hide her glee because Daddy could never get really angry with her, and she was so excited for the day to end: she'd already decided her next move. Sneaky and awesome!

They babbled so happily about her new school that she couldn't help feeling not so terrible about it, in spite of her determination to maintain a mask of so what. Things in the building had surprised her, reminding her of the Children's Museum. Stuff to play and interact with. And it was so near the playground—maybe she'd get to play there every day. But the other children. They might be a problem. They looked stupid and, in some cases, deformed. One of them was floppy like her stuffed bunny. Another had knees like a kangaroo and walked with the aid of a four-wheeled walker. She heard howls and yowls coming through some of the doors; no wonder Mr. G was so placid about her barking. She'd give it a day or two to study the terrain, then decide what to do.

Just thinking about the other children ruined her good mood; if only they would all die and she could have the school to herself. She'd seen little blips on the news about mass shootings and had heard Daddy rant about the gun problem "not everyone needs a gun, *children* do not need guns!" But maybe Daddy was mistaken. Maybe the other children weren't clever enough to conjure ways to handle their problems. A vengeful pit grew inside her and it remained to be seen how it would grow—very possibly into a tree with snaking branches and claws. How fun it would be to be such a tree, looming like a giant on a neighborhood street. People would pass beneath her, and the ones she didn't like—*snap snap crunch!* She'd snatch them up and tangle her branches around them, and their bones would break with little crunches that would be mistaken for the snap of a twig. Her bark-self would absorb their yummy blood and the tree would grow and thrive.

"So, Hanna, remember how Daddy talked to you about having your very own person to talk to? Someone who'd focus their attention just on you?" Mommy glanced at Daddy and he stopped chewing for a second. He swallowed; his food and the surprised look slipped in tandem down his throat.

"Right, *lilla gumman*, we talked about that. Because maybe you're thinking things and need a better way to express yourself. Remember?" Then Daddy turned back to Mommy, like he didn't know what to say next.

"Well, I talked to a very helpful woman today; her name is Beatrix. She's very, very nice. And it just happens that she has some time to see you on Monday."

"Wait—doesn't she start school on Monday?"

Daddy blinked at Mommy and for a minute both forgot about Hanna, who watched them volley back and forth in a friendly ping-pong match that risked becoming something more serious.

"Yes, the appointment's after school."

"Isn't that too much? Too many new things for one day?"

"It's when she could see her—she had an opening and I didn't see the point in waiting."

Daddy shook his head. "I just think . . . She's going to need some down time, it's already a big—"

"I know, but it might be good too. If she has any reactions about her new school."

"Maybe."

"I didn't want to put it off, I thought we'd agreed."

Daddy nodded at his plate and stabbed at his noodles. Hanna knew he would always defend her, but Mommy was such a bossy boss and always wanted her own way. It was hard to read the weird vibes passing between them. They tried to speak with their eyebrows instead of words.

"It'll be good," Mommy told him like a fish surfacing for air. "And I was very impressed with her. She's so sweet and nice."

"Someone named Beatrix," Daddy said to Hanna, "must be nice. It isn't humanly possible for someone with such an adorable name to be anything but kind. Right?"

Hanna gave one of her single, assertive head bobs.

After supper Mommy suggested that Daddy play a board game with Hanna while she cleaned the kitchen.

"Sure you don't need any help?" He tucked his body behind hers, kissing the exposed skin on the back of her neck as she rinsed the dishes. "This is my new favorite spot," he said.

Mommy looked way too happy as Daddy kissed her neck again. Hanna grabbed the Spot It! tin from a lower cabinet and ran back to the table, where she slapped the lid to get everyone's attention.

"I think I'm being paged," said Daddy, drifting toward the table.

"Is it okay if I use your laptop for a little bit?"

"Yeah, sure. We never did replace your old one—we should."

"Also, I wanted to do some shopping this weekend— get some things for Hanna, some special school supplies and a backpack, maybe some clothes. She might like that."

"Sounds like a plan."

Mommy turned off the faucet, and with her hands still wet she used her shoulder to rub something on her cheek, an itch or a splash of water. "I'll be upstairs while you guys are playing."

"Come join us when you're finished."

Hanna hoped she wouldn't join them. Maybe, if her plan worked, Mommy would spend the entire weekend sick in bed—or maybe forever sick in bed—and then she and Daddy could do whatever they wanted. She placed one round card in front of each of them, then tidied the draw pile into a neat stack, ready to play.

When it was time for bed, Daddy brought her a special present.

"Don't tell Mommy," he whispered in her ear. "She'll think we're weird."

It was a potato. A funny-shaped raw potato still cold from the refrigerator.

She giggled and hugged it to her chest. She and Daddy knew what would happen: the potato would become the body of her very own UnderSlumberBumbleBeast. She wasn't quite ready to leave it to its destiny, though, so she slept with it in her fist, cuddled up so close to her nose she could inhale its earthy origins.

At three A.M. her alarm clock rumbled to life. First it flashed its lights, then it tolled its harmonic bells—which she'd set at a very low volume. It had been a very special Christmas Eve present from her grandparents and made her feel so grown-up. But she rarely needed to set it or get up by herself. Sometimes she set it anyway, for random times, just to make sure it would chime at whatever hour she appointed. But tonight she actually had a mission.

She grabbed her flashlight—another of her most favorite items. It fit perfectly in her small hand and she could set the brightness for low, medium, or high with just a press of her thumb. She put it on low and opened her door. Everything was dark and quiet. Her parents' bedroom door was shut and no light glowed from beneath. She made her way downstairs as silently as a worm. She'd met a few cats in her day and they weren't as quiet as everyone said. They purred and meowed and made thumping noises when they jumped off things. But a worm. She'd never heard a worm utter a sound even as faint as a breath.

It slightly concerned her that turning on the kitchen light would somehow awaken her parents, but she needed to see to do her work. The hardest part was lugging a chair over to the counter—if only Marie-Anne had a physical self and could help her. It was heavy, and she didn't want to make any noise or leave scuffs on the floor or bang it into her chin or knee. The chair bumped against her a few times, but she finally got it right against the lower cabinet and then stood on the seat.

She used her flashlight to better illuminate all the medications Mommy kept in the cabinet. Some were just over-the-counter ones, like the chewable Tylenol she took when her throat hurt. She didn't want to mess with anything that she or Daddy might take, so she concentrated on the clear orangey bottles that had Mommy's name on the sticker. The pen thingy she injected into her belly would be too hard to tamper with; she'd already ruled that out. And she wanted something that Mommy used every day—unlike the pen thingy. She looked at one of the packets she'd seen Mommy mix with water, like instant lemonade. Could she poison it with something? But if she tore it open, there'd be no way to reseal it. Her best choice would be the little plastic-looking two-tone brown pills. Mommy took one with both breakfast and supper. She couldn't pronounce the name of it, but the label said, "Take one capsule by mouth every four to six hours as needed for diarrhea." She'd seen a commercial on TV where, by magic, a capsule opened and a million tiny balls spilled out, so she knew they could be pulled apart.

The bottle was a bit tricky, but she imitated how Mommy pressed her palm into the top of it, then turned. After a few tries, she got it to open.

She held one of the capsules between her thumb and forefinger. It looked so small, not at all like the animated thing she'd seen on TV. But she soon found that with a little twisting, it popped open. The capsule wasn't filled with tiny balls as she'd expected, but with a fine white powder that looked exactly like flour.

For a moment, she weighed her options. Her original idea had been to dump out all the medication into the sink, but the capsules might feel too light if she left them all empty. Getting a tiny drop of flour into each one would be hard to do without making a mess, but it might be worth the effort. She tried putting the two halves of the capsule back together, just to verify that it would work. Easy peasy. It looked good as new. Testing it, she pinched it between

her fingers and it squooshed, flat and empty. Nope. Definitely have to refill them.

She grabbed the fat canister of flour with both hands
and tugged it over. The smallest-tipped object she could
think of was a teeny tiny plastic-handled paring knife—
she'd used it before, standing at the counter on a chair like
she was now, slicing bananas and melon chunks on her
own special cutting board. Daddy liked fruit salad. Very
quietly, she slid open the drawer and found the knife.

For the next two hours she painstakingly sabotaged
her mother's pills. The process was too exhausting and
boring for her to do all of them. But she scooped up the
ones she'd altered and put them back in the bottle so all the
ones on top were flour instead of medicine. The sink was
filled with white powder residue, so she turned on the faucet and let the water wash it all away.

She yawned. Silently as a worm, she put everything
back where it had been, turned off the light, and returned
to bed.

Everyone seemed a bit groggy at breakfast. Mommy swallowed her pill. Hanna tugged her pajama collar up to cover
her mouth, hiding her grin.

They all went to the office supply store, and it was hard to
tell which one of them was having more fun. Daddy liked
trying out the different ergonomic chairs. "Not the best
they make, but still comfy," he said. Hanna tried them all,

too. They took turns spinning each other. She was surprised to see that Mommy was attracted to the same things she was, colorful packs of everything you could think of—card stock, Post-its, highlighters, and especially the metal binder clips.

"You're a big girl now," Mommy said. "Kindergarten students don't need their own notebooks and supplies, but first graders do."

Mommy and Daddy had a list of things she needed, and she got to pick her favoritest of each item. She chose a purple backpack, a red lunch cooler that reminded her of Daddy's, a yellow binder and some three-ring lined paper, a matching yellow pencil case, pencils with swirly patterns around them, gummy erasers that looked like flowers (she couldn't wait to toss one under her bed), a rectangular plastic container with a magnetized rim that kept a zillion colorful paper clips from falling out ("To use at home," Mommy said), a pack of fat highlighters, an adorable jar of thumbtacks, and a square bulletin board ("We can put it right on your wall," Daddy said). Plus all sorts of random objects because no one could stop oohing and aahing over all the rows of stuff. Daddy got a heavy bundle of paper for his printer and Mommy got some Post-its and a giant sketchbook.

The parking lot was a death trap of monstrous bugs: hulking SUVs in endless rows. The sky hung low in thick gray stripes and people scampered in and out of cars and stores like they were afraid the rain would come and wash them all away. After they put all the stuff in the trunk Daddy pointed at another store and said, "We could get you a computer."

"I'm not ready," Mommy said. "Not sure what I really want. A tablet? Don't know yet."

Daddy took Mommy's hand, so Hanna took his other hand. "Clothes then? Some new school clothes, squirrely girl?"

Hanna usually fussed when she went shopping with just her mother, but it was a treat for Daddy to come along. But once they were inside he went off to the boring men's section to look for gym pants, even though Mommy asked if he really needed them. Hanna tried to follow him but Mommy called her back. Hanna ignored her, but then Daddy told her, too, and suddenly the store wasn't nearly as much fun. Stupid Mommy and stupid clothes.

Mommy clicked her tongue as they strolled past the racks. "It's all for summer."

Every building in the mile-long complex was the opposite of their house. Vast quantities of everything, enough for twenty cities of a million people on display in each one. Hanna squinted, picturing how different it would be if the place were empty. If every store had only a single item hanging among the circular racks. Shopping would be a treasure hunt then: If you found the item in ten seconds and if it was your size, you could keep it; otherwise you had to leave it behind. She hated how much everything there was in the everywhere outside of the house. Too much and too much. Sometimes she wished she could turn off her eyes instead of her mouth.

"What do you want to wear to school on your first day?" Mommy asked.

Hanna held a polka-dotted bathing suit against her

body. It had a navy-blue background and dots of different sizes and colors. If it was almost summer, she'd get to go swimming soon. *Farmor* and *Farfar* would come. They would go to the park with the lake.

"You can't wear a bathing suit," Mommy said as she looked through a rack of sale items.

Hanna bounced a little, clutching the colorful bathing suit.

"No, Hanna." She picked out a simple pale-yellow dress with a white collar. "This looks like something you'd like."

"Mmmmnnn," Hanna whined. She made angry or whining noises at everything Mommy pulled off the rack.

"You don't want something new for school?" Hanna rubbed her eyes, her face in a grump. "Okay. We won't get anything. Let's go find Daddy."

Hanna ran ahead of her.

"You didn't find anything?" he asked when they found him looking at a folded wonderland of T-shirts.

"She didn't want anything."

Hanna's face crumpled like she was about to cry. "What's wrong, *lilla gumman*?" She pointed back toward the kids' things.

Mommy gave one of her annoyed sighs. "She wanted a bathing suit. I think she's tired."

"It'll be summer soon. Does she need one?"

"We haven't tried on her old ones yet."

"Nothing's expensive here. Did they have her size?"

Daddy, Daddy, Daddy! She gripped his hand and jumped up and down. She led the way to the polka-dotted bathing suit. She glanced back at Mommy, who trailed behind them with a pinched face. Daddy wasn't looking, so she stuck her tongue out. Mommy scratched the tip of her nose with her middle finger—the bad finger that meant a bad word. She couldn't quite tell if Mommy was just fixing an itch or giving her the bad-word finger. It didn't matter. Daddy bought her the bathing suit, so she won another round.

Otters swam like ripples of fur, peering at her through the glass. She liked them best, so far. She held Daddy's hand the whole time and didn't have to compete with Mommy, who stayed home. Not feeling well. Hanna was very proud of herself. She didn't need Marie-Anne to do all the sneaky things. She almost wished she could tell someone how clever she was.

The elephants looked like boulders with fat stumps for legs. She wanted to climb a giraffe's neck, its spots like a ladder. The peacocks strutted and showed the world their rainbows. They were very arrogant. Hanna wanted to wrap her fist around one of their delicate heads and squeeze. Would it crack open like an egg? The monkeys bore wise, sad faces that told the truth. She wasn't fooled by the way they played, climbing with their four identical hands while their tails asked, *Why? Why? Why?* It was like watching babies in a prison.

Maybe someday there'd be a zoo full of people. Just ordinary people sitting at a dining room table with a meal they hated. The free people would stand on the other side of the glass, watching them sniff their food in misery. In another room, children in bunk beds would have to wear pajamas all the time. They'd sleep so much they wouldn't grow, and parents would say to their own kids, "That could be you, if you aren't good." In the last room would be a solitary woman, bony and dirty, orange haired like an orangutan, sitting in a big stuffed chair watching the same three hours of television over and over, day in and day out. Poor monkeys.

"Have you ever said anything to Mommy?" Daddy asked. "Spoken to her?"

She shook her head. They walked along the plant-lined path on the way to the food stand, where Daddy promised her some french fries.

"Are you sure? Not even once or twice? When you were bursting with words and just couldn't hold them in anymore?"

She furrowed her eyebrows and stuck her lips out, shaking her head. If she had anything to say so badly, she'd say it to Daddy, not Mommy. And she couldn't be held accountable for Marie-Anne.

"But if you had anything to say—really, really important, or even just really, really silly, you know you could come to me, right? You know I'd listen?"

It was like he could read her mind. She kissed his hand, then gripped it in both of hers and did a little skip. Daddy skipped, too. They skipped all the way to the french fry place.

SUZETTE

SHE'D TRIED TO explain the pain to him, back when she was pregnant. At first they just thought it was another strange consequence of her ever-changing hormone-infused body. So she didn't mention it right away. Then it became almost too difficult to speak, too difficult to swallow food. She ate a lot of nondairy ice cream and little else. It melted in her mouth and slid down her esophagus. It did nothing to ease the pain.

It was as if someone had shoved straight pins through the back edges of her tongue. Both sides. She'd looked in the mirror so many times half expecting to see the tiny silver pinheads. She wanted so badly to pull them out and make the pain go away, return her tongue to its natural flexible state. But as hard as she looked, there was nothing to see. She didn't know how—or to whom—to report such a pain. The agony in her throat was somewhat different, as if she'd swallowed a razor blade and it stuck there, unwilling to budge up or down. Every time she swallowed even her own saliva, the razor blade screamed, Gotcha!

The pain had been relentless, a torture beyond what she'd previously been able to imagine. She googled *mouth sores* and found lots of gross pictures of inflamed cankers, but nothing in her mouth looked like that. Finally, she found a post that revealed the answer. By then she'd had Crohn's disease for nearly fifteen years, but her symptoms had always been confined to stomach pain and cramping and diarrhea—all of which she was already experiencing; she'd never heard of anyone having excruciating but nearly invisible sores in their mouth. Though six months pregnant, she'd lost ten pounds by the time she knew to go back to her gastroenterologist. Dr. Stefanski recognized what was happening immediately: it was another symptom of her flare-up. Because of the pregnancy, he still wouldn't start her on one of the biological drugs, even though the pain was relentless. She'd been reluctant to take even Tylenol, but she needed to gain weight during her last trimester, so Dr. Stefanski wrote a prescription that helped with her symptoms until the baby was born.

She leaned over the bathroom sink, trying to turn her cheek inside out. Maybe she'd just bitten it while chewing or in her sleep. She could feel the spot with her tongue but couldn't see anything in the mirror. It could be nothing, but there was a chance that her body could develop antibodies that would render her injections useless. Usually she tried not to think about it because the drug worked so well and she prayed it always would. Even after her recent bowel resection she'd only needed a few Imodium a day and was pleased with how quickly her digestion got back to normal. She'd been prepared for the worst; for months following her adolescent surgery she took the maximum dosage— eight Imodium a day—and still worried about straying too far from a bathroom every time she left the house.

Maybe it was just an upset stomach. Maybe she'd eaten something iffy at that chain restaurant they'd gone to for lunch the day before while they were out shopping. She was distrustful of restaurants in general; they could bury cheap ingredients with salty, fatty sauces. She took an extra Imodium at lunch and another before heading upstairs for the night. Maybe in the morning everything would be back to normal. No mouth pain, no fucking diarrhea. Blips happened.

But what if what if what if it was happening again, everything going awry, a new fistula about to announce itself? It shouldn't happen again, her inflammation was under control and the surgery was supposed to make everything better. But Crohn's was notoriously unpredictable, and what if she wasn't in the majority percentage, and what if they'd made havoc of her delicate system in spite of it being "only a few inches." Maybe she shouldn't have trusted the surgeons. It was so easy for her worry to run out of control . . . *defective no hope more cutting amputation of lower ileum what would be left would it be enough oh God* . . . Stop. Stop. Stop.

She lifted her flimsy T-shirt. Her scars lay there quietly, nothing to say. Not even a tingle beneath her skin. Their silence was a relief, a comfort even. She tousled her hair. Did she look younger? The shorter length revealed the tiny scar on her jugular vein, though only she would care about the pinkish speck. Too many things in her life were tinged with horror. She told herself not to think about it, and turned off the bathroom light and slipped into bed.

While Alex and Hanna were at the zoo, she spent the

day alone. It was nice, like a staycation. She binge-watched
TV shows and started reading a long novel about a
decades-spanning friendship that made her wistful. Alex
gave it to her for the fifth night of Hanukkah, which
was always their Book Night. Sometimes she thought
about reconnecting with friends she'd made at the Art
Institute. Being a mother—homeschooling—sapped her
energy for other relationships, but at least she had Alex.
The book, enjoyable as it was, made her feel lonely, so
she set it aside and spread out, taking up more than her
share of the bed. Hanna was asleep; Alex helped with
her bath and got her ready for bed, as had become their
routine. He was upstairs working, and she knew she
had no reason to feel neglected—he'd kept Hanna entertained all day so she could rest. But she wanted him. She
couldn't risk calling out and waking Hanna, so she called
his phone.

"Hey—you almost finished?"

"I'm never really almost finished."

"Could you come to bed?"

"What did you have in mind?"

She heard the flirty smile in his voice but didn't want to
disappoint him by telling him the truth: she just wanted to
talk. "You'll see." Her voice sounded sleepy, not the least
bit seductive. But Alex said he'd be right down.

She turned off her lamp, leaving the room in the warm
glow of his bedside light. It was easy to picture him, in the
room above her head, in the cool glare of his computer
screen, saving his work to the cloud. There'd been no porn
on his laptop and no links that suggested such an interest,

though she found the website where Hanna acquired her pictures of dead people—a Victorian phenomenon she had to admit was morbidly fascinating. She felt relieved rather than guilty about checking her husband's search history; she was only confirming what she already knew. It was asinine that she'd doubted him, even for half a second—that, too, she could blame on Hanna's machinations. Alex was not a depraved man, and surely Hanna would make him an object of her wrath if he ever harmed her in any way. Still, it bothered her to see how selective Hanna had been in choosing her pictures.

Many on the website were of children, from babes to teenagers, and a few were of men. But Hanna was interested only in the dead women, most of whom, thanks to the washed-out black-and-white photography, appeared roughly the same age: midthirties. A long-dormant memory came to her of the anger that sometimes seethed when she lay awake as a teenager, her stomach roiling. There were moments when she contemplated sneaking into her mother's bedroom and plunging a knife into her sleeping heart.

Did Hanna harbor such fantasies, too? Sometimes Suzette was afraid the girl could read her thoughts: The regret she fought to keep from surfacing; the love that she hoped would overshadow her otherwise tepid feelings (if only Hanna were more likeable); her desperate need for her own time and space.

A minute later she heard Alex on the stairs. Even when he tried to be quiet, the weight of his body, his low center of gravity, made the floors groan. He whipped off his

T-shirt as he came in the room and tossed it onto the floor. He shut the door behind him and launched onto the bed beside her.

"Hej, älskling."

"Hej." She snuggled next to him, trailing her fingertips in random patterns along his back. "I missed you."

"Feels nice. Feeling better?"

"Not really."

"What do you think's going on? The surgery?" He leaned on his elbow to look at her.

"Don't know. Maybe something I ate? I do blood work the end of next week, before my appointment with Dr. Stefanski. But it shouldn't be inflammation."

"There's been a lot going on. With Hanna."

"Could be that. A little stressful."

"What time is her appointment on Monday?"

"Four. I'll go right from picking her up at school."

"Do you want me to meet you there?"

"Can you?" It was a surprise that he even asked. He always left all of Hanna's appointments—doctor, dental, school, hair—to her.

"I could probably leave about then, get there by four-thirty."

"If you want to."

He tucked a piece of her hair behind her ear. "Won't . . . Beatrice—"

"Beatrix. Dr. Yamamoto."

"Won't she want to talk to both of us?"

In that instant, she couldn't determine if it was a great idea or a terrible one that Dr. Yamamoto would hear them describe two entirely different children. A part of her wanted Beatrix all to herself. Alex didn't even know about the most recent event—she'd dealt with it with Dr. Yamamoto instead. And she didn't know how much of the appointment would be just the doctor and Hanna.

"You're hesitating," Alex said without judgment.

"I honestly have no idea if she wants to talk with us, both of us. We didn't talk about that on the phone. I'm sure she will at some point."

"Do you want me to come?"

She couldn't say no, so she said yes.

She tried to look more grateful than she felt. For a minute they just dream-gazed into each other's eyes. He nibbled her lips. She let him, but made no effort to move things along.

"Tired?" he asked.

"Do you miss it? When we used to talk? About everything?"

"Sure. Sometimes. But life progresses."

"Have we progressed?"

"Sure, as a family."

"But we only talk about Hanna now. What about us—you and me. Have we progressed?"

"It's different now. We have more responsibilities."

"I don't feel like I've progressed," she said. "As a person. I've slid. Laterally. I'm sliding. Down a gradual slope."

His already crowded face drew together even tighter with sympathy. "You're a good . . . mom, wife, partner . . . But I know, I understand if you want more than that."

"I do, but . . ." She turned slightly onto her back and looked at the ceiling, trying to wrangle her feelings into something she could explain.

"What do you want to do?"

"I don't know. That's just it. This . . . directionless feeling. This . . . going nowhere."

"Hanna will be in school. I'd love to work with you more, if you want to." He inched closer to her, but she wasn't ready to engage in a more intimate way. What seemed like such a simple solution to him only complicated her nebulous uncertainties.

"I just remember . . . Before Hanna. And I loved my work, and working with you. But I'd get so obsessed. Thinking about a project all the time, and I have this compulsion, you know. Everything has to be finished, I can't rest until everything's done. And I didn't want to think then, how I couldn't do things because of my health. But I'm older now. And I don't know if I should be cautious? Or throw caution to the wind. Maybe I missed my chance to be fearless. I'm too aware now, of how things can go wrong."

"I think you can have both—do something you're passionate about, that makes you feel fulfilled, and not have it be something that makes you unwell."

"I just wish I knew . . . I don't know what that is." She turned onto her side to face him, their noses just inches apart.

"Very, very, very soon—soon—like really soon, you're going to have more time to yourself."

"Soon?"

"So soon it's almost here. Tomorrow. Start thinking about it tomorrow. You know I'll support you and encourage you—if you want to try something, or pursue something." Now it was his turn to trail his fingertips up and down the exposed skin of her arm. It tingled.

"I think . . . I miss being more creative. I always imagined . . . I thought Hanna and I would do art projects together. Make stuff with paper plates and noodles and paint, I don't know. Paper flowers. Tie-dyed T-shirts. Little felt animals, holiday decorations. I had these ideas of how it would be, the two of us. Making stuff. If she'd just shown any interest—any interest, ever. I thought that would be the creative part of being a mom, fostering that in her, coming up with things, seeing her develop, seeing her make discoveries. She keeps everything to herself. Everything."

"I know."

"I have no clue. Who she is. What's going on in her head?" A tear slid sideways across her nose. Alex gently stopped it with his thumb.

"I know, *älskling*. I don't want you to be eaten up, again. Like when you were young and no one cared about how you felt—"

"You care."

"I do care. And I'm sorry, that I waited so long, that I didn't see it sooner, that this situation with Hanna is more than just . . . waiting. It's eating you up and that's partly my fault."

"It's not, I just. Reached a breaking point."

"Okay. Well, I don't want you to break. I'm in it, I'm

here. You worked so hard to find a place for Hanna. So let's focus on you now. You. What do you want? What do you need? What do you miss? What will make you happy?"

She sniffled up the last of her tears and slid her leg between his. Her hand glided over his elbow and she felt so close to him, like she was inside him and he inside her. Their hands moved in tandem, seeking each other, and she brought his to her mouth and kissed his hairy knuckles.

"Sometimes I think . . ." It was so new, the idea. She hadn't really considered voicing it. Maybe Hanna had felt the same way, the first time she'd spoken. Maybe it had come as a surprise to her when the words emerged, revealing something that had existed only inside her. It wasn't impossible that her idea would sound as strange to Alex as Hanna's first words had been.

"I've been thinking about a book, for a while now. Not writing one. But an art project, with different pages. Different textures. Different kinds of paper. And some of the pages have miniature paintings, and others are like a photo album, and others like a . . . I don't know, a scrapbook of found objects. I just have this idea. About creating something that opens."

"Then you should make something. That opens." And he kissed her.

For a moment she was transported to the early days. The early nights. When he was everything. When she was someone. When the two of them were enough. And having a child meant the exponential increase of their love, because they wanted more ways to express it. Now they knew how a child divided them, as individuals, and a couple. She wanted them back, the couple they had been. But she couldn't . . . not right then.

"Shhh, sweetheart . . ." She made the words a whisper, as if she could quiet his longing. "I'm sorry . . ."

"I don't want you to be sick."

"I don't either." She resented her body's betrayal. She still couldn't express how insecure it made her, how she lived on a precipice. The most basic parts of her could fail, and there was nothing she could do to stop it.

He switched off his lamp and held her in the dark. He stroked her back while she silently prayed. She resolved to begin her book the very next day, sketching out the ideas that had terraformed from nothingness as she washed and folded and scrubbed and chopped. Someone else could finally quiz Hanna on her spelling and explain the fundamentals of math and read with her the biased accounts of the history of the world. She would make something. Something else. Something better than Hanna.

Looking at her daughter in the rearview mirror, she almost felt sorry for her. Hanna sat somberly, buckled in like a prisoner on her way to be executed, no hope for a last-minute reprieve. Suzette was grateful for her passive acceptance, even though it registered in the girl as defeat; she didn't have the energy to argue or wrangle with her. All morning, while trying to keep things moving along— making sure she got dressed and brushed her teeth, fixing her hair and lunch, chatting lightly over breakfast—she'd needed to run to the bathroom. Her stomach wasn't better at all, and mornings were always the worst. She'd have preferred not to leave the house, but at least she'd have the bulk of the day to herself. She made a list in her head of the beige-colored foods she fell back on when her digestion was at its worst: baked chicken and white rice, oatmeal, noodles, potatoes, toast with peanut butter, bananas. She'd stop at Giant Eagle on her way home and stock up.

Hanna perked up when they drove past the playground, her eyes on the climbing rig. It saddened Suzette to see so clearly, for once, what her daughter was thinking, what she wanted, knowing she couldn't give it to her. She couldn't deny that school was the end of a certain kind of freedom.

"It's normal to feel a little nervous on the first day. But you're going to have fun. You'll get to do all sorts of things that you can't do at home."

Hanna didn't acknowledge her.

She parked a half block from the school, behind a long caravan of other parents. Some of them still escorted their young children, while others sat and watched, pulling away only when their sons or daughters disappeared inside. Suzette didn't take Hanna's hand, sensing how the girl was bracing herself and in need of her own space. They walked side by side, each consumed in a personal gloom.

Just inside, Mr. G was waiting to greet them. He stood beside a tall, fifty-ish woman with rosy cheeks and untended hair who looked as if she'd just gotten out of bed. Her jeans were tucked into a pair of colorful rubber boots and she had chapped, red hands. Everything about her made Suzette think she should be on a muddy farm, wrangling piglets instead of children.

"Good morning, Hanna! Hi, Mrs. Jensen."

"Oh, are you okay?" Suzette asked Mr. G. At first glance she'd hoped he was merely dressing up as a pirate, but there was an actual bandage beneath his black eye patch.

"Minor accident. One of those weird things, nothing to worry about."

"That's good. I think Hanna's all ready."

"Great—this is Ms. Atwood," he said to Hanna, even though she wouldn't look at him. "She's going to be your primary teacher." He turned to Suzette. "And she'll keep you informed of Hanna's progress."

"Thank you. Nice to meet you." Suzette shook Ms. Atwood's hand. The teacher had a very strong grip.

"Likewise. We're really excited to get to know Hanna. Want to see your homeroom? I can show you where to put your things." Hanna dropped her chin against her chest. "Follow me."

Somewhat to Suzette's surprise, Hanna followed a few steps behind Ms. Atwood, her big backpack bobbing along, and allowed herself to be led away.

She breathed a sigh of relief. "I think that's actually a really good start."

"I think a part of Hanna really does want to explore some other options. She's in good hands, don't worry."

"Thank you."

"See you at three-fifteen?"

She waved at Mr. G and headed out. Behind her,

Mr. G greeted other students. The hallway filled with a cacophony of sounds—more varied than the typical school chatter of her youth. Hanna, apparently, wasn't the only one who preferred noises to actual words.

Before she started the car, she sent Alex a quick text: so far so good.

She put the groceries away. More things for Hanna's lunches: little tubs of organic applesauce, sliced cheese for her sandwiches, a big bag of the dried fruit and nut mixture she liked. And her personal stockpile of beige food.

Afterward, devoid of the ambition she'd had the previous night, she lingered barefoot in the middle of the downstairs. With all the lights off, subdued daylight filled the great room. She'd helped in designing the space and the decor was all hers, but she didn't always feel a sense of ownership, a sense of belonging. The yard beyond the glass looked more hostile and wild than usual. She decided it was a trick of the light that made the tall hedges look dark and savage. It was such a different space in the sunshine, but Pittsburgh was susceptible to heavy, overcast days. It affected her mood and made her think of her mother: maybe she could have been cured with more light—bigger windows, better lightbulbs.

Maybe not. It might have helped. But it wouldn't have been enough. Her mother needed the heat and hope of an internal sun, but she exuded the nothingness of a distant and dead planet.

Think of the book. Pick a page. Make a sketch.

But all that came to mind was Hanna's room and the number of days since she'd been in there to clean it. She fought herself for a while, standing there like a misplaced statue. She should go dig out the rest of her art supplies, the professional-quality paper and pencils she kept in a tub in her closet. It wouldn't be hard; she had a storage system for everything in the house and knew where everything was. But she couldn't quite get herself motivated. The silence was distracting, not inspiring. She told herself it wasn't wrong to do what she most felt like doing in that moment. And what she wanted to do was clean. And perhaps then, inspiration would come.

She dusted the shelves above Hanna's bed that held her nighttime things: her clock and flashlight, the night-light she didn't use anymore, a few books and stuffed animals. She flitted the duster over the bare top of her dresser, then moved on to the storage shelves that held the rest of her books and all her cubbies. She shifted them to get between the cracks, then peered into each one as she swept over her things. Hanna loved receiving the art supplies, but Suzette couldn't understand why she wouldn't use them. It occurred to her to raid her daughter's supplies as a starting place for her book. But Hanna, like she did, kept her things in very specific places; she would notice if anything went missing. And thievery was beneath her.

When she finished dusting, she grabbed the dry Swiffer mop from where it leaned by the door. She loved Swiffering the floors. She moved with grace, like a dancer with a partner, collecting all the stray hairs and nearly invisible bits of debris. When she pushed the mop under the bed, it came out with bits of paper clinging to it. From the collage of dead people, she assumed. When she reached in again, the mop caught a barrette and three of her new paper clips. Suzette puzzled over these objects as she picked them up and wiped them off. Hanna's room was never in a state of disarray. She'd respected Alex's moratorium on staying out of her room for a few days, but how had so much stuff come to be under her bed in the meanwhile?

She got down on her hands and knees to get a better look. What the fuck was that?

Using the Swiffer, she fished for a lumpy object that tumbled forward. A potato?

Reaching back under, she secured the rest of the detritus—small objects that couldn't have collected in the far corner by accident. Was her daughter hoarding things? Stashing them away for some future obscure purpose?

She picked up the potato from the floor and examined it more closely. Things had been stuck into it, like a real-life Mr. Potato Head. It had two pencils, golden and brown, inserted at the bottom like legs, and a rudimentary partly drawn face: a smile and a mustache rendered in heavy black pen. One of her new flower erasers sat glued on top at a jaunty angle, like a hat. It had a green thumbtack for the right eye. But the left one . . .

"Oh shit."

The mangled left eye dripped red crayon blood and the red nub stuck out of its carved socket. If it had been a different color, or if Hanna hadn't drawn red, oozing drops, it might not have reminded her of a wound—of Mr. G.

But Mr. G's bandage and patch were over his left eye and she couldn't help making the connection to his injury.

Had her daughter made a voodoo doll?

And if it wasn't a voodoo doll, it was still hideous. That Hanna paired the almost-cute flower hat with a bloody gouged-out eye made her want to weep for her splintered child. Why would she do such a thing? She had nice toys, many that she never played with.

The more she looked at it, the creepier it seemed. She shuddered as ghosts tapped her shoulder. Was this her new ploy for getting out of school? Harming her principal?

Impossible. She didn't believe in witches and voodoo dolls.

Did she?

What was it doing under the bed?

Why did Hanna make it?

Why, after years when she wouldn't even doodle, was she suddenly making sick, disgusting things?

"Why couldn't I have a fucking normal daughter?" She ripped out the crayon and the pencils and threw the monstrosity to the floor. It bounced, leaving a wet splat, but she didn't bother to wipe it up. The little flower hat tumbled off.

The thing made her skin crawl and she wanted to extract it from her mind. She grabbed her cleaning things and stormed out, leaving an uncharacteristic mess in her wake. At the head of the stairs she froze, bucket of supplies in one hand, mop in the other. It was all too much—the rage, the frustration. But she was alone, and could finally let it out. She screamed and stomped her feet. In a fit of rebellion, she pitched her bucket down the stairs and threw her dry mop like a javelin after it.

After a minute she stopped, but her echo rang in the house.

She felt better. Empty. Drained of poison.

She trudged down the steps one by one. Gathered up the rag. The spray bottle. The duster. The mop. Dropped them in the kitchen. Too depleted to slog back upstairs for a nap, she threw herself onto the couch, her arm over her eyes.

Her body relaxed in the plush comfort and her spinning thoughts unwound. It was nothing. Mr. G said he was fine. Her daughter couldn't have made a voodoo doll because such things were superstitious nonsense. Besides, Hanna was a witch, not a . . . *Shut up*. It was a ridiculous waste of precious energy.

The world cooperated, grew quiet, and disappeared. She slept for hours.

HANNA

SHE DIDN'T UNDERSTAND why she was being punished. Every stupid person she'd met throughout the stupid day thought she, too, was stupid. They couldn't stop asking, "Can you do that?" even though a second later Ms. Stinky Breath or Mr. Do-Goody would add, "I know you can!" They thought she was a dumb baby who couldn't add or subtract or read. They wanted her to point to cards.

"Can you show me the color blue?"

"Which of these has wheels?"

"What is $3 + 7$?"

"Does one of these words begin with *K*?"

"Which one says *dog*?"

Early in the day, she tried her stare-and-glare technique, but the questions persisted. Finally, she started slapping at the right cards.

"Good job!" they said a million times.

It was maddening enough to make her scream, but she didn't. Finally, she grabbed a pencil and a piece of paper and wrote *Jag kan läsa!* in big angry letters.

That stopped Ms. Atwood for a second. "What does that mean?" she asked.

Hanna scribbled over a second sheet. *Je peux lire*.

"Is that French? What's this one?" She held up the first sheet.

Svenska! She wrote over it.

Ms. Atwood squinted, looking at something inside her brain. She mouthed the word *svenska*. "Your father . . . I think Mr. G mentioned he was Swedish? You know Swedish and French?"

Hanna shrugged.

"That's very impressive. And English too. So this is all too easy." She gathered up the stupid flash cards with the stupid words, the third stupid set Hanna had slapped at that day. If anyone else put cards in front of her, she'd stab them in the eye.

"And I'm glad to see how well you communicate with writing. Your mom said you'd come really far with your workbooks at home, but she also said you don't like to have a conversation that way."

Hanna crossed her arms.

"You have done so well today, do you realize that? And I promise you, when we all have a better sense for what you know, we'll have much more-interesting projects for you."

So it went throughout the day. Sometimes she just had to sit there in a circle with a bunch of weird kids and listen to a teacher blather on, reading them a book, or showing them pictures of animals. She practiced lowering the volume on her ears, determined to enclose herself in a bubble of silence. Sometimes she shut her eyes; somewhat to her surprise, no one bothered her or poked her or said, "Hanna, pay attention!" like her mother.

The worst part of school was she was never alone. Kids,

teachers, aides. They hovered like wasps and it didn't matter how far she ran—they always caught up, buzzing and stinging, and complimented her on her speed. The stupids thought it was a game.

At lunch, a girl sat beside her and peered into her lunch bag as soon as Hanna unzipped it. "What do you have?"

She tried to take out Hanna's sandwich, but Ms. Atwood dashed over. "Remember what we always talk about, Emily? About your things and other people's things?"

"I can touch mine but not others'."

"Right, and that's Hanna's lunch."

"Hanna's lunch."

Ms. Atwood sat there at the big cafeteria table with them and supervised, watching as Emily and Hanna ate their sandwiches. Hanna wasn't used to being watched so closely. She didn't like it. And Ms. Atwood really didn't need to worry; if Emily—or anyone else—tried to take her things she'd punch them in the nose.

In the afternoon, they tried to get her to sit around a big parachute with the other kids and play different games while they gripped it. Hanna hugged herself and jumped in her pouting way until an aide let her sit on the gym floor, away from everyone else. She watched them make the parachute billow up in the air. Sometimes they'd get underneath it and let it fall over them like a jellyfish and they giggled, but she didn't think it was safe. Jellyfish had invisible stingers, long threads that they sent out into the ocean to paralyze the little creatures they wanted to eat. Hanna thought all the children might die under the parachute, and she started to panic and fret: maybe the tendrils would get her, too. The aide took her to the bathroom and she was very, very glad because she needed to pee, and at home she knew where to go but at school she wasn't sure what she was supposed to do.

It was an exhausting day.

At two-thirty she put her head on her desk. After Ms. Atwood got the other kids settled, she came over. She led Hanna to the corner where there were some big beanbag chairs, and Hanna curled up and took a nap until it was time to go home.

Mommy and Ms. Atwood lingered by the door talking about *her-Hanna-she-her-Hanna* when all she wanted was to *get out out home out away away home*! But then Mommy reminded her that they weren't going straight home. Beatrix was expecting them, and Daddy would meet them there later, and it struck Hanna that this new routine was very, very bad and wasn't going to work. She'd tried her hardest but she just didn't have the vim to do that every single day.

In the car, Mommy gave her a granola bar and some cherry juice. Mommy looked a little different than she had in the morning. She'd put on some makeup and her favorite necklace. Hanna liked the necklace, too—a yellowy disc on a fine chain. Daddy said it was amber, but to her it looked just like a butterscotch candy. Every time she saw it, she wanted to rip it off and pop it in her mouth.

Mommy blathered as she drove away.

". . . is so nice and it sounded like you had a very good—"

"One of them will have to die."

She met her mother's startled gaze in the rearview mirror. "Excuse me? What did you say? Hanna?"

"*Je suis Marie-Anne.*"

Her mother flicked her eyes between the road and the mirror and didn't say anything right away. Her hands tightened on the wheel, but she surprised Hanna.

"*Excusez-moi, Marie-Anne.* I didn't hear what you said." Her French sounded exaggerated, like the puppets on *Sesame Street.*

Hanna sighed impatiently. "If you make me go there again, I will cast a spell on one of them. One of them will die."

In the mirror, her mother chewed her lip, weighing how to respond. "Which one?" she finally asked as they inched along Forbes Avenue.

Hanna glanced at the shops outside her window, bicycles and shoes and ice cream. That was a good question. It might not be such a bad idea to put a spell on the parachute, turn it into the jellyfish it so resembled, and let it devour a class of eight all at once. A teacher and a couple of aides might perish, too.

"I'll pick them off one by one," she said. "It will be your fault."

"If you end up in jail it won't be my fault—that's what happens to people who hurt other people."

"A jail can't hold me."

"Okay, if that's what you want. Personally, I think school is a better option than jail."

Her mother's responses weren't what she was expecting. It felt almost good to talk back and forth, but that was enough. Marie-Anne tucked herself away, and Hanna made her face look unaware, disinterested.

"So, Marie-Anne, I'd love to know how you make one of your spells. Do you need a big pot—a cauldron? And toads and bats and eyeballs?"

What a foolish woman. Hanna let the words float out the window. They were meaningless; Mommy knew nothing about being a real witch.

Mommy tried a few more times to continue the conversation. Hanna wiped a dribble of juice from her chin, then licked it off the back of her hand. Mommy kept talking to herself. She went on and on. ". . . mumble mumble . . . grumble grumble . . ." Like a crazy person.

Beatrix lived in a big house on Wightman Street. They went to the side entrance where she had a rectangular sign the color of a dirty penny with her name and a bunch of letters that didn't spell anything. Beneath it was a doorbell. Mommy pushed it and then Hanna pushed it again, because she wanted to.

"We might be a little early," Mommy said, checking the time on her phone.

A woman with black hair, bony like an insect and older than Mommy, came to the door with a smile.

"I think we're a little early," Mommy said, fretting in her Mommy way.

"No, good timing, come on in."

More introductions and Hanna wouldn't look at her: she already knew her name was Beatrix. They walked down a hallway, and Beatrix explained if she were busy she would just buzz them in and they could sit in the chairs by the door until she came out. She led them to a window-less room that, shockingly, was filled with toys. Games on the shelves. Arts and crafts stuff on a cart against the wall. A low table sat in the middle, surrounded by small chairs. Stuffed animals and giant cardboard building blocks were scattered around the floor. On one wall was a blue nubby sofa, and on the opposite wall was a big mirror.

"Do you think you can find something in here to amuse yourself with?" Beatrix asked.

Hanna went into the room, alone, and looked around. Not bad. Nice colors and stuff to play with. And *no* children.

"I'm going to be in the next room, talking to your mom—right there, on the other side of that mirror. So if you need one of us, just wave and we'll see you, okay? And you can play with anything in here by yourself for a few minutes, is that all right?"

Finally, she'd be alone. She found a tub of Legos on the shelf and took them to the table. The door closed behind her and for the first time that day it was quiet. The jangled-up day—colors and noises and words and people—slowly disintegrated, like white paper dissolving in a puddle of blue ink, and her heart returned to normal. Soft bumps instead of hammering thumps.

Better better better she chanted silently, fluttering her tongue like a snake.

SUZETTE

THE COZY OFFICE had one big window flanked by two gargantuan tropical plants. Beatrix crossed behind her desk to pull the curtain closed and dim the room. Then she raised the blinds that revealed the playroom. They could see Hanna, framed within the window, stacking Legos—something she enjoyed doing in Alex's study, where he didn't mind her leaving pieces all over his floor.

Beatrix came back around her desk and joined Suzette in the living-room-like area where Suzette had taken a seat on the couch next to a bright decorative pillow. There were also two armchairs and a solid Craftsman-style coffee table with a box of Kleenex and a bowl filled with cat's-eye marbles. The walls were decorated with watercolors, mostly of landscapes with trees and cerulean pools of water.

"Did you make these?" Suzette asked, studying the artwork.

"Yes. A hobby I've been doing for many years." She sat in a chair with the draped window at her back, and glanced at Hanna through the one-way glass at her right. In form and posture Beatrix looked like a ballet dancer, but her sharp movements lacked grace.

"You're really good. They're quite beautiful." Simple and clean. The word *haiku* came to mind, as if the paintings were also poems.

"Thank you." She crossed her legs and angled herself toward Suzette. "I always like to talk with the parents for a short time during each session—"

"My husband will be coming a bit later. Do you talk to Hanna"—she pointed toward the playroom—"in there?" The therapist held a Moleskine notebook and a pen in one hand. Suzette noticed the thin gold wedding band and wanted to ask her if she had children of her own, but didn't.

"Sometimes, it depends on the child. Some prefer this room. While I'm talking with her I'll have you wait by the entryway. I do honor the children's privacy and I won't reveal the specifics of what we communicate together. That trust needs to be there between me and Hanna—"

"Of course."

"—but I also will keep you and your husband apprised of anything that you need to be aware of. And based on things I learn from Hanna, I might sometimes need to talk to both you and your husband. I view the family as a holistic unit and you're all affecting one another. So, in a way, this isn't just a process for Hanna but for all of you."

"No, that's good. I feel like, as a family, we're really isolated. Like, we look a certain way when people see us, who don't know us, but what happens at home . . ."

"So . . ." Beatrix breathed in and relaxed, smiling at Suzette. "How have things been since we talked? Better? Worse?"

"Okay. I haven't been feeling that well, so Alex was with her most of the weekend. And she started school today."

"How did that go?"

"According to her teachers? Pretty well. Maybe a little better than expected. She actually wrote something out on a piece of paper, which she doesn't do with us. I guess she was really frustrated. She wrote one sentence in Swedish, and one in French. But then, on the way here . . ." It almost struck her as funny. "She told me, as her alter ego Marie-Anne, that she wanted to put a spell on one of the kids at school and kill them."

"She's just started talking—you said within the last couple of weeks?"

"Yes, as this other person." Suzette found herself resorting to old, anxious habits—twisting her purse strap. She pushed the purse away, but doubted it was far enough to quell the temptation.

"It's really . . . I know from your perspective it's probably not fascinating, but I can almost see how, after not talking for so long, that this is protection for her, on some level. Hiding behind someone who can talk, so her identity of herself as someone who doesn't talk is still intact." She finally opened her notebook and jotted something down.

"It doesn't sound at all frightening when you put it that way. It's still only to me. She doesn't pretend to be a witch with Alex. I tried to handle it a little better this time; I tried to engage her instead of freaking out."

"How did that work?"

"Not bad. A weird conversation, but I guess that's what it was."

"It may not seem like progress, but it sounds to me like she really is trying to reach out." Suzette winced. "No? You don't interpret it that way?"

"It's the other things. The savage dog, the weird acting like the devil's fucking her—I never told my husband about that. I even looked for porn on his computer, to see if that's where she saw, or found out about sex, but . . ." Conscious of the therapist's intense, evaluating gaze she fought the urge to drag her purse back over. She pressed her hands tightly together instead.

"Are there a lot of things you don't tell your husband?"

She considered the question. What did she tell Alex? The easy things, mostly. "Maybe, I guess . . . Early on we shared everything, but over time . . . From his perspective, I think he'd say he has everything. A fulfilling career—meaningful, runs his own business, loves his coworkers. A good relationship with his parents. A beautiful house, a devoted wife, an adorable child. He has enough money, and still has free time—goes to the gym, does what he wants. He loves me, and I love him . . . But . . . I can't do this without him, and sometimes . . . You know, it's just important . . . I don't want him to lose faith in me."

"Why would he lose faith in you if you told him everything that's going on?"

"Because he doesn't see it. I've always been the one who's home with her all day—taking care of her, feeding her, schooling her, trying to keep her entertained. Keep her safe, healthy, well behaved. I bear the burden for raising her, really. Alex loves her—deeply, deeply loves her. But he only has to do it for tiny spans of time. Make her giggle. Read her a bedtime story. Maybe play with her a little on the weekends. She loves everything she does with him, and he feels like a hero—he feels her love."

Beatrix nodded. "It is the curse of the caregiver. But surely Alex recognizes the important work you—"

"Yes, absolutely. But this—" She threw her hand toward the glass pane. "I seriously thought she was going to attack me, and bite me." Suzette told her the rest—putting Hanna in the backyard to cool down, the marks on her arm, Alex's hostile response.

Beatrix jotted down a few more notes. "Would you be uncomfortable if we talked about the sexual incident with Alex? I'd like to hear his thoughts."

"He's going to wonder why I didn't tell him."

"Maybe. Might be a chance, in a safe place, for you to talk about it."

Suzette hadn't expected to feel like the one on trial. She worried about what Beatrix had written in her notebook, what conclusions she was drawing. That she was abusive. A bad mom. A bad wife. A liar. Another broken, dysfunctional family hiding behind the façade of better-than-average accessories. Waiting by the door in one of three matching chairs, she pressed on her stomach, on the thing that was turning over and over, getting thicker and harder with each revolution. She felt it vibrating, threatening to rupture. It didn't matter what she did, it was always the mother's fault.

She had vowed to do better than her own mother—had been certain, for a long time, that she was earning a passing grade. But every time she talked about what was going on . . . Insanity dipped around her like a swarm of frenzied bats.

What were Beatrix and Hanna doing in there? Would the therapist ask her yes and no questions, prying information from her child's vaulted mind? Would she ask her to draw a picture? Would Hanna do it? Would she nod yes and no like she did when she wasn't being Marie-Anne?

A door buzzer announced Alex's arrival. She stood and peered through the window. On time as he'd promised, he smiled and kissed her when she let him in.

"Hej, älskling."

"Hey."

He glanced at the chairs, the hallway.

"She's talking to Hanna right now."

"How was school?"

"Promising, actually."

"That's good news."

Beatrix popped out of the playroom. "Just checking, heard the door," she said, seeing Alex. She turned back to the room, to Hanna. "A few more minutes on your own? Is that okay?" Hanna must have nodded, because Beatrix smiled. "Good." She shut the door and gestured for Suzette and Alex to join her.

Round two. Suzette settled back on the couch. Alex and Beatrix shook hands and made their proper introductions. Before joining Suzette on the couch, he peered through the one-way glass, where Hanna played with Legos. Beatrix checked her watch as she took a seat.

"So we only have a few minutes, but—" she looked at Suzette "—I'd like to get Alex caught up."

Suzette put her hand on her belly again, trying to keep the heavy thing from churning. Maybe it would sound better, less ridiculous—crazy—coming from the therapist.

"So Suzette has informed me of a couple of incidents. The dog barking—" Alex nodded. "—which was quite alarming to Suzette, because of how intense it was and she had concerns for her own safety." Now it was Suzette's turn to nod. Alex glanced at her, but she couldn't read his expression. Concern? Regret? Doubt?

"But Hanna is exhibiting other disturbing behavior as—"

"What kinds of disturbing behavior?" he asked, annoyed. Skeptical.

Beatrix continued. "There was an incident where she acted out sexually—"

Alex snapped his head toward Suzette. She hoped Beatrix read his anger, his unwillingness to believe what he didn't want to be true.

"Just because she's a child," he said to the therapist, "doesn't mean she can't have sexual feelings."

"I agree. But the incident Suzette described—your daughter claimed, in that moment, that the devil was having intercourse with her."

"What?"

His face bloomed red as he glared first at Beatrix, and then at Suzette.

"I told you, she's . . . She thinks, or is pretending, to be this witch—"

"But you know she's not a witch."

"No, she isn't," said Beatrix. Suzette looked to the therapist, hoping she had a special technique for smoothing things over, for talking offended fathers down from a defiant ledge.

"My opinion is that this alter ego is a way for her to break the ice, of sorts. She's adopted a persona who is allowed to speak, to be demonstrative, in a way that Hanna still won't permit for herself. It doesn't mean she's a witch. But we do need to understand what this behavior means, and what your daughter's trying to express. She's a very precocious girl who's built a wall around herself—and we don't know why she felt she needed the wall, but I think she's trying to find a way over it. And right now, this is manifesting in some new behaviors."

Thank God. Beatrix and her art of rationalizing. Of being reasonable. Of being clinically professional in the face of deviance. Even Alex relented. His body relaxed. She slipped her hand into his, and was relieved when he squeezed it.

She should've taken that moment to tell them both about the voodoo-doll-potato thing, to hear Beatrix justify it as another attempt by Hanna to find a way over her wall. But the moment felt too precarious, and she didn't want Alex to pull his hand away. And maybe, after all, Hanna hadn't made an effigy of Mr. G.

Beatrix was on top of things. And Tisdale seemed to know how to handle Hanna.

They left a few minutes later after scheduling another appointment for the following Monday. Hanna monkey-climbed up Alex as soon as she saw him. He carried her to his car, babbling his Good Daddy babble, and she giggled, and both of them forgot about her. Suzette got in her own car, alone, aware of Beatrix standing on the stoop, arms crossed, watching the family dynamics on display. It was just as well. It confirmed everything she'd tried to say. From afar, father and daughter appeared so normal. Because that's what the daughter wanted everyone to think. Still, Suzette knew it made her look bad, made it seem as if the problem existed only between mother and daughter.

It was hard to pour endless love into someone who wouldn't love you back. No one could do it forever.

Alex sat double-parked with his flashers on, waiting so she could pull into the driveway first, and then backed in behind her. On the cramped city street, even with their double lot, they lacked the space for a garage. At the front door, Hanna scuffed her feet back and forth along the welcome mat, eager to get inside. Suzette was afraid he was angry, but he wrapped his arm around her as they crossed the stone-paved walk.

"You need to keep me fully apprised of what's going on. I felt so stupid, not even knowing—"

"I want to, it's not that I don't want to."

He unlocked the door. Hanna barged past, kicked off her Keds, and slunk off to her room. Alex and Suzette slipped out of their shoes, too, leaving them in a tidy row by the closet.

"Some of the things that happen . . ." She tried to figure out how to explain it. He patiently waited. "I find myself . . . I get so caught off guard, so freaked out. I know how crazy it sounds. And I don't want to cast Hanna, in your eyes, as crazy—or myself."

His fingertips sought hers and for a moment he seemed intent on reading her through touch. But before he could say anything, a high scream, as piercing as a Klaxon alarm, shattered the air. Startled and terrified, they both followed the noise, charging up the stairs to Hanna's room.

"*Lilla gumman?*" Alex said, tearing past the corner into her room. "What's wrong?"

Suzette pushed in beside him.

Hanna stood there holding the half-mashed legless potato in her hand. As soon as she saw her parents, the scream turned into a wail. Tears cascaded down her cheeks.

Alex fell to his knees. His hands wandered over her, making sure she wasn't injured. "What happened?"

She held up the potato and scooped up the pencil legs and the flower hat, crying as she had never cried before.

Her daughter's pain punctured Suzette's chest, sending panic through her veins. Hanna uttered breathless, open-mouthed wails—the kind that turn a child's face scarlet and wound a parent's heart.

"Your UnderSlumberBumbleBeast?" Alex asked.

Oh God. Regret sliced through Suzette as efficiently

as an executioner's ax. She'd forgotten about the creatures in Hanna's favorite book.

Hanna's head was almost too heavy for her to nod. She tried to show him where the legs went, where the hat went. She picked up the red crayon and tried to stick it back in its broken hole. The horrible keening noises she made sounded like a dog that had been hit by a car. She threw the useless appendages back onto the floor.

"I don't understand what happened." Stricken and desperate, he sat on the bed and pulled Hanna onto his lap, trying to comfort her. She squirmed away on her hands and knees. Alex looked to Suzette and she, too, gaped in horror. Hanna had never thrown such a fit, and her breathing was so erratic, and the noises so fitful, so agonized.

"It was me—it was me." Suzette fell to the floor, scrambling. She wrapped her arms around Hanna, rocking her. "It was me—it was Bad Mommy." Alex looked confused. "I found it and it scared me," she told him. "I didn't know what it was, I thought maybe it was a voodoo doll."

Hanna fought her way out of her mother's arms and crawled to her father. He scooped her up and cradled her, but his hard eyes stayed on Suzette.

"It's from the book we always read. It was her friend—she made it!"

"I didn't know, I forgot. I'm sorry. At school, Mr. G—the principal—had an eye patch, over the same eye as . . ."

"As a potato?"

"I wasn't thinking, it was the first thing that came to mind and—"

"What's wrong with you?"

"I know! But she said she was a witch. And she drew blood, dripping out of its eye . . ."

Hanna held the ruined beast clutched to her heart. Alex gently encouraged her to show it to him. She pointed to the red marks she'd drawn on the potato, then gestured to her own tears. Then pointed and gestured again, imploring for her father to understand. But even Suzette grasped it: they were tears, not drops of blood.

Suzette collapsed into sobs. She hadn't meant to destroy something precious. She hadn't meant to wound her child. They didn't know the rage it had triggered, how she'd screamed and thrown her own tantrum. Jealous of Alex's sympathy for Hanna, she questioned if he would have comforted her in that moment, when she'd been so over-whelmed. She read condemnation on his face as he held Hanna like a baby, rocking her as her wails subsided to hiccupping sobs.

"Sshh, *lilla gumman* . . . Daddy's squirrely girl . . ." He cooed so softly Suzette couldn't hear everything he said. But Hanna quieted. She looked so tiny in his arms, a rag doll.

"I'm so sorry." Suzette steepled her hands against her mouth. She knew she looked pathetic, on her knees, guilty, beseeching their forgiveness.

Alex planted kisses on Hanna's tear-streaked face. "We'll go upstairs to Daddy's room?" Hanna nodded. He eased the ruined potato out of her hand and held it out for Suzette.

With her head bowed, she had no choice but to take it. The punishment. The reminder of her foolishness. He carried Hanna away and she couldn't look. She heard him climbing the stairs, mumbling something. Probably about getting away from Bad Mommy.

Bad Mommy wiped her nose on the back of her hand. She gathered up the detritus she'd discovered under the bed. She considered what to do with the pencils, the flower eraser, the broken crayon, aware that they weren't just objects, but body parts.

Once, in second grade, she'd taken one of her beloved stuffed animals to school. Baby Bear was actually a mouse, but she'd named him as a three-year-old and no one corrected her. He spent most of the day at the bottom of her backpack, and when she got home she realized Baby Bear's face was streaked with blue ink stains—scars from a leaking pen. She tried to wash them off—gently with water and a Q-tip, and then more vigorously with a soapy washcloth—but the stains wouldn't come out. Holding back the tears, she went to her mother, parked in front of the TV, and asked for help.

"It's just a stupid toy," her mother said.

But Baby Bear wasn't stupid, or a toy. In fact, young Suzette ascribed to him more empathy and nurturing capabilities than the human she lived with. He watched over her. He cared about her feelings. She'd damaged Baby Bear and, consumed with guilt, could do nothing but curl up with him on her bed and cry.

A good mother would have known what the Under-SlumberBumbleBeast was. A good mother would have recognized how, in a child's eyes, it might be a cherished friend.

She left the little body parts in a neat row on the shelf above Hanna's bed. She carried the rest away, cupped in her hands like a delicate bird that might yet come back to life.

HANNA

THEY HAD A party on the open sofa bed. She'd always been intrigued by it because it looked just like a couch, but when *Farmor* and *Farfar* came, it transformed into a bed. Now it was an island where she and Daddy were the only inhabitants. He laid a blanket over it so they wouldn't get crumbs everywhere while they ate their open-faced sandwiches and watched episodes of *Star Trek: The Next Generation* on his laptop.

When Mommy came up, Hanna dived into the ocean and hid, treading water while itsy-bitsy fish tickled her toes and ankles.

"Mango sorbet?" She handed two bowls to Daddy. "How's she doing?"

His big shoulders went up and down. "That was way not cool."

"I know . . . If only she would show you her witch side . . . Maybe you'd understand how I get so creeped out."

"We'll talk later."

Mommy nodded and left, and Hanna climbed ashore. She wanted to tell him about the baby fish, who had such bright colors and flashed to one another like Christmas lights. She didn't know why the words, so clear in her brain, always stopped in her mouth. She just couldn't. And the more she thought about it, the worse it became. In that regard, she was a little jealous of Marie-Anne.

They gobbled up their mango sorbet.

"Yummy yummy."

She agreed. She and Daddy had a secret language like the fish and their flashing lights. He always saw her, no matter how lost she was in the dark, and figured out what she meant.

At bedtime Daddy didn't make her go to her own room. She tugged on his arm and he understood.

"Okay, I'll sleep up here too."

She curled up with a smile and closed her eyes, even though she wasn't that tired yet. They would sleep side by side, like a married couple. Like they would all the time when it was just the two of them. Daddy turned off one of the lights, and the bed jiggled as he sat beside her and stretched out his legs. She heard him turn the pages of a book. She was just starting to plot her revenge against Mommy when she came shuffling up the stairs with her scaly feet.

"You aren't coming down?" she said in a whisper from very near the island.

"I told her I'd stay."

Mommy exhaled through her nose. "Aren't we going to talk?"

She couldn't see how Daddy responded, but it wasn't

with words. Mommy didn't give up. "I called Dr. Stefanski's office. They said to double up on the Imodium, which wasn't helpful because I've already been doing that, and I'm going in on Thursday."

They couldn't see her face, buried in the pillow away from them, so she smiled. Mommy was getting sicker. She deserved it. But then Daddy got up and waded to shore, and she was afraid he was breaking his promise, betraying her to go downstairs with Mommy. But they only went to the top of the stairs.

The whispering continued.

"Did he think it could be the surgery? You just need more time to heal?"

"I don't know, I only talked to the nurse. I'll do my blood work tomorrow so they'll have the results."

They went quiet. Maybe Daddy was thinking of pushing Mommy down the stairs. But there weren't any screams or blumping bumps, and then Daddy started talking again, a little louder than a whisper.

"I want you to write out every single word she's said as Marie-Anne."

"I already have—I wrote it down for Beatrix. I'll send it to you."

"And tell me every time it happens again. I need to know."

"I will. I promise."

"Okay. And maybe . . . Try to stop being afraid of her—she's trying to communicate with us, with you. Frankly, I'm kind of envious. And you're not even appreciating—"

"It's hard to appreciate, the way she does it. I don't think you'd really like it."

For once, she had to agree with Mommy. Daddy hadn't done anything to deserve Marie-Anne's wrath. And if ever she could find a way to speak as herself, those words would all be for Daddy.

"I have a hard time accepting that."

"Clearly. But Alex . . . You could give me the benefit of the doubt. I take care of her all day. This is beyond fussing or whining or some little temper tantrum."

"Beatrix said it was a process. A process that took time to develop and will take time to undo. I know you're having a hard time, but I don't want you losing patience with her."

"I'm trying. I think we did better today. And Beatrix. And Tisdale's going to help."

Pissdale most definitely was not going to help. She needed, with Marie-Anne's assistance, to step up her game against Mommy, and they could make Mommy's life more difficult if they were at home. She had to figure out something bad enough to get her expelled from a school for bad children. And the murder of her UnderSlumberBumble-Beast hurt like her heart had been tossed in a blender. Mommy needed to know what that felt like.

"I like Beatrix," Daddy said.

"Me too."

They smoochy-kissed. Then Mommy went away and Daddy slipped back into bed beside her. She wanted—so wanted—to stay awake and enjoy his company and ponder all the things that she needed to ponder. But sleep stole her, the greedy thief, away into the darkness.

The next couple of days were school and more school. The Bouncy Room wasn't nearly as much fun with other people there—mutant children and clownlike adults with painted smiles. She didn't like being in regular classrooms where all the surfaces were too hard and, ideally, she was to remain seated. She couldn't understand why she was supposed to be a robot and follow endless hours of obeying an evil master's routine—even more rigid than Mommy's. She wanted to be master of her own schedule, decide on her own when and where she sat. To think that children everywhere sat at similar desks in similar rooms following similar routines like they were all supposed to grow up and become the same person.

Her only good discovery was the Quiet Room. It was intended to be a punishment, a place to go when she needed to "collect herself." She had tried sitting like a statue, unmoving and unresponsive, but they didn't like it when she ignored everybody—the robots were supposed to follow orders, not play dead. But sometimes she went too far in the other direction and jumped and waved her hands and made noises. If she couldn't settle down, they escorted her to the Quiet Room, which wasn't, in her mind, a punishment at all but a reward. They let her sit on the big cushions and read a book. Usually an aide stayed with her, but sometimes they ducked out and for a moment she got to be alone. She tried to have at least two to three outbursts a day.

Ms. Atwood and the other stupid-heads were unimpressed by most of her efforts to ignore or get away from them. And other students made equally disruptive noises. One boy would vocalize only as a police siren. One girl liked to imitate animal sounds and went way beyond barking: she quacked and mooed and snorted and trumpeted like an elephant. Hanna hadn't figured out—yet—how she was going to get thrown out. Maybe Marie-Anne would come up with something.

She had a setback with Mommy, too. She spotted a rosy bruise on Mommy's forearm where a needle had poked her, sucking out her blood. Hoping it was terribly painful, she pressed on it, but Mommy just slapped her hand away. She told Daddy at supper what they'd found—hadn't found— lurking in her blood.

"No real inflammation, so that's the good news."

"So the shots are still working?"

"Guess so. Dr. Stefanski said I was healing well, everything looked good. We couldn't really figure out why the Imodium isn't helping anymore. Told him I've been a little stressed, could be that. But there are other things to try—he wrote me a prescription for Lomotil. Picked it up before I got Hanna." She put a tablet on her tongue and swallowed. "I can experiment with how many to take, but should know soon enough if it helps."

Hanna scowled. The new pill was tiny and solid and couldn't be opened and dumped out. And it sounded like Mommy's insides weren't going to rot away; she seemed in little danger of dying. Hanna cursed her missed opportunity to fill the capsules with poison. She couldn't let her make another move—or worse, win another round.

"How about you, squirrely girl, how was school?"

She made a sound in her nose and pushed away her plate. Daddy looked at Mommy.

"Ms. Atwood assured me that they're really getting to know her, what she likes and doesn't like. They all find her to be very teachable."

"That's because my squirrel's so smart." He reached out to tousle her hair.

"She is smart." Mommy seemed happier. Hanna didn't like it.

"Did you start your project?"

"Not really. Well, sort of. Just a few simple sketches."

"That's a good start, right?"

"I'm not sure what direction to take yet, like, if I should work around a theme."

They talked back and forth like everything were normal. Like Mommy had been forgiven for being so bad bad bad. Hanna squirmed, twisting in her chair. She put her feet on the seat and pressed against the table with her knees.

"Are you finished? You know how to ask," Mommy said.

Rules. Everyone and their stupid rules. She put her feet against the edge of the table and made more noises in her nose. She liked the way it vibrated and sometimes she wished her nose had lips and then she'd talk that way. Daddy grabbed her feet and pushed them down.

"No feet on the table, you know better. You want to be excused? Listen to Mommy."

She hated him for a second. But just a second, because Mommy could cast spells, too, and sometimes she made Daddy do things he didn't want to do. But she had a thought—one she got from Mommy and her sketchbook, because she understood that's where you put ideas that weren't fully formed yet. So she got up and stood obediently beside her chair.

"Thank you," said Mommy. "Yes, you may be excused."

She crawled up the stairs like a tiger, stayed on all fours, and prowled to her room. Once there, she poked her head out to make sure no one had followed her and quietly shut the door.

One of her cubbies was for different kinds of paper. Construction paper. Origami paper. Tracing paper. Graph paper. She liked the perfect tablets almost as much as her pens and pencils. But just as she had sacrificed two pencils and a crayon for the sake of her now-murdered Under-SlumberBumbleBeast, she was ready to surrender one of her notebooks. She picked the one that was very much like Mommy's, with a big spiral on the edge and thick pages, and dug through her purple backpack until she found her yellow pencil case. She selected the pencil with the sharpest point.

In case anyone found her project—like snooping Mommy—she decided to make it in code, like Egyptian hieroglyphs. Then nobody could ruin her idea. The page would look like random marks and no one would know what they really were: ways to hurt Mommy.

First she drew three small, wobbly circles. That stood for her medication. It worked really fast last time, but she didn't know how to tamper with the new pills. She drew three dots after the circles which meant: think about it.

She crossed one leg over the other and gazed up at the ceiling. What else could she do? Maybe Marie-Anne had some ideas . . .

Sometimes Mommy sewed a button on a shirt, or a hem on Hanna's skirts if they started out too long. Sewing looked easy. It would be very nice to sew Mommy's mouth shut, but there was the problem of getting her to stay still through the procedure. She drew a one-inch line that represented a needle, and next to it a pair of *x*'s that symbolized Mommy's eyes—unconscious? asleep? And then three more think-about-it dots.

While it was very easy to think of ways to harm her, it was very hard—even with Marie-Anne's help—to think of things that wouldn't immediately give her away. Mommy would see if she pushed her down the stairs, but Hanna didn't think the fall would do much more than annoy her. She could stab her in the heart while she slept and then carefully wipe her fingerprints off the knife. In the TV show she'd watched with a hapless babysitter, the murderer was caught in the end. She'd tried over the years to think about how it could have been done better, without leaving any clues behind. Worth thinking about.

She drew what looked like an arrow to represent a knife. Next to it she made what looked like a capital

T—which was code for a hammer. She could hit her in the head with a hammer. It might be hard to break through her skull so she'd probably have to hit her hard, a few times. It sounded kind of messy, but she left it on the list as a possibility.

Maybe if Mommy fell asleep while taking a bath she could drop something in the water and electrocute her. To do that, it would have to be something that plugged into the wall. A hair dryer maybe? She'd have to turn it on right before she dropped it in, because the noise would alert Mommy to the danger. Still not a great idea, but she drew a series of wavy lines to represent both the bathwater and the hair dryer.

Though Mommy usually used vinegar to clean, there were more-toxic products in the house—like what she used in the toilets. If she could find a way to put it in her food it would make Mommy sick really fast . . . but even Marie-Anne didn't know how to cook, and what would they mix the poison with so Mommy wouldn't taste it right away? And could she keep Daddy from trying it?

Still, she put a frowny face on her list—which looked sort of like Mr. Yuk. There were green Mr. Yuk stickers on products all around the house—nail polish remover and dishwasher detergent and lots of stuff that lived under and around sinks. She hadn't been tempted for many, many years to drink from any of these containers, but Mommy and Daddy still had so many stickers that they put them on everything. She'd have to look for them and get more ideas.

Daddy's heavy footfalls grew louder as he came up the

stairs, so she quickly stuffed everything into her backpack. He poked his head into her room.

"*Lilla gumman?* Read before bedtime?"

She nodded in eager agreement and fished out clean pajamas from beneath her pillow.

"Want to pick something out?"

She blinked at him, confused by his confusion, and pointed at the shelf above her bed.

"I thought you might not want to keep reading that if you were still sad about your UnderSlumberBumble-Beast."

Her pajama top was covered with rocket ships and she held it against her chest with her chin, considering Daddy's words. She was sad, but she wasn't without hope that she could still have an under-the-bed friend. She point-pointy-pointed to her book again.

"Sure? You have lots of other books, with lots of other fun characters?"

She snatched up the book and thrust it out to Daddy. "Okay, then." He sighed, and it bothered her that he wasn't entirely pleased.

She whipped her shirt off over her head and replaced it with the rocket ships, then wriggled out of her leggings and jumped into the rocket ship pants. She liked nightclothes much better than day clothes because they were always comfy and patterned with things she liked: planets and ladybugs and hedgehogs and sea horses.

They were at the part in the story where the little girl starts to hear noises in the basement. The little girl also had a bad Mommy, who made her clear out all the "junk" from under her bed, but instead of throwing it away, the girl stashed it all in the basement. After that, things were quiet under her bed, but Hanna already knew what the girl was going to discover when she crept down the dark stairs. Not spiders or monsters, but new configurations of friends called CraggyCellarDragonDwellers. Lollipop Hand was there among them, better than ever, though he'd outgrown his sky-blue knitted shorts.

She snuggled under the covers so Daddy would finish reading the story.

Ms. Atwood held her hand and dragged her down the hallway. Hanna tried to pull away, tried to pry her fingers off, screeching like a wounded bird.

"You were told many times. No Google searches when you're supposed to be doing your work."

The other kids liked working on the computers because everything looked like an animated game. But Hanna didn't like how the rabbits and frogs bounced around on the screen. She closed the program and tried to do some research on ways to start fires. Usually she liked the Quiet Room, but the research was important: Marie-Anne had a great idea.

"Listen." Ms. Atwood stopped. She put her hands on her knees so they were face to face. "I know you need your breaks throughout the day. I know you like your quiet time. We'll have to come up with a way—you and me—to signal when you want some alone time. We don't need you acting out or doing things you're not supposed to be doing. We can behave like civilized people and find a way so you, in your way, can say 'Hey, Ms. A, I need a little break.' So let's work on that."

Hanna listened to her very intently. She couldn't deny it was a reasonable suggestion.

"I think we have a deal." Ms. Atwood ushered her into the Quiet Room, where the aide, Kenzie, was sitting on a pillow beside the boy with the red helmet.

"Room for another one?" Ms. Atwood asked.

"Of course, Hanna and I are getting to be old friends."

Hanna didn't share her opinion. To her, Kenzie was a mere fixture of the room, of significantly less interest than the shelves full of books or the big pillows. At best she registered with the ugly rug or the unfortunately bright overhead light. A female blob in tight jeans with sticky-out hair.

"See you in a bit."

Hanna didn't wave. She got a book off the shelf, right where she had left it, her bookmark still in place.

"This is Ian," Kenzie said. "Ian, this is Hanna."

Neither of the children looked at each other. Ian was sitting on her favorite pillow—the red one. She moved the blue one so it was far away from him and sat on it as if on a nest. She opened the book to where she'd left off and tried to read, but she was curious about Ian. He distracted her. In her peripheral vision, he ran his hand over the wall, touching the knobbly, paint-covered cinder blocks. Then he tapped his helmet against it a few times. He must have liked something about it—the way it felt or the way it sounded—because he smiled. But Kenzie wasn't amused. She knelt beside him.

"Hey. Ian?" He stopped tapping his helmet against the wall and looked at her. "None of that, that's not a good use of your energy. Are you ready to go back to class?" He shook his head. "Do you want something to read?"

Ian glanced at Hanna, sitting so perfectly with her open book. He opened his mouth in a wide grin, revealing gummy walls with crooked tombstone teeth, and nodded. Kenzie went to the bookcase. "Come and help me pick something. What do you want to read?"

The boy pointed toward the open door. Hanna couldn't help looking toward the hallway beyond the door, trying to discern what was of so much interest to him. Helmet Head was a fascinating specimen.

"What's out there?" Kenzie asked.

"My book my book my book!"

"Did you leave your book on your desk?"

"My desk my desk my book."

Kenzie knelt to address both of them. "Okay, I'm gonna leave you two for *one* minute. One minute equals sixty seconds. And then I'll be right back with Ian's book. And you'll both be on your best behavior?" Ian nodded happily. Hanna just stared at her. "Okay, I'll be right back."

Hanna turned to Helmet Head the second the aide was gone. He pointed at her.

"Hanna Hanna Hanna."

She barked in reply and he dropped his hand. She got on her hands and knees and faced him, snarling. Wide-eyed with fear, he pushed himself back against the wall. And started banging his helmet.

An idea came to her and she smiled at him for a moment. Then she inched forward and unfastened his helmet. She lifted it gently off his head and tossed it aside. His face fluttered with confusion.

She sat back on her haunches and studied him. Then she unleashed the dog—snarling and yapping. Helmetless Head opened his mouth but no scream emerged. He knocked his bare head against the wall. Pleased with his response, Hanna lurched forward, growling, lashing out as if to bite him.

The boy whimpered in terror, bashing his bare head against the wall.

As the dog became more and more threatening, gnashing its teeth within inches of his face, the boy worked himself into a frenzy. Slobber drooled from his mouth and he struck his head against the wall again and again.

Hanna glanced toward the open door, unsure of how much time she had. Satisfied as Helmetless Head continued thrashing and moaning, she returned to her pillow and crossed her legs. She was just opening her book when Kenzie raced back in.

"I heard a dog . . . !" She flung Ian's book aside and scrambled to him, pulling him away from the wall. "Peter!" she called toward the hallway. "Peter!"

She took Ian onto her lap and gingerly examined his head. She glanced at the smears of blood on the wall, at the helmet near her feet. At Hanna.

"What happened? I heard barking!"

Hanna continued reading her book. Another young aide rushed to the doorway. Peter quickly scanned the scene: the thrashing boy in Kenzie's arms; the blood trickling down the side of his head, dribbling along his jawline; red smudges on the wall.

"Call nine-one-one and get Mr. G!"

Peter dug a phone out of his pocket and darted back out.

"What did you do?" Kenzie asked Hanna.

She calmly turned to the next page and pretended she was sitting atop a giant mushroom, in the middle of a magical forest.

SUZETTE

SHE COULDN'T EVEN look at her husband, so she stayed focused on Mr. G, who—no-nonsense, no longer so friendly—had introduced himself to Alex as Dr. Gutierrez moments before. He still wore the black eye patch. Alex sat like a wary lion about to rise and annihilate a spindly-legged gazelle.

That they were both called was an indication of the severity of the situation.

"I think you need to state some substantive facts before you claim that my child is beyond hope," roared the lion.

"I didn't say—" Mr. G flicked his eyes—eye—toward Suzette, who couldn't muster an emotion beyond fear.

What had Hanna done now? Could they get a second chance?

"I said we weren't the right school for her. A boy was injured while the two of them were in a room together. He struck his head against a wall, repeatedly, and we've known Ian for three years . . ." He stopped himself and took a slow breath. When he resumed speaking his voice was less steely. "Three years. And he has never removed his helmet on his own. It's like his superhero costume, he would never take it off. And Kenzie—Ms. Johnson—said she heard Hanna, barking like a savage dog, when she was coming down the hall."

She glanced at Alex. A vindictive part of her rejoiced: he'd have to believe her now. Their daughter was capable of savagery; other people had witnessed it. The beast of prey in him retreated a little.

"Why were they alone?" he asked.

Mr. G considered his folded hands. "That's something we'll have to address internally. It was just for a moment, and we'd seen no signs previously that Hanna was violent—"

"She's not."

"—or might provoke violence. This was very unexpected, for all of us."

Suzette said, "We still don't know, not really . . ." Both men turned to her. "She might not have meant to hurt him, maybe she was curious about his helmet. She might not have known what would happen if he didn't have it."

"Still can't prove she even did it," Alex muttered.

Mr. G grew even more serious. "Mrs. Jensen . . . Knowing the intelligence of your daughter, it seems likely that she was trying to find out. That she understood on some level—between the removal of the helmet and the barking—that she was provoking a reaction. Ian needed stitches. He's still at the hospital, with a possible concussion."

"I'm sorry." She felt badly for the injured boy but worse for herself. She feared Hanna was saving the real anger for her. *Hide the scissors.*

"So . . . She needs more supervision. She shouldn't be left alone. This isn't entirely her fault."

"I agree," Mr. G said to Alex. "And we will likely alter staff policy because of this incident. But a child has been hurt. And your daughter . . ."

Alex was already shaking his head. But Suzette knew it was too late to try to defend Hanna. She shook her head, too, desperate to stop Mr. G from announcing his conclusion.

". . . requires a type of therapy and supervision that we can't provide. We know kids lash out sometimes, spur of the moment, but we're not prepared to manage children with severe . . . This was a calculated incident and I don't think we can give your daughter the help she needs."

Alex burst from his chair. "She isn't violent! You make it sound like she's a psychopath."

"Please, Dr. Gutierrez. She was doing so well here." The thought of having her home, all day every day . . . Suzette couldn't, not anymore. Her nerves were singed, her patience obliterated. "We've started taking her to a therapist—this is something we can work on. Please!"

"I'm glad, that's good, I'm glad Hanna is getting help. I know how incredibly difficult it is for parents, with a child who has violent outbursts. And I'm sorry, because I know it limits where—"

"Please, I can't—"

"No." Alex held out his arm, stopping Suzette. "We're not going to beg—to keep our child in a school that blames her, that thinks she's a monster. Maybe you need to train your staff better."

"We just can't risk putting other children in danger—"

Alex stormed out. Suzette couldn't erase her pleading look when she turned back to Mr. G.

"I'm sorry," he said. And the matter was finished.

Alex wouldn't even wait for Hanna, who scampered behind him down the hallway trying to catch up. He marched toward the exit. Suzette slunk after them, face toward the ground, shame seeping through her pores. Ms. Atwood intercepted her.

"Mrs. Jensen? I'm sorry this didn't work out. I know it's hard, but Hanna really is a special girl."

"Thank you." It moved her almost to tears that Hanna's primary teacher seemed sad to see her go.

"Don't give up, it'll work out."

Suzette thanked her again and walked out of the school hugging her arms across her body, relieved that it was too early for other parents to witness them walking the plank.

Alex waited on the sidewalk, coiled tight with fury. Hanna jumped over the cracks in the pavement, humming, as her big backpack flopped against her.

"She did it again," she said, shaking her head at her happy, victorious child. She was almost impressed by Hanna's genius, if only it weren't so devious. Suzette couldn't dislodge the unease that it was part of Hanna's master plan, that the girl was plotting something bigger. Something worse.

"I don't want to talk about it."

"Now you see her manipulative behavior. This is what she does to get out of school. We finally found a good—"

"This was not a good school—this was not the right school for her." She cowered, not expecting Alex to direct his anger toward her. Hanna stopped jumping and watched them. "This is what she's learned being in a school with other kids who can't behave properly—she learned this here."

"She's done variations of this at every school, at home—Alex, for fuck's sake, how can you be in such denial?"

"I'm done. This was a mistake." He strode off toward his car. Hanna chased after him. To Suzette's shock, he turned on Hanna. "Go home with your mother."

Hanna stopped, lost in an empty space between her two parents.

"She wants to go with you, I think it's better—"

"Take her home, I'm going to the gym." He slammed his car door and started the engine.

"Come on, Hanna." The girl looked back at her father, watched him pull out and drive away. When she turned to Suzette, her face bore a bewildered expression. Suzette fought the urge to taunt her: no pet names or special coddling from Daddy. Unlike after the Green Hill Academy expulsion, Suzette wanted Alex to stew in it this time, to really think about what the professionals were saying about his child. Hanna chewed on her lip, her face an open wound as Alex's car disappeared. Even in Suzette's worst moments she didn't like to see Hanna in pain, though she knew Alex's rejection of her wouldn't last. "Daddy's upset. He'll come home when he's feeling better. Come on."

She opened the back door for her, and Hanna traipsed over. She threw her backpack into the car.

"You did this to yourself. I know you didn't want to come here. And now you won't be back. And now your parents are all pissed off, so."

Hanna buckled herself into her car seat, and Suzette closed her door. As they drove home, she monitored Hanna in the rearview mirror, half expecting Marie-Anne to make an appearance, but she only tapped the window with her finger.

"Is this your doing, Marie-Anne?" Suzette couldn't stop herself from trying to needle her. "I really wish you'd leave my daughter alone. Hanna doesn't like it when her Daddy's mad at her, and now he's really mad."

Hanna's eyes met hers in the mirror. They burned with hatred. "You know nothing."

In a cloying voice, Suzette dug in deeper. "I know Hanna's daddy wants a good little girl—a good little girl who goes to school and grows up like a normal person. He wants to be proud of all her accomplishments. It's hard when the girl won't do anything—color a picture, or write a story, or say a single word to her favorite person. It hurts Daddy's feelings, that Hanna's talking to me and not him."

Hanna bared her teeth, grunting out screams. She kicked at the seat in front of her.

"Daddy pretends to himself that Hanna's still a little girl, a baby. The picture he keeps of her on his desk at work is so old, from when Hanna was three—back when we still thought she might turn out all right. Hanna's been a disappointment and Marie-Anne, you are not helping. If Hanna were as smart as I think she is, she'd send Marie-Anne away."

Hanna pounded the back of the passenger seat with her Mary-Janed feet. Suzette let her; it was satisfying to know Hanna could be provoked, and the seat was a harmless outlet for her aggression. Maybe the girl's outbursts could be manipulated, and Suzette could get her to reveal her true self to Alex.

Periodically, she came over to the glass wall to check on her. Since getting home, Hanna had been outside abusing her Hula-Hoop. Sometimes she used the palm of her hand to keep it upright as she rolled it around the yard. Sometimes she tested its ability to bounce and threw it against the ground from various angles. She invented a game that seemed to involve trying to get the hedge to play catch with her. She tossed it at the thin branches and sometimes they held on for a few seconds before the hoop fell off.

Suzette remembered being alone as a child. She'd longed for a sister, someone to play with—someone to understand what she endured as the daughter of a depressed mother. When she was Hanna's age she had an alter ego named Danielle. Sometimes when she played a board game behind the closed door of her room, she controlled two colors at once—red for herself, blue for Danielle—leaping from one side to the other, pretending she wasn't alone. Oh God. She couldn't bury the empathy after it surfaced.

She inched open the door. Arms crossed, she poked her head and shoulder out, ready to dart back in if Hanna made any sort of threatening move.

"I'll play catch with you if you want."

Hanna continued playing by herself.

"I can blow up the beach ball." That seemed like the least dangerous toy to offer her; she certainly didn't want her daughter hurling a Hula-Hoop toward her face.

Hanna abruptly stopped playing. She glared at her mother for a second, then very deliberately scratched her nose with her middle finger.

"Suit yourself." She ducked back in and shut the door.

It was hard to imagine sitting at the dinner table that night, pretending everything was fine. If Alex was still angry, their usual light chatter might be reduced to smoke signals sent from warring continents. Hanna would sit there, watching them, trying to decipher the puffs of smoke. How much had her young brain already misconstrued? Observing, absorbing. Warping, twisting. Drawing conclusions about everything they did. But there was nothing Suzette could do to fix it—her, him, anything—so she started making supper. Her stomach was feeling a bit better but she wanted mashed potatoes. The peeling and chopping would help ameliorate her volatile mood. And though Alex shouldn't have bolted, maybe he'd come home restored after his workout. Maybe they could talk about their options later without him jumping to Hanna's defense. Or running out of the room.

* * *

His hair was still wet from his post-workout shower. He leaned against the counter, watching the pot of potatoes bubble. Suzette flipped on the oven light and cracked the door to check the breadcrumb-Parmesan topping on the chicken cutlets. Out of the corner of her eye, she spotted Hanna on the other side of the glass door, watching them.

"Sorry," Alex said, halfhearted and reluctant.

"I can't fix this myself." She closed the oven door harder than she'd intended, letting it punctuate her despairing mood.

He noticed Hanna and waved her in. She slipped inside and stood across the room, wary. Her caution agonized her father. His posture drooped and his eyebrows flagged his regret. He moved away from the counter, beckoning her with his hands. The scene reminded Suzette of a bad commercial uniting two lost lovers.

"Oh, *lilla gumman,* I'm not mad."

And then Hanna sprang into motion and the sappy music rose. Alex took her in his arms.

"I'm sorry, sweetheart, I'm not mad at you. I was mad at the school, and mad that this happened . . ." He glanced at Suzette, his face more apologetic than his words to her had been.

Hanna clung to his neck and he held her like he'd never let go. "Hanna, look—look at me." He carried her around, talking to her like she was a much younger, much more innocent girl. "You've been misbehaving. And Mommy and I . . . We have to get to the bottom of this. It's not good for you, you need to be in school. I love you—we love you—so much."

Hanna tried to wrap her arms around his neck again, but he resisted. He wasn't finished. "This is serious. You're a big girl now. And we have to figure out what's going on. Okay?"

For a minute, Hanna just sat stiffly as he held her, her face blank. She glanced at Suzette, who watched from the kitchen. Then her expression turned hard and she pushed at Alex, eager to get away from him. He set her down and she ran off and thundered up the stairs.

It was Suzette's second small victory of the day: witnesses to Hanna's savagery followed by the limits of her tolerance for Alex.

She drained the potatoes as he came over, rubbing his beard and groaning.

"I'm glad we have Beatrix. To talk to. She has an appointment on Monday?"

"Yep, same time."

"Look, this doesn't mean . . . I'm still not convinced she meant to hurt that boy. But . . . I know they were doing well with her. I shouldn't have said that about the school."

"It's not just me." She smashed the potatoes. Soft skyscrapers oozed through the masher.

"Why does she do that? Bark like a dog?"

She felt him at her side, needy. She abandoned her work and turned, taking his hands. "I don't know. But she does. And she does other things too. You can't help—her, me—if you don't accept that it's actually happening."

"It's hard . . . She's not a savage," he said, tears in his eyes. "She's a little girl, our little girl."

"Honey, I know . . ."

He embraced her and she felt him trembling. Her shame returned. It was a wretched milestone, his realization that something was wrong with Hanna. He rested his head atop hers, and she gripped him tightly in her arms so he would know she was there for him. Would always be there for him.

"We'll fix this," he said. "We'll help her. Beatrix will help us."

She heard him trying to convince himself. She couldn't tell him how the day had turned her thoughts toward the apocalyptic. The walls were crumbling. Hanna would shake the house until Suzette lay beneath the rubble, buried alive. And the word *psychopath* had come from Alex's own lips, like maybe it was a thought he harbored, even as he defended his daughter. Maybe it was too late. Maybe no one could help Hanna. But what did that mean—for any of them?

She stirred, troubled in her half-consciousness that it was too early. Darkness lingered in the world beyond their room, but Alex's lamp was on.

"What's going on?"

He came and sat on her side of the bed, knotting his tie.

"Sorry, you were already asleep last night when I got the email. WTAE's coming in this morning to do a story about us."

Suzette forced herself to sit up, blinking in an effort to get her vision in focus.

"Today?"

"Yes. They'll run it tonight."

"What kind of story?"

"Not completely sure. We sent out press releases about what's being called the Skinny Building. But it sounded like they were interested in more than that. The evolution of green materials, the future of architecture."

"Sounds ambitious for the local news." Alex and his partner, Matt, had been interviewed by many local outlets—press, radio, TV—over the years. "Why's it always have to be so early?"

"They're a spontaneous bunch. Deadlines, I guess. Go back to sleep." He kissed her cheek.

"I was hoping you'd stay home today."

Alex tucked in his shirt as he went to the closet to retrieve his suit jacket.

"Did you hear me? Honey?"

He emerged from the closet, tugging on the lapels to adjust the jacket. "Because of Hanna?" he asked as he wandered back over to the bed.

She touched the fine material of his suit. "I'm just worried. I'm not her favorite person."

"Well, if you're right—and I suspect you are—she'll probably be in a good mood. Happy she doesn't have to go to school."

"Maybe. You look smashing."

He grinned and planted a kiss on her hair. "Go back to sleep."

She lay back on the bed, groggy. "Come home after?"

"Call me and let me know what's going on. I'm not sure how long the crew will be there."

"I can get up and make you coffee." She meant it, even though her eyes were already closing.

"*Jag älskar dig,*" he said, switching off his lamp.

She mumbled something that might have been half Swedish, half English in reply. The door opened, closed, as she rolled onto her side and tucked the pillow over her shoulder. A little more sleep. She needed it, deserved it. Especially if she was to survive the day alone with Hanna.

HANNA

DADDY LEFT EARLY early. Hanna had set the soft chimes of her alarm, because she and Marie-Anne had some thinking to do before Mommy woke up, and she heard him going down the stairs. It was a tremendously good sign and bode well for her plan: it might take time for Mommy to bleed to death. Hanna saw more and more how Daddy was teeter-tottering. She'd always been able to count on him to be there for her, to take her side even if he had to pretend with Mommy. But things were changing, she could tell (and Marie-Anne agreed). He was asking questions. He was looking at her with ghost eyes instead of sparkly ones. Mommy was getting under his skin, burrowing like an icky worm. Maybe she would munch-munch on his brain until he couldn't think or move.

Hanna hoped she was strong enough to do what needed to be done. Helmetless Head was a productive exercise, beyond getting her kicked out of Pissdale. Skulls were hard; a lot of force would be required to crack one open. It would expose her, but when Daddy returned to his unspelled self, his eyes bright and full of love, he would understand why she had to do it. Why Mommy had to die so he could be saved. In the end, he'd thank her.

Not wanting any of her favorite pajamas or clothing to get stained with blood, she put on a dress she didn't like. She considered the shoes in her closet—she needed something to protect her feet. Her Mary Janes and Keds were down by the front door, and as much as she liked her ladybug rain boots they'd be hard to tiptoe in. Still in her socks, she slipped out into the hallway and monitored Daddy's movements in the kitchen. His coffee was already smelling up the whole house. She heard the rising tone, glurg-glurg-glurg, as he filled his mug, and saw him pass beneath her on his way to the door. She waited a second after he left to make sure he was really gone and not coming back for something he forgot. Then she made her way downstairs.

After putting on her sneakers—and hoping they wouldn't squeak—she went to the utility drawer and rummaged around. Daddy always kept a few basic tools there: a couple of screwdrivers, an adjustable wrench (which she liked to play with, tightening the clampy parts around her finger), and—there it was—a big claw hammer. It was heavy—heavy enough that if she dropped it on her foot, even with shoes on, she'd probably break a toe. She carried it back upstairs in both hands, holding it as she would in the decisive moment before she smashed it into Mommy's head. That was Part Two of her plan, because she wasn't confident that she could knock Mommy unconscious with one blow, and she didn't want Mommy wresting the weapon from her.

She left the hammer just outside of Mommy's bedroom door, then snuck back to her own room to get what she needed for Part One. It was a very funny plan, really. But Part One might just make her go *Aaaaaahhh! Ooohhhhhh!* and flop around and whack her chin on the floor, maybe knocking out a tooth or biting through her lip. If Hanna was very very lucky, Mommy would knock herself unconscious, bonking her head on the bedside shelf. And if that happened, Part Two would be so much easier—she'd just have to burst in and whack away with the hammer until her brains started to ooze out.

Save Daddy. Even if it didn't go the easy way, even if she had to look Mommy in the eye and hit her again and again, she had to save Daddy.

Mommy was breathing loudly when Hanna cracked open the door: not quite a snore, but a throaty sound. It was enough to cover the pit-pat of her shoes as she crept over to Mommy's side of the bed. Marie-Anne kept an eye on Mommy as Hanna executed Part One. When Mommy started moving, Hanna hunkered down, hiding. But she was just turning over. Mommy let out a little fart and Hanna almost lost it. She laughed silently and got back to work.

When she was finished, she snuck back out and shut the door so so softly. She took up her position outside Mommy's room, hammer in hand, ready to charge in. She wasn't sure what time it was, but Mommy, even though she slept later than everyone else, was usually up by 7:15.

Time dripped by and Hanna feared she might die of boredom. Or curl up beside the hammer and fall asleep, missing her cue. She poked her head in a couple of times and didn't even try that hard to keep from making

SUZETTE

SOMETIMES SLEEP WAS a commanding presence, a magician in a heavy cloak. Sometimes the sleeper was the cloak itself, soft as water, heavy as the ocean's depths. There was no stirring from such a sleep. Not yet.

After what felt like hours in a coma of ecstasy, intermittently aware of the depth of her trance, Suzette started to become aware of the light, brightening the room. On the verge of opening her eyes—

A heavy crash. Then the shattering of glass.

Fully awakened, she readied herself, alert to the possibility of her daughter in peril. Then it came—a piercing cry, followed by sobs. She could already see it: Hanna alone in the kitchen, trying to get something from the cabinet. On a chair. The chair wobbled under her shifting weight, sending the bowl, the chair, her daughter sprawling to the floor.

Suzette tossed back the sheet. Did she hit her head? Was she bleeding? She threw her legs over the bed. Stood.

What . . .

Pain shattered her vision. Cut off her daughter's cries. She collapsed back onto the mattress. Unable to fully decipher what was wrong.

She lifted her left foot, the one that hurt the most. Through the blurry vision of her tears she saw what looked like bright M&Ms stuck to her foot. Her heel was full of them—green, yellow, orange, red. But pieces of candy wouldn't hurt. There were some on the ball of her foot, too. She gently lowered it and lifted the right one. More colorful dots of pain, not as deep as the left. She blinked away her tears, the pain still a shock wedged in her throat.

Something dotted the floor. In a tight cluster beside her bed. A welcome mat of torture.

She leaned over, cautious of her balance and her feet that couldn't bear any weight, and picked up one of the shiny objects. But it was shiny only on one side—the pointy side. The other was a pretty shade of cobalt blue. Thumbtacks. The thumbtacks they'd purchased for Hanna from the office supply store.

Hanna.

Devilish bitch.

Suzette froze, listening. The crying had stopped. Were those footsteps? Hanna hurrying up the stairs? She eased herself back onto the deeper safety of the bed and took a second quick look at her feet. More than a dozen thumbtacks in her left foot, and the ones in her heel went all the way in. Her right foot hadn't taken as much weight and they were only halfway in. But standing or walking . . . Droplets of blood trailed around the colorful tack heads and Suzette fell against the bed, suddenly nauseated.

She reached for her phone, sensing Hanna on the other side of the door.

Hanna threw it open.

For a moment they each stared at the other, taking in their respective weapons: Hanna double-fisting a hammer, Suzette with her cellphone.

"What are you doing?" She could almost see the intention in her daughter's face, a murderous gleam. But Hanna took only one step into the room.

The girl's eyes widened as she stared at the buttons of color on the soles of her mother's feet. For a second there was only silence, and the beating of their two scared hearts. A ripple of uncertainty softened Hanna's stance. Seeing her daughter's resolve waver, Suzette lurched up onto her elbows.

"You fucking little monster!" She would have thrown something. A knife. A grenade. "You fucking little—I'm calling the police!"

Hanna abruptly stepped out and yanked the door shut; it reverberated like gunfire. Suzette lost all her energy. She flopped onto her back and wept.

Her feet throbbed and her soul churned. Defeat spread through her limbs. Though she'd anticipated some form of retaliation, the manner of it made her skin prickle. Her young daughter clenching a hammer. Had Hanna thought of killing her then, while they shopped for school supplies? Suzette felt defenseless, but instead of calling the police, she speed-dialed Alex's number.

He didn't pick up. Maybe the news crew was still there, making him and his friends feel adulated and important, clever and conscientious. She called the main number, knowing Fiona, their office manager, would answer it.

While it rang she tried to remember when she'd last had a tetanus shot. She'd have to call her doctor.

"Jensen and Goldstein."

"Fiona, this is Suzette."

"Hi—" The manager's voice turned from professional to bubbly.

"I need Alex, it's an emergency."

From bubbly to scared. "Hold on. Hold on, I'll try to get him."

"Don't . . . !" Suzette held back a scream as Fiona put her on hold.

She pushed herself up so she was leaning against the headboard. While on hold, she considered taking a photo of her injured feet—proof, should Alex need it. But she changed her mind; the damage would be enough evidence. And she didn't need to memorialize the event. It wasn't as if she were going to share the depths of her daughter's savagery on Instagram. The thumbtacks had to come out; she couldn't put it off forever. There was nothing handy to use to sop up the blood—she couldn't even reach the box of Kleenex on Alex's side and it wasn't worth the effort to shimmy over. She stripped the pillowcase off his pillow and gently dabbed at her left foot.

Taking a few deep breaths to steel herself, she gripped a yellow-headed tack between her thumb and middle finger. She pretended she was giving herself an injection and made herself relax. Then she pulled.

It popped right out. After a quick bloom of new pain, that one tiny spot felt a little better. She pressed the pillowcase against the pinprick to stanch the blood. Just as she was readying to yank out a green-headed tack, Alex came on the line.

"Suzette?" His voiced sounded taut, like he was bracing himself for whatever she was about to unleash.

She started crying again. "Come home—she hurt me, Alex. Thumbtacks on the floor, I'm bleeding all over the place. I can't be alone with—"

"Thumbtacks?"

"In my feet. They were beside the bed. She came into my room with a hammer! I can't walk!"

"I'll call nine-one-one."

"I could've done that myself—I need *you*."

"I'm coming, I'll be right—"

"And get bandages, and gauze and Neosporin—I can't get to the bathroom—"

"I'll stop on my way—twenty minutes, I'll be right there."

He hung up, and she tossed the phone aside. Crying made her body tighten, which made her feet hurt even worse. She wanted a drink of water, but had to settle for a few sticky swallows of saliva. Still, it helped her regain some sense of control. Removing the first tack hadn't been as bad as she thought it would be. But she had twenty-odd more to pull. She told herself it would feel better, so much better, when they were out.

But first. She couldn't stop eyeing the door. What if Hanna got her nerve back and tried to finish what she started?

The pain and tacks would have to wait.

She draped the pillowcase around her neck. Once she got to the door, she'd stay there until Alex came. She whistled her breath in and out a few times, a gladiator readying for battle. Using her forearms, she maneuvered herself to the end of the bed—away from the tacks that still littered the floor. Slithering down, she soon found herself in a position like a push-up, with her hands on the floor and her feet on the bed. She didn't have the upper body strength to hold the posture for long, so she tried to lower only her knee to the ground. It was too far and she collapsed. Her feet bent instinctively, and she cried out as her left big toe broke her fall.

But at least she was off the bed. She scrabbled for the door on her hands and knees, reached up, and flicked the lock.

With her legs outstretched and her back against the wall, she took a moment to breathe. Her feet pulsed and she wondered if she made the wrong call: she could have dialed 9-1-1. No. She didn't want other people in the house. Witnessing her misery. Questioning her deplorable parenting. How had her child ended up like this? Maybe they'd take Hanna away. Foster care? A prison? Were there prisons for mute first graders?

"I'll get my house in order," she said, her voice hoarse with emotion. "I'll get my house in order."

She took the pillowcase from around her neck, ready to use it as a giant bandage, and started pulling out the thumbtacks. One by one. Quickly. Angrily. It hurt less that way.

* * *

She heard him thundering up the stairs, calling her name. It struck her that he still had his shoes on. Swedish State of Emergency. She giggled.

"Hold on," she said as he jiggled the knob, pushing against the door.

He fell to his knees beside her the minute she unlocked the door. Her feet were bundled together in the pillowcase, soaking up the blood.

"What happened?"

"Where is she?" Suzette countered.

"I didn't see her—I came right up."

She took the Rite Aid bag from his hand and pointed—toward the blood droplets on the bed, the scattered thumbtacks on the floor beside it, her feet. His face absorbed a terrible story as he took it all in—twice, three times—trying to edit or reconfigure the obvious.

"Hanna couldn't . . ."

"And when she was sure I stepped on them, she came in holding a hammer."

"But why . . . ? Why would she do this?" He sounded more baffled than angry.

Suzette wanted to grab his shoulders and shake him, but she couldn't spare the energy. "Something's wrong with her. Worse than . . ."

"Hanna?" Alex called, turning to face the hallway. "Can you come here, please?"

"Wait, just . . ." She reached down and unwrapped her feet. They were puffy and peppered with tiny congealing scabs. Alex and Suzette winced in unison.

"Should we go to Urgent Care?"

"They're shallow, I'll be fine."

She let him tend to her feet. He dabbed on the Neosporin, smearing it gently with a sterile pad. Tears flickered in his eyes. He sniffled, taking a second to wipe his cheeks with the back of his hand. He lay the pads on the bottom of each foot, securing them by wrapping gauze around and around. Suzette tore off strips of the medical paper tape and handed them to him.

"You're very good at this," she said.

Silently, he lifted her in his arms and carried her to the comfy chair that looked out over their street. Unable to speak, he balled the bloody sterile pads in his hands and gathered the thumbtacks that had been in her feet. He knelt beside the bed to gather the rest of them.

"Careful," she said.

He headed for the bathroom. She heard the tinny rain of thumbtacks as Alex dropped them into the mesh garbage bin beneath the sink.

"Is there a mess in the kitchen?" she asked when he came back in.

"I didn't even look." He stripped the sheets from the bed. "You're not going to be able to walk. Maybe for a few days. Can Beatrix come? Here? Maybe this afternoon?"

"I'll call her. My phone's . . ."

He found it among the bedding and carried it over to her. Shame pulled his eyes downward and he wouldn't make eye contact with her. He hurried back to the bed and bundled the sheets together.

"Should probably just throw them away. Stained . . ."

"Alex . . . Alex . . ." She reached out her hand.

He came to her like a wounded boy, his face pink and fragile. They gripped each other's fingers.

"I don't know what to do," he said.

"You have to find Hanna, make sure she's okay." He nodded. "And I need something to drink. And maybe a banana? Feeling a little weak."

"Of course." He strode to the door, then stopped. He fiddled with the doorknob, tossing glances toward the hostile world beyond.

"What should I say to her?" he whispered. "What sort of punishment . . . ?"

"Let's not antagonize her, for now. She's always good with you. Just be normal."

"Can you ask Beatrix? What we should do?"

"Yes, I'll ask her."

Alex went out into the hall, calling Hanna's name. He made it sound like a question, scared and uncertain. Suzette realized then that their daughter had effectively made an attack on both of them. He wasn't so sure anymore, who his daughter was. It was a bittersweet triumph, but worth the pain if Alex finally understood the extent of their troubles.

At her request, Alex left the bedroom door open so she could monitor what was happening elsewhere in the house. She heard him talking from the foot of the attic stairs— Hanna must have taken refuge in his study. He told her he would make them all some breakfast soon. Pancakes. And then they'd have a little talk. No response from Hanna, and Alex went downstairs alone. Then came the clinking clatter of a shattered something as it was swept up and thrown away.

Suzette checked her phone. Still so early, not yet 8:30. She called Dr. Yamamoto.

"Beatrix? This is Suzette."

"Is everything all right?"

As she finished telling her what had happened at school the previous day, what happened that morning, Alex slipped back into the room, a tumbler of water in one hand, a banana in the other.

"Is that Beatrix?" he whispered. Suzette nodded. He closed the door halfway with his foot.

"Alex just came in, I'm going to put you on speaker."

He handed her the water and sat on the arm of her chair.

"The first question, I guess—do you two feel safe? Are you concerned about your safety?"

Suzette finished gulping the water. "No, not with Alex here. She won't do anything to him." She set the glass on the little table and took the banana from him.

"What about you, Alex?" Beatrix asked.

Suzette consumed the banana in big bites, watching as elemental forces clashed within her husband. A grown man shouldn't be afraid of a young girl, but there was fear in his eyes.

"I don't know what to think," he said. "She's never done anything to me. But I didn't think she could do something like this."

"It's unusual to have a child committed," Beatrix said

in her composed way. "But it's an option you have, to take her to a hospital, if you ever feel you can't handle what's going on and have concerns for your safety, or hers."

Alex and Suzette gazed at each other, mirror images of dismay and bewilderment. They both shook their heads a little.

"She'd be so scared in a hospital," Suzette said, her own past encroaching on her thoughts. "How would that help? She'd be scared and confused—"

Alex cut in. "That's not—we're not to that place, are we? Can you just come here, and talk to us—her?"

"That's just an emergency option, if you need it. Most parents are reluctant, for the same reasons you are." Beatrix sighed. They sat there, in need of her words, her guidance. "She's going to need a full mental health evaluation, I don't want to make a hasty diagnosis. So I can't recommend prescriptions, or specific therapy just yet. I'm still gathering information. Do you have a sense . . . Was there an inciting incident? Something Hanna could be reacting to?"

"Yes." Alex looked surprised by Suzette's quick confirmation. "I think there's been so much going on, and I was so determined to get her into school. I mean, I caused major upheaval in her life. That's the truth. Even taking her to you. And maybe . . . With that toy," she said to Alex. "I ruined one of her toys; I thought it was a voodoo doll and she was very upset."

"You think this was revenge?" he asked.

Suzette felt a black fog of guilt spreading in her chest, snaking into her belly, entwining itself with whispers of hate. Maybe it was true that things wouldn't have gotten so bad if she'd managed her frustrations with more grace. But it was normal for a child to go to school, make friends, grow toward an independent life. Under such conditions, could *any* mother have done better?

"Some of this was my fault. It's been too much for her and I kept pushing. And I kept pushing because I . . . She was getting worse so I wanted a solution, and she'd push back against my solutions and get even worse, so I was even more desperate to do something . . . She and I are in this bad cycle . . ." It was as conciliatory as she could get, since going back in time and forgoing her pregnancy with Hanna wasn't an option. Alex rubbed her back.

"I think that's an important realization." Beatrix spoke with caution. "But her ability . . . The way she plans and carries through with these aggressive . . . Maybe, Alex, if you feel comfortable, you can try talking to Hanna one-on-one? See if she'll admit to any of this as the source of her frustration?"

"Okay." He seemed reluctant. "You can't . . . Suzette can't even walk."

"I'm sorry I can't see you before Monday, but it'll give me time to look into some things. I might be able to see you earlier on Monday? Let me check." Again, they waited for her to toss them a lifeline. "Nine? Is that too early?"

"We'll take it," Alex agreed without hesitation.

"I'll have more info for you then, about ways to proceed. And in the meanwhile—Alex, you'll be home all weekend?"

"Yes."

"I know this isn't much comfort at this moment, but some of the families I've been acquainted with over the years—the children lash out explosively, throw things—knives even—threaten younger siblings, hit and punch and can't be controlled. Hanna's actions are more thought-out, less spontaneous. But also less disruptive, less volatile in a way. It's possible she'll have a good weekend with you, home—where she seems to want to be. Try to talk to her, but try to avoid being too punitive, too angry. The calmer you can keep the household, the easier it will be. And we'll start finalizing a diagnosis and treatment plan. And you know you have the hospital as an option, if at any point during the weekend things escalate."

"Thank you."

"Thank you," Alex echoed.

After they got off the phone, he went to the bathroom linen closet and came back with a fresh set of sheets. He made the bed with quick and sure movements that filled Suzette with envy; she'd lost all sense of being competent or purposeful.

"Maybe I should try talking to her," she said, half thinking aloud.

"I don't think that's a good idea. Don't think Beatrix would think so either."

"Not to antagonize her. Maybe I owe her an apology." It wouldn't help, but it would cleanse the part of Suzette's conscience that wasn't completely ready to give up.

Alex tucked a pillow under his chin and stuffed it into a clean pillowcase. "I'd like to keep the two of you apart until Monday."

"I don't want to stay cooped up all weekend. I'd feel better being with you—and you can't leave Hanna alone the whole time."

"I'd feel better if you saw a doctor."

"This is superficial." Her head only wobbled in dissent, but her voice was firm. The pain in her feet hummed in a shallow way, entirely different—and less frightening— than feeling her innards twist or swell.

He fluffed the pillows. "Do you want *in* the bed or *on* the bed?"

"On. Can you bring me my sketchbook? I left it downstairs, on the shelf next to the TV."

"I'm going to make you a real breakfast too." He carried her over to the bed. "I'll bring my laptop, you can watch stuff online. Anything else? Should I call my mother?"

"Tova? Why?"

"She would come. For an emergency. Help us out." He sat beside her and she felt him bursting with need—for Tova, or Beatrix, or her. Maybe for anyone who could help fill up the house and spare him from facing his daughter alone.

"I'll be up and about tomorrow."

"You don't know—"

"And Beatrix is on top of this—she's going to help us. Your exact words."

"That was last night."

She didn't want his mother to come—his perfect mother who believed in the perfection of her son and might not understand how Suzette had bungled the raising of her own child. And the fog of guilt wouldn't disperse. She hadn't meant to ruin her child, or overlook a legitimate mental illness, but the shame stung nonetheless. Maybe, in all her efforts, she'd only made things worse.

Maybe she'd over-parented, trying to compensate for her own mother's lack of parenting. Had she given Hanna too much organic food as a toddler? Not enough? She did the baby-mommy movement classes, the baby-mommy yoga, the baby-mommy let's take a nap at the same time because Mommy needs a rest. They read books to her every day, limited her amount of screen time, made sure she played outside. Maybe they should have insisted on preschool earlier, when she might have been more malleable. Should Hanna have had less of a regular routine? Should they have let her stay up as late as she wanted? Did they say no too many times? Yes too many times? It was impossible not to doubt the way she—and Alex—had parented.

A sliver of her still hoped Beatrix was right, that they were working on modifying the family's behavior. Maybe there were steps she and Alex could take—new patterns, things to change—that would turn Hanna into a normal little girl. Maybe they'd always punished her incorrectly (that she enjoyed her time-outs might have been an indicator). Maybe they were too soft, too hard, and with some adjustments Hanna would come around.

"What are you thinking about?" Alex asked.

"Maybe it's not too late."

"Well. We can keep my mother in mind, if we need to."

Suzette almost laughed. Alex had no concern for his

mother's safety, no fear that Hanna might hurt her *farmor*. He grasped an important truth, but wouldn't admit it: Hanna's sights were on a particular target. Why was he even pretending to be afraid?

"We'll figure this out. Remember? You told me just a couple of days ago not to be afraid of her."

"Things have changed. You aren't scared?"

She didn't want to tell him the relief she felt. That at last it was out in the open. Irrevocable proof. And her husband had finally trudged at least partway over to her side. Maybe she should have told him more, sooner, or been more emphatic about the troubling differences Hanna had always exhibited toward them. But it still nagged at her that out-of-control Hanna was her fault. Incompetent, stupid, paper doll of a mother. She'd never wanted Alex to see her as flimsy, or lacking in the basic substance that every mother should have. But maybe . . . Maybe she wasn't the only one with an unreliable backbone. Why hadn't either of them ever stood up and demanded more of Hanna? Was their illusion of family so fragile that neither of them could confront the specter of imperfection? It was possible that now, with the surface cracking, the family dynamic would finally change, and improve.

"A little. But we still have to believe . . . She's trying to say something." *I hate you.* But maybe that wasn't the message at all. She could believe that something hurt inside Hanna, something the girl couldn't name. Something Suzette had inadvertently planted. If they could just find it, identify it, maybe they could yank it out and Hanna would be free to grow outward and upward, not inward and twisting.

The calmness that descended over her was irrational, like she'd become invincible by having survived her daughter's attack. And for the moment, instead of it severing her attachment to Hanna, it somehow strengthened the umbilicus. They were combatants, two parts of a whole, and Suzette's last weapon was empathy. "She's been alone for hours now. I don't know if she's eaten. She'll be an angel with you, Alex."

He nodded. But didn't let go of her hand. "I used to criticize my father. For being so unobservant. My mom and I used to joke about rearranging the furniture. We knew he'd crash into it before even noticing that anything had been moved."

"You're not like that—you're very present with us."

"Present, but oblivious. Half on, half aware. Half always thinking about other things—projects, things that need to get done. I notice when my car isn't running well, but not my family."

"Don't do this to yourself." She pressed closer to him and he rested his forehead against hers.

"I love you so much," he said. "Remember when you asked if I'd thought we'd progressed? As a couple? Honestly . . . I tried to let my love for Hanna fill the gaps I sometimes felt, between us. Not that you were moving away from me, but . . . She pushes. And I accepted it, because she's a child, and it's our job to put her first. But maybe she's been pushing us in . . ."

He wouldn't say the rest. So Suzette did. "In different directions."

Suzette clutched him around the neck, burying her face as she sobbed. It was the first he'd ever hinted that maybe Hanna was coming between them.

"We're gonna be okay," she said. And the strength of Alex's arms convinced her: with the two of them united, maybe all wasn't lost.

HANNA

WHEN DADDY CAME looking for her, she sent one of her rubber balls bouncing down the attic steps so he'd know where she was. She didn't come down, and Daddy didn't go up. It had all turned out so badly. Mommy wasn't supposed to end up on the bed—how could she tower over her with the hammer? And with a phone to call for help. It was a stupid mistake, and she should have stolen Mommy's phone when she had the chance. Her feet hadn't bled as much as she thought they would, but it still scared Hanna a little. Seeing the blood. Knowing she caused it. It made her so grumpy thinking about it: Daddy was still fully under Mommy's spell, but now he knew his *lilla gumman* wasn't always a sweet little girl.

She waited as long as she could. Cooked buttery smells wafted up, and Daddy called her name from the kitchen. She hid the hammer behind some of his books.

Daddy came in from the garden with a cut daffodil as Hanna slunk into the room. He glanced at her, his face closed and hard like a brick, then finished making up his fancy tray. Pancakes. Coffee. The flower.

"I'll be right back." He carried it upstairs for Mommy.

Hanna sat at the table waiting for him to come back.

She was hungry. And now he was only concerned about Mommy—doing everything for Mommy. Like this wasn't all Mommy's fault and how could he forgive her so easily for murdering their UnderSlumberBumbleBeast?

Daddy jogged back down the stairs, and she slumped in her chair, her eyes so close to the table it was just a blur. He stopped, and she knew he was watching her, but she couldn't tell if he looked like Daddy or an imposter. Was he angry with her? Would he become more and more like Mommy— disappointed and demanding—with every passing minute?

But then he came over and sat across from her.

"*Lilla gumman?* Are you feeling bad?"

Hanna nodded.

"Because of what you did to Mommy?"

She sniffled up a tear. No, because she hadn't saved Daddy.

Daddy put his face close to the table, so they could look in each other's eyes. They were crinkly, concerned eyes, and the sight of them gave her hope.

"I'm sorry that you're feeling so frustrated. I know there's a lot you probably want to say. I'm sorry we don't understand everything you're thinking, feeling. But that's not the way to express yourself."

Her tummy gurg-gurgled Feed Me!

"Hungry?" Daddy asked.

She nodded.

He went to the griddle and buttered the remaining pancakes. Usually he let her sprinkle them with powdered sugar, but he did it himself and rolled them up. He put one on each of their plates.

She liked to cut hers with a fork even though Daddy always said she could pick it up with her fingers. But pancakes were especially easy to cut and she liked how the metal fork sliced through the rolled dough.

"Good?"

Hanna grinned and nodded. She looked at him, but his face still didn't seem very happy. Inspired, she scooted out of her chair and ran around to his side of the table. As she leaned in to kiss him, Daddy leaned away. Then he stopped and let her kiss him. She didn't know what to make of it, but she was glad he was downstairs with her again.

"Eat your pancake."

She plodded back around to her chair. Daddy chewed and shoved the pancake into his mouth like he was eating the connected cars of a train. Suddenly there was only one bite left. He licked his thumb and fingers. She ate much more slowly.

"Want another one? Are you still hungry?" She shrugged. "Can we talk, *lilla gumman*? A real talk?"

She gave him a big nod and hoped everything would get back to normal. Maybe he'd talk about the transporter on *Star Trek*—explain how their molecules got all sorted out so their clothes and boots and communicator didn't end up fused in their bodies. Fabric instead of skin and electronic components poking out of their ears. She loved the transporter and the thingy that replicated all their food. It would be tricky to use the Replicator without talking. But the idea of having mint chocolate-chip ice cream or bubble-gum flavored jellybeans whenever she wanted might have tempted her to hazard whispering to such a machine.

Daddy pushed his plate away, resting his elbows on the table.

"So. You can be honest with me, right? We're honest with each other."

The conversation already made her wiggle and squiggle. She stacked two bites of pancake on her fork and stuffed it in her mouth. Honesty was not an altogether solid subject in her mind; it was a vapory thing, like smoke that was present one minute and began drifting away the next. Keeping things to yourself was more important than honesty, but it was bad to lie, and Daddy was the last person she'd want to think of her as bad.

"Did you hurt Mommy because of what she did to your UnderSlumberBumbleBeast?"

She weighed her options, and nodded. She had nothing to lose because Daddy—smart Daddy—already figured it out. And he would see that it was fair—more than fair—because her UnderSlumberBumbleBeast was dead and Mommy remained very much alive.

"Come here." He scooted his chair over so it was closer to her, and tugged hers around so they were knee to knee. "Hanna, this is very important. I know how hurt you were, when Mommy broke your toy. But you understand, don't you? A potato—even one you turn into a friend—doesn't feel things the way a human being does. Do you understand that?"

Yes. No. Of course a potato doesn't feel pain—but she wasn't a potato, and she felt it, Mommy hurting her. Daddy would understand, if only she could explain it better. But everything got so jumbled in her head that she started to cry.

"Maybe you thought it would be funny, playing a joke on Mommy? But what you did hurt her—physically hurt her. Scared her. And it scares me, hurts me—that my squirrely girl . . ."

She looked at him as his voice broke, astonished by his tears. She touched his cheek, then shook her head, hoping he understood: *don't cry, Daddy.*

It made him cry harder, and he scooped her onto his lap and held her tightly.

"See? You're my loving little . . ." He kissed her head.

She loved being in his arms. His heart bu-bumped against her ear, and she tapped her middle finger against his chest, thumping along in unison. But then Daddy took a deep breath and set her back on her chair. He wiped his eyes, and she looked at him with big question marks.

"Daddy's upset. You can't hurt people anymore—no one. It's not allowed. See, we have a problem now, and I don't know how to fix it. It's like you . . . You're two different little girls. Is it . . . Marie-Anne? Does she make you do these things?"

She squirmed again, and pressed her finger into a blob of sugar that was left behind on her plate. Licked it off. She'd been very proud of herself that, in fact, the thumb-tack idea had been her own—Marie-Anne had just been the lookout. And what happened at school . . . She considered that nothing more than a series of fortunate coincidences. Being left in the room with Helmet Head. Him tapping it on the wall. Him allowing her to remove his helmet without protest or complaint. The vicious dog. Maybe Marie-Anne helped with that a little.

It occurred to her for the first time that Marie-Anne may have overstayed her welcome. That Mommy didn't like Marie-Anne was fine, but if Marie-Anne was getting between her and her father . . . Hanna wanted her old Daddy back, the one who never shied away from her kisses.

"Can you make Marie-Anne go away?" he asked.

She grinned. He could still read her mind. But then she shrugged. She'd invited Marie-Anne, after all, because she wanted a bestest friend. She really didn't know how to make her leave.

Daddy sat there thinking.

"What if . . ." He kept looking like he was about to say something; his mouth opened and closed like a hungry goldfish. "What if I help you?"

Help her? The idea intrigued her. She stood in front of her chair, in front of Daddy, her weight on one leg, alert to what he'd say next.

"Sometimes . . . When there's something troubling us, we can cast our troubles away."

Did he want to cast a spell with her? She screwed up her face in confusion.

"So I'm proposing . . . We could cast Marie-Anne away. Would you be willing to do that?"

She nodded. Did Daddy have magical powers, too? She held out her hands: how?

"Sunday is *Valborg*—Walpurgis. And we'll have our

own backyard fire. Sometimes, when people want things to go away, they toss their worries into the fire."

Could they toss Mommy into the fire?

"So maybe . . . You could draw a picture. Of Marie-Anne. And on Sunday evening we'll cast her away."

She chewed her lip. It didn't seem entirely fair, considering Marie-Anne had been burned to death once before. But if *that* Marie-Anne really had been innocent, Hanna's interpretation of her proved to be a bit more dangerous. And Hanna didn't really need her anymore—talking was overrated, and most of their best witchy things had been Hanna's ideas. She jutted out her chin and bobbed it a few times.

"Good girl. So we'll have a very special Walpurgis this year, and afterward no more Marie-Anne, just my *lilla gumman*."

She threw her arms around his neck, relieved. He didn't want Marie-Anne coming between them. He wanted Hanna all to himself.

She sat on the floor with the sketchbook on her lap—the one in which she'd drawn her secret symbols. It was hard, trying to conjure an image of Marie-Anne. She wasn't used to drawing, and after a few attempts her hand started to feel like a stiff claw and she could barely hold the crayon. It didn't help that she really didn't know what Marie-Anne looked like. A girl, with blackened flesh like the chicken Daddy once burned on the grill. But what she drew on the paper looked like a messy egg with sticklike arms and flippers for feet. If only she had a photograph.

The thought stopped her.

She did have a photograph of Mommy. She and Daddy had printed a few copies, until it was the size and shade she wanted for her collage. The collage had disappeared, but she still had the extra pictures. She dug through the cubby where she kept her secret things, all carefully stashed between ordinary things that wouldn't attract anyone's interest. The pictures were kept with some other pages she'd printed, information she'd found on the internet about How to Cast Spells of Vengeance and Attack. The article had very big, and sometimes very weird, words in it, but she understood the general idea: through a series of intentional actions and thoughts a witch could do harm to another person.

Bursts of sound—a big voice and lots of people laughing—drifted into her room, and she stuck her head out the door to investigate. It gouged at her heart that Daddy was in his room with Mommy, watching stuff on his laptop. When he was home during the week he usually went to his study and didn't mind if she played on the floor while he worked at his desk. It was a sign of how strong Mommy's spell on him was, that Daddy stayed by her side.

Well, she'd get him all to herself soon enough. He'd be happy when she showed him the drawing of Marie-Anne. He left her alone in her room so she could work on it, and she planned on making it as good as she could. The Casting Out might go badly if the girl at all resembled Hanna herself, so she would draw her with different hair, a thicker body, in colors she never wore. But first, while safely alone, she wanted to work on the spell against Mommy.

She wasn't absolutely certain what the spell was supposed to accomplish, but "Vengeance and Attack" sounded good. She had no idea what widdershins meant, or Saturnian. Or circumambulations or thurible. But she interpreted that destroying the photograph of the intended victim would somehow damage the victim, especially if she did it while repeating her own heartfelt curse—an example of which was included in the article.

The curse was supposed to be said aloud, but Hanna knew she'd become a most special witch and that mouthing the words would suffice. She read the pages carefully to get a sense for what she was supposed to say. The article recommended destroying the photograph slowly, over many days, but Hanna wasn't concerned about deviating from the internet's instructions.

She sat cross-legged and tore a tiny corner off the picture of sleeping Mommy. In her mind, she willed it to be a picture of dead Mommy and mouthed her spell.

I inflict this curse on you.

Piece by piece, she tore apart the picture, making a pile of paper bits in her notebook. She mouthed her spell over and over.

It was so clear in her mind. In two days Daddy would build a fire and sing his odes to spring. Hanna would place her drawing of Marie-Anne on the flames, where it would curl and blacken and disappear. And then she'd toss the bits of Mommy like confetti into the fire. She could already feel Marie-Anne, redundant and unnecessary, leaving her;

SUZETTE

ALEX SLIPPED BACK into the room, easing the door shut behind him.

"She's asleep," he said

"Thank you." It was 8:09, right on time. With a nimble determination, he'd managed to keep the household entertained—and free of drama—while maintaining Hanna's regular routine.

He ducked into the closet and emerged with a pair of clean socks, then sat on the bed to put them on. After a surprisingly pleasant afternoon and evening—the pain in her feet notwithstanding—with Alex close and attentive to her needs, Suzette felt a surge of dread. She shook her head, not wanting to believe what was happening.

"You're going out?" She pushed herself away from the headboard, her muscles taut and anxious. Was he running away to the gym? To work, for something Matt could do, or Alex could do on another day?

"Two quick stops." He grabbed his wallet from his bedside table.

"Why? No. Alex, no."

He stood, tucking his wallet into the back pocket of his gym pants. With his fingers he combed his hair.

"Just for a minute, to get a few things."

"What things? No."

He came around to her side of the bed, cozying next to her. Where before she'd seen compassion and concern in all his efforts, now she read selfishness. Condescension. Even in the way he took her hand.

"We need a few things, for the weekend. It'll be——"

She withdrew her hand. "Fine? What if she wakes up? Finds me here alone? At least . . . Leave me with a weapon or something." She regretted the words the minute she said them. "I'm . . ."

Such pain on his face. She felt it, too. Everywhere. Her feet, her heart. Her body, stiffened by a day of cautious movement.

"I was going to get you a pair of crutches."

"Oh."

"So you can get around better."

"Tired of carrying me to the bathroom?" She wanted it to sound light, but the reminder of her incapacitation only increased his torment. "Sorry. Maybe . . . We could put a bell on her door, so I can hear if she gets up." She was thinking of his string of brass bells that dangled from his bookcase—a souvenir from his parents' trip to Nepal.

He nodded, but didn't get up to retrieve them. "Maybe I could jury-rig a lock of some kind."

"Lock her in?"

He shrugged, and his powerlessness sparked a new ache within her.

"The bells will be fine," she said, reluctant to admit she'd feel safer with a hockey stick, or a rolling pin, or an electric cattle prod. Maybe after he left, she'd hobble to the closet and dig out his old tennis racket.

As much as she didn't want him to leave, the thought of them all as prisoners, trapped within the walls of their energy-efficient dream home, was equally undesirable. He left the bedroom door open and she watched him tiptoe past Hanna's door, aware of his own heaviness even as his socks muffled his footfalls.

Weapons, locks, bells. Her failures pierced her in obsidian shards. What would come next? Straitjackets? Padded rooms? A lobotomy? Her thoughts waffled between wanting to help her daughter, and wanting to be free of her. Maybe a mental institution could accomplish both.

The ceiling creaked as he walked across the floor above her head, followed by the tinkling of bells. A minute later he was back in the hallway. Cocooning them in his hands, he hung the bells from Hanna's doorknob, snuffing out their chimes as they cascaded to the floor.

He held his long limbs stiffly as he came back in, shutting the door behind him and exhaling with relief.

"I feel like a thief," he whispered, sitting on the bed's corner, elbows on his knees, massaging a great burden from his scalp. "I don't even know what that means. I don't know what we're doing."

"The best we can." She wanted to comfort him but couldn't reach him where he was sitting, not without moving.

"This is so fucking . . ." He pushed the thought aside. "So anyway." He angled toward her. "Crutches from

Rite Aid, maybe replenish the medical supplies, and a quick stop for some firewood, then I'll be right back."

"Firewood?"

"It's *Valborg*, day after tomorrow."

His eyes looked sunken in, skeletal, and she saw not his exhaustion but how he would look as an old man. Frail. Tottering. Oblivious.

"We're not celebrating Walpurgis." It was so final, the bite of her words. Yet he protested.

"Why not?"

"A fire? In our backyard? With how she's been? You didn't want to believe it but she likely *did* set that garbage can on fire when she was in—"

"It's not just for her, it's a tradition, welcoming in the spring—"

"Walpurgis? Witches' Night? You can't be serious."

"It's a bit of home," he said, his face so innocent and needy. Though the way they celebrated it was nothing like home, where communities gathered in the parks, singing, eating, drinking, tossing the debris from their gardens into a massive bonfire.

Imagining their reduced ritual suddenly saddened her. The three of them gathered in the backyard around their copper fire pit, Alex singing alone in Swedish. It felt wrong to deny him such a paltry celebration.

"Once upon a time . . . Wasn't it about warding off witches and evil spirits?" she asked, seeing a relevant application for the old pagan holiday.

Alex gave her a devilish half grin. "I already thought of that. I sort of made a deal. With Hanna."

"What kind of deal?"

"To get rid of Marie-Anne."

"Like an exorcism? Are you fucking insane?" Not that it was an inherently bad idea, but what did either of them know about exorcising a witch from a seven-year-old?

"No! Like when you wanted to get rid of negative thoughts, leave things behind, and you wrote it all down—I don't know what you wrote. And tossed it into the flames. Like that. Maybe Marie-Anne's like . . . her bad side. So I told her to draw a picture, and on Sunday we'll burn it. It might help, you don't know."

If it wasn't for her child's ability to cause harm, it almost seemed like a reasonable plan. But something about her daughter near fire troubled her.

"Maybe she's become dependent on her," she said, thinking about how Beatrix had described Marie-Anne as an aspect of Hanna's personality.

"Exactly. And we can encourage her, in a really harmless way, to get rid of her. I want Hanna back. Sweet Hanna. Maybe not perfect; there'll still be things to work on. But maybe we can purge this violent side of her."

"You really think it's that easy?" She fought to keep the disbelief from her voice. "She carried out a sophisticated, well-planned attack—"

"I know! I'm not forgetting what she did—but what are we supposed to do? Tiptoe around her and pretend like nothing happened?"

"Isn't that exactly what you've been doing?"

"And that's why I'm trying to *do* something! She's our child. She needs us to *help* her."

For a moment they were both silent, lost in the magnitude of their child's disrepair.

"Do you really think . . ." Her anger dissipated. She wanted a dram of Alex's optimism. "You think that could possibly . . . make a difference?"

Alex's eyes wandered, lost, and he shook his head. But he tried to talk himself into it. "Maybe this, everything— maybe she really is trying to communicate with us, and it's all going wrong. For what it's worth, when I talked to her—she seemed remorseful. Sad. I don't want her to think we've abandoned her. If she's . . . sick . . ."

No, Suzette couldn't do such a thing, either. Their daughter's sickness—her impending diagnosis—sat between them like an expanding tumor, threatening to smother them all. Hanna probably didn't even understand what her father had asked her to do. But a purge was harmless, if ineffective.

"Have to keep a close eye on her," she said, relenting for the cause of Alex's well-being, his need to not be helpless.

"Obviously."

"Really close. Don't want her burning anything else."

"I'll be right there the whole time."

"What about the champagne and strawberries?" she asked, swallowing her misgivings, and trying to lessen the sense of doom. In previous years he'd insisted on the traditional *Valborg* breakfast.

"I'll have to make another stop for that," he said, sidling up to her, pressing his cheek to hers as he kissed her ear. "You'll be okay here?"

She smiled and nodded, and grabbed up her cellphone, holding it in both hands like it would save her in an emergency. She almost laughed, imagining herself calling 9-1-1 to say that her demonic daughter had arisen and was threatening . . . oh, never mind, she was just heading to the bathroom for a pee.

"Hurry back," she said.

He gave her another quick kiss and sprang from the bed.

"Leave it open?" she asked as he started to close the bedroom door.

"Back soon," he whispered, leaving the door fully open. He jogged down the stairs. Keys jangled, and the dead bolt clicked into place.

A minute later his car started. The house loomed heavy as a grave, and her arm hairs prickled with the thought of her daughter emerging from her room, white-eyed and alien, her teeth transformed into daggers. She experienced for a moment the dream sensation of floating, knowing this is how her daughter's body would move. Toward her. Smiling.

She wanted to close her door, have a barrier between her and the monster that might yet awaken. She'd asked Alex to keep it open so she could keep an eye on the hallway, but now she couldn't stop staring at the bells. Anticipating the slightest movement. Her vision grew blurry with the effort and she considered calling him, telling him she'd changed her mind. Come home.

But she didn't.

Marie-Anne had died once before in a fire, an

injustice of her time. They had to try. And justice was on their side this time. Once there'd been a baby named Hanna who smiled at the sun. A baby who flapped her arms when she saw birds. A giggler. Hanna wasn't happy. And no speech-language pathologist or pediatrician had ever diagnosed a reason for her mutism. Suzette couldn't gauge how prepared Alex was for their child to be declared mentally ill, though Dr. Yamamoto had all but said it. They'd finally have something to work with—and the common goal of helping Hanna.

She tried to quell her nerves with the mantra *sick not demonic*.

A shriek wafted in from the street, followed by a chorus of laughter. A carefree group heading to one of the local bars, she supposed. Ready to get drunk. Ready to get laid. In spite of her worries she didn't envy them. There were no answers out there—in the communal obliteration, or the heartless sex, or the determined separation of self from reality. She had people she loved, people worth fighting for.

Maybe she should offer Hanna help in drawing Marie-Anne. Maybe it could be their first real mother-daughter art project. She could say through her actions: "I am helping you excise your inner demons, because I love you. And I'm sorry for your terrible, unreachable pain."

That's what she would say if the bells jingled, if the door opened, "I love you, no matter what you do."

HANNA

SHE WATCHED FROM the kitchen table, slurping up the last of her banana slices and milk, as Daddy helped Mommy hobble down the stairs. Everything since her revenge with the thumbtacks had been weird and wobbly, like the whole house was on a seesaw that wouldn't level out. No one yelled at her or threatened her with punishment. But she'd spent most of the previous day alone as Daddy made only cursory checks on her. She liked her aloneness best when it was of her own choosing. Daddy had barely helped with her bath, and didn't bother to comb her hair so it didn't hurt. And then he'd refused to read from her favorite book. He picked one instead, and it was boring and babyish, and she just stared at him while he hurried through it.

When she emerged from her room the door exploded with noise, and she stood there frozen for a moment, afraid that her face or hands would fall off. Then she saw they were just the bells from Daddy's study, bells she liked to tap with the tip of her finger while they hung in their rightful place upstairs. She could make them sing a tiny song, like the music fairies or insects might make. Daddy came into the hall, rubbing his eyes, and she pointed at the bells. Were they a gift? Who had moved them? Why?

"*Gomorron*," Daddy said. He scratched his beard and ignored her silent questions.

She got dressed and he fixed her breakfast, but he sliced her bananas thicker than Mommy did, and she liked them thinner so she could break them easily with her spoon.

Mommy's crutches were mesmerizing, like an extra pair of giant robot arms. She wore her exercise clothes—stretchy but formfitting—which she also wore to clean the house, but it didn't seem likely that she could do either. Daddy glued his eyes to Mommy as she set the crutches on the step beneath her, placed one flat foot on it and then the other. Again and again, until she'd made her way down the stairs. Daddy walked down the steps backward in front of her, holding his hands out like he was afraid she would fall.

"How is it?" he asked.

"Not too bad. Won't be going up and down too much, though. But the crutches really help for moving across the floor."

Daddy ran down the last couple of steps and darted over to the table to pull out a chair. They watched together as Mommy swung her legs between the crutches, making surprising speed.

He tucked Mommy into the table across from her and dashed off to the kitchen.

"Coffee? Cereal?"

"Yes to both. You don't have to run, I'm here, I'm not going anywhere. For a while."

And then Mommy looked at her. It was the first time they'd seen each other since the thumbtack incident, and

Hanna still expected Mommy to call her a fucking-this-or-that. But she just sat there with her chin in her hand, studying her.

"Morning."

Hanna sucked a banana slice off her spoon.

"So . . . We have to make things better. Between us. I'm sorry if I pushed you too fast. I wish you could understand. School, and how important it is. If we're together so much and I'm teaching you at home . . . And what you really need is other people. We're just at cross-purposes, and that's why I was trying to get you into school."

Daddy brought over a mug of coffee and a bowl of cinnamon Puffins and set them in front of Mommy.

"Thank you."

He stroked Mommy's ugly hair and kissed her head. On another day those pets and kisses would have been for her. He pulled out the chair from the head of the table and sat with his legs wide apart, a stance that made Hanna think of lions, comfortable in their territory. It bothered her, how united Mommy and Daddy were. They looked at her like they were the rulers of the kingdom and she was the ant who'd crawled under the door, lost. They both acted dopey-clueless about the other things Mommy needed to apologize for: the tug-of-war she insisted on engaging in with Daddy's heart, when it was so obvious that she, the daughter, was worthier of his love; the warm bumpity-bump love Mommy owed her on principle, after all the years Mommy had spent either pushing her away, or hovering like a flying saucer, mangled and about to crash. Mommy was only a shell of a person with nothing to give.

She was like a store full of bright and tempting candies held captive behind a thick, transparent wall. It wasn't like Hanna hadn't tried to tap on the glass and grasp what was inside.

"Daddy told me about the arrangement the two of you made, for getting rid of Marie-Anne."

Probably Mommy had dragged it out of him, like a magician pulling endless handkerchiefs from her sleeve, while Daddy was under her spell. Hanna lifted her bowl, rolling the last few drops of milk around the bottom. She had to accept that Daddy couldn't help giving up their secret, and maybe it was better if Mommy knew: then she wouldn't be surprised when Hanna started tossing things into the fire.

"We're both really glad that you're ready to let go of Marie-Anne. I'm glad she helped you find your voice, but I know you can do it again without her." Mommy dunked her Puffins under the milk, drowning them before taking a big bite.

"I can't wait to hear you speak," Daddy said, and his eagerness made her want to swallow every sound she'd ever uttered. She didn't like that they were both focused on her; their misguided expectations formed a black hole in her gut. Black holes were dangerous; they absorbed everything around them, and maybe some parts of her that she needed would tumble into the abyss.

She got up and stood beside her chair, her gaze on the floor.

"You may be excused," Mommy said. "But first . . ." She reached out for her as Hanna started to flee.

Hanna stopped, but kept out of range of Mommy's touch.

"I know you're working on a drawing of Marie-Anne, for tomorrow's fire. I know you're . . . a little bit of a perfectionist? So if you need help—"

"Mommy's very good at drawing," Daddy added.

She considered the two of them, and Mommy's offer. She'd tried again with her egg-shaped girl and it still barely looked like a person. Mommy wanted to help her—but more important, Daddy wanted her to accept Mommy's help. She could see it all over his face. If Mommy participated in the drawing, a part of her would end up in the fire, too—the lines she drew on the page, and some of her cells that rubbed against it. Maybe she'd leave fingerprints behind. And when Hanna tossed the Mommy-confetti into the flames, her spell would be twice as strong. She stuck her finger in her mouth, feeling the ridges of the new tooth that was poking through her gum. And gave one assertive nod.

Daddy brought down one of Mommy's sketchbooks and two sets of her pencils—one with lots of colors, and one in which the pencils all looked alike; Mommy said those were different shades of gray, rated by hardness.

"The softer the graphite, the darker the line. So when you want just a very light sketch, you use a harder pencil." She pointed to the 7H printed near its blunt end.

Daddy set up his laptop on the kitchen counter, but kept glancing over at them. Hanna knew what he was thinking: some of the pencils were very sharp. She could stab them into the back of Mommy's hand until it was stuck to the table. She grinned at him so he would know she was enjoying herself and wouldn't cause Mommy any further harm. Yet.

He winked at her, then grubbled up his eyebrows as he studied something on his screen.

"Do you want to show me what you've drawn so far?"

Hanna shook her head.

"People are hard to draw."

Hanna nodded.

"So I'll show you how. And I'll do it very lightly, and then you can color it in, or try it on your own, okay?"

She sat on her knees and leaned on her elbows, her eyes on Mommy's sketchbook.

"So I like to start by drawing two little lines—just slashes, really. One here where the top of the head will be, and one here for the feet. This way, you know your whole figure will always fit on the page and you won't run out of room. Then I make two more slashes—one near the middle, where the waist will be. And one up here for the shoulders.

"I like to proportion a human figure off the size of the head. So I draw an oval for the head . . . and then a neck . . . and, including the head, the whole body will be about seven to eight ovals of about the same size."

She ogled at the shapes that emerged beneath Mommy's pencil, so faint but confident.

"So I draw three ovals beneath the neck, and there's the torso—and you see the last oval straddles the line I drew for the waist. And then four ovals on either side of that. And these are the legs. Smaller sideways ovals for the feet.

"Then I go back to the line I made for the shoulder. I draw a smaller circle on either side of the upper torso—those are the shoulders. And you see how they line up with the hips and legs? Then beneath the first shoulder I draw an oval—same size as the others. A little circle—that's the elbow. Another oval, another little circle—that's the hand."

She repeated her series of circles and ovals and created the right arm, and then sat back. Hanna's eyes and mouth became big O's. Like magic, Mommy had drawn a recognizable, well-proportioned human figure. She didn't even mind the way Mommy was gazing on her, her face alert and pleased.

Daddy came over and twirled a piece of Hanna's hair in his finger. "Mommy's pretty good at this, right? *Älskling,* we should find a spot for you to use as a studio. Even the upstairs hallway in front of the window, or up in my study."

Mommy beamed at him, but Hanna thought it was a terrible idea. The very thought of Mommy invading the best room in the house—Daddy's room—made her want to tear up the sketch. But she didn't. She needed it.

"Do you want to try it?" Mommy asked as Daddy gave her shoulder a squeeze and returned to the counter and his work.

Hanna shook her head and pointed to the colored pencils.

"You just want to color it in?"

She nodded.

"Okay. Well then I'll pick a slightly darker pencil"—
she exchanged one gray pencil for another—"and sketch
out some clothes, and it'll be like a coloring book. What
should she wear? Is she a girl of olden times? Does she
wear a dress?"

Hanna nodded enthusiastically and reached for a
rusty-orange pencil. She pointed to her own head and then
the head on the page.

"Does she have red hair?"

Big nod.

"Well, I'll draw an outline, and you can color it in."

It was going better than she ever could have expected.
Faint memories swam in her mind of being very little.
Mommy with a sketchbook on her lap. Showing Hanna a
perfect rendering of the room they were sitting in. And
sometime else, showing her a sketch of a child's face—
hers—intense but unsmiling. She hadn't realized then that
Mommy's drawing was a real talent.

She watched as her hand lightly skipped around the
page, leaving behind textured clothing and beat-up shoes,
loosely held fists and a stern face. She was particularly
interested in the fleshy side of Mommy's hand, the way it
touched the paper but didn't smear it, coating it with invisible bits of her skin. The fire would get a taste of her before
Hanna mumbled the final words of her spell. Maybe
Mommy would burst into flames with the drawing and
the confetti. Spontaneous combustion. That happened
once in a cartoon. Poof! A black cat turned into a black
cloud. And then it disintegrated into a pool of ashes on the
floor.

When she tore the page from the sketchbook and handed it to her, Hanna was almost afraid to touch it. She wasn't good at coloring and didn't want to ruin Marie-Anne's likeness—and she was certain they'd captured her likeness perfectly, from her thick hair to her tattered clothes. Like Marie-Anne had separated from Hanna and stood by the table to model for her own portrait. Once again, Daddy was right: sending Marie-Anne on her way would work better with such a realistic drawing. And maybe a part of him understood it would help get Mommy out of the way, too.

She worked on small areas with as delicate a touch as she could manage. When she approved of a preliminary section, she went back in and made the color bolder. With tremendous pride, she stayed within the lines and Marie-Anne became even more lifelike. Mommy glanced over at her from time to time, encouraging her with compliments, but soon became absorbed in her own creation. They all worked on their individual projects, and Hanna felt as yellow as her favorite sunshiny pencil.

Her family deserved a short hour of perfection.

SUZETTE

FOR THE SECOND day in a row, she sat at the table and had never been more grateful for the glass wall that filled the room with light, diffused but bright given the cloudiness of the day. Maybe the whole house would become her artist's studio, maybe that had been its purpose all along. Sometimes she drew in her tiny sketchbook and sometimes in the big one, a foot and a half by two feet. But the standard-size one, in which she'd drawn an effigy for her daughter to burn, held no further interest. Her mind traveled to petite ideas—phantasmagoric animals with swirling horns and folded wings—or large ideas—shafts of light piercing a box or a room as if it had been attacked by arrows or a barrage of bullets—and nothing in between. She worked in pencil and charcoal and forgot about her feet, her daughter, her husband, and the ritual they would soon perform.

Suzette sipped from the goblet, the champagne long since turned flat and warm, and noticed the halos of green leaves—the tops of eaten strawberries—left scattered on the plate. The champagne and strawberries appealed to her rejuvenated artistic side—like the emancipation of a suppressed debauchery—and she'd snacked on them throughout the day.

Outside, Hanna ran around the yard gathering twigs like they were Easter eggs, Hanukkah presents, wishes left by leprechauns. Alex did the heavy work, raking under the shrubs and trimming dead limbs from overhanging trees. He'd already gotten out their copper fire pit and placed it on its solitary stone paver. The patio chairs formed a triangle around the pit, drip-drying after he'd hosed away the winter grime. It felt a bit strange to be so unhelpful and removed from her family, yet she liked watching them from afar.

She'd been surprised by Hanna's attentiveness the previous day as she composed the effigy of Marie-Anne, and the girl's determination to make her alive with color. Suzette took a picture of it when it was finished, a bit remorseful about having to burn it. After a hesitant start, Hanna colored very well. It made her wistful for all the projects she'd given up on when Hanna showed no interest. Valentine's Day cards and Halloween decorations. Three-dimensional wonders made of recycled oatmeal canisters and egg cartons.

A part of her hoped it was the beginning of better things to come. Another part of her worried that her parental license would soon be revoked—especially if Hanna ended up being diagnosed with something Suzette should have recognized sooner. But mostly, she couldn't shake the unease that the weekend had gone too well, too smoothly. It was odd timing—and odd circumstances—for family bonding.

She didn't like the clippers that Alex used on the trees; it was too easy to imagine someone—Marie-Anne/

Hanna—using them to snip off one or all of her fingers. But Alex swore he'd lock them back in the toolshed when he was finished. He was so happy in his element, and she could hear him humming, mumbling the words of *"Vintern Rasat"*—the folk song he would boom in his baritone when it was time to lay the first log on the fire.

They came in sweating and smiling, with pungent earth embedded in their hands, their clothes. It reminded her that she intended, every spring, to plant vegetables, but somehow never did. Hanna hopped on one foot as he sang, *"Himlen ler i vårens ljusa kvällar, solen kysser liv i skog och sjö . . ."* He raced her upstairs, challenging her to see which one could get cleaned up and changed first.

Suzette sniffed her armpits. Her natural smell was barely masked by the powdery perfume of her deodorant. She hadn't showered in days, and didn't really want to soften the comforting scabs that had formed on the soles of her feet. She couldn't remember when last she had gone so long without cleaning—herself, or some part of the house. The thought wasn't unappealing that vines could grow up through the floors, snake along the walls, fill the house like a jungle. And she, in her rags, could climb them and find a perch on the ceiling. In that savagely deconstructed domesticity, there'd be no need to speak. She'd reek of musk and Alex would fuck her from behind. Maybe there'd even be a place for Hanna there, barking like a chimpanzee, a wild child, a happy pet.

She closed her sketchbooks and repackaged all the supplies, tingling with the mindfulness that the weekend had changed her. Without the damage to her feet she would have bustled around with her everyday obsessions.

The calamity of their failed parenting would have pressed in, suffocating her. Maybe it was the tipsiness of a day spent sipping champagne, but it felt manageable now; they would survive this. She would selfishly shut doors, or leave things undone, to have her hands look as they did now. Blackened by her art.

She gazed at them as if they were sculptures, not her own body. These were hands that did important things. These hands followed the will of vision, of spontaneity. They caressed dreams from the dark fold.

Had she wanted something once? Other than stability? The reassurance of one person's infallible love? These filthy hands were up to the task of finding out.

Her feet, however, were not. She stood, intent on hobbling over to the sink, but immediately collapsed back in the chair. Her hands would dirty everything—the crutches, the dish towels. She continued gazing at her hands as she waited to ask Alex for help.

In the university town of Lund, where Alex grew up, people would drink and barbecue during the day, then wait until the sun slipped below the horizon before lighting the bonfires. At the Jensen home in Pittsburgh, they started feasting too late and burning too early. Theirs was a supper celebration, a picnic around their own portable hearth.

Bathed and freshly dressed in gray comfy pants and a pale blue zip-up jacket, Suzette sat planted in her chair, facing the back of the house, her crutches on the ground beside her. They were all too buoyant. Her own pent-up energy could be explained by so much sitting; she fought the urge to spring up and help lay the kindling, help prepare the food, help bring out the plates. Alex's energy might be explained by his verve for the holiday—the Swedes liked their festivities, even ones who had been removed from their culture for nearly twenty years. Hanna followed her father like a devoted puppy, keen to do everything he asked her to do. She carried out the Brita pitcher, followed by two bottles of their preferred red wine, setting them on a folding table just beyond the double doors. She brought out a serving spoon for the cucumber salad, cloth napkins, the corkscrew for the wine—each item retrieved and placed one at a time before she bounded back in to take Alex's next order.

Suzette wasn't altogether happy to see her daughter's slavish devotion to her husband. The weekend seemed to have eased his fear and confusion, and she found his optimism—his belief in Hanna's remorse—unsettling. Hanna hadn't done anything wretched for two whole days, but they couldn't use that as a barometer.

Alex proudly carried out the food: the cucumber salad that he'd made himself, sliced rye bread with both butter and cream cheese, steamed asparagus, a big platter of cured salmon and pickled herring flanked by sliced tomatoes and onions. He'd ducked out to their favorite deli that morning to procure the fish. She remembered being shocked the first time he'd said the Swedish word for salmon— *lax*—as it sounded almost like lox, a Jewish staple of her childhood. He'd come to adopt lox as a favorite, even though it wasn't the smoked salmon of his youth, and he, too, marveled that the Jews and Swedes enjoyed so many crossovers in their taste for "stinky fishes." They were having rye bread instead of bagels, but their open-faced sandwiches would be a blend of their two cultures.

"Light the fire, then eat?" he asked.

"Sounds good. Pretty hungry." Her stomach growled in confirmation. She gave silent thanks to the gods and goddesses of intestinal matters that the new medication had kicked in. Her helplessness would have been worse if she'd needed Alex to help her to the toilet every hour.

The kindling was ready; all he had to do was strike a match. Hanna huddled beside him, hands on her knees and her face too near the copper pit. He gently guided her back toward her chair.

"Not so close, *lilla gumman*."

The dry leaves caught right away, and fed the slender twigs.

"You have your fire stick?"

Hanna ran over to the pile of wood and grabbed a stick that had been whittled of its branches.

"We'll just poke it a little as we lay some bigger wood on," he whispered, like the process was so delicate and the fire would expire if he raised his voice.

She watched her daughter stab the fire tentatively with her special stick. Suzette's body tightened, and she had the instinct to move her chair back, away from the growing flames. Alex kept a hand on Hanna's free arm, keeping her safe.

When the fire became a sure thing, he deposited Hanna into her chair and went to get the first real log.

"Vintern rasat ut bland våra fjällar, drivans blommor smälta ned och dö . . ."

Suzette grinned. Alex had an imperfect voice, but he sang with exuberance. She clapped her hands to the beat of his music, wishing she'd made more effort to learn the whole song. She felt a moment of pride for her family, celebrating spring on an overcast, soon-to-chill evening, feasting and singing in spite of the troubles they faced. She joined in for the last few lines, which, in their repetition, she'd learned over the years.

". . . se dem än som i min barndoms stunder följa bäckens dans till klarnad sjö . . ."

His face lit up as she sang along. Hanna bounced a little in her chair.

When they finished singing, they all clapped. Suzette was struck, again, by the abnormal normality of the entire weekend. Were they all merely acting?

Alex served the food. He brought her over a generous, but not heaping plate, cognizant of her never fully robust appetite. He set wine and water at her feet, served in identical fat-bottomed tumblers.

"Tack så mycket," she said. He kissed her forehead and went back to load up a plate for himself.

As they ate, Alex periodically tended the fire, prodding it with his own stripped-down stick, rearranging the branches and logs.

Hanna nibbled on bread coated with a thick layer of cream cheese, and ate both the cucumber salad and tomato slices with her fingers. Only Alex ate the pickled herring, which he gobbled up in big mouthfuls, murmuring with delight.

"Mm, mm, *mums*!"

Suzette enjoyed her open-faced lox sandwich, chewing slowly, as the dancing fire lured her into a contemplative daze.

She reflected on a dream she'd had the night before. In it, a friend she hadn't seen since elementary school—now grown up—told her to keep an eye out for Greta, a young woman unknown to Suzette who was asleep in another room.

"She's blind, but she won't admit it," said the friend, heading for the door.

Apparently they all lived together in an apartment that, in the way of dreams, was excessively large and both resplendent and run-down, with damask-upholstered curving couches and ceilings rotten with water stains.

"Greta needs assistance, but don't be fooled by her confidence." And the friend left.

Dream-Suzette waited for the mysterious Greta to emerge, and when she did, she realized the full extent of Greta's disabilities. Emaciated and petite, the young woman looked as if she'd been consumed in a fire. The flames had eaten away most of her feet leaving only nubs, and all her exposed, scarred skin lay in pink folds. Atop her head she wore a synthetic cherry-colored wig, and her eyes had melted in the fire; what Suzette saw in Greta's face were glass prosthetics.

Greta wore black and green velvet with great aplomb and hobbled on her ruined feet.

"I need to get to Seraphina's," she said. "I have an appointment."

Seraphina was known in certain circles as an expert and expensive dominatrix.

Suzette grasped that the apartment belonged to Greta, and she and her friend were merely guests, or squatters, because only Greta had means—wealth acquired through a lawsuit from the devastating fire.

"Can I call you a taxi?" Suzette asked, remembering her friend's instructions. She was glad Greta couldn't see her face. It was a struggle to hide her confused thoughts. Why would a girl who had obviously suffered immeasurable pain, and maybe still did, seek the services of a woman who inflicted pain for a living?

"No, I'll walk," said Greta. "I just need the address. And then point me in the right direction."

Suzette looked it up and Seraphina's was more than a mile away. She offered again to call a taxi, unable to imagine Greta hobbling on her stubs for a mile, up and down concrete hills. Greta, again, declined. Suzette followed her outside, noticing that Greta didn't hold a hand in front of her, but walked without hesitation, as if she could see.

Suzette pointed her in the right direction and bade her farewell. Greta headed away, limping but determined.

The dream troubled Suzette, and she'd thought about it many times throughout the day. Why *would* a girl who'd suffered through so much seek the services of a woman who promised to hurt her more?

The fire popped, sending up a spray of glowing bubbles. Alex and Hanna both gazed into the fire as they ate. It had a mesmerizing effect on everyone.

And then it dawned on her.

Greta needed her pain to become pleasurable.

It was the only way she could face the future.

The timing of the dream was obvious; fire had been on her mind. Witches' Night. And the wrongful killing of a once-innocent girl, Marie-Anne Dufosset. Her subconscious was always working in the background, and the dream rekindled an awareness that she preferred to suppress: except for Alex, she'd remained nearly friendless as an adolescent and an adult. But it was Greta, the inspiring centerpiece of the dream, who gave her the most to ponder. Something horrible had happened to her, but she refused to be a victim. She sought to overcome the bane of her existence, and possibly even make it a source of joy.

"Need anything else?" Alex asked, breaking Suzette's reverie, as he got up with his empty plate.

"It was delicious, thank you. We owe Daddy a big thank you, don't we," she said to Hanna. "He did all the work. And you helped."

"Happy to do it." He took her plate. "Should I leave everything out in case we want to nibble a little later?"

"Sure."

Hanna scampered after him as he carried all their dirty plates into the kitchen. Suzette watched them through the glass. She'd always felt of vital importance, with her shopping and cleaning, laundry and cooking, the maker of lists and the runner of errands, the hand-holder for the occasional crying girl or fretting man. But they were managing so well without her.

When Hanna came back out she headed straight for the

fire, which she poked, more confidently, with her stick. Alex brought over the bottle of wine and refilled their glasses.

"What do you think? Before it gets too late, should we say our goodbyes to Marie-Anne?" He spoke the words to Hanna, who, for the first time all day, didn't spring to his suggestion.

Suzette was relieved he was still determined to follow through with it.

"You don't need her anymore," he said, reading Hanna's hesitation. "Go get your drawing, and we'll have a goodbye ceremony."

She obeyed, but the lowered angle of her head, the lack of zip in her walk, revealed her doubt.

Suzette waited until Hanna disappeared inside. "I was afraid you'd forgotten."

Alex sighed, his face heavy with worry. "No. Trying to keep things light. I don't want her to know. What I really think."

"What do you really think?" He only shook his head, and though she was desperate to know, she loved him too much to poke at his tender places. "It's been okay. The weekend. I took a picture of the drawing."

He nodded, but he was still inside himself, maybe regretting that he'd hinted at having negative ruminations about his daughter. The mood between them turned funereal. They sipped from their wine and didn't speak again until Hanna returned, holding the picture.

"Ready?" Alex moved his and Hanna's chairs out of the way, so they could stand but still be safe from the lapping flames.

Suzette set her wine on the ground and used the chair arms to help her balance as she pushed onto her feet.

"*Älskling!*" He rushed over to her.

"I want to stand too." What she really wanted—what she'd wanted all evening—was to move back from the fire. Her feet, still bandaged and in padded socks, weren't as sore as they had been, and it felt good to stand. Stretch her legs. Alex moved her chair aside, then picked up her wine. She took it as he held on to her elbow.

"Okay?"

"Yes, I'm good." She could flee if she had to. It felt much better than sitting.

He went back to his place on the other side of the fire, stick in one hand, wine in the other. Hanna gripped her picture, looking at her father for instructions.

"We gather here on *valborgsmässoafton* to send Marie-Anne back to her realm . . ."

He spoke in a deep, priestly voice. Suzette fought a deranged urge to grin; it was no longer clear which of the three of them was most in need of professional help. Alex was a better actor than she'd ever guessed—what they were doing was lunacy—but he played it straight and somber. It would be worth it if Hanna really dissolved her attachment to Marie-Anne. Suzette held out hope that someday the girl would speak in her own voice.

"Marie-Anne tried to be a friend to our dear Hanna, but she is too mischievous a girl, and Hanna doesn't need a friend who gets her in so much trouble . . ."

An execution and funeral for their daughter's invisible friend. Suzette masked her snort of nervous laughter with a cough. Everything swirled for a moment, too much champagne and wine, but she steadied herself. It seemed proper that they should stand and be solemn and she didn't want to ruin the ceremony.

"And so we say goodbye to Marie-Anne, and in doing so we embrace Hanna—who can think for herself, and do things for herself, and speak for herself, and doesn't need a naughty witch for a companion." He gave Hanna one of her signature singular nods, and she nodded back.

"Can you poke your stick through the paper and hold it over the fire?"

This was the part Suzette had been dreading. She half expected, when the paper ignited, that it would burst into a fireball, or that a smoke-enshrouded demon would emerge from the flames.

But Hanna handed the stick and the picture to her father and let him puncture it. While he did that, Hanna reached into her pocket and brought out a handful of what looked like confetti. After tossing it into the flames, the girl reached out and took her stick back. The bits of paper burned like a meteor shower. Suzette only half-questioned their purpose, enthralled for a moment by the specks of light.

She thought it should have been a hot dog or a marsh-mallow dangling over the blaze, not a girl sentenced to burn for the second time. But nothing monstrous erupted as the edges blackened and singed. Then the fire caught it and ate around the paper's margins.

"Goodbye, Marie-Anne." She prayed the witch would really leave them.

The paper started to curl, engulfed, and Alex stepped over to help Hanna free it from her stick. He knocked the stick against the side of the copper bowl, making a tolling sound. Hanna grabbed for it, eager to have it back. As the thick paper turned to ash, succumbing to the flames, shrinking into feathery pieces, Hanna banged her stick against the pit's rim, gonging out the death knell.

It was as if she were speaking. Good. Bye. Good. Bye.

Alex sank back in his chair, tugging it closer to the fire. Suzette read exhaustion in his body, and understood then how hard it had been for him, pretending for days that he wasn't upset or worried, and trying to keep everyone calm.

She took a sip of wine. Her feet howled with pain and the prolonged pressure of standing. As she stepped back—bending her knees, ready to sit—her foot encountered something unexpected. It was just a bit of twig, but her foot protested and she lost her balance. She tumbled onto the ground beside her chair, uttering a surprised yelp, spilling her wine down the front of her clothes.

Alex was at her side in an instant, his hands under her arms, lifting her.

"Are you okay?"

"Yes. Stepped on something."

He helped her back into her chair. "Did you hurt your feet?"

"They'll be okay. I just tripped." Splotches of dark wine seeped into her jacket and down one of her pant legs. "I made a mess."

"I'll get you a cloth." He dashed into the house.

"And a bowl of warm water, with a little salt in it," she called after him.

She angled herself in the chair, partly to keep all the weight off her feet, and partly so she could examine the stains by the light of the fire. Out of the corner of her eye, she spotted Hanna, gazing at her in an intense, unsettling way. The girl crept forward.

She extended her arm, pointing at Suzette with two fingers.

Hanna mouthed silent words, over and over.

A chill radiated from Suzette's spine, prickling her skin like a million tiny scorpions. She pressed herself into the chair, wanting to get away. Suddenly the girl was beside her. When Suzette looked in her face she saw the whites of her eyes. In dead sockets.

And the fingers. Pointing. Accusing.

Marie-Anne was not gone.

HANNA

ACCELERANT. THE RESEARCH she'd started at school had been cut short, but she knew alcohol was an accelerant. The fire had its taste of Mommy—yummy, yummy, *mumsig*—and wanted more. The fire wanted to eat her!

It was clear now. The spell of Vengeance and Attack made Mommy stumble. The spell coated her with alcohol. Fire accelerant.

It was up to her to do the rest.

Mommy pulled up her feet, shrinking into the corner of her chair, eyes big and afraid. Hanna kept her spell focused, directed at Mommy through two outstretched fingers, and mouthed the words. *Suffer and cease to be. Suffer and cease to be.*

She prodded the flames with her stick. Fished for a burning branch. And flung it out of the copper pit.

Mommy screamed as it landed in her lap. She scrambled out of her chair. Fell. Pushed the burning branch away with her bare hands.

Hanna used her stick like a shovel, gripped in both fists, scooping out burning embers. They landed on Mommy's legs. Her foot. Mommy squealed and kicked, trying to wriggle away.

She swept more embers out of the fire, hurling them at Mommy.

They attacked her like vampire lightning bugs.

Mommy howled and cried.

The tip of her stick glowed a molten orange, and Hanna knew just what to do. Mommy's hands were flapping at her pants, trying to extinguish some burning threads. Hanna aimed the stick right at Mommy's eye, but at the last minute Mommy looked up and Hanna's aim went awry. She plunged the fiery stick into her cheek, where it made a sizzling sound. Mommy screamed, and wrenched the weapon from her hands.

In the next instant Daddy was there, a bowl in his hands. He tossed it on Mommy, on the fluttering, enflamed bits.

He picked up Hanna. And threw her.

She came back to herself, as the cool air sailed past.

Had she gotten too close to the fire? Was Daddy saving her?

She landed splat on a muddy patch of grass and rolled. Stunned. Something tore inside her wrist, the one that she'd held out to break her fall. Her thumb was going to come loose and fall off. She screamed.

But Daddy and Mommy didn't run to her.

Instead, Daddy ran to the table and grabbed the Brita pitcher. He poured it on Mommy and stomped on the embers. Mommy wailed and curled up in a ball.

"Where does it hurt?"

"My face! More water!"

Daddy lifted Mommy into his arms and dashed into

the house. Hanna held her left arm against her chest, still sobbing, and trailed after them. She almost whimpered "Daddy," but it sounded like a broken-up, tear-filled squeal.

She couldn't understand what happened. The spell had gone so well. And she did it all herself, without Marie-Anne. It was almost finished, Mommy had been squirming on the ground, about to catch fire. And then Daddy ruined it. It wasn't possible he could love Mommy more than her. Was it? He *threw* her. Threw her away.

"Why?" she cried through her tears, her French accent abandoned, but neither parent heard her.

Daddy put Mommy on the big table and wiped at her with wet dish towels while Mommy held a wet cloth to her face and wept. Her head fell against the table and Daddy yelled, "Should I call nine-one-one?"

Mommy shook her head, but couldn't stop crying.

The drama of it scared Hanna a little, her parents in such disarray, their movements so out of control. She blinked and blinked while hugging herself with her one good arm.

As Mommy started to wiggle out of her ruined pants, Daddy helped and yanked them off.

"This spot here." She pointed above her knee. "And my hands." She used her elbows to push herself into a sitting position, and let Daddy wrap the wet cloths around one hand, then the other.

Daddy scrambled in the cabinets until he found more dish towels. He plunged them under the kitchen tap, moving in clumsy jerks, like a strange creature she'd seen on

Star Trek, jolted by bolts from a laser gun. He looked nutso whacko and she didn't like it.

He wrung the wet rags over Mommy's exposed skin, then draped them on her leg. "Are there more burns?"

What a mess he was making. Mommy wouldn't like it. Even Hanna felt the urge to rush in and sponge the water off the floor. She jumped up and down a little—look at me, look at me! Another whimper escaped her throat, but Mommy and Daddy still acted like she wasn't there.

"My face."

"We should go to the emergency room."

Mommy shook her head. "Urgent Care, it'll be faster, and it's not . . . I don't think they're too bad . . ."

Hanna crept in closer. Mommy wasn't crying so much anymore; she lifted the compress off her cheek and showed it to Daddy. "Is it okay?"

"Holy shit . . ." Daddy couldn't stop zip-zip-spazzing. "We need to get to the doctor's!"

"Is it that bad? Oh God! I'm not going anywhere without pants—grab me some shorts?"

Daddy charged up the stairs. That's when Mommy finally noticed her. At first Mommy froze, big-eyed and ready to flee. Hanna inched over, mewling a bit, clutching her arm beneath the swollen part.

"Hanna? Are you hurt?" Mommy swung her head around, like she couldn't decide which way to go—she looked up the stairs, toward the front door, and finally back at Hanna. As she gazed at Hanna her face went from frightened to concerned. "What were you doing . . . ? Is it broken?"

Hanna stood beside the table and extended her arm. Her wrist had fattened into a plummy bulb.

Mommy's mask slipped off and her gaze turned hard, mean, like she couldn't pretend anymore that she wasn't really Bad Mommy. "That's what you get . . . Hurts, doesn't it?"

The stairs rumbled as Daddy thundered down.

"Hanna's hurt," Mommy said. Her face flipped back to normal then, the way she got whenever Hanna had a fever or a tummy ache.

"What's wrong?"

"Her wrist, I think it's broken."

Daddy's eyes and mouth popped like an alarm.

"Get her an ice pack . . ."

As he handed Mommy the shorts, she had to put down the cloth she'd kept against her face. Hanna gaped at the wound on her cheek as Mommy shimmied into her clothes. A big fat circle, black and red, and Hanna thought of the erupting mouth of a volcano. Daddy, poor Daddy, couldn't stop the panic mode. He leapt to the freezer and grabbed up a dry dishcloth that had slipped onto the floor.

"I'm so sorry—"

"What happened?" Mommy asked.

"I wasn't thinking, I just . . . I had to get her away from you." He turned from Mommy to Hanna. "Baby, I'm so sorry!" Daddy gently wrapped the towel-covered ice pack around her wrist. "Holy shit, I can't even believe this is—"

"Honey, it's okay, we're okay . . . But we can't leave with the fire going."

Daddy, all-a-shambles, hurried out back and used the hose to put out their little fire. He scrambled back in, carrying a few plates of food that clattered when he shoved them on the counter. Hanna still didn't like how zonkers he looked, out of control and barely aware of what he was doing.

"Okay, everybody ready? Hanna, *lilla gumman*, I'm so sorry . . ."

Hanna wanted him to pick her up and carry her to the car. But he carried Mommy instead. She whimpered. The ice pack made it worse; her wrist still throbbed but now it pulsed in sharp, frozen shards.

"Come on, Hanna," Mommy said over her shoulder. "I know it hurts, but we'll be at the doctor's really soon."

It only took a few minutes to get there, and Mommy spent most of that time being rather good Mommy-like and saying over and over that everyone was going to be okay, take some deep breaths, and she didn't sound mad or even like she was hurting. Sometimes Daddy had to brake really hard because he was driving very fast.

The sign—Shadyside Urgent Care—looked bright against the darkening sky. The parking lot was pretty empty.

In the waiting room, Daddy put Mommy in one of the very ugly olive-green chairs and rushed to the desk and spoke so fast about "his wife" and "his daughter" that Desk Lady asked him to slow down.

Desk Lady said it would just be a few minutes. Daddy sat on Mommy's other side, filling in paperwork, leaving

Mommy in the middle. Her eyelids fluttered as she pressed the folded cloth to her cheek and gripped Daddy's forearm with her free hand. She was as colorless as the cloth.

"I can't believe she would do this," Daddy said.

Hanna knew he was talking about her, and frowned very big so her lip stuck out. She'd failed again. As he scribbled on the papers, Daddy sometimes glanced at her, his face a puzzle of mismatched pieces. Hanna wanted to tell him that she'd tried, she followed the will of her spell. But Mommy was so much stronger than she'd anticipated. She didn't burn up like the confetti or the drawing. She didn't poof disappear into a cloud of ash. The spell wasn't supposed to cause crying and stupid ouchies, it was supposed to make her gone. It was supposed to free Daddy, yet somehow he was in more pain than either of them.

He handed Desk Lady the clipboard and sat back down in a huff of too-long limbs.

"Don't be too angry with her . . ." Mommy gripped his hand. Her eyeballs wobbled around and Hanna inched away from her, afraid Mommy was going to throw up. "She doesn't understand. She doesn't understand right from wrong. Good from evil. To her, what's play is real and what's real is play. There's no point in being mad if she doesn't even understand."

"What's wrong with her?"

It was weird, the way they looked at her, talked about her. Like she was someone else. Or someone who shouldn't be able to see and hear them. Hanna looked down at her legs, her smudged shirt, worried she might have turned invisible. But she could still see herself, and hear everything

Mommy and Daddy were saying. She snuffled back her tears.

"Something's wrong inside her. Some chemical thing. Something got twisted," Mommy said.

"How do we fix it?"

"I don't know."

They called Suzette first and brought over a wheelchair when they realized something was wrong with her feet. Daddy wanted to follow Mommy, and Hanna thought they were going to abandon her in the waiting room.

"Stay with Hanna," Mommy said. "You'll have an X-ray, baby—it won't hurt, and then they'll see what's wrong with your wrist, okay?" And they wheeled Mommy away.

She moved over to be beside Daddy, though what she really wanted was to sit on his lap. No. What she really wanted was for him to scoop her onto his lap and murmur all the sweet things that made her feel bloomy and good. But he didn't. He gazed at her, his forehead and eyebrows wrinkly with anguish.

"My *lilla gumman* . . ." But he sounded a solar system away. She looped her right arm around his bicep. Together? We're okay? She loved him so so much. "We're going to make sure you get the help you need, okay? So you'll be okay?"

She nodded. Her hand didn't even hurt that much anymore.

After they did the X-ray, she sat on the paper-covered table and was very glad Daddy stayed so close, shoulder to shoulder.

"Good news," said Dr. Something as he bustled through the open doorway. "It's not broken. Just a sprain."

Dr. Something spoke with an accent much stronger than Daddy's.

Daddy breathed a big gush of relief. The doctor turned on him for a moment with his very dark eyes. But for her, his eyes went smiley again.

"So, I'll just wrap it for you, in a big stretchy bandage." He started at a point below her wrist and wrapped it around and up and over her thumb and back down and around. "So, let me guess—did you fall off your bike? Or was it some other daring feat of bravery?"

Hanna liked the way the bandage felt, all snug and secure around her sore wrist.

"She doesn't talk," Daddy said.

"Oh. Ever?" He gave Hanna a big teasing smile, like that would unlock her years of withheld words.

"No. Well . . . not to me."

Dr. Something looked at Daddy, very very not smiling. "I understand your wife was brought in too? Some sort of accident in the backyard?"

"Our fire pit."

The doctor nodded. "So . . . What happened with your daughter?"

Daddy hesitated. "Part of the same accident."

Hanna didn't like the way the doctor was two people rolled into one—lighthearted with her; super serious with Daddy.

"So, I suppose since she doesn't talk, Miss Hanna can't explain her side of the story. That's very convenient."

The two men stared each other down like a pair of cobras.

Daddy shifted his weight, moving in closer to Hanna. She was very glad he knew she was on his side. She couldn't even stay mad at him for throwing her because he was still under Mommy's spell.

"I didn't hurt my family," Daddy said, his jaw tightening.

Hanna's mouth dropped open; she didn't realize that's what the doctor was hinting at. But she snapped it shut and scowled at the doctor. She threw her arms around Daddy and he picked her up, carrying her on his hip.

"Okay, but you understand it's part of my job to make sure—"

"Is she ready to leave? It's past her bedtime."

Though she wasn't tired, she laid her head on Daddy's shoulder, pretending to be sleepy. He was still and always her most favorite person and Dr. Something didn't have a clue about the who or why of their botched execution.

"They'll print up aftercare instructions for you when you check out."

Daddy strode out and Hanna liked being in his strong arms. He'd regained his strength—for her. Fully back on her side. She loved how deep their understanding was. They could each make little blunders, but in the end they were a team.

Now what were they going to do about Mommy?

SUZETTE

SHE WAS STRUCK by the doctor's youth and beauty. Her magnificent thick hair and coppery skin. Suzette wanted to ask where she was from, unable to pinpoint her ethnicity by her name or coloring. But she knew such a question was impolitic, and would likely yield a truthful but unhelpful answer: Berkeley, California; Newark, New Jersey; Columbus, Ohio. Likely she had parents or grandparents from one or several other parts of the world, but Suzette accepted the irrelevance of her own curiosity. More important, the doctor had a delicate touch and a soothing manner.

The doctor confirmed the wounds above Suzette's left knee and on her cheek were worse than the burns on her hands. Thankfully, only a tiny piece of fabric had to be separated from her skin. Her hands, swaddled in gel and gauze, barely stung anymore—she'd acquired a worse injury after taking a heavy dish out of the oven with a frayed hot mitt. But she was warned her knee might scar a little. And her cheek. The doctor had tended to it first as Suzette lay on the exam table, fighting a wave of nausea.

"How bad?" Suzette had asked.

The doctor had continued working for a minute, gently cleaning the edges of the wound. "It'll be fairly symmetrical, about the size of a quarter. I'm glad this black stuff—it's just charcoal, not dead skin. You might be left with some puckering or a little discoloration after it fully heals. I can refer you to a plastic surgeon, but with a second-degree burn like this, I don't know if they can help."

Suzette lost herself for a spell, cataloging her body's road map of scars. It seemed fortuitous that she'd so recently had her gaping abdominal scar repaired. The new abdominal incision, and the laparoscopic ones, were healing in tidy lines; in combination with whatever would remain on her leg, the collection of them was still less terrible than what the reminder of her fistula had been. But what of the scar now marring her face? How prominent would it be? Would everyone's eyes go there first? Would they ask what happened, or would they turn their gaze in pity? And what could she ever say if they did ask? Oh, my sweet little girl tried to incinerate me while we were having a picnic.

And what would Alex think? He might say she was still beautiful. But it would forever remind him of sick Hanna and all their parental failings. It was easy to imagine him never looking her in the face again. For the same reason, it was easy to imagine herself avoiding every mirror and reflection. The ugliness aside. Irreparable harm. Internal, external. That's what Hanna had done: irreparable harm. It was unforgivable. Even if she'd mothered imperfectly. She didn't deserve to wear her failings like a brand.

It was bandaged for now, in thick gauze that both collected the wound's watery ooze and kept all the healing ointment from seeping out. Maybe she'd always keep a bandage over it. Pretend it was a new injury in the process of healing. That seemed more acceptable to her: a misfortune that might yet heal, rather than a scar that would remind her forever of the demon she'd given birth to. Would it be better for Alex that way, too? Easier for him to still find her attractive? She'd tried so hard to keep herself beautiful for her husband. Never again would she let Hanna threaten the one relationship that had been strong and true.

As the doctor finished treating her leg, they made light banter about summer plans. The doctor wanted mountains. Suzette couldn't think of anything beyond her in-laws' July visit; Tova and Bernt made their house a regular stop on their annual return trip from Europe. Their conversation went silent for a moment.

"So, there are some standard questions we ask everyone who comes in. Have you had any serious falls in the last six months?"

"No."

"Have you been depressed?"

"No. A little. Not depression exactly."

"Is anyone hurting you at home?"

"Is that one of the standard questions?" Tendrils of anxiety radiated through Suzette's gut. Had the pleasant conversation been an attempt to earn her trust, in anticipation of this one inquiry? Her shoulders tightened, alarmed that she'd exposed herself and her family to the type of scrutiny she'd sought to avoid.

The beautiful young doctor smiled at her. "Yes. But in your case, it seemed especially relevant."

"Because of my feet?" Suzette, needing help onto the exam table, had explained how she'd stumbled by the fire because of her previously damaged feet, which she'd downplayed with a vague "stepped on something." She'd declined to have the doctor check them.

"You have multiple injuries, some preexisting. And your daughter was brought in as well."

Suzette frowned, aware of how Alex would feel if he was being put through a similar line of questioning. He didn't deserve the accusations, but she appreciated why they had to ask, had to make sure. Would Alex get angry and make himself look more suspicious?

"It's not my husband. He'd never hurt me."

"Is someone else at home? Hurting you?"

Her adrenaline plummeted; Suzette didn't want any more of the doctor's compassion or concern. She wanted to go to their imperfect home and sleep an imperfect sleep. She heard herself trying to explain, in a defeated and distant voice, worried they'd call Child Protective Services or some other agency that would condemn Alex.

". . . You wouldn't understand. It's complicated."

"You're safe here. I don't want you going home if you're in danger . . ."

"You don't understand. It's my daughter . . ." There was too much to tell and this wasn't the place, so she shook her head. Her breathing grew shallow as the walls pressed in. *Please, let us go* . . . They'd deal with it with Beatrix, who already knew something about them.

"Your daughter is in danger?" More head-shaking. Suzette couldn't even look in the doctor's perplexed face as she tried to piece it together. "Your daughter . . . hurts you?"

With the words formed in someone else's mouth, the reality came fully into existence, too. Hanna had dark intentions toward her, maybe even murderous ones. Something inside her burst and crumbled—their precious fortress of denial and hope. Her limbs went loose, her head dropped with the weight of defeat.

"I don't know why," she said, the pain of it greater than even her throbbing cheek. "I don't think I ever did anything that terrible . . . Not intentionally. We—my husband and I—know there's something wrong, we're trying. We have an appointment with her therapist first thing in the morning."

The doctor nodded, stunned into silence. Suzette read the fear, the newness of such a dilemma, in the doctor's face.

"Well, if there's anything we can do to help . . ." But it was an empty offer, and the doctor was already moving away from her, peeling off her blue nitrile gloves. Her body language changed, closing herself off from the situation. It was all too weird, too foreign, too diabolical.

Suzette brought her trembling fingers to her mouth. It was a mistake to have said anything. She and Alex could never pretend again. Violent children only grow up to be serial killers. It was a fear she couldn't resolve.

A few minutes later, they wheeled her into the waiting room where Alex sat with Hanna on his lap. On his lap, like nothing happened. They got their aftercare info and Suzette's referral, and Alex folded the papers and stuffed them into his pants pocket.

Hanna grabbed the wheelchair handles and started pushing.

"Hey, not so fast—you can't use that hand. It's not broken, but it's sprained. You have to let it rest," Alex told her.

"Just use your right hand and Daddy will get the other side," Suzette said. Her daughter's effort to help was sweet—as she could sometimes be—unless Hanna meant to push her in front of a bus.

They maneuvered her into the parking lot. Alex whispered in her left ear, "They thought I was abusing you."

"I know. They asked me about it too."

"What did you tell them?"

"The truth."

When they got home from Urgent Care, Hanna plodded off to her room. Neither of them thought to follow her up or make sure she brushed her teeth. Alex brought in Suzette's crutches and the remnants of their feast. The dishes stayed on the counter, spoiling. They collapsed together on the couch, huddled in each other's arms like refugees.

At dawn, the bells chimed upstairs. Hanna had awakened.

"Go. Take a shower," Suzette told Alex, stretching out the night's kinks. He hesitated. "We can't fall apart."

Hanna snuck down while Alex was in the shower. After surveying the piled-up dishes in the kitchen, she wrinkled her nose; it stank of fish and onions. Suzette disapproved somewhat of her daughter's wardrobe choice—a slightly-too-big summer dress and color-coordinated but mismatched yellow knee socks—but at least Hanna appeared to be reasonably clean. Her wrist remained bandaged, but Suzette was relieved that she no longer seemed protective of it.

"Hungry?"

Hanna shrugged.

"Want to get your brush and I'll fix your hair?"

Her daughter turned and clambered back up the stairs.

Suzette groaned a little, easing herself into a sitting position. She straightened out her shirt. She'd slip on a bra later before they went out. And a loose pair of long pants, which would cover the bandage and discolored marks on her legs. Couldn't hide her face, though. And probably wouldn't wear shoes, just slippers. She'd gotten used to clothing that was the equivalent of pajamas over the last few days. It felt good to be comfortable.

She was hobbling back from the powder room after a quick pee when Hanna returned holding a brush and two red hair bands. Suzette limped over to the table and sat down. The puddles from Alex's efforts to cool her burns had dried. The abandoned dish towels were stiff mounds.

Hanna knew the routine; she stood between Suzette's legs, facing away from her.

"I'll just give mine a quick brushing first." With the purple sparkly brush gripped gingerly between her least-sore fingers, she ran it through her hair a few times. Better than nothing.

Their glamorous days were over. She didn't care if she showed up at the therapist's looking like the type of people she used to complain about, who went about in public as if the whole world was their bedroom. Why couldn't other people be bothered to put on proper clothes? She saw them everywhere. At Starbucks. Rite Aid. The Giant Eagle. People who looked as if they were just going to, or just getting ready for, bed. Now she knew what it took for her to abandon the basics of propriety. Was everyone's life in such a state of ruin? Were they all just barely going through the motions?

She ran the brush through her daughter's hair, careful not to cause the slightest bit of discomfort. Hanna held up the hair bands, one in each hand.

"Braids? Pigtails?"

Hanna nodded at the second suggestion. Suzette parted her hair down the back, sweeping one section away.

"You know, I wish I knew what I did. I'd undo it." She spoke to her softly. "You have to believe me. I don't want you to be in pain, but you can't keep hurting me."

There was nothing else to say. Hanna remained silent.

The pigtails sat high on either side of her head, parallel and perfect. Not a hair out of place. Suzette nudged Hanna's shoulders, and the girl turned to face her. Suzette gave the bottom of each pigtail a twist, so each settled in a curl. A dread descended; everything was about to change. What would Beatrix say about their daughter's future? Hanna had laid her own path, but where was she leading them, and could they ever recover? It felt awkward, but Suzette needed to do it: she wrapped her tentative arms around Hanna's rigid and resisting body.

"I remember," Suzette whispered. "Being young, and feeling so alone. I promise. It won't always be this way."

She kissed her daughter's rosy, perfect cheek. Sat back and looked at her adorable face. Hanna remained expressionless. Suzette remembered a few mornings when she was little and her mother wanted to snuggle in bed. Suzette lay with her mother's arm beneath her head, but wouldn't roll in for a cuddle. Her mother spoke in a babyish voice as Suzette lay stiff as a board, aware of the body beside her as if it were component parts of rotting flesh and unyielding bone, and waited for the affection to be over. Maybe her mother had tried. Maybe Suzette rejected her love. Maybe her mother gave up. They hadn't bonded well, but she'd needed her mother to keep trying. It was a child's selfish desire, but mothers were meant to be selfless.

She thrust her arms around Hanna. A genuine embrace, tight and heartfelt.

Suzette and Alex were both anxious; the pot of coffee, shared in silence at the table, didn't help. Hanna nibbled on her cereal, so cautious with her spoon that it made no sound against the bowl. Her exaggerated care suited the mood. Suzette couldn't shake the sense that something was about to break. One of them would speak and the entire room—the house—would splinter into a million pieces, shattering the illusion they inhabited. Suzette and Alex kept glancing at their phones, eager to leave.

They arrived at Dr. Yamamoto's fifteen minutes early. Hanna ran ahead to the door.

"I guess she likes her. Or the toys." Suzette kept her arm threaded through Alex's. The crutches weren't the fix they'd once been, not with having to put pressure on blistered finger pads and palms. She walked slowly, careful not to step on a stone or a crack, feeling doomed and ridiculous with her gauzy hands and slippered feet. Hanna still wore her mismatched knee socks and opted for ladybug rain boots, in spite of the clear weather. Suzette had her put on a cardigan for the morning chill, but Hanna pushed up the sleeves. Because she was too warm, or eager to show off her bandaged wrist? Even Alex didn't look as sharp as usual, though he was probably the cleanest of the three of them. He opted for gym pants, with a buttoned shirt worn open over a blue T-shirt. His beard was raggedy, the lines around his eyes more pronounced.

Hanna held her finger over the doorbell, looking to her mother for permission. When Suzette nodded, Hanna pushed the bell. She and Alex weren't yet to the door when Beatrix opened it. Her welcoming smile melted as she took in the three of them. The limping. The bandages. The rumpled mess.

"Oh dear. Not the best weekend, I take it?" She glanced down at Hanna with a warm smile. "Good morning, Hanna. Do you want to go into the playroom?"

Hanna grinned and skipped inside.

As the adults moved down the hallway, slowly to accommodate Suzette's hobbling, Hanna disappeared into the playroom.

"These look like new injuries. Is everyone okay?" Beatrix asked.

"We had an accident—"

Suzette cut Alex off. "Hanna's trying to kill me."

They hovered in the doorway to Beatrix's office. Alex and Suzette just looked at each other, wearing matching expressions of wounded, but not angry, acceptance.

"We've had so little time together," said Beatrix. "But I made note during our first session of Hanna's Callous-Unemotional traits."

"What does that mean?" Alex asked.

"Perhaps I should speak with her first today, and see if I can uncover a bit more."

HANNA

BEATRIX SAID SHE'D be right back, that she needed to lower the blind in the other room so they would have privacy. Hanna found a puzzle of a real-life castle and brought it over to the table. A minute later Beatrix came in and shut the door.

"I'm glad to see you." Beatrix had a nice voice, like honey and daisies. She got paper and a plastic box from the cart against the wall, and sat near her in one of the little chairs.

"You'll have lots of time to work on a puzzle when I talk with your mom and dad. Do you think you and I could do something together for a few minutes?"

Hanna liked that she used the word "together." Beatrix had a very nice way of making Hanna feel like she listened to and understood her, and without stupid questions or flash cards. She reminded Hanna of a character she'd liked in a book, who was the grandmother of the world and all its natural creatures. Sometimes the old woman in the book looked like a fairy godmother with smiling dimples, and sometimes she looked like the waves of the ocean, or a tree with beckoning limbs. She knew everything and saw the goodness in everyone. Beatrix made her feel like a chest filled with shiny treasure, so she nodded and pushed the puzzle box away.

"It looks like you hurt your wrist. Are you okay?"

Hanna nodded. She didn't even think of it as Daddy's fault anymore. In that moment he was a puppet, with Mommy yanking his strings.

"I'm thinking you all had a pretty dramatic weekend."

Big nod.

"I hope it wasn't too scary?"

Hanna tilted her head a little and let it wobble while she rolled her eyes. Beatrix smiled, and then Hanna smiled because she made Beatrix smile.

"Are you too brave to get scared?"

Big noddy nod.

"Well, here's what I was thinking." Beatrix laid out some pieces of construction paper in different colors and popped open the plastic box, which was filled with crayons and pencils. "I was hoping you could draw me some pictures. Like, can you draw me a picture of Mommy?"

Hanna scrumbled up her face, confused. She pointed to the other room.

"I know, she's right in there—and you're probably thinking I already know what she looks like, right?"

Hanna nodded. Beatrix was super smart.

"But you know what: sometimes people see different things. And I want to see how *you* see your mommy."

Oh yes, so so smart. Beatrix understood that Mommy always wore a mask; she wanted to know what was beneath it. Hanna grabbed a piece of red paper and a black crayon.

She couldn't draw people very well—in spite of Mommy's helpful lesson—so she just drew her face. Fat blobby head. Mean little eyes. A snarl. Some teeth sticking out. Then, so Beatrix couldn't mistake it, she drew a big triangle hat with a wide brim and viciously colored it in. She pushed the paper around so it faced Beatrix.

"Is that a witch's hat?" she asked.

Yup yup yup.

"Is Mommy a witch?"

Bingo!

"Now, she told me about Marie-Anne—I thought Marie-Anne was the witch."

Nod.

"And she was helping you?"

Yes. But. She tap tap tapped on Mommy's hat with her black crayon.

"But Mommy is a witch also?"

Hanna made her eyes go big and round and she nodded slowly so Beatrix would understand the gravity of the situation.

"Is Mommy a scary witch?"

Oh yes. Hanna took up a pencil and used it like a wand, trying to show Beatrix how Mommy cast spells. She made her face pinched and mean and jabbed with the pencil-wand.

"Is that a wand? Does Mommy cast spells?"

Instead of answering, Hanna grabbed up another piece of paper—a light-blue one—and used a darker blue crayon to try to draw Daddy. She made him with long legs so Beatrix would recognize him, and scribbled a beard around his chin.

"Is that Daddy?"

Nod. She pointed to the picture of Mommy, then thrust out the pencil-wand, banging it on Daddy's picture.

"Did Mommy cast a spell on Daddy?"

Yes!

"Oh my goodness, that sounds very serious. Why did Mommy do that?"

With a red crayon, she drew a wobbly heart in the middle of Daddy's chest. Then she put her hands, one on top of the other, over her own chest. She pointed from Daddy's crayoned heart to her own real one, back and forth.

"Daddy loves you. He loves you very much."

Hanna pointed from her heart to his.

"And you love him."

Big nod.

"Hanna, I just want to say, you are doing such an excellent job of expressing yourself."

Grin.

Explaining the next part was a bit harder. She panto-mimed the love she and Daddy had, making her hand move back and forth between their two hearts. Then, frustrated and angry, she picked up Mommy's wand and slashed with it like a sword, cutting the love she shared with Daddy.

Beatrix frowned. Hanna made the slashing gesture again, waiting for her to understand.

"Do you think your mom wants to stop your dad from loving you?"

Hanna's body flopped with relief. She hopped up and gave Beatrix a kiss on the cheek.

"It feels good for someone to understand, doesn't it?"

So so yes.

"I know you're not quite ready, but someday, after you get over some hard things, some other things might become easier. Like, it might be hard to become someone who talks and interacts, but when you do, you might be rewarded by how other people respond, and how good it feels for other people to understand."

Hanna shrugged, not quite able to imagine herself blah-blahing back and forth like everyone else. And still a little afraid that her most important words might yet come out as dead bugs, frightening nonsense that would earn her nothing but strange looks. She folded her foot under her and sat back down.

"So let's get back to your drawings. Can you tell me why you think Mommy doesn't want Daddy to love you anymore?"

Hanna picked up Mommy's drawing in one hand and Daddy's in the other. She had them face each other, then pressed them together.

Beatrix looked confused.

Hanna grabbed up a piece of yellow paper and a purple crayon and drew a little stick figure with two ponytails. She pointed to herself, then the picture.

"That's you."

Right. She turned over the pictures of Mommy and

Daddy so they were face up. Picked up a pencil while pointing at Mommy. And cast a spell by tapping it onto Daddy. She picked up both pictures again and smooshed them into each other, twisting them a little like they were smoochy smoochy. She puckered up her lips to make it clear. Snatching up the picture of herself, she tore it into big messy chunks and swept them onto the floor. She made Mommy and Daddy's pictures move like they were walking—walking away from the pieces of her scattered on the floor.

"So you think . . . Mommy cast a spell on Daddy. You don't think she loves you?"

Big no.

"And the spell makes Daddy not love you anymore. And the two of them go off together, and leave you behind. They don't want you?"

Sad no.

"That must feel very bad. I can imagine how sad I would feel."

Sighing yes.

"So if I'm understanding everything right . . . Then you're trying to hurt Mommy so Daddy will always love you?"

A nod. A shake. Not hurt. She drew a big X over Mommy the Witch's face. Then slowly tore the paper down the middle.

"You want Mommy gone? Dead?"

It was necessary.

"You spend a lot of time with her—do you think you would miss her if she wasn't around?"

Nope. She pointed at Daddy's picture.

"You'd have Daddy then, all to yourself."

Exactly.

"I want to thank you for sharing all of this with me. I'm glad you trust me."

Beatrix was her second most favoritest person. And she understood everything. Without words. Hanna thought of Mommy—the way she liked to draw, and buy her coloring stuff for presents. Had Mommy known all along that pictures could be substitutes for words? Hanna tapped a finger on one of her half-grown-in teeth, considering the possibility of creating her own language out of colorful splotches. She could teach it to Daddy, and they could communicate that way.

"It's important to me that you know that I care about you, and I only want to help you, and I'll try to do what's best for you. Okay?"

Hanna felt all singing and ringing inside. Because Beatrix knew what was best for her, and maybe with the help of a big person like her, they could finally make Mommy go away.

SUZETTE

SUZETTE SAT WITH her legs stretched across the couch, Alex perched at the other end, waiting in a miasma of private thoughts. The cloudy blind covered the playroom window like a cataract. Somewhere her vision had failed. Once Hanna had been a balloon calmly suspended at the end of a string. When had the balloon twisted away in a rill of turbulent air? Why hadn't she noticed?

After a passage of swampy time, Beatrix came in. She raised the blind, and there was Hanna on the other side, unboxing a puzzle. Beatrix sat, monitoring her three clients from the chair between the mirrored window and the sofa.

"Was she . . . ?" Suzette didn't finish the question.

"Quite eager to communicate," Beatrix said. "Surprisingly adept at it, even without words."

"Did she tell you . . . ?" Alex cringed. "It wouldn't have happened—it was my fault, I shouldn't have gone through with the Walpurgis celebration."

Beatrix's brow furrowed, her lips parted, but before she could speak, Suzette jumped in and caught her up. About how they celebrated the Swedish holiday. Their attempt to help Hanna let go of her dangerous other self. The fire. Urgent Care.

"I should never have planned an activity for my family around fire. It was stupid, I don't know what I was thinking." His hair flopped over his hands as he held his head.

Suzette wished she could comfort him, but he was out of reach.

"It was a creative idea," said Beatrix. "And all things considered—"

"I could've gotten Suzette killed . . ." Alex said, cutting her off.

"I'm fine." Suzette couldn't explain it, but she felt calmer, less conflicted than she had in months. Even the twinges in her stomach were gone. Though she fought the urge to keep one hand protectively against her bandaged cheek.

"And Hanna . . . I don't know, maybe she really is possessed . . ."

"No, she's not." Beatrix spoke the words with a contemplative drawl. "We have a lot to talk about. If the weekend had gone differently, I might have had a different course of action for you—the evaluations I talked about. But I don't think we can take the time for that."

"What are you suggesting?" Suzette asked.

"Remember on Friday? I said I wanted to look into something? A few years ago I had a family with a violent child. The child needed to be removed from the household. I did a lot of research at the time, and I called the facility on Friday. Just to see, in case we needed that as an option. I think we do."

Alex finally looked up. Suzette struggled to read his expression. She knew a part of him would always be loyal to Hanna. He fed on her adoration and sweetness. But where did he stand now? Hanna's behavior pained him in such a personal way. He'd been lied to, betrayed. They couldn't continue without intervention and help. Suzette shut her eyes, relieved that her fantasy might come true—that Hanna could be sent away, at least for a short time—but she didn't want Alex to see her relief, or the glee bubbling beneath the surface.

"Removed from the household?" he asked.

"Yes, an inpatient facility."

"Like a mental hospital?"

"Not like what you're thinking."

"Is Hanna . . . Is she a psychopath?" His voice broke. He brought a fist to his mouth and cleared his throat, fighting to get himself under control. Was that what he'd been pondering the previous night? That their child might be the worst of the worst, a violent monster?

"I want to explain everything to you about my preliminary diagnosis. And Marshes—the facility." Beatrix stood. "I'm going to run into the kitchen for a minute. To cancel my ten o'clock. And send a quick email off to Marshes. Okay? I'll be right back."

Beatrix left the door open, and they watched her head down the hallway—delicate like a dancer, even with the angular swing of her arms—and retreat into the main part of her house. Suzette slid her feet off the couch and scooted over, taking Alex's hand.

"What are you thinking? About an inpatient facility?" she asked.

"I don't know. We don't really know anything yet. I

mean . . . Is that where we are? I guess it is. I just . . . She's seven. How can she not live with us?"

"She can't, Alex." She softened her tone, aware he was still several paces behind her. "I don't think she can. Look what she did to me. We don't know how to handle her—"

"That's why it all just seems so hopeless. This is hopeless." Tension coursed through his body. Suzette loosened his tight grip on her fingers.

"It isn't. If Hanna's sick . . . We'd help her if she had asthma, or leukemia. We'd be in it for the long haul. We'd do everything to help her get healthy. Right?" She owed her daughter that.

Alex rubbed his eye and looked at her. "What if she can't get better?"

There it was, the wound he'd been nursing. The fear of a monster that couldn't be vanquished.

"What if she can?" Suzette had to believe it was possible. She knew for herself how even incurable conditions could be managed. They didn't have to spend their lives being terrorized by their child. And Hanna didn't have to be condemned to an inner nightmare of turmoil and confusion. It was hard for Suzette to forgive herself for not recognizing the symptoms sooner, but being good parents meant getting Hanna the care she needed. Even if that meant sending her away. It wouldn't be forever.

They sat in silence, watching their daughter in the other room, content and unaware as she put her puzzle together.

* * *

Beatrix returned a short time later carrying a tray of tea with the balmy aroma of chamomile. "I brought herbal tea and bagels. You aren't gluten-free, are you?" They shook their heads. She set the tray on the coffee table. "You look like you could use something warm and hearty. Has Hanna eaten?"

"She had some cereal," Suzette said.

"Well, help yourself."

"Thank you." Suzette sipped from one of the mugs. "Oh, nice."

"I'll just take her in a snack and tell her we'll be talking for a while." She spread strawberry-jam cream cheese on a half bagel, and slipped out.

Again, they watched the therapist interact with their child. Hanna looked so darling, so polite, as she took her bagel and gnawed on it with her half-grown-in teeth. Beatrix came back in and closed the door.

"Right, so. First let me say that mental illness is as real as any other illness. But it can be scarier, because of how it manifests." She folded one leg over the other, a Moleskine notebook on her lap and a pen in her hand. Alex and Suzette each prepared a bagel, and nibbled and drank with their eyes fixed on Beatrix.

"So, after speaking with her . . . Had it just been her drawings, I might have concluded there's something going on that's making her jealous, or some sort of more typical mother-daughter, caregiver-child issues . . . masked in a kind of fantasy play. And maybe there is a bit of a struggle, with reality. But this is more than even severe Oppositional Defiant Disorder. The drawings she made really clarify the intent behind the actions you've described—the thumbtacks, the fire. Your injuries." *Your ruined face*. "And I think we need to take those intentions very seriously, especially seeing how quickly things have escalated.

"Marshes is a unique facility that I found, as I said, a few years ago for another family. It's modeled after a facility in the UK, and provides immersive treatment for children with severe behavioral issues. She'll live there. Go to school there. Have her therapy. And she'll have one-on-one supervision twenty-four hours a day. She'll have someone with her in class, someone monitoring her playtime, someone available to her at night—"

"It sounds like a prison," Alex said, hostile, his mouth full of bagel.

"Marshes has developed a very effective strategy. Part of that is removing the child from the environment that may have exacerbated their problems." She took a moment to consider each of them. "I won't lie to you—some of the kids at Marshes come from extremely abusive households . . ."

Suzette stopped chewing, a knot of panic in her throat. She'd thought the diagnosis of a mental illness would get her off the hook, remove her parenting from blame. She glanced at Alex, half expecting him to erupt. He kept his glowering eyes on Beatrix, but listened without interrupting.

"The children have anger issues, bonding issues. And a lot of them have problems communicating. But sometimes . . .

"One of the things we've come to understand is, there's

an environmental component to a lot of children's behavior, but each child is also hard-wired in their own way. Sometimes the combination of environment and hardwiring doesn't work, and that's where a place like Marshes can be helpful. They'll figure out how to understand Hanna and get through to her, and then they can communicate that to you and help you figure out how to make it work at home."

"That sounds really good. That's what we need," Suzette said with more enthusiasm than she felt. But Alex didn't look won over.

"Isn't there just something . . . If she's sick, isn't there a medication we can give her?" Alex asked.

Beatrix fidgeted with her pen, her eyes darting between the two of them. "I'm sorry, it's not that simple. For some conditions, that's part of the therapy. Others require more in the way of behavioral modification. The psychiatrists at Marshes may yet recommend something, once they've done a full evaluation. Marshes is experienced with treating children that fall within the sociopathic/psychopathic diagnosis—"

"You think that's what's wrong with Hanna?" Alex asked.

His posture held an alertness, a desperation to have a name for the problem.

"Hanna's situation is . . . unique. She seems to function well much of the time. Even tempered, well behaved. Perhaps a bit withdrawn. But the mutism. Did she speak at all over the weekend? Did her witch-self say any last words?"

"No, nothing," Suzette said.

Beatrix made a note before continuing. "I've given Marshes some preliminary information about what I know so far—elements of delusion, psychosis. She's a child with a great imagination, so what could seem like illness in an adult could be something quite different for a child. But the great concern is the calculated nature of her violence. Her clear intent and determination, and her overall lack of remorse—"

"She's not—she regretted what she did," Alex said.

"No, she regretted not being able to finish the job." Suzette gazed at her husband, willing him to see the difference.

"I can't make a clear diagnosis right now. She may have some empathy—or some kind of emotion—toward Alex, but it doesn't extend toward you. But we don't really understand . . . what she understands, or what she thinks she's experiencing. So psychopathy can't be ruled out."

"Oh no," Alex groaned. Suzette wrapped her arm through his, pressing herself tightly to him. Alex took in quick, shallow breaths.

"Is that curable?" Suzette asked, her voice high and tremulous. She loved Hanna too much to wish any of her own fate on the girl; she wanted Hanna to be all right. It horrified her to think of her child with an endlessly rocky future, always threatened by an abyss.

"Hold on—I see the panic in both of your faces. Let's take this one step at a time. We're learning more about this all the time. I believe there are differences between being a sociopath and being a psychopath, and I also believe receiving the diagnosis as a child is ultimately helpful—children with these conditions are more treatable than adults. They're still developing and new patterns can be nurtured—through behavioral modification and the reinforcement of empathy skills. The effort is to reignite that part of their brain.

"Now, my delineation for a sociopath is that it's more often an acquired behavior—that can originate from abuse, or a brain lesion of some kind. Sociopaths are liars who manipulate toward a desired outcome, but they tend not to be as callous as psychopaths. Psychopathy can be genetic, the structure of the brain, and it can include chemical and physical components—a lesion on a particular part of the brain, not unlike the sociopath—but it's marked by more-aggressive, remorseless traits: where a sociopath might manipulate, the psychopath attacks."

Suzette saw a way out—a reprieve from the worst diagnosis. "Would something show up on a CT? A lesion? She just had a CT and there was nothing wrong."

Beside her, Alex's face grew brighter with hope. But Beatrix frowned.

"Typically, these abnormalities are found using a contrast-enhanced MRI. It's an option that could be considered for the future."

Deflated, Suzette and Alex nodded.

"I know how it sounds, but especially in the young, these behaviors can be modified; they can *learn* to understand empathy, even if it isn't something that comes naturally to them. So these diagnoses, while frightening, don't mean all is lost. Especially in the young. It's a long road, just as it is when you're dealing with any chronic condition."

"Like my Crohn's," Suzette said to Alex, not wanting him to lose all hope. "It's hard, but she might learn how to manage it." When he glanced at her, his eyes glistened.

"You know Hanna has a joyful side, an engaged side. You've had real pleasure with her, and she's so creative and intelligent," Beatrix said, emphasizing all the positive words. "There's something real and encouraging to work with here. All is not lost."

Alex nodded, looking more optimistic than before. But Suzette couldn't relinquish the fear that she'd done something—something the therapist and Marshes would deem abusive—to turn Hanna into a sociopath.

"How did it turn out for the other family?" she asked. "Are they back together, is the child okay?"

"They are. They're doing okay."

Suzette hated how tepid and cautious Beatrix sounded. The whole prospect of Marshes appealed to Suzette because it fulfilled two primary functions: get Hanna out of the house for a short time, and return her when they were all better equipped to live happily ever after. "Okay" smacked of mediocrity. "Okay" wasn't a promise of future happiness.

"Isn't there . . . anything else?" Alex asked. "Out-treatment?"

"Regular therapy sessions . . ." Beatrix shook her head. "It's not enough. Suzette's life will be in real danger if Hanna remains in the house. That, more than anything else, is crystal clear."

Scarcely breathing, Suzette waited for Alex to look at her. Who would he choose? She dreaded the possibility where, to spare Hanna an inpatient facility, he'd suggest that Suzette move out. Leave them.

But he looked at her with longing, with tears.

"I should never have doubted you," he said. "Maybe it's my fault, that staying home isn't an option for her anymore. If I'd listened to you sooner . . . I just couldn't believe . . . anyone, when they said how bad she was, at school, everyone. And sometimes—I could never say this, I can't say this—I've missed you so much, and I felt guilty. Guilty because you were right: being parents changed us, the two of us. And it killed me to think how it had been between us, before Hanna. You, all to myself. Then I felt like I owed her *more*, because what sort of father has moments of regret . . ."

"Oh Alex!" She pressed her forehead against his, gripping his hair like she could pull him from an abyss. That they had been so in sync all along, and both of them too aghast to admit it.

"And then last night . . . He didn't believe me, but the doctor couldn't prove it. And Hanna played him. Snuggled up like I was her hero, even after what I did . . . I saw it, and wondered how many times . . . And you've told me for years . . . All that time I just wanted to protect, what we had—what we were supposed to have. I don't even know what that is anymore. But I have to protect you. I'm sorry, I'm sorry." He sobbed, and collapsed in Suzette's arms.

Beatrix gently pushed over the well-placed box of Kleenex. He grabbed up a handful and blew his nose.

Suzette held him, squeezed him, rocking him a little. How many people had sat on Beatrix's couch and wept in realization that their sense of loss, of bewilderment, could not be wished away? Perhaps other parents had unraveled in the same way, sitting just as they were, facing a frightening diagnosis as their ephemeral hope was dismantled by reason.

"I know it's hard," Beatrix said. "But you won't be alone. I continued to counsel the other family while their child was away, and I'd like to do that with you as well. I still don't know very much about your family dynamics, but if you allow me to share what I learn with Marshes, that could be very helpful for them in understanding Hanna."

"Of course," Alex agreed without hesitating, sitting up, wiping the tears from his pinked cheeks. Suzette envied him. Ultimately, if Hanna were diagnosed as a psychopath, neither of them would be at fault. But if they decided her problems were a result of a dysfunctional household or bad parenting, Suzette would take the bulk of the blame.

"So what do we do next?" she asked.

"You're on Marshes' radar, and I'll let them know when to expect you. They prefer to do intakes on Wednesdays and Saturdays, but if you needed to take her today or tomorrow—"

"Wednesday's in two days—" Suzette was surprised by how quickly everything was moving.

"She doesn't know anything about it, she's not packed," Alex said, his voice rising in protest.

"I wouldn't recommend waiting," Beatrix said. "It's not impossible that Hanna will make a more direct attempt on Suzette's life."

That silenced him. He swallowed hard. "I'll stay home. The whole time, until then," he said to Suzette.

"Where is it? How often can we visit her?" she asked.

"It's just outside of Harrisburg, so about a three-hour drive. The grounds used to be a working farm, so they have a fair bit of land. It's quite a beautiful setting." Beatrix hesitated. "Marshes will determine a visitation schedule, based on what they think will work best for Hanna. I don't want to sugarcoat it—they may only suggest three or four visits a year. Sometimes family visits are disrupt—"

"A year? A *year*?" Alex couldn't hide his shock. "How long will she be there?"

"Again, I don't want to lead you astray. But a typical stay at Marshes is one to three years."

Suzette's mouth dropped open. She couldn't imagine not having Hanna under their roof again until she was ten years old. That's not what she wanted. She needed a break, a few weeks, maybe a few months. Not a few years.

She and Alex looked at each other.

"Are you okay with . . . ?" he asked.

"What else are we going to do?" An unforgivable thought wormed its way in: would it be so terrible, just the two of them again?

"What if she doesn't like it?" Alex asked Beatrix.

"None of the kids like it at first. She'll need some time to adjust. I know this is hard. The situation at home is difficult, but sending a young child away—"

"There's nothing closer?" Suzette asked.

"Marshes is a very specialized facility, and really, we're lucky to have one so close. I have colleagues who have to recommend out-of-state options for their clients; sometimes they end up relocating the whole family. I know how it seems—but it's not a punishment. For her, or you."

Suzette found some comfort in that. But Alex had one last grasping concern.

"But . . . If she doesn't adjust . . . At some point, there has to be an agreement . . . We can't just send her off to be miserable and not care what happens after she's gone. If she's miserable, if she's worse—"

"She's not going to prison. They'll communicate with you. Plus, you can both see me—and I can communicate with them. And there will be visiting opportunities. If she speaks . . . supervised phone calls, and Skype chats can be arranged too. You're helping Hanna, because you love her. And you want her to have the best possible future."

"We'll get her through this. We're not giving up on her." *We're saving us.* Suzette squeezed Alex's hand. She had to get the words right. She had to get him to accept what was happening. Maybe her face would heal better than she hoped, but until then . . . She couldn't have Hanna around as a constant reminder. A constant threat. And the possibility of having Alex back—the two of them, as they were before Hanna—filled her with a giddy longing.

Bleary-eyed, he nodded mechanically. "What do we tell her? To get her ready?"

"Don't tell her too much; there's no point in making her

anxious or upset. Tell her you'll be taking a drive on Wednesday. To a new school. A quiet place in the country. I sense she likes quiet places." She gestured with her head toward the glass, through which they could just make out Hanna humming as she worked on her puzzle.

"Do we tell her we're leaving her there?" Suzette asked.

"We can't just drop her off," Alex added.

"You'll help her pack a few things. You don't need to pack everything; you'll be able to take more clothes, seasonal, as she needs them. I know your instinct is to be honest. To prepare her. But Hanna doesn't react to things as a typical child would, and we don't want to make things harder than they already are. For any of you. On Wednesday morning . . . Focus on the positive. A nice drive. Off to meet nice people. They have therapy horses on the property—I've never met a little girl who didn't like horses. Don't go into details she might not understand, or you might provoke a reaction that you can't control. Let Marshes handle that at the other end."

Beatrix showed them the facility's website on her computer. There were photos of the lush, sweeping grounds and a cluster of buildings, old and modern. From inside, the rooms looked bright and inviting, very much like a boarding school, not a medical facility. Alex and Suzette filled in an online form, which they would sign in person, giving the school various permissions and providing insurance and payment details.

Suzette felt gutted and in desperate need of a nap. It was all too much to think about; her thoughts whirled. She might have failed as a mother in certain ways, but she would never deny her child the help she needed. An angry flare shot up within her: maybe if her own mother had made any effort at all, Suzette could have learned from her instead of being left to cobble together the mother persona for Hanna that she had wanted for herself. Maybe it wasn't rational, after hearing Beatrix's pre-diagnosis, but she couldn't help thinking that maybe, with better mothering, she would have been a better parent and none of this would have happened.

Lists formed in her head, things she wanted to make sure Hanna had with her. Her favorite clothes and pajamas, her yellow comforter, her pillow. Her toothbrush and her monkey washcloth. The special fragrance-free, dye-free soaps. She should take a few stuffed animals, but Suzette wasn't sure which were still her favorites. Ducky? Hazel, the rabbit? *How could she not know?* And that book she liked so much. Or would it make her homesick? Or make Hanna hate her even more?

By the time she limped away from Beatrix's house, she had no energy to speak. Alex walked between them, holding one of her hands and one of Hanna's. He reeked of guilt and would probably fuss over Hanna for the next two days. Good. She was okay with that, now that she understood how he'd tended, all these years, toward over-compensation. Such days were numbered.

Alex dropped Suzette at home so she could take a nap while he ferried Hanna on to the playground, to ease the burden of his shame. He wore his pain so openly that she couldn't look at him, not without tumbling into grief.

"See you later," she said, getting out of the car. "I'll start getting some of her things together."

He nodded, then turned to Hanna in the backseat. "Ready to have some fun?"

The child who responded, jiggling with glee in her car seat, didn't need a mental hospital.

Maybe Hanna had been right all along in trying to get rid of her. *Maybe I'm the real problem.*

She let herself into the empty house.

HANNA

HOME GOT STRANGELY better in spite of everything that happened. Daddy and Mommy wanted to please her and it was like they were on holiday. Maybe it had been a mistake, trying to set Mommy on fire. If only she'd known how long it took for things—or people—to fully ignite. She wouldn't try such a spell again until she was a stronger witch and could call down a bolt of lightning. She ruined their picnic and made Daddy mad. And now he was giving Mommy extra attention. The downstairs ended up all a-jumble, and even after they cleaned it up she was sure she could still detect the stinky fish. But she actually liked the springy bandage around her wrist; it made her feel like she could punch something and not get hurt, or ward off a beam from a laser gun. It was already getting dirty, but she hoped she could keep it for a long time.

Sometimes Daddy caught her staring at Mommy's face, which had a gauze pad on it, held on with tape.

"Mommy's going to be fine, just a little circle . . ."

But Hanna could tell he was saying it for Mommy's benefit, not hers. When Mommy's mask slipped off, she looked like she was going to cry. Hanna wondered if her skin had melted and maybe the gauze was covering a hole.

Maybe she'd be able to see Mommy's teeth, and maybe food would dribble out when she chewed. Surely Daddy couldn't love her anymore—not with her smelly butt and that horrifying face. But Mommy tried hard to keep her mask just so, where she didn't look angry or I'm-gonna-kill-you.

Hanna was certain she had Beatrix to thank for how smoothly everything was going. Beatrix was a fairy godmother with her own sort of magic. She wasn't sure if Daddy quit his job or if Beatrix had used her special powers to make it so he didn't need one anymore. She liked having him at home, and he spent so much more time with her and played with her all day and said, "We'll just let Mommy do what she needs to do upstairs" like he didn't want to be with her, either.

They came in from playing football—his name for it really did make more sense because you kicked the ball with your feet—when it started to sprinkle. Mommy looked happy to see her and smiled.

"There you are," she said, like she hadn't been able to see Hanna through the glass.

Mommy had all sorts of stuff on the table, crafty stuff like scissors and thread, scraps of fabric and felt, and a jar of mismatched buttons.

She and Daddy left their shoes by the double doors, then ambled over to see what Mommy was up to.

"Making something?" Daddy asked.

"I thought *we* could make something, together, all of us." She turned to Hanna. "I've learned enough from your book to understand that UnderSlumberBumbleBeasts are made from bits of this and pieces of that, so I got out some bits and pieces. And needle and thread. I thought we could make you your own special UnderSlumberBumbleBeast."

Hanna's eyes lit up. She turned to Daddy; he must have been thinking the same thing: is this really Mommy? Mommy with a good idea?

"Fantastic, *älskling*." He kissed Mommy's cheek. The good one.

She didn't have her hands and feet all wrapped up anymore, so Hanna took that as a sign that everything was almost fine. It was time for her to figure out what to do next—her biggest, bestest attack yet. If she were Mommy, she probably would have stayed mad a bit longer. Maybe Mommy was still planning some sort of future revenge. Hanna would keep an eye on her, just in case, but she felt safe with Daddy there, and she really really really wanted her own BumbleBeast.

She scrambled onto a chair. Daddy sat beside her, reaching for the felt and fabric.

"So, what do we do? Where do we start?" he asked.

"First, Hanna can pick which fabric she wants for the body—we have old blue jeans, a snowflake sock, felt . . ."

Hanna grabbed for the blue jean scraps—they were soft and so faded they were almost gray. More important, they had belonged to Daddy once, before he cut them off for shorts.

"What sort of shape do you want? Round? Oval? Square? Rectangle?" Mommy asked.

Hanna made a figure in the air with her finger.

"So . . . a rectangle, with soft corners?"

She asked her lots of questions. For once Hanna didn't

mind nodding and shaking her head and pointing and making lots of fast decisions. Mommy did all the sewing parts, but Hanna did all the picking parts. Daddy helped by cutting things out with the big scissors.

Mommy sewed two almost-alike buttons on the creature's face for eyes, and a tiny half-dome bobble of a button for a nose, but Hanna refused all the questions about what the mouth should be like. No no no. It didn't need a mouth. She picked two little yellow pom-poms—from a hat she'd worn as a toddler—for the feet. Daddy doubled-over strips of red felt to make lanky arms, and Mommy stitched them up and put light-blue felt hands on the ends that looked like big gloves.

When it was almost sewn all the way around, Mommy turned it right-side out and let Hanna fill it with dried black beans. Then she stitched it closed.

Hanna rolled up the snowflake sock and set it on the BumbleBeast's head like a winter hat, and Mommy and Daddy gushed about what a good idea that was. She felt so rosy inside, she wanted to fold into herself and go away for a minute, but she stayed because she didn't want to miss anything. Mommy stitched the little hat so it wouldn't fall off.

When it was finished, Hanna plopped the Bumble-Beast on his feet and bum and he sat up nicely, weighted by his beanbag body. She clapped his hands together and kissed his nose; she loved him so much. He whispered his name in her ear—Skog, the Swedish word for forest. Giggling, she held him in the crook of her arm like a baby, and her head bobbed around as she listened to him chatter.

"You like your little friend?" Daddy asked.

Hanna responded by kissing Skog's belly. She lifted him in her outstretched arms and danced around the room, making a noise that, to her, was almost like a song.

Daddy stood behind Mommy's chair and they watched her, looking like statue people with no muscles and frozen smiles. On another day, Hanna might have skipped up to her room so they couldn't watch her, but she didn't care now that she had Skog.

"Great idea," Daddy murmured to Mommy.

Mommy wiped something from her eye and gathered up the scraps and bits they hadn't used.

"If only this had happened before . . ." Her voice sounded broken and high, almost like a whining child.

Daddy whispered something to her, and Mommy wiped her eyes again and walked in her new way, flat and awkward, toward the stairs.

"I have to finish her laundry . . ."

Then it was just Daddy, and she didn't mind if he watched her dance forever. Skog was a good partner so they twirled and twirled.

Wednesday was Go for a Drive Day. While Daddy put stuff in the car, Mommy brushed her hair. Mommy was back to her old self, making everyone look fancy, and they all wore clothes they couldn't play in. Mommy's hair looked shiny and she smelled sweet—fruity and flowery— like the special bottles she kept in their glittery white bathroom. She had on her butterscotch-candy necklace and when Mommy turned her around to finish her hair, it was only inches away and Hanna wanted wanted wanted so badly to lick it.

"They have horses there," Mommy said in a sickly, singsong voice. "Horses just for the children to ride. Remember when you rode the pony? When we went to that country fair, a long time ago? We're going to the country again."

The country was where large animals lived, because there was no room for them in the city because the cars and buses ate all the grass. Hanna liked grass and animals much better than noisy farting trucks and cars. The country sounded like a nicer place to live. Beatrix's name had popped up over the last couple of days, and it seemed likely that Go for a Drive Day—the country in general—was some part of her fairy godmother's magic. First Daddy stopped working, and now they were leaving the city for a quiet place with horses and trees, with no people around for miles. She even had her very own BumbleBeast. Beatrix's magic was better than her own. Hanna felt all glowy, and even Mommy wasn't so bad when Daddy was around, and she hoped they were going to live in a cottage made of iced cookies with gumdrops on the roof.

She buckled herself in, and Daddy shut the door. She let Skog sit on her shoulder so he could see out the window as they chug-chugged along in a sleepy snake of slow-moving cars. Daddy played some music he liked.

"Instrumental," he said. And catching her eye in the rearview mirror he added, "That means no words. We don't need words all the time." And he winked at her.

She didn't like the sounds the cars made when they went really fast. And she didn't like the way the concrete roads were hemmed in on the sides. It would be much better if they could float in the air, or travel in a rocket ship above all the chaos until everything below them became tiny. Tiny things weren't scary because you could step on them or hide them beneath your hand—or even one of Skog's hands—if you didn't want to look at them anymore.

She fell asleep and when she awoke, Skog was napping in her lap and there was more green out the windows. It smelled funny, like poop that doesn't exactly stink, and she saw cows with brown and white shapes like puzzle pieces, huddled together so the pieces didn't fit. She held Skog up to see, and he thought they were marvelous, too. She imagined how the cows all fit together, and how some would have to lie down and some would have to stand on their heads to get the puzzle right. Skog laughed and jumped up and down.

They stopped for an early lunch, and Daddy got two orders of bacon and Mommy said she didn't feel very well. She ordered toast, and told Daddy it wasn't her stomach but her head.

"Allergies, probably," she said.

Hanna knew better than to order pancakes or french toast because they were always better at home—buttery, not soggy and bland. She got grilled cheese and french fries, which Daddy stole one by one from her plate. He pretended he wasn't stealing them, which made it all the more obvious and she couldn't help laughing at his silly faces. Skog ate her pickle slices.

Just when it was seeming like there was too much driving and not enough arriving, the car turned up a narrow road where some buildings sat at the top of the hill. They drove past tumbling meadows and Skog whispered "Maybe we can roll down them!" and she tickled him for having such a good idea. At the top of the hill was a parking area, and she unfastened her buckle as they pulled in, ready to leap out.

A smiling man came to greet them and Hanna guessed he was a farmer. He wore muddy jeans and a sweatshirt with pushed-up sleeves and ripped pockets, and he shook hands with Daddy and Mommy.

"Can I carry your things up for you?"

Daddy popped the trunk and the farmer nodded toward the biggest building, the boxy modern one with reflective windows that didn't look like it should be in the country, and told them which door to go in.

Hanna tugged Daddy's hand and pointed toward the scalloped hills, so green and inviting.

"You'll get to play outside soon," he said. But he looked grim when he said it. Mommy wouldn't even look at her as she walked gingerly across the pebbled lot in her flat shoes.

They went inside and Hanna hated it immediately because it looked too much like an official place, a school, with handmade things on the walls and echoes of voices coming down the hallways. They went straight into the office and she dreaded what would come next—another principal, another interview. She weighed her options— barking and snarling were always good. Except that she never behaved like that in front of Daddy and wasn't sure she wanted him to see her that way.

Two blah-blah old women greeted them in the office. One had teeth that were a little brown and the other had teeth that were very white.

"We've been expecting you," said White Teeth.

More handshaking and hellos and lots of smiles. Hanna stamped her foot. Even Skog gurgled his displeasure.

"Why don't we leave them to this boring adult stuff and we can go look around. Sound good?" Brown Teeth had twinkly eyes and Hanna liked how they smiled at the corners. "Say goodbye?"

Hanna waved at Daddy but he surprised her by dropping to his knees and giving her a big hug and kiss. "Love you, *lilla gumman*, love you so much."

She hugged him back and raised the volume on her pitter-patter heart so he could hear her love.

Mommy's goodbye was less forceful. She held a wisp of Hanna's hair between her fingers. Kissed her cheek. "See you later, alligator."

As Hanna started toward the door with Brown Teeth, Mommy burst into giggles. Everyone looked at her, and Mommy had to clamp a hand over her mouth and mutter some apologies. Hanna couldn't make sense of her parents' tangled-up emotions so she shook her head a little, trying to clear it of confusion. Brown Teeth extended her hand, wanting her to take it. She didn't, but she followed her, hoping they would go outside. Maybe her fairy godmother had a hut made of twigs nearby. But when they left the building it was only to cross a short covered walkway into another building. Up some stairs. Down a hall.

"My name is Audrey," said Brown Teeth. "We're going to get to know each other very well. I'm going to be here for you as much as you need."

She led her into a room with a bed and a window, a desk and a chest of drawers.

Hanna stopped, pointing at the bed. She recognized the folded bundle of her comforter, her smiling daisy pillowcase. Why were her things in this strange room? It wasn't her room. Brown Teeth unzipped the suitcase and Hanna spotted her robot pajamas, her ladybug rain boots . . . She stepped closer. It was filled with her things.

"We can put your clothes in the drawers—do you want to organize them yourself?"

Hanna scrumbled up her face and pointed to the next room. Would that be Daddy's room?

But Brown Teeth didn't understand. "Do you have to go to the bathroom? You'll share one with three other girls—and your night monitors. It's right here." She went to the doorway and pointed to something Hanna couldn't see.

Hanna shook her head and stamped her foot. She shouldn't have left Daddy. With Skog held tightly under her arm, she ran from the room. Brown Teeth chased after her.

"Hanna?"

Across the hallway. Down the steps. She pushed open the door and for a second it was better: she was outside again where the air reminded her of solid, earthy things. She saw horses in a paddock snorting messages to each other. She saw flowers blooming in front of buildings that looked smaller and kinder than the one she left. Brown Teeth stood patiently beside her while she looked around.

"Do you want to see the horses?" Brown Teeth had a nice voice, soothing like a cup of hot chocolate.

Skog wanted to pet the horses' long noses, but she told him he had to be more patient. They needed to find Daddy. She walked around to the front of the building, toward the graveled lot. Brown Teeth followed along.

"I'll let you explore. And I'll just tag along and make sure you don't get lost, okay? There's lots to look at . . ."

Hanna switched off her hearing. Her eyes swept the parking lot but Daddy's car wasn't there. Then she spotted it, rolling down the narrow road. It was already almost to the bigger road. She uttered an alarmed squeal and took off running.

Wait! Wait!

She almost wanted to yell. She tried to find her voice but it rattled around in her head, pinged back and forth across her tongue until it felt like a mummy in her mouth, bandaged and unmovable.

Brown Teeth was faster than she expected her to be. She kept right up.

"Wait! Hanna, little bear—wait!"

Daddy's car turned onto the bigger road and sped away. Hanna stopped. A thunderstorm roiled in her throat, big black clouds full of hail and lightning.

"Uhhhhn!" she screamed, pointing at the car. "Daaaaaaaa!" The tears made her vision blurry, flooding the road, erasing the way back home.

"I know, little bear." Brown Teeth sat on the road and took her onto her lap. "Your parents love you and they want what's best for you. And you'll be with them again. Promise, promise." She rocked Hanna as she wept.

Skog climbed up and tucked himself between her chin and shoulder, trying to comfort her. But a part of her was still attached to Daddy, stretching as the distance grew between them, ripping away her insides.

She surrendered to Brown Teeth's embrace, certain she would bleed to death, and unable to fathom why Daddy would leave her to die with a stranger.

SUZETTE

WITH THE DRAPES fully open, the window to the play-room was nothing but a square of shimmering glass. Her child wasn't in there and the impulse to jump up and look for her made her muscles twitch. It felt unreal, driving to Beatrix's without Hanna. Often she had the impression of a ghost sitting in the backseat. The whole week had been similarly odd. She hadn't thought much about it before, how much noise her mute child made. Up and down the stairs. The comforting chatter of cartoons on the televi-sion. Her bouncy balls. Her little chirps and squeals, the way she hummed and sang to herself in a language with-out identifiable words.

Catching her gaze, Beatrix glanced at the empty playroom. "You're struggling with her absence?"

Suzette shrugged. "It's weird. I keep thinking I need to buy her some bananas and cheese. I go to her room and stand in the doorway, expecting to tell her something. I catch myself about to call up to her when I'm fixing a meal. We've had a routine. For a long time." She didn't say how free she felt, without the routine.

"Is Alex struggling too?"

"I guess. At bedtime the most. He wasn't with her

during the day, he's busy at work again. I think the sight of the empty bed. That bothers him. She's not hiding behind the door, she's . . ." Much to her surprise she'd slept well all week. Unburdened.

"You seem . . . contemplative. Are you feeling depressed? Is that something you've struggled with in the past?"

"It's not depression, it's . . . everything else. I'm not sure if I'm still a mother. It's like when you're a kid and someone asks you what you want to be when you grow up. I feel like that, in a way I never did. I'm not sure who I am, but . . ."

"I know it's hard to not feel guilty, but you didn't—"

With an adamant shake of her head and a bitter laugh, Suzette silenced the therapist. "I haven't tried to do that many things in my life, not really. With my health, I've always been kind of a recluse. And I'm just left thinking of . . . I make lists in my head of all the things I should have done differently. For my life. And hers. Things I should have said and shouldn't have said. When I should have been more patient, or more firm, or more . . . Over and over."

"You wouldn't blame yourself if she had, say, a hearing impairment." Beatrix tilted her head, offering an encouraging smile.

"I would. I probably would." She gave the therapist a sardonic smirk. "I'd wonder what I exposed her to that damaged her sensitive baby ears. Or I'd blame myself for some genetic anomaly. You know, before we got pregnant, I told Alex my big concern was that she'd get Crohn's disease—I was afraid I'd pass it on to her. And he reassured me, said if she did we'd know how to handle it, because of my experiences. And she'd never end up isolated, suffering. But she did. That's exactly where she ended up. Maybe we never understood her at all. Maybe she was always trying to say something else. Now it's Marshes' turn to figure it out."

Beatrix considered her for a long, silent moment. She sat forward in her chair.

"I'm going to ask you a difficult question. Since you're focusing right now on the things you think you did wrong, I'm curious if there's one particular thing that stands out."

Suzette turned her head toward the window, but what she gazed at was farther away than the trees beyond.

"When we found out we were having a girl, I wanted to give her a Swedish name. An unusual name. Matt, Alex's partner, had twins not that long ago. A daughter named Stryker and a son named Sound. Alex thinks it's a bit weird. But I kind of understood, this image Matt had for his children. A girl named Stryker is not going to be defeated, by anything. And a man named Sound would be calm. Reasonable. Strong.

"I guess the names I liked were a little odd. Saga. Blix. Majken. Solveig. Alex really didn't want her to have a name that everyone, in this country anyway, would mispronounce—we always have to correct people with *Yensen*. I don't know why but I didn't want her to have an ordinary name. Sometimes I wonder if we'd named her something else, would she be someone else? But that's not . . . What I really didn't want . . .

"She was born with dark hair. My hair. I needed to look at her and see Alex—I wanted baby Alex. But she looked like me, like my mother. I let him pick her name, so I'd always remember she was Alex's child. Alex, Alex who I love. It was Alex I wanted. All along."

The first week was hardest; after saying goodbye at Marshes, she managed to keep her giggling fits private. The relief and disbelief and disgrace sometimes burst out—a happy and sad eruption of "Is this really happening?" By the second week their parental anguish softened. Enough so that time passed at an ordinary pace, not the surreal, dragged-out rate of the intermittent mourning created by Hanna's absence.

Suzette stood at the counter, barefoot, head bowed over a recipe. Her hair fell around her face and she tucked it back behind her ears, concentrating. She wore a loose T-shirt, soft as a spider's web, and jeans rolled up to the knee; a youthful outfit that suited her mood. The garden lay in sunlight and the breeze coming through the open door rustled the sketches that covered the table. She'd placed them there to gain perspective on a series of drawings: a progression of views through a doorway. In some the door was only open a crack, in others the viewer seemed about to step through into another place. But she set them aside after Alex, home from the gym, went up for a shower and she had a different type of inspiration. Those cinnamon buns she'd been meaning to make. It would cheer him up.

Baking didn't come easily to her and she knew she had to follow the recipe exactly—no extra pinches or experimental flourishes. She wanted them to be as much like his mother's as possible, picturing in her mind a lazy afternoon in the backyard with their own little *fika,* enjoying their coffee and *kanelbullar* over a winding conversation. They needed to relearn how to be together. Every day. Just the two of them, without Hanna. She would help them find a new routine, new joys.

Alex jogged down the stairs, trailing clean, soapy aromas from his shower. He struck a pose, and waited for Suzette to look over. When she did, she squealed with delight and threw out her arms. She stood on tiptoe to wrap her arms around his neck, taking in the smooth feel of his cheek against hers. Then she stepped back to admire his pink, bare-shaven face.

"I didn't think you hated my beard that much," he said, mockingly hurt.

"No, it isn't that. But I love this face, this smooth face." She held his cheeks in her hands. "This is the face I fell in love with." And it struck her that he was trying, too, in his own way, to make a difference, to break away from old routines and embrace their household of two.

"Do I look younger?"

"You look less like a hipster."

He laughed. "It was getting to be too much. Every guy at work has a beard now, and Matt is sporting a waxed handlebar mustache." It was Suzette's turn to laugh. He gathered her toward him. "Look at you, so beautiful, so young. I love this makeup-free, carefree you."

Her cheek had stopped oozing, and though she'd been instructed to let it heal the rest of the way uncovered, she wore a Band-Aid whenever she was with people, even Alex. She believed it was the large square Band-Aid that made her look youthful, but she appreciated Alex's devotion. They kissed, and their bodies connected with a crackle of desire, but she resisted and pulled away. "Okay, I'm not quite ready to make love on the kitchen floor. I'm on a mission."

"I could make a pun about that." He followed her back to the counter. "What are you making?"

"A surprise." She wriggled away from him.

"A yummy surprise?" he asked, trying to read the recipe over her shoulder.

"Maybe, if I'm not distracted."

"I like yummy surprises." He wandered over to the table to study her drawings.

With the clang of glass against glass, Suzette took the largest Pyrex mixing bowl out of its nest of bowls. She dragged the canister of flour across the counter, then reached into the cupboard for a package of yeast and both the white and brown sugar.

"These are really interesting." He straightened the pictures where the breeze had made them crooked and overlapping. "I've never seen you draw stuff like this before—where your design, architectural skills blossom into something totally different."

"I can't really explain it, but . . . When I start one I get all these other ideas. I'm just going with it."

"You should, they're really cool. Your gray work is so detailed."

She laid out a collection of different sized bowls, intent on preparing a complete *mise en place* before mixing any ingredients. She'd learned from past mistakes where she'd found herself short of an ingredient or two deep into her preparation process. Flour billowed up in a poof as she dumped first one cup, then another, into the bowl. Just as she was about to drop in a third cup, she caught sight of something in the flour.

At first, she thought it was an insect of some kind and she grimaced, digging it out with her fingers. It was smooth and brown, and the right size to be the husk of some sort of bug, but on further inspection . . . No legs. Too smooth.

She sucked in her breath, realizing what it was.

"What's wrong?" Alex asked, alerted by her gasp.

"Look." She wiped it off so he could get a better look. Back at her side, he squinted, trying to understand what she was showing him. "It was in the flour."

"What is it?"

"It's half of an Imodium capsule. Remember when my medication seemed to suddenly stop working?"

A light dawned on his face. "She . . ." But he couldn't say it.

"I wasn't getting sick. I thought maybe I'd used loperamide for too many years, but it wasn't . . . Hanna tampered with my medicine."

He took the empty half capsule from her, like he needed its solidity to make what she was saying real. His face registered pain, then resolve. With a tiny nod, he opened the cabinet beneath the sink and dropped the capsule into the garbage.

"It means . . ." She's a diabolical monster.

But before she could find a better answer, Alex pulled her in by the elbows and rested his forehead against hers.

"It means we did the right thing. Our girl needs help. She needs to learn right from wrong. They're going to help her. They'll teach her. And someday she'll come home to us, when she knows . . ."

"They'll help her," she agreed—convinced, at least for a moment, that it wasn't her fault.

He held her in his strong arms and she let her past doubt and misgivings dissolve. When she really considered it, the last couple of weeks hadn't been so bad. She didn't have to do as much laundry or cleaning. No one bothered her during the day, and she liked the time alone. A magical thing happened when she lost herself in her sketches: they came from nowhere and afterward their existence surprised her. And it wasn't as if they'd lost their child permanently. Hanna was alive and they would see her again. And they could hold out hope that their future life together would be better than it had ever been.

Things weren't so bad. They were getting better.

Dr. Stefanski had referred her to a hematologist after another round of wonky blood work. The hematologist believed he had a solution for Suzette's chronic low energy: she was extremely anemic—with rock-bottom levels of B_{12}, iron, and vitamin D. She'd likely been deficient for years, a malabsorption issue common for anyone who'd had intestinal surgery. Suzette remained ambivalent about Dr. Stefanski's historic disinterest in her energy issues, but at least someone was finally on top of it. The following week she'd have her first iron infusion and B$_{12}$ shot, and she'd already started on D$_3$ supplements.

It was almost too much to hope for—feeling well—but she hoped anyway.

Meanwhile, she and Alex would finally, blissfully have time, like they'd once had. Before . . . They'd strengthen their relationship. They'd work with Beatrix and learn better parenting strategies. Marshes would untangle their daughter's convoluted wiring and in a year—or two, or three—they'd all know how to communicate with one another.

She contemplated these things as she and Alex held each other. And later she gave them voice because it was likely that she hadn't shared enough—with him, with Hanna—and she vowed to amend her ways.

"It's going to be so much better," she said. "My health. Us. And she'll come home when she's ready and we'll all be . . ."

As he hugged her tighter she felt his body agreeing, accepting. The separation was better for all of them.

"As good as my mom's!"

It was a generous assessment on Alex's part, though the cinnamon buns turned out better than she'd expected. As she'd hoped, they lazed all afternoon and evening in the yard, talking about Alex's progress with the Skinny Building, the merits and uses of laminated strand lumber, the possibilities for constructing semi-floating furniture out of repurposed sailing canvas, the goings on in the White

House, the newest scandal in the EU, and the unlikelihood that they'd ever commit to growing vegetables when it meant giving up a portion of their precious green space. After the sugar crash made them more sullen and vulnerable, they spoke less and watched the sky change color.

"This one's my favorite," Alex said when it turned a sharp blue.

Suzette waited until the purple crept in. "I like this one."

Under the cover of darkness, safe from having to see too much, she admitted to always being a little jealous of Hanna's love for Alex—and to some extent, his love for her. And Alex admitted that he was envious of her seemingly effortless ability to run a household.

"My brain fixates on imagining structures, putting things together. It's an endless puzzle. But it's all . . . mechanical. But you imagine a home, an environment, how people will live and function inside a space."

"But I don't see the real people."

"We're dreamers." Their fingers danced a courtship as their arms lay flopped over the lounge chairs.

"You're a really good father. I should have said it more."

Barks of protest and laughter drifted in from the street and neither of them spoke until it was quiet again.

"We should take a trip this summer. A real trip. A few weeks," he said.

"Yeah?"

"Want to?"

"Yeah." And the more she thought about it, the more

she really wanted to travel. It wasn't something she'd felt comfortable with when they were younger, when her Crohn's still wasn't well controlled. But it seemed possible now. Exciting, even. "Where should we go?"

"Wherever you want. Think about it, and we'll start making plans."

She clapped her palm against his, grinning.

It was almost eleven when they dragged themselves up the stairs, heavy with cinnamon buns and sunshine and the soporific lullabies of night insects. When they reached the top, Alex stopped.

"What?" she asked.

He went to Hanna's room and just stood there for a moment, peering in.

Then he shut her door.

HANNA

IT WASN'T SAFE at Marshes for little Skog. The other children lumbered like monsters, their movements wild and exaggerated. Half of them yelled and the other half growled or looked out from suspicious eyes, ready to bite. Savages, all. Even the way they laughed was barbaric, shrill like a fire alarm. She wanted him with her every minute of every day, but she feared for him, so delicate and defenseless. When she had to leave her room—for school or therapy or meals or playing—she left him nestled between her pillow and the wall so he would be hidden but could still see what was going on. No other children ever came into her room because of The Rules, and the adults were respectful of everyone's Personal Items, so he was safe, in theory. At night, they whispered together. Sometimes he dried her tears with his felted hand. He told her what she already knew: She'd messed up with Mommy's spell; Marshes was Mommy's revenge.

Hanna spent most mornings with a woman whose clothing often matched her orange hair. Her name started with a *T* so Hanna called her Tangerine. She made a lot of statements like "It makes me sad when I see someone crying." Hanna was supposed to slap one of the cards on the table in front of her—the True card or the False card. Most of the time she needed a third option, a What Does This Have to Do With Anything card. So she smacked the False card.

I feel happy when my mother gives me a hug. False.

I feel sad a lot of the time. True. False. True.

I like myself. True.

I make friends easily. False. True—if Skog counted. But she knew how adults thought. They liked what they could see right in front of them, solid things. They encouraged imagination but hated anything imaginary. Hanna knew they didn't understand how reality was malleable. It flowed on a wave in front of Hanna's eyes, and she could choose to be outside or within it. Parents and schools wanted her to be within it, because it was easier for them and they'd forgotten how to swim to other planes. That's why she was sent away. She didn't think her actions strayed so far from okay-normal-enough. But now she understood that everyone else disagreed.

Still. Marshes seemed like an unfair punishment.

So much for her fairy godmother, Beatrix. Wicked witch after all.

At playtime, she liked to see how far she could wander from whoever was in charge of watching her. One day, while Brown Teeth was distracted helping another aide with an angry boy, Hanna slipped past the play yard and down a hill. She considered running past the wooded area, across the meadow and all the way to the road—maybe she could run all the way home. But she couldn't leave without Skog. And at least the trees gave her something to hide behind. A fat black trunk loomed in front of her, and she ducked behind it to catch her breath and decide what to do next. But she found an older girl sitting there, her face like a pug's, and her arms starred and striped with pale scars.

Pug Face jumped to her feet, grabbed Hanna by the arm—harder than Mommy ever did—and spun her back in the direction of the play yard. Hanna hesitated, intrigued by the puckers and lines on her arms, and their shared desire for privacy.

"Did your parents do that?" Pug Face asked, jutting her chin toward Hanna's still-bundled wrist.

Hanna touched the stretchy bandage, now raggedy and blackened by time. Is that what everyone thought? She'd never ratted on Daddy; she kept it only because she liked it. But maybe they wouldn't let her go home until . . .

Pug Face pushed her again, then punched her shoulder blade. "Probably deserved it. Now get going, twat!"

Hanna ran away, back up the hill, her shoulder a bloom of pain. She unwound the filthy bandage and tossed it away. It flagged on the spindly branches of a dying tree. She tried to reach the sore spot on her back to rub it. It made her think of Skog and tears rushed to her eyes. Was he really safe? Would Pug Face or another brute find him eventually? They'd rip his arms off. Pull out his eyes. Stab him in the belly so his beans spilled out. It would be even worse than what Mommy did to the potato because Skog was a really real friend, and she couldn't survive Marshes without him.

She needed to get him someplace safer, but where? If

she kept him with her she might accidentally leave him somewhere, or he might fall from her bag, or tumble out of her shirt if she tried to keep him tucked against her body. The monsters would see him only as something to destroy. Children know where other children are vulnerable; the more she loved him, the greater his peril.

Maybe it was already too late.

Maybe, in her absence, they'd already seized him.

She ran as fast as she could, determined to rescue him.

Panicked and bawling, she ran across the play yard, indifferent to the shouts of protest as she plowed through a game of kickball. All she could see were Skog's amputated hands and feet, his black-bean organs and blood scattered irreparably all over her floor. As she raced for the dormitory, Brown Teeth chased after her.

"Hanna, wait! Little bear, what's wrong?"

Hanna shoved open the doors and charged up the stairs.

Brown Teeth caught up with her on the landing. She scooted in front of her and got to her knees, holding Hanna's arms.

"I have to make sure you're okay. Are you hurt? Did something happen? Is your wrist okay?" She caressed Hanna's bare skin, now exposed by the removal of the bandage.

Hanna wailed and pointed toward her room.

"Okay, we'll go to your room. And we'll make sure everything's all right."

Brown Teeth wanted to hold her hand but Hanna

couldn't slow down for her. She burst into her room, crying and breathless, and flung herself onto the bed.

There was Skog, unharmed, right where she'd left him. She clutched him to her heart and couldn't stop crying.

"Oh, little one . . ." Brown Teeth sat beside her, rubbing circles into her back. Hanna flinched when she touched the new bruise. "I wish you could tell me why you're so upset. I'm sorry you're having such a hard day."

Skog told her again and again that he was okay. But the terror wouldn't leave her, now that she'd imagined the worst. He would die here, and she couldn't live without him.

She told him in her anguished cries how she missed everything. Her room and her comfy bed. Her bins of colorful treasure. The big glass wall that fed her sunshine. Daddy's study and crawling around on his feathery carpet. The squishy couch in the living room that held her like a hug. The refrigerator where she could get her favorite snacks, whenever she wanted. Watching TV by herself, or *Star Trek* with Daddy. Daddy reading her bedtime stories. Daddy hugging her, talking to her, playing with her. She even missed . . .

It was true, she even missed Mommy. Well, not Mommy exactly.

Mommy made her food just how she liked it; she knew what Hanna liked and didn't like. Mommy sometimes gave her space, unlike the flying gnats of Marshes who were always up her nose, down her throat, dive-bombing into her eyes. They never left her alone no matter how much she swatted them away. And worse worst worstest of all: no one understood her. Daddy always knew what she was saying—even Mommy wasn't clueless all the time—but the people at Marshes were stupid and wanted to use their ears when their eyes were just as good. Even now, Brown Teeth, the nicest of the people, didn't grasp anything about the danger she and Skog were in.

Her face swelled up, puffy and tight, and it started to get too hard to cry. She snuffled and breathed through her mouth. Brown Teeth brought her a tissue and wiped her nose and told her to blow. As she slipped off her Keds and set them on the ugly floor, Hanna curled up on her side, face to the wall.

"I know it's hard, little bear. I know . . ."

Hanna felt the hand on her arm, her back, drawing circles in an empty universe, warm circles like good planets full of growing things. She drifted toward sleep. How long had it been since she slept through the night? Maybe maybe it was all a bad dream and she would wake up at home, in her own bed.

"You could be better if you tried," Skog told her.

She agreed. If she couldn't dream away Mommy, maybe she could dream away Marshes. Dream it away and maybe everything would get back to normal.

"Okay," said Brown Teeth, reading her note. "We can do that."

Hanna was in her robot pajamas. Brown Teeth told her

to put something on her feet so she put on three pairs of socks. Brown Teeth waited patiently, her mouth a moon of amusement, then held out her hand. Hanna took it after getting Skog settled in on her pillow.

They walked past silent rooms and Hanna hoped everyone was dead, but knew the younger children were probably just sleeping. Brown Teeth led her to an office and turned on the light, which made them both blink blink their startled eyes. She sat behind the desk and dug out a file while Hanna waited beside it.

"Here it is," she said, scrolling her finger down a list. "Daddy's number?"

Hanna nodded.

Brown Teeth picked up the phone and dialed.

SUZETTE

ALEX SLID HER to the end of their magnificent tree-slab table and she supported herself on her elbows. She threw her head back, intoxicated, as usual, by the feel of his cock making its entrance—her favorite, favorite thing. He thrust and they gasped and her body tingled with the sureness of her passion, his love, their connection. She'd never fucked another man and never wanted to.

Afterward, they sat naked at the table and shared a carton of brownie fudge ice cream—the real stuff. It was an impulse purchase, and she'd been pleasantly surprised when it didn't upset her stomach. After years of shrinking, the world was getting bigger again. The wall beside them displayed a haphazard arrangement of her drawings. Alex studied them while he waited for Suzette to dig her spoon out of the chocolatey goop.

"I started my book," she said.

"You did?" He took his turn, and licked from his heaping spoon.

"These are just the sketches. It's a slightly bigger format than I originally imagined. But this is the theme"—she gestured toward the series of doors with her spoon—"and on some of the pages the point of view will be like you're approaching the door. And then the door starts to open. And on some pages it'll be like . . ." She searched for a word. "A pop-up book, I guess. Three-dimensional, the stuff on the other side of the door. A lot of surreal things. Dreams and nightmares. For contrast, I might use a few photographs too."

"It sounds really awesomely cool. I can see where you're heading with these."

Suzette shrugged. "It's something."

He nodded, and though he still gazed at the pictures, his look went vacant. She felt it as their connection broke and his thoughts drifted elsewhere.

"I miss her less, now," he said. "I like the two of us. I don't have to just ruminate about it anymore. Does that make me a bad person?"

Suzette pushed down a wicked smile. "It was a necessity—for her, for us. It's good we can adjust. But sometimes it doesn't feel like we've moved ahead, you know? Sometimes it's like we've gone into the past, the way we were. Before."

"And we were great. We are great. *Förälskad.*"

"*För alltid.*"

"Forever and ever and ever."

They contemplated each other, dreamy and satisfied.

A cell phone sang out its cheery tune.

"That's mine," Alex said, looking around.

"I think it's by the door."

Suzette smacked his bare ass as he shuffled past her.

"I'll get you for that." He found his phone on the entryway table and checked the incoming number. "Hey, it's Marshes."

She turned to watch him answer, concern on her face. "Hope nothing's wrong."

"Hello?" He made his way back to the table. "Yes . . . Okay . . ." He shrugged at her in confusion. "Said somebody wants to talk to me . . ." His jaw dropped. "Hanna?" His eyes bulged as he looked at Suzette. "Hanna, *lilla gumman*, is that you? Hold on, I'll put you on speaker."

He set the phone on the table between them.

"*Jag älskar dig*, Daddy—so you know it's really me."

Her words sounded perfect, the French accent gone, her voice small and fragile. Suzette thought of a sparrow, not a witch. Not Marie-Anne.

"*Herregud*—holy shit," he said.

They gaped at each other, shocked.

"Hanna, baby?" she said.

"Hi Mommy."

"Oh Hanna, it's so good—"

"—so good to hear you." Alex's eyes shone with tears.

"I miss you." Her childish voice through the speaker sounded so sad. But to hear her—and her unexpected words—made them laugh and clutch at each other's hands.

"We miss you too, *lilla gumman*, we love you so much."

"How are you? Are you learning a lot at school?"

"She's talking!"

It was all over his face, the giddiness that she also felt. The miracle. Marshes had gotten through to her, such progress after only a month.

"I'm sorry I was so bad."

Now it was Suzette's turn to tear up. She never expected

to hear such an admission. The remorse came flooding back—that she'd ever thought of her child as a demon, blind to the possibility that Hanna's bad behavior might have been an illness. If Suzette had taken action sooner, could she have spared both of them years of hardship?

"We're so glad you're doing so well," Alex said.

"I don't like it here. I want to come home."

They frowned at each other.

"You're still getting used to it," he said.

"It's a big change, it'll take time but you're doing so well—"

"I'm really sorry and I promise I'll be good," Hanna said.

The excitement that had briefly ignited the room dissipated. Suzette and Alex looked to each other, unsure what to say. A part of her was overjoyed that Hanna was getting better. But a larger part of her simply couldn't conceive of having her back home. And Hanna couldn't possibly have been cured—not so soon. What if everything went back to how it was?

"Daddy? Can I come home? I miss you."

"We miss you too . . ." He faltered. "But you need to be at school—"

"I don't like it here and the kids are mean. Please, I'll be good, I promise."

The surface of Suzette's heart started to peel away, like the skin of an apple beneath a skilled knife. Their child wanted them and missed her home. The longing in her voice was so plaintive. Yet Suzette felt herself readying to snuff Hanna's wishes. She and Alex still had so much work to do with Beatrix, and the initial reports they'd received from Marshes were a mixed bag, at best. Hanna was capable of emotion, but her moral compass was savagely askew. She had a high IQ, but problems with defiance and impulsivity. After weeks of testing, her therapists had barely begun to implement the behavioral modification strategies that they hoped would help her gain crucial emotional and social skills, and build up her ability to empathize. And they hadn't ruled out the possibility of a psychotic disorder to explain her delusions.

Suzette shook her head. Glanced at her sketches with fear. The book was barely started. She had Alex back—all of him, even the parts Hanna had stolen away. They were going to travel, the romantic adventures she was finally ready for. It was selfish, but she wasn't ready to give it all up. If her daughter came home, Suzette would lose herself. She was certain of it. The new parts of her would shrivel— her passion, her health; she wasn't strong enough yet to have Hanna back in the house.

"I can't," she whispered to him. "We can't. She's just trying to manipulate us, testing the waters. Beatrix warned us."

It probably was a new method of manipulation. Beatrix, indeed, warned them that Hanna would want to come home. All the children said that, even the ones from the most abusive families. But she never guessed Hanna would call them and say everything they'd wanted to hear. Mommy. Daddy. I love you. I'm sorry. Out loud, in an adorable voice with perfect pronunciation.

Suzette prayed Alex wouldn't cave.

He covered the lower portion of the phone so Hanna wouldn't hear. "*Älskling*, I know. The school is doing great—they're helping her."

Her entire body flushed, feverish with disgrace. "She needs more time there, they've only started . . ."

Please let reason be enough. She couldn't tell him how easy she'd found it, after the first week, to start discarding her mothering self. Couldn't say—to Beatrix or Alex or anyone—what a relief it became, the unmothering. Like a slow undressing, a peeling away of layers and dropping them to the floor. She wasn't ready to step back into her costume of domesticity, and feared she never would be.

She shook her head again, a hand pressed to her mouth, afraid she'd blurt out her unforgivable thoughts.

"Mommy? Daddy? Are you still there?"

Alex gripped Suzette's hand and nodded, like he agreed with what she was thinking.

"We'll get to see you soon," he said.

Something exploded inside her. Suzette jumped to her feet, lurching away from the table. "Don't tell her that!"

"Why?"

"We can't . . ."

Alex covered the phone's microphone again. "They'll let us visit soon, if she keeps doing so well. And maybe she really will be able to come home sooner—"

"No!" With one hand protecting the delicate new skin on her cheek, she inched away from him. "After all I've been through—doctors slicing open my neck, the loss of my adolescence, a hole in my stomach for four years, my own daughter tormenting me, branding me—it could've been my *eye*! Enough! I can't take it! I don't deserve this! We deserve a happy life. I deserve to love you, and be loved, and not have this—her—fucking up our lives."

Alex buried the phone in his palm and came toward her, a man intent on calming a terrified beast with the intensity of his stare.

"It's okay—"

"It's not! My own mother didn't care if I lived or died, but I chose to *live,* and I won't let my daughter be my undoing. This is *our* life again, the life we should have had. Please, Alex, let me—us—live . . ."

"Okay, okay . . ." He reached her, and enveloped her. Suzette pressed the full of her skin against his and sobbed.

"Daddy?"

"Let her go," Suzette whispered, pleading. She looked up at Alex just as he licked away a tear that had traveled all the way down his cheek. He held up the phone.

"We're here, and we love you very much," he said. "But you need to stay in school—"

"No," Hanna wailed.

"—I know you're homesick, but you're doing so well and Mommy and Daddy are very proud of you."

"Please, I won't be bad anymore. I promise," she cried.

Suzette pressed herself against him, so grateful that he would be the one to end the conversation. And surely it cost him, as she knew how much he'd longed to hear Hanna's voice.

"It's past your bedtime, *lilla gumman*—"

She marveled at how well he played the father, how he knew every word of an invisible script.

"I want to come home! Don't you miss me?" she sobbed.

Alex's expression froze. And then as his face contorted, his body began to contract. Suzette gasped, seeing her husband shed his own costume. For so many years he'd seemed to play the character so well, but now she understood what a strain it had been. Wearing his mask of smiles, always weighted by guilt.

"I can't . . . What if she hurts you again? I can't . . ." He shoved the phone to her, and stumbled back to the table where he crumpled into the nearest chair, whimpering. Ashamed, and left with nothing but his guilt, he covered his face and wept.

Suzette stared at the phone in her hand. It had, after all, become her responsibility.

"Daddy, what's wrong? Mommy?" Suzette turned off the speaker so Alex wouldn't have to hear his only child begging. Only she heard Hanna's final words.

"Don't you love me?"

The pained wonder of her question was too much. Like she'd suspected it for a while. Suzette wasn't sure if she could keep loving her child unconditionally, not after she'd seen Hanna with the hammer in her fists. Hanna mouthing a spell that was intended to dispose of her as readily as she'd annihilated a character on a piece of paper. Would a part of Suzette always be afraid of Hanna? Was Alex grappling with it, too, now that his daughter had a taste of blood? Animals were put to sleep, irredeemable after breaking human skin. Would Hanna always keep a part of Marie-Anne in her heart?

"Not enough," Suzette said, barely giving breath to the words. She disconnected the call and dropped onto Alex's lap. His skin was a balm, his warm breath made her tingle as they held each other.

"We'll be okay," she said. "She belongs there."

His tears fell onto her breast. "I know."

She straddled him, knowing in a few minutes he'd be inside her again. They'd both feel so much better.

HANNA

"HELLO? MOMMY? DADDY? Hello?"

"Did you lose them, little bear?" Brown Teeth asked, taking the receiver from her hand.

Hanna nodded, unblinking. Stunned. She'd been certain her voice would be enough. Her insides ignited and she melted to the floor. Their hesitation was unmistakable. Even Daddy didn't want her anymore.

Mommy proved herself to be the strongest witch after all: she set Hanna on fire, even from afar.

Tears came like lava. She slumped against the cold metal of the desk, pressing her cheek and palms to it to soothe her molten despair. Brown Teeth got on her knees, always ready to console her.

"There, there, little bear. You'll get another chance, don't worry."

Brown Teeth's cool knuckles felt good against her hot, wet cheek. Sniffling, smearing her tears against her shoulder, she let Brown Teeth take her hand and lead her back to her room. Where Skog waited.

Delicate little Skog. Her bestest and only friend in a cruel and mangled world.

Stupid stupid, she raged at her own stupidity. Getting

her out of the house forever had probably been Mommy's plan all along. Of course hearing her voice wouldn't persuade bewitched Daddy to let her come home. Daddy was an island that seemed like paradise in her desire, but was nothing more than a rocky crag that couldn't save her from drowning. Not with Mommy beside him. Hanna wiped her eyes and settled into bed. Skog climbed up on her chest to comfort her.

"I'm sure you made Mommy and Daddy very happy tonight. That is such a big step, to use your voice." Brown Teeth tucked her in. "You keep being so brave and learning so much and you'll get to go home before you know it."

Is that what it took to go home? Bravery? Learning?

Brown Teeth shut the door, leaving them in the dark.

"They can't keep us here forever," Hanna whispered.

"We have this time to plan," said Skog.

She'd be a good student—just like everyone wanted—and learn ever so much. She'd build up her strength and resolve; she'd be ready for Mommy on her first day back. Daddy shouldn't have betrayed her, but with Hanna out of the way, Mommy's magic was too powerful. Daddy couldn't even choose his own words anymore. Hanna couldn't let Mommy win, not when all of Daddy's goodness was at stake.

"I've been so selfish," she said. "Daddy needs me."

"He's waiting for you—"

"I know."

"—to take care of Mommy."

"We have to save him, Skog."

"We will."

"I have to be very very good now. So I can go home."

Skog fell asleep with one soft hand on her cheek. But Hanna stayed awake. She'd conjured so many ways to be a bad girl, but maybe that strategy had made her too visible. Mommy caught on to all of her tricks; so did all the teachers. Hanna needed a sneakier approach—for school, and home. It might take some time—she couldn't unleash her new plan all at once or it wouldn't seem convincing. But she knew what she needed to do, and who she needed to become.

The best girl ever.

ACKNOWLEDGMENTS

I will forever be grateful to my agent, Sarah Bedingfield, for finding me in her inbox and seeing in my work what no one else had previously seen. Her passion allayed some of my fears that I was a crazy person on a solitary mission who had nothing of value to share. Loud and clear she said, "I see you. I get what you're saying." And then she promptly proceeded to sell my book. Sarah, it has been the joy of my life to share this process with you.

I am similarly grateful to Jennifer Weis of St. Martin's Press, who promptly proceeded to buy my book. Your excitement and faith in this story have meant everything to me. It is humbling to have so many people working behind the scenes on my behalf to bring my words into the world. Thank you Sylvan Creekmore, Lisa Senz, Jennifer Enderlin, Sally Richardson, Tracey Guest, Brant Janeway, Erica Martirano, Jordan Hanley, and Olga Grlic. Thank you, also, to Francesca Best and the folks at TransWorld, who came on board so quickly and enthusiastically.

I am indebted to Pitch Wars—to Brenda Drake in particular, and the greater community in general (especially Nikki Roberti, Heather Cashman, Michael Mammay, Rachel Lynn Solomon, Rebecca Enzor, Kellye Garrett, and Kristen Lepionka). My mentor, Margarita Montimore, was the first person to pluck my work from the slush, and she consistently had more faith in me as a writer than I had for myself—thank you for pushing me to make my manuscript the best it could be. I didn't fully understand what line revisions were before your mentorship, and now I know that's where the magic happens: I'm a better writer because of you. I couldn't have gotten through those crazy two months without my fellow mentees, Class of '16 (too many to name)—I'll always be rooting for every single one of you.

The writing community on Twitter has proven to be an amazing resource for information and encouragement. I have learned so much from so many writers—thank you all!

Thank you to beta reader and cheerleader extraordinaire Kim Chance: our writing journeys took different paths, but I'm so happy 2018 is a book celebration year for both of us.

I started writing novels while I was a part-time employee at Monroe Branch Library in Rochester, New York. It was inspiring to be around so many books—and so many lunatics. Thank you to my co-workers and friends who were such a part of my Rochester life, especially Mary Clare Scheg and Chris Price.

Thank you to Scott Keiner, an early champion of the earliest version of this story; you made me think I might be on to something.

Thank you to my guardian angel, Manya Nelson, who nursed me in spirit when I was ill, and made sure I had a computer to write on.

Thank you to Kathryn Markakis, who listened to me like no other doctor ever had, and kept me sane and well enough to keep pursuing my dreams.

Thank you to Eva Albertsson for answering my Swedish usage questions. If any mistakes remain in my Swedish, the fault is entirely mine.

Thank you to my dad, John Stage, who's been game for every rough draft of almost everything I've ever written, starting when I was a teenager. It took me a long time to grasp all of your allusions to Stephen King, but I think I finally got it: make sure the readers keep turning the page! And also, thank you to my mum, Ruth Stage. My parents gave me a love of books, and the Smoky Mountains, and the Grand Canyon, and trees-mountains-sky, and the big world of ideas and wonder. It wasn't always easy, but somehow you provided the right upbringing for a writer.

I couldn't live without my bestest friends, Lisa Ricci and Paula D'Alessandris. We may have started with a common love of theater, but we evolved in so many other directions. I'm so grateful for the decades we've shared. You've helped make me who I am, and have been there for all of life's victories and mishaps, for serious talks and goofy exploits.

And finally, thank you to my sister, Deborah Stage— the singularly most important person in my life. You have been part of my consciousness for as long as I've been conscious, sharing in the perils, silliness, and adventures of growing up, and growing older. You've encouraged me in all of my creative endeavors—and participated in quite a few of them—though we will overlook that this one slipped into the world without your fingerprints ("too scary"). There is no one I'd rather laugh with, or sit in silence with, or play a board game with, or gaze at the stars with. Though I've often felt lost in this world, with you I am always "home."

While I've been writing and creating for many, many years, this book came together suddenly and unexpectedly, and has been a life-changing event. I am grateful beyond what I know how to express.

ABOUT THE AUTHOR

Zoje Stage is a writer and former filmmaker. She was a 2008 Fellow in Screenwriting from the New York Foundation for the Arts and a 2012 Emerging Storytellers Fellow from the Independent Filmmaker Project. She lives in Pittsburgh, Pennsylvania. *Bad Apple* is her first novel.

Visit her blog at zoje.blogspot.com
and find her on Twitter @zooshka
and Instagram @zoje.stage_author